# ROBYN CARR

## SUNRISE POINT

MIRA®

ISBN-13: 978-0-7783-1914-6

Sunrise Point

www.MIRABooks.com

**Printed in U.S.A.**

# SUNRISE
# POINT

TOWN OF VIRGIN RIVER

Nick & Jo Fitch's House

Ricky's House

Beryl's House

Connie & Ron's House

Corner Store

Jack's Bar

P P P

Church

Noah's House

Doc's Clinic

N NE E SE S SW W NW

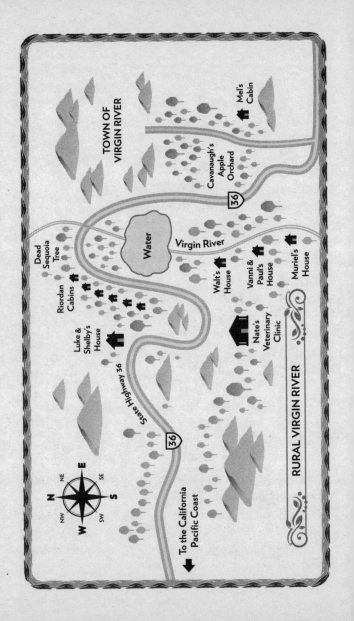

# One

There was a small note on the bulletin board at the Virgin River Presbyterian Church. *Apple harvest to begin at Cavanaugh Orchard. Apply in person.*

Virgin River newcomer Nora Crane studied the board regularly and, when she saw the notice, asked Reverend Kincaid what he knew about the job. "Very little," he answered. "It's a fairly long harvesting season and the Cavanaughs like to add a few full-time workers to their staff. Not many, though. I hear they pay pretty well, it's very demanding work and it's all over in a few months."

*Pay pretty well* stuck. She was holding her two-year-old daughter's hand and carried nine-month-old Fay in her backpack.

"Can you give me directions to the orchard?" she asked.

He wrinkled his brow. "Nora, it's a few miles away. You don't have a car."

"I'll have to go there, find out what the pay and

hours are. If it's a good job with good pay, I bet I can afford day care at the new school. That would be so good for Berry," she said of her two-year-old. "She's almost never with other children and needs socialization. She's so shy. And I'm not afraid of walking. I'm not afraid to hitch a ride around here, either—people are generous. And a few miles—that's really nothing. I'll get some exercise."

Noah Kincaid's frown just deepened. "Walking home could be tough after a long day of physical labor. Picking apples is hard work."

"So is being broke," she said with a smile. "I bet Adie would love a little babysitting money to add to her budget. She barely squeaks by. And she's so wonderful with the girls." Adie Clemens was Nora's neighbor and friend. Although Adie was elderly, she managed the girls very well because two-year-old Berry was so well behaved and Fay didn't get around much yet. Fay had just started crawling. Adie loved taking care of them, even though she couldn't take them on full-time.

"What about your job at the clinic?" Noah asked.

"I think Mel gave me that job more out of kindness than necessity, but of course I'll talk to her. Noah, there isn't that much work available. I have to try anything that comes along. Are you going to tell me how to get there?"

"I'm going to drive you," he said. "We're going to log the miles and get an accurate distance reading. I'm not sure this is a good idea."

"How long has that notice been up?" Nora asked.

"Tom Cavanaugh put it up this morning."

"Good! That means not too many people have seen it."

"Nora, think of the little girls," he said. "You don't want to be too tired to take care of them."

"Oh, Noah. It's nice of you to be concerned. I'll go ask Adie if she can watch them for a little while so I can go to the orchard to apply. She always says yes, she loves them so much. I'll be back in ten minutes. If you're sure you don't mind giving me a lift… I don't want to take advantage."

He just shook his head and chuckled. "Bound and determined, aren't you? You remind me of someone…."

"Oh?"

"Someone just as unstoppable as you. I fell in love with her on the spot, I think."

"Ellie?" she asked. "Mrs. Kincaid?"

"Yes, Mrs. Kincaid," he said with a laugh. "You have no idea how much you two have in common. But we'll save that for another time. Hurry up and check in with Adie and I'll take you to the Cavanaugh orchard."

"Thanks!" she said with a wide smile, dashing out of the church and down the street as quickly as she could.

It would never occur to Nora that she had anything in common with the pastor's wife. Ellie Kincaid was so beautiful, so confident and the kindest person she'd ever known. And by the way Noah looked at his wife, he adored her. It was kind of fun to see the preacher was a regular man; he gazed at his wife with hunger in his eyes, as if he couldn't wait to get her alone. They weren't just a handsome couple, but also obviously a man and woman very deeply in love.

Nora went straight to Adie Clemens's door.

"Just bring me some diapers and formula," Adie said. "And good luck."

"If I get the job and have to work full-time, do you think you can help me out a little bit?"

"I'll do whatever I can," Adie said. "Maybe between me, Martha Hutchkins and other neighbors, we can get you covered."

"I hate to ask everyone around here to take care of me…." But, hate it or not, she didn't have many choices. She'd landed here with the girls and hardly any belongings right before last Christmas—just one old couch, a mattress that sat on the floor and the clothes on their backs. It was Adie who alerted Reverend Kincaid that Nora and her family were in need, and the first gesture of help came in the form of a Christmas food basket. Through the generosity of her neighbors and the town, a few necessary items had been added to their household—an old refrigerator, a rug for the floor, sheets and towels, clothes for the children. The church had regular rummage sales and Mrs. Kincaid skimmed the used clothing to help dress Nora, as well. Her neighbor three doors down, Leslie, invited Nora to use her washer and dryer while she was at work and Martha offered her laundry, as well.

She'd never be able to repay all these kindnesses, but at least she could work to make her own way.

Picking apples? Well, as she'd told Noah, she'd do just about anything.

Noah drove a beat-up old pickup truck that Nora thought might be older than she was, and it definitely didn't have much in the way of shocks. As they bounced along the road out to highway 36, Nora had the thought that walking probably wouldn't be as hard on her spine. But as they trundled along, she became increasingly intimidated by the distance, farther than she expected. She wasn't sure how long it might take to walk it. She'd have to get the mile count from Noah once they arrived. If the odometer actually worked in this old heap of tin.

They turned off 36 and drove down a road, through a gate that stood open and down a tree-lined lane. Nora became distracted by the sheer beauty. There was something so pure and homespun about row after row of perfectly spaced apple trees, the fruit in various stages of ripening hanging from the boughs, some still small-apple-green while others wore a slight blush of red. And at the end of what seemed a long driveway through the orchard stood a big house—a white fairy-tale house with red shutters and a red front door and a wonderful wraparound porch with chairs separated by small tables. She couldn't even imagine the luxury of relaxing on such a porch at the end of a long day. At wide spaces in the road there were large bins, probably for collecting apples. They passed by a forklift tucked into a row of trees and a bit farther down the road, a tractor.

As the house grew closer Nora noticed that there were two large buildings behind it—either barns or very large storage sheds or... Ah, the housing for machinery and farm equipment, she realized, looking into some large open doors. One of the buildings bore the sign Cavanaugh Apples.

For a girl who grew up in a small house on a busy street in Berkeley, she looked at this house, land and operation in both fascination and envy. A person would be very lucky to grow up in such a place.

There was a collection of pickup trucks and four men standing outside a door at the end of one of the buildings.

"Nora?"

She turned toward Reverend Kincaid's voice.

"You probably should get going. While you go talk to Tom Cavanaugh, I'm going to pay a visit to Maxie, the lady of the house. She's almost always in the kitchen or on the porch."

"Where should I go?" she asked, suddenly far less sure of herself.

He pointed toward the short line of men. "Looks like that's the place."

"Right," she said. She got out of the truck, jumped down, but before she closed the door she peered back inside. "Reverend Kincaid, if I need a recommendation, will you give me one?"

She saw him frown again; she knew he was worried about how in the world she'd manage a job like this. Then his frown melted into a smile and he said, "Of course, Nora."

Noah pulled away from her to park on the drive near the house and she went to stand with the men. "Are you applying for the picking job?" she asked.

All four turned toward her. Only one nodded. Feeling a sense of competition, she assessed them. One was an old guy, and old was relative—he was balding, what was left of his hair was wispy and thin, but he stood straight and tall and appeared to have wide, strong shoulders. One was a teenager, around sixteen years old, good-looking and buff. One was a short Mexican man in his twenties, healthy and hearty, and the fourth looked as if he could be his father. "Am I in the right place to apply?"

The older man frowned, the teenager grinned, the older Mexican man looked her up and down and gave her the impression he was merely judging her ability by her size, which was small. And the man who could be his son said, "This is the place. You ever pick before?"

She shook her head.

"Want some advice? Maybe you should tell him you have."

"Why? Is it hard to learn?"

The men chuckled together. "Hard to *do*," the teenager said. "I'll show you the ropes if you get hired." Then he looked her over from her head to her feet, but his appraisal was a little more personal. "You sure you're up to it?"

She sucked in a breath. She'd do anything to take care of her girls. Mel Sheridan and Reverend Kincaid had helped her get some county assistance—food stamps and Medicaid—but that wasn't enough to live on. She'd been getting by on that plus part-time jobs at the clinic and the new school's summer program, but it was very part-time, given her small children.

She wanted to earn her own money. There just hadn't been much opportunity.

"I'm stronger than I look," she informed him. "I am. I can't lie about my experience, though. I have this…" *This deal I made with God,* she thought dismally. Nora was trying so hard to rectify past mistakes, she wasn't about to make more along the way. "When I make a commitment, I'm good for it. I'll take any advice I can get, though. Did you guys see the notice in the church?"

"We pick every year," the teenager said. "I've been picking since junior high. Jerome has been picking for a hundred years," he said, indicating the older man. "Eduardo and Juan live down in the valley and the apples here pay better than the vegetables. Juan's wife has her own little business—they're doing pretty good these days, right, Juan?"

The older Mexican gentleman nodded solemnly. Proudly.

"Tom usually works around the grove—it's usually Mrs. Cavanaugh and her foreman, Junior, who handle the hiring." The boy put out his hand. "I'm Buddy Holson, by the way."

She took the hand with a smile. "Nora," she said. "Nice to meet you."

The latch to the door finally unlocked; the door opened a crack. Jerome went in first. He came out just a moment later and then Eduardo and Juan entered together. They were out in a second.

"We've all worked here before," Buddy explained. "Everything is on file for the regulars. Good luck."

"Thanks," she said. "Hope to see you around."

"You bet. Me, too," he said, giving his hat a little touch. And Nora realized, he probably thought she was much younger than she was. It would never occur to him she was actually a single mother. "You must live around here."

"Virgin River," she said.

"I'm in Clear River. I better go in—see you around." And he disappeared inside, but was back out in just seconds, slipping a piece of paper into his pocket. With a handsome parting smile and another touch to his hat, he headed for the last pickup parked there.

Nora took a deep breath and pulled open the door. The man behind the desk looked up at her and she froze momentarily. For no particular reason, she'd been expecting a much older man—the husband of the Mrs. Cavanaugh who usually managed the hiring. But this was a young man. And so handsome that he almost took her breath away. He had wide shoulders, a tanned face, brown hair, expressive brows and the kind of dark brown eyes that would glitter in the sun. His features might be ordinary, but put together so perfectly, he was hot. A hunk with that dangerous wholesome look about him—the look that had trapped her in the past. Her face probably flushed before going completely pale. She had had bad luck with such men and had no reason to assume her luck had changed.

"Can I help you?" he asked.

"I'm here about the job. The apple-picking job."

"You have experience with apple harvesting?" he asked.

She shook her head. "I'm a very fast learner and I'm strong. I have tons of energy. And I need a job like this."

"Really? What about this job seems right for you?"

"Reverend Kincaid says it pays pretty well and is kind of short. I'm a single mother and I can probably get help with the kids for a while, then I have two part-time jobs in Virgin River to fall back on when the harvest is over. Sounds perfect for someone like me."

"Well, it might be longer than you think. The end of August to almost December, most years. So I guess it wouldn't be right for—"

"I might be able to do it—there's a new day care and preschool in town, if I can afford it."

"How old are you?" he asked.

"Twenty-three."

He shook his head. "Already a divorced mother at twenty-three?" he asked.

The surprise showed on her face for less than a moment. She stood as straight as possible. "There are some questions you're not allowed to ask me," she informed him. "It's the law. If they don't pertain to the job…"

"It's irrelevant. I'm afraid I've already hired my max—all people with experience. I'm sorry."

That took the starch out of her. Her chin dropped and she briefly looked at the ground. Then she lifted her eyes to his. "Is there any chance something might become available? Because there aren't many job openings around here."

"Listen... Your name?" he asked, standing from behind his messy desk and proving that he was taller than she even guessed.

"I'm Nora Crane."

"Listen, Nora, it can be back-breaking labor and I mean no offense when I say, you don't appear to be strong enough for a job like this. We generally hire very muscled men and women. We haven't ever hired kids or slight women—it's just too frustrating for them."

"Buddy's been working here since junior high...."

"He's a great big kid. Sometimes you have to carry fifty pounds of apples down a tripod ladder. Our harvesting season is grueling."

"I can do that," she said. "I've carried my nine-month-old in a backpack and my two-year-old in my arms." She flexed a muscle in her upper arm. "Motherhood isn't for sissies. Neither is being broke. I can do the work. I *want* to do the work."

He stared at her in shock for a moment. "Nine months and two years?"

"Berry will be three before long. They're beautiful, brilliant and they have a terrible addiction to eating."

"I'm sorry, Nora. I have all the people I need. Do you want to leave a number in case something comes open?"

"The church," she said with disappointment. "You can leave a message with anyone at the Virgin River Presbyterian Church. I'll check in with them every day. Twice a day."

He gave her a very small smile. "I don't expect anything to come up, but I know the number if something does." He wrote down her name and referenced the church phone number beside it. "Thanks for coming out here."

"Sure. I had to try. And if you hear of anything at all, anywhere at all…"

"Of course," he said, but she knew he didn't mean it. He wasn't going to help her get a job.

She left that little office and went to wait by Noah's truck, leaning against it. She hoped he had a nice visit with Mrs. Cavanaugh since she had inconvenienced him for no reason. No matter what Tom Cavanaugh had said, she knew he had rejected her as not strong or dependable enough for apple picking.

Life hadn't always been like this for Nora. Well, it had been difficult, but not like now. She hadn't grown up poor, for one thing. She'd never been what one could call financially comfortable, but she'd always had enough to eat, a roof over her head, decent if inexpensive clothes to wear. She'd gone to college briefly and during that time had had a part-time job, no different from most students. She'd had an unhappy family life, the only child of a bitter single mother. Then she'd found herself to be very susceptible to the flirtations of a hot and sexy minor league baseball player with no earthly clue he'd turn into a hard-core drug addict who would dump her and their two children in a tiny mountain town with no money, their possessions having been sold for his, um, hobby.

Even though times were about as tough as they could get as income went, she'd been lucky to find herself in Virgin River where she had made a few good friends and had the support of people like Noah Kincaid, Mel Sheridan and her neighbors. It might take a while and a little more luck, but eventually she'd manage to pull it together and give her girls a decent place to grow up.

She heard the slamming of a door—it had the distinct sound of a wooden screen door. There was laughter. When she looked up she saw Noah with an attractive woman with thick white hair cut in a modern, short, blown-out style. She was a bit roundish with a generous bosom and just slightly plump hips; her cheeks were rosy from either makeup or sun and her eyebrows shaped and drawn on with a dark brown pencil. She wore lipstick and laughed, showing a very young, attractive smile. Nora couldn't guess her age. Fifty-eight? Sixty-four? She looked like she should be hosting a country kitchen cooking show. And then she let go a big laugh, leaning into Noah's arm as she did so.

Nora straightened, since they were walking toward

her. She smiled somewhat timidly, feeling so unsure of herself after being rejected from the job.

"Nora, this is Maxie Cavanaugh. This is her orchard and cider operation."

"It's a pleasure to meet you, Nora," Maxie said, putting out her hand. Nora noticed that she had a bit of arthritis that bent her fingers at the knuckles, but her nails were still manicured in bright red. "So you're going to pick apples for us?"

"Well, no, ma'am," she said. "Your son said he had enough pickers already and couldn't use me."

"Son?" Maxie asked. "Girl, that's my grandson, Tom, and I raised him. Now what is it Reverend Kincaid told me? You have a couple of little daughters and only part-time work at the moment?"

"Yes, ma'am, but I think I'll get more hours in the fall when they need almost full-time help at the new school. I'll get a discount on day care, too. Thing is, it's a brand-new school and still needs all kinds of certification so we won't get help from the county for a while and I got all excited about a job that could pay pretty well for a couple of… But if there are already enough pickers…"

"I bet there's room for one more," she said, smiling. "Wait right here a minute." And she strode off across the yard to the big barn and its small office.

Nora turned her eyes up to Noah's. "Grandmother?" she asked. "How old is she?"

"I have no idea," he said with a shrug. "She's full of life, isn't she? It keeps her young. She's been a fantastic supporter of the church, though she doesn't go to services very often. She says Sundays are usually her busiest days and when they're not, she reserves them for sleep. Maxie works hard all week."

"And that's her grandson?" Nora asked.

"Yep. She must've gotten started early. I think Jack put Tom at about thirty."

"What's she going to say to him? Because he doesn't want to hire me. He took one look at me and pronounced me not strong enough, which is bull, but... But for that matter, you don't want me to get the job because even you think it's too much for me."

"It's between Maxie and Tom now. And I might've been wrong about this idea. Let's see what happens."

Tom Cavanaugh sat at the old desk in the cider press office for a while after Nora left, completely stunned and disappointed. When she first walked in, he thought she was a fresh-faced teenager and his immediate prediction was that Buddy would be after her. She was so damn cute with her ponytail, sweet face and petite body. When she admitted to being twenty-three with two children, he couldn't hide his shock. But worse than the shock—if she'd told him she was twenty-three and not a single mother, he'd have followed up with some kind of advance that would lead to a date. He wouldn't have hired her because that could have been problematic, hiring someone who sent little sparks shooting through his body. It would eventually lead to love among the trees, something that was strictly prohibited. Mostly.

Tom had spent a lifetime on this orchard and he was aware of certain employees falling in love among the apple blossoms and harvest bins, but Maxie had always warned him about the foolishness of that sort of thing. She said it could be pure bliss, unless it went wrong and turned into pure lawsuit. But lectures or not, Tom's first intimate experience with a girl had happened in this orchard on a sultry summer night right before he went off to college. The memory could still make him smile.

And the smile turned to heat as he replaced the young girl of his past with Nora in his mind.

Damn, that little Nora was lust at first sight. Her bright eyes, soft, full lips, splatter of freckles across her nose... Just his type, if she weren't married, mothering a couple of kids and divorced by the age of twenty-three. He was looking for a different kind of woman, a woman more like his grandmother— settled, smart, a strong moral code. Maxie had been married exactly once, to his grandfather. She'd been widowed since Tom was in college and had never re-married, never shown an interest in men after her husband passed. Not that there were many eligible men in Virgin River.... Maxie had long been dedicated to the business, the town and her many friends.

The office door opened and speak of the devil herself, there stood his grandmother, who he had always called Maxie rather than Grandma. She tilted her head and twisted her glossed lips. "You didn't hire that girl, though she desperately needs a job. She has children to feed."

"She probably weighs a hundred and ten pounds soaking wet."

"We don't hire by weight. And we can afford to be charitable. I'm going to tell her she has a job. When are you starting the harvest?"

"Maxie…"

"When?"

"I don't think this is a good idea, Maxie. She could distract the pickers. The men."

Everything inside Maxie seemed to twinkle and Tom knew at once she was on to him, that she knew exactly who Tom was worried about. But she didn't say anything. "Okay, we'll dock her pay for being attractive. When?"

"I think August twenty-fourth. My best guess. But, Maxie—"

"It's done. She's a good girl, Reverend Kincaid vouches for her and I bet she works harder than anyone. Young mothers can be fierce. Hell, Tom, I still pick apples and I'm seventy-four! You can be a little more generous."

And then she left his office.

# *Two*

It was three-point-four miles to the Cavanaugh Orchard. Nora did a dry run, which was when she learned that some of what she thought were her best ideas were her worst. She had considered saving for a used bicycle. It was over three miles *down* to a lower elevation where the trees were happier, closer to the river. And then it was three-point-four *up*. She could make it to the orchard in just over an hour, but getting back to town, uphill, was another story. The idea of a bicycle wasn't going to be that helpful on the way home, especially if her legs were tired.

Rather than a used bicycle, she spent what little money she could scrape together for some of the rubber boots Maxie suggested. She had a small, used umbrella stroller she could give to Adie for the baby. Adie Clemens wasn't strong enough to carry Fay around in the backpack; Fay weighed eighteen pounds already.

They had worked out a system for babysitting—Adie would walk three houses down to Nora's in the early morning and stay with her sleeping children, give them breakfast, dress them and walk them down to day care, pushing little Fay in the stroller. "This will help you commit to your walking every day even if I'm not here to remind you and walk around town with you," Nora said. "Your blood pressure and cholesterol is so much improved since we started walking."

"Oh, yes, ma'am," Adie teased.

The early hour was no strain on Adie because she was an early riser; she'd come at 5:00 a.m. with her book or morning paper and her cup of tea. It was perfect as Nora wanted to be extra early at the orchard to prove a point—that she'd do everything possible to do a good job. By Nora's calculations, she could afford day care, barely, plus give Adie twenty dollars a week for her help. Adie was just squeaking by on her Social Security income. She said she didn't want any money, but Nora knew it would help. Adie could use a little more money each week for necessities.

Then came the real miracle. Reverend Kincaid told her he had arranged a partial "scholarship" for day care for Fay and preschool for Berry. It nearly brought tears to her eyes and she couldn't believe it, but apparently the church had taken on the challenge of helping some of the local working mothers to afford help with the children so they could work. It was a healthy discount and made Nora's challenges so much more manageable. "There's no question in my mind, once you're on your feet, you'll be joining the cause and helping others," Reverend Kincaid said.

"You can count on that," she said. "I just can't believe every break I get from this town. I know I don't deserve it."

"We're going to work on that attitude. You deserve it as much as anyone," he said.

That first morning of work, as she left Adie before dawn, she said, "I'll get a phone number at the orchard that you can call if you have problems." But she wasn't sure what she'd do if a call came. Where would she be? Out in the trees somewhere, far away from the house and office? And if it was important, was she going to run home? Uphill? "Of course if you have an emergency, you'll call Mel Sheridan at the clinic, right?"

"I wish you wouldn't worry so much," Adie said. "I'm not as wimpy as I look. I have phone numbers for people in town. I'll take the girls to the school at 9:00 a.m. and Martha and I are going to pick them up at five and bring them home for a snack. You'll be along about that time or soon after, I expect." Then she smiled. Adie had the sweetest smile. "We'll be fine."

Sometimes Adie seemed so old and frail, unlike Maxie Cavanaugh who looked like she would probably live forever. Just the news that Martha was going to pitch in gave her a little more peace of mind.

It was her plan to arrive at the orchard before the sun was up, before any of the other workers, and it hadn't been easy. It was scary descending the mountain in the darkness, the fog gathering around her as she got lower and lower. She heard lots of rustling, hooting, squeaking—the birds were just waking up and she wasn't sure who else was out there, concealed in the trees, thinking about breakfast. She was terrified of being eaten by some wild animal, so she kept her head down and her feet moving rapidly.

Finally the gate and orchard came into sight and she relaxed for a moment. There were some lights on in the back of the big house when she got there, but no movement anywhere else. Nora went to the building that held the office and sat on the ground, leaning against the door. She wanted to make a point to Mr. Cavanaugh, that she'd go the extra mile. And she got her wish—he came tromping out of the back porch of his big house followed by a golden dog, appearing through the morning mist as he walked toward the barn. She stood up from the ground.

He stopped short when he saw her. "Why are you here?" he asked.

"Did you change the starting date?" she returned.

"It's today. But we don't pick apples in the dark unless there's threat of a freeze."

"I… I wanted you to know I was serious about the job."

"Well, it looks like I can count on you to stand around doing nothing until the others get here, since you haven't worked the harvest before and don't know where anything is."

*Oh, he was so ornery,* she thought. *Very difficult to please.* Well, thanks to her mother, she knew how to deal with that type. "Is there anything I can do to help out until they get here?"

"Do you know how to make coffee?" he asked.

"I do," she said. But she wasn't sure she could make *good* coffee. "Where's the pot?"

"In the break room. Behind the office."

And she immediately thought, *I'm such an idiot.* There was a break room, a *lunch*room! And lunch had never even crossed her mind. Well, she'd sneak an apple or two and tomorrow she'd bring a sandwich. In the break room was a large thirty-cup pot and she tried to remember how many scoops per cup of water, hoping for the best.

"Holy crap!" Tom Cavanaugh exclaimed. "Think you got enough coffee in this brew? My spoon could stand up in it!"

"My dad used to like it strong," she said, squaring her shoulders, though she had no idea if her father even drank coffee.

"Go to the house," he ordered. "Maxie is in the kitchen. Ask her for cream and sugar."

No *please.* No *if you don't mind.* "Sure," she said.

And rather than walk, she jogged. Then she knocked on the screen door. "Come on in, Nora," Maxie said. She was still wearing her robe and slippers, sitting at the kitchen table with her own coffee and a paper folded open to a crossword puzzle. "What can I do for you?"

"I've been sent for cream and sugar for the coffee. So far today I've failed in arrival time and coffee that's too strong."

Maxie laughed. "Is that right? Drain a cup or two and add water. That should shut him up. What was wrong with your arrival time?"

"I guess I got here too early and since I don't know

where anything is, I'm useless. Except for destroying his coffee."

Maxie got a weird look on her face. "Sounds like someone got up on the wrong side of the bed. I'd be likely to admire that in an employee. The early arrival part, I mean. By tomorrow, you'll know where things are. And he can make his own coffee." She pointed to the counter. "There's the cream and sugar. Which, by the way, Tom forgot to take with him." Nora lifted the small pitcher and bowl and Maxi said, "I'm probably going deaf, but I didn't hear a car or truck."

Nora turned back. "I don't have a car. Or truck."

Maxie regarded her steadily. "I see. Quite a long walk, isn't it?"

"Three-point-four," Nora said. Then she smiled. "I made very good time. I won't come so early tomorrow, since Mr. Cavanaugh isn't in the mood for company first thing in the morning."

Maxie grinned and said, "Fix the coffee like I told you. The first couple of days on a new job are always kind of sketchy. You'll be fine."

"I'll try. And thanks for the job—I know it was your doing. I can't tell you how much I—"

"A long, long time ago, many years before you were born, when I didn't have a pot to piss in or a window to throw it out of, some old woman gave me a job picking apples and it was the best job I ever had. I hope it all works out for you."

And that brought a very grateful smile out of Nora. "Thank you, Mrs. Cavanaugh."

"I'm Maxie, and that's final. You're entirely welcome."

\* \* \*

The knee-high rubber boots were an excellent investment in keeping her feet dry. The ground beneath the trees was sometimes very soggy. She wore the boots over her tennis shoes. But it was cold on the wet ground, especially in the early morning, and rubber boots did little to keep her feet warm. Her toes were icy cold and when she took her lunch break, she pulled off the boots, the socks and tennis shoes she wore inside them and gave her feet a rubbing, trying to warm them.

The other pickers, all men, wore their rubber boots over expensive, steel-toed, lace-up boots. They didn't need to rub the life back into their toes.

Nora ran into trouble with her hands, feet, arms and shoulders. She got blisters on her hands from toting the canvas bag she looped over her shoulders and after a few days of picking apples, the blisters popped, bled and hurt like the devil. She cut her hands on wooden crates and bins if she wasn't careful. The men wore gloves most of the time; she didn't have gloves and her hands took a beating. She had matching blisters on her heels, just from more walking than she'd done in her life. Although she was armed with Band-Aids, they rubbed off too quickly. Even though she was in good physical condition, carrying almost fifty pounds of apples up and down a ladder in a sack that strapped over her shoulders took its toll on her shoulders, back and legs. Her right shoulder was in agony from picking, but she didn't dare let it slow her down. She was just plain sore all over.

She had to work hard to keep up with the men. She was no match, that much was obvious. But Buddy praised her efforts now and then, telling her she was doing great for a new picker. Of course, Buddy clearly wanted a date, but she tried to ignore that since it was never going to happen.

After the first day, she didn't walk to work in the pitch dark anymore, but she did set out in early dawn and all the same suspicious animal noises haunted her. She managed to get to the orchard just as full morning was upon them so she could make the coffee, which she had perfected. She brought a sandwich everyday—apples were on the house. And she was always the last one to leave—home by six.

By the time she got home everyday, Adie had joined forces with Martha to get the little girls home from day care, bathed and fed, a contribution so monumental it nearly moved Nora to tears, she was so grateful.

"Adie, you must be exhausted," she said. "They wear *me* out!"

"I'm doing very well," the woman replied. "I feel useful. Needed. But I'll be the first to admit, they're quite a lot to manage in the tub. They like the tub."

"Thank God for Martha!" Nora said. She tried not to let it show that she had a little trouble lifting the baby into her little stroller, but Adie wasn't paying attention to that, thank goodness.

"You know what's wonderful? How excited they are when I come to school to pick them up," Adie said while Nora readied her children to go home. "The teachers say the girls do very well—they eat well and nap well and seem to love being there."

Almost more important than the added income, her girls needed to be around loving adults and other children in a safe environment. "Is Ellie Kincaid there sometimes?" Nora asked.

"I see her every morning. I think she's some kind of official sponsor of the day care and preschool," Adie said. "She welcomes the children and makes a big fuss over them every day. I'm volunteering to help with milk and cookie time and watching over nap time."

"Oh, Adie, you're priceless."

"Why not? I have the time. And I love the children."

Nora didn't see Tom Cavanaugh much that first week and when she did, they didn't speak or make eye contact, not even when she arrived early enough to be sure his coffee was made. This suited her fine. She wasn't prepared to have him judge her weakness by her wounded hands or her slow movements and winces due to muscle pain. She saw him talking to other harvesters from time to time, saw him using the forklift to move full bins, saw him in the cider press area. But they didn't work together nor chitchat. Why would they?

He never complained about the coffee again. And he had remembered the cream and sugar every morning.

By the end of the week she was so tired she believed she could fall down and sleep for a month. Mr. Cavanaugh told the harvesters it was their choice whether to work or take time off on the weekend; they weren't in a critical harvesting situation like over-ripening or an impending freeze. He paid overtime, so even though Nora could hardly bend her fingers from the tightness or lift her right arm, her picking arm, she signed on and hoped she could get a little help from Adie and Martha with the kids, or maybe Ellie Kincaid or one of the local teenage babysitters. Overtime, that was juicy.

On her walk home, alone on that long uphill trek on a Friday night, she allowed herself to fall apart a little bit. She hurt all over and faced another long seven days of work. It was hard for her to hold her little girls; she ached when she lifted them and there were a couple of spots on her hands that bled if she didn't wrap them in bandages. If Adie and Martha hadn't managed the bathing before she got home, Nora didn't know how she would. For her own daily shower, soap and water stung so badly tears rolled down her cheeks. And she was going to have to beg the use of someone's washer and dryer during an evening soon—the laundry was piling up and they didn't have much wardrobe.

Because no one could see her, she did something she hadn't done in so long—she let herself cry for the first time in months. She told herself this was good work and she was lucky to have it, her hands would heal and callus, her arms and legs would build muscle and get stronger—all she needed was courage and time. She hadn't taken the job because it was *easy*.

She heard the engine of a vehicle and had no idea who it might be. She was always the last of her crew to leave so no one would notice she walked home. It was a matter of pride; she knew she was destitute and the charity she had to take for the sake of her girls was hard enough. Nora quickly wiped the tears off her cheeks and stuffed her sore hands into the center pocket of her hoodie. Looking at the ground, she stayed to the side of the road and made tracks. And the truck passed.

But then it slowed to a stop. And backed up. Tom. Because luck hadn't exactly been her friend lately. Like in twenty-three years.

Of course it was a new, huge, expensive pickup. It probably cost more than the house she lived in. She'd seen it before, of course. It said Cavanaugh Apples on the side and had an extended cab with lots of apple crates in the bed. She kept her eyes cast down. She sniffed back her tears and hoped there were no tracks on her cheeks. She was far too self-conscious to be caught sniveling in self-pity, especially by him.

He lowered the window on the passenger side. "Nora?" he called.

She stopped walking and looked up. "Yes?"

"Um, sore?"

"A little," she said with a shrug. Oh, the shrug hurt. "It's my first time," she added, as if an explanation were necessary. "I'll develop muscle."

He looked away just so briefly, then back quickly. "Let's see your hands."

"Why?"

"Let me see," he commanded. "Come on." She pulled her hands out of her pockets and splayed her fingers but kept them palms down. He rolled his eyes impatiently. "Flip 'em over, Nora," he said.

"What for?"

"I bet you stuffed 'em in your pockets because you have cuts or blisters or something. Come on, flip 'em."

She groaned in irritation and looked away as she turned her hands over.

Then the voice came a bit more softly. "Raise your right arm for me," he said.

Driven purely by pride, she lifted it high.

"Come on," he said. "Get in."

Her eyes jerked back. "What?"

"Get in. I know what to do about that," he said. "You think that's the first time I've seen that? All you've been doing is changing diapers. Your hands and shoulders weren't ready for the trees, the bins, the ladders and heavy sacks. Your rotator cuff is strained from picking and hauling. Get in, I'll get you fixed up. You should've told me."

She was reluctant, but just the suggestion that he could make this pain go away, that was enough for her. She opened the heavy truck door, which hurt like a demon, and hoisted herself up and in.

Tom Cavanaugh made a difficult U-turn on the narrow drive, heading back toward the house and office. He looked over at her. "Why didn't you tell me?"

She stared straight ahead. "You didn't want to hire me. Your grandmother made you. And you weren't all that friendly. I figured you'd just fire me."

"For hurt hands and sore muscles? Jesus. Do I really seem like that kind of brute?"

"You said you didn't think I was up to the job. I didn't want to prove you right."

"Listen to me—you got the job and I can see that you do your best." She shot him a glare. "Okay, you do pretty well," he added. "But it's dangerous to walk around a farm or orchard with injuries that go untended. You have to pay attention to that. You're a mother, right? You wouldn't let your child walk around with a wound that could get infected if left untreated. Would you?"

"I know medical people in town," she said. "If I thought there was an infection, I would have talked to someone."

"At that point, you might've waited too long. That would be bad for both of us. Now let's agree, you and I, that from now on you'll let me know when you have a problem."

That would be very hard to do, she acknowledged privately. But to him she said, "Okay."

He pulled up to his back porch. "Come into the kitchen," he said, not waiting for her to follow. He was up the porch steps and into the house before she was even out of the truck. By the time she joined him in the kitchen, he had opened a cupboard and was emptying supplies onto the counter. "Just sit at the table, right there."

She took a seat and waited tensely.

Tom filled a silver mixing bowl with warm, soapy water. He spread a towel over her lap, put the basin on her knees and said, "I know it stings, but I want you to soak your hands for a minute, get them very clean. Just grit your teeth and do it, please."

She'd be damned if she'd let an ounce of discomfort show on her face. She plunged her hands into the water and bit her lower lip against a wince. She couldn't keep her eyes from filling with tears from the sting. He didn't notice; his back was turned while he put out his first-aid supplies. Then he began transferring the stuff to the table. There was an old-fashioned-looking tin can, a tube of something or other, some gauze, another towel, a small bowl and spoon, latex gloves. He scrubbed and dried his hands as if he'd be performing surgery. And then he pulled a chair toward her, his long legs spread so that her knees were between his.

"We don't know each other, so let me explain a couple of things. I don't have much use for excuses, but hiding real issues from me isn't good. If you're going to work for me, you have to be honest about stuff like this. Got that?"

"I don't make excuses, I'm always honest and I need the job," she said, insulted and defensive. "I have just as much of a family to support as the men."

"Fair enough. But the men have been working in lumber and agriculture for a long time. Their hands are rough and callused. Tough as leather. And their muscles are strong now." He showed her his own calluses but thankfully didn't flex anything. Then he picked up a towel and gestured to the bowl. "Let me see the right hand."

"They're just blisters," she said, not mentioning

that the joints in her fingers were so stiff she hated to bend them.

"Left untended, they won't heal for a long time. I can help with that." He held out the towel. She lifted it and he very gently patted it dry. It wasn't too bad—a couple of blisters and two cuts from the rough wooden edge of an apple crate. Then he asked for the left and she put that one in the towel. The basin went away when he placed it on the table.

"Let your hands dry a little more, palms up on the towel," he instructed. Then he went about the business of mixing up some goop from the tin can and the tube. "This is bag balm and an ointment that vets use sometimes…" She visibly withdrew and he chuckled. "Maxie swears by it, especially for arthritis, and I've seen it work wonders."

When his concoction was mixed, he gently smoothed some of the salve over the sore places on her palms. He dipped his fingertips into the mixture and his touch was so gentle, it sent shivers through her. She had expected it to hurt, but it was sweet and light; she let her eyes fall closed and just enjoyed his ministrations. He didn't talk, thank God. She stayed quiet also. She hadn't been touched in this way in so long, she couldn't remember the last time. And how bizarre, it should come from someone she hated.

Well, maybe she didn't hate him, but she didn't like him much. He'd been either hostile or completely ignored her.

He wrapped gauze around her hands, then slid them

into the latex gloves. Right about that moment, Maxie walked into the kitchen, the yellow dog at her side. She smiled as she obviously recognized the procedure. "Want me to take over, Tom?" she asked.

"I'm fine," he said. He shook a couple of pills into his palm and handed them to Nora. "You need to take this for muscle pain," he said. "It's just over-the-counter anti-inflammatory and pain relief, but I'm giving you a bottle to take home. I'm afraid you're going to have to skip the overtime this weekend, you have to heal or you'll make things worse. I'll give you balm, salve, gauze, ice pack, extra latex gloves, anal-gesic, everything you need. Sleep in the gloves. Wear them when you come back to work. Keep salve on your hands—change the gauze wrap and apply new salve mornings and evenings. Take the pills every four hours—your muscles will recover."

Then he put a little cream from the tube on his fingertips and slid them under the back collar of her shirt. Without the least hint of embarrassment, he slid her thin bra strap down over her shoulder and began to massage the cream into her shoulder and scapula.

"Oh, that's going to help you so much," Maxie said. "When my hands get bad, I use that liniment—it's miraculous."

His big, callused hands on her shoulder and upper back were so firm, so gentle, so wonderful. Slow, circular strokes with the tips of his fingers—pure luxury. It only took him a few minutes to rub it in. After he pulled out his hand, he went to the freezer to withdraw a cold pack, placing it gently over her shoulder.

"And now ice. You'll be good as new," he said. "And when you come back to work on Monday, wear work gloves. I'll give you a pair." A glass of water appeared for her to take her pills. "How are your feet? Blisters?"

"My feet are fine." They were sore and there were blisters, but she wasn't going to have him touching her feet. Although the thought had merit—his roughened hands gently smoothing salve on her sore feet could be heaven.

When he had a small brown bag stocked with everything from salve to gloves, he handed it to her. "Come on, I'll give you a ride home."

She stood up. "I can walk just fine."

He gave a smirk. "I'm headed for town, Nora. I'll give you a lift. And it might be a good idea to ask around if anyone is going your way, hitch a ride. You could meet Buddy—he'd be more than happy to—"

"We shouldn't encourage Buddy. And I don't mind walking," she insisted. "I make good time."

He held the back door open for her. "If you run into a mountain lion, you'll make even better time, too."

She stopped in her tracks and looked up at him. "Funny."

He just lifted one brow and smiled.

"See you Monday, Maxie," she said.

"Have a nice weekend, Nora," the woman returned.

# *Three*

Nora hated to part with overtime pay by taking the weekend off. Overtime sounded delicious—her budget was beyond tight. But she took her girls to the gym set at the elementary school, pushed Fay in the baby swing while Berry played on the slide and rings. She consoled herself that there would be more overtime coming her way when she was healed enough to take it without crippling herself for life.

It was so early that she was surprised to see Noah Kincaid coming her way. "Hey," she said. "Out for a morning walk?"

"Kind of," he answered, flashing her that handsome grin. "I was looking for you."

"Me?"

"Maxie called me this morning—she's an early riser. She said they were picking this weekend and you'd been refused overtime because of job related injuries. She suggested I might check on you, see how you're doing."

She sat on a swing next to the baby swing. She stopped pushing the baby and gave a little laugh and held out her gloved hands. "It's true. And as much as I hate to admit this, Tom Cavanaugh probably did the right thing. My hands are sore. I'm nursing some blisters from doing work I've never done before, not to mention sore muscles from picking for hours. My right shoulder was on fire. Don't you dare tell him this, but the blisters on my feet were probably even worse than on my hands, but that stuff he gave me for my hands, that goop, wow. I'm almost as good as new." She turned her hands over a couple of times so he could see the latex over gauze. "This is a pretty amazing cure."

"The shoulder?"

"Better. Ice packs, anti-inflammatory and a little downtime does the trick." She tsked. "It killed me to give up the money."

Noah leaned against the side of the jungle gym next to Fay, belted in and safe between them. Berry ran around crazily, up the stairs on the slide, down the slide, a swing on the ropes, singing and talking to herself the whole time. But Berry was not the least bit interested in Noah. She was a little on the antisocial side, Nora feared.

"We started to talk about this a couple of times before," Noah said. "Do you have family who would be available to help you get over this rough patch? I mean any family at all?"

"We didn't get far on that subject because there

were too many immediate issues, like the fact that a few months ago my drug-crazed ex-boyfriend showed up here looking for money, attacked me and everyone who was trying to protect me. And that was a situation I got myself into at the age of nineteen."

"Well, he's in jail and out of the picture, thankfully. Family?" Noah asked again.

"There's no one," she said.

"As in…no one? Or no one you're not too proud to call on?"

"I told you—I got myself into this mess and—"

"I know, we don't have to go over all that again—I'm up to speed on Chad and pregnancy and getting mixed up with the wrong crowd. You probably think you're the first person to ever carry that load, but you're not. I'm interested in knowing more about your family—parents, aunts, uncles, siblings, et cetera. Someone you trust who loves you or at least has enough sense of responsibility to lend a hand."

She took a deep breath. "My father left us when I was six. My mother, who was abandoned and stuck with me, struggled for years to make it on her salary alone. We lived from paycheck to paycheck. Right there you have several reasons why she was angry and very bitter. The great irony is, she earned her living as a—are you ready? As a counselor. And when I went home from college to confess I was in trouble in a million ways and needed help—I was flunking out, pregnant, had played around with pot and beer with the boyfriend—she told me to get out and never come

back. That's where we left it. She threw everything that
had my fingerprints on it out the front door onto the
lawn, Chad drove me away and stuffed me into a flea-
bag motel where he left me. I went to Student Services
who sent me to the county welfare office and…" She
gave her shoulder a little lift—half a shrug.

"But you stayed with him?"

"No," she said softly. "Not really."

"But there's Fay," he said.

She nodded but couldn't meet his eyes. She finally
looked up, but all she could muster was a hoarse whisper. "He came and went. And I was so lonely and vulnerable after Berry was born. Chad was manipulative.
Sometimes he gave me money, for which I was so stupidly grateful, but I didn't know until I was ready to
have Fay that he'd been thrown off his professional
baseball team over a year before." She shook her head.
Then she glanced at Fay and said, "But how can I regret her?" And on cue, the baby gave them a brilliant,
toothless smile and Nora nearly cried.

Noah couldn't resist touching Fay's pudgy hand.
"Where did the abuse begin in your life, Nora?"

"According to my mother, it began with my father,
I don't remember anything about that. I was al-
six when he left, but my memory of life before
pretty spotty, which my mother said is typical.
She says I have buried memories."

"And you were in therapy for this?"

She smiled. "Of course not. My mother is a therapist. I will tell you the truth, Noah—I went to talk

with you on Mel Sheridan's recommendation because you're a minister. I have no experience with church and I had this idea you could somehow show me forgiveness for all the mistakes I've made. Although it was hard, I was open to the idea of charity. But I've learned to be wary of therapists. When you told me you were a licensed counselor before becoming a minister, I almost bolted."

"What do you think of your mother's decision to never put you in counseling for these so-called buried memories?" he asked her.

"I think she's incompetent. And I'm not convinced I have buried memories, either. According to my mother, there's no other family anywhere. No grandparents, aunts, uncles. But I think I have pretty screwed-up parents."

He gave her a small smile. "Think we should explore this further?"

"Probably," she said. "But the very thought makes me far more exhausted than picking apples for ten hours a day."

He laughed. "Don't worry, Nora. There won't be that many hours of daylight before long—fall is here and winter is coming. The days are growing shorter."

"Fortunately that leaves very little time for discussing my dysfunctional parents."

"But would you like me to contact your mother?" he asked.

"God! Perish the thought. When we have several hours to chat, I'll tell you all the details of my whole life's story and all about my mother—she's *brutal*. I spent my whole life being afraid of her, and surprised and so grateful during her brief affectionate or kind moments. I learned to step very lightly."

"And your father? Would you like to know what's become of him?"

She thought about that for a moment. "I've been curious, but not curious enough to look for him and certainly not enough to forgive him for leaving us the way he did. But there have been times I've wondered if he was dead… I have these snatches of memories of times with my father that aren't scary or terrible. Not a lot, but a few. Like bowling—isn't that a kick? A six-year-old, bowling? Learning to ride a bike with training wheels, doing dishes together with me standing on a stool at the sink, cutting the grass and planting flowers. My mother says none of those things ever happened—no bowling, et cetera. She claims I invented those memories just like children invent imaginary friends. But I have no dark or eerie or scary memories or dreams about him. I have warm memories. But if he was a good person, he wouldn't have left me…."

"I could do a little research," Noah said.

"Could you find out if he's dead? Without making me…"

"Vulnerable?" Noah finished for her. "You are always in control, Nora. If you tell me his name and last known address, I can probably find out if he's alive or dead, where he is, if he's remarried, if there are children, what he does for a living, that sort of thing.

But there's no reason he'd have to know you're even involved."

She thought about this for a minute. "Then okay," she said. "I'd like to know if he's alive. And maybe someday, I'd like to know why he ran out on me. I mean us." She swallowed. "His name is Jed—Jedediah Crane. And he was a history teacher at UC Berkeley. My mother said he was fired and left us high and dry."

"A professor?" Noah asked. "Did they divorce?"

"She always called him a teacher. Oh, of course they divorced—and it must have been bitter. As a girl, dangerously curious, I searched through files and stored boxes in the attic and even in my mother's underwear drawer for some evidence of him, of them. Of us. Of anyone—even my mother with her family. There was not so much as a picture! If you'd known my mother as I had, you'd have expected at least a lot of photos with my father's face cut out of them! And there were no documents of any kind—I don't even have my own birth certificate."

Noah smiled. "We'll get that taken care of, as well. That's a simple process and you don't have to have the permission of your parents to get a copy."

"Noah…" she said hesitatingly. "There's something you should take into consideration before you walk down this path. My mother… Not everyone knows what she's really like. She has friends. Not a lot, but some—she had things to do, although she mostly went to work and came home to spend the evening alone in front of the TV. She's very funny. She could make people laugh. She fell out with the neighbors and they stopped talking years ago, which of course was *their* fault, but she had friends from work, from other places. People to talk to on the phone, that sort of thing. It used to amaze me how funny and charming she could be with some people and how completely insane she could act at other times. If you met her by some chance or investigated what kind of person she is, you'll probably think I'm just a bratty, ungrateful kid. And I've admitted—I was trouble. Yes, I was—I made so many mistakes."

"Where is she a counselor?"

"The community college in Berkeley. People Services. She helped students get through their crises, referred them, helped them get their lives together." She laughed resentfully. "I wonder if she ever did it by throwing everything they owned on the front lawn. But then, I probably deserved it…."

Noah smiled patiently. "I don't think you need forgiveness, Nora."

She laughed humorlessly. "You don't have to be so nice. I know how many bad things I did."

Noah ran a hand over Fay's smooth, round head. The baby beamed at him. "I think you've redeemed yourself."

One of the convenient things about living in a place that catered to hunters and fishermen from out of town, were the heavy-duty Band-Aids at the Corner Store for those sportsmen who were just breaking in their new boots. Armed with large canvas protection on her heels and palms, Nora lit out for work early Monday morning. She went down the road from Virgin River to 36, ready to take on another week.

The work was physically demanding, but it was refreshing to a city girl. If she hadn't been distracted by soreness and the fear of not being able to keep up, she would have been thoroughly into the experience. The apples smelled heavenly. The breeze wafting through the trees was refreshing, the sound of the swaying branches and rustling leaves as calming as a lullaby. And the industry all around her, plus the weight of her bag filled her with a sense of accomplishment. She loved the sacks full of apples adding to the bins, the forklift taking the full bins away, the watering and aerating going on all around her while she stood on her ladder and picked, the trucks taking crates and boxes of apples to vendors. She caught sight of Tom and Junior repairing the tall fence that surrounded the orchard, not once but twice, right in the same place. And every now and again she could hear people talking or laughing off in the distance and the occasional bark of that yellow dog.

Nora wouldn't trade her children for anything, not even for an easier life leading up to their births, but if she weren't a single mother constantly worried about money, this job outdoors in the beauty of a northern California Indian summer would seem like a gift. It was September and the afternoons were still warm.

A couple of days into her second week, when she arrived at the juncture of the road from Virgin River and Highway 36, there sat a big white truck. And outside the cab, leaning against the driver's door, was Mr. Tom Cavanaugh. His long legs were casually crossed in front of him and he was looking down; he appeared to be cleaning his nails with a pocketknife.

She looked at him for a moment. *Appreciated* him. It seemed such a distant memory when she'd gotten mixed up with Chad. Chad had seemed like such a catch, slated for the big time. Now, looking at Tom, she saw stability and success, not to mention power and beauty. Yes, he was a very beautiful man. And she wondered what it must feel like to be the kind of girl someone like him would want.

She shook it off. Then she put her head down and walked on by.

"Hey," he called.

She turned back. She tried a small smile. "'Morning," she said.

"Where are you going?" he asked.

"To work," she said.

"Well, jump in. I'll give you a lift. Why do you think I'm here?" he asked.

"I have absolutely no idea. I don't need a ride. I'm perfectly capable of walking."

"I know, Nora. Humor me."

"I don't think it looks good," she said. "Getting a ride with the boss. What will the others think?"

"There are no others yet," he said with a chuckle. "You're always the first one to get to the orchard. Come on. No strings."

She thought about it for just a second, but there was really no way to refuse a kindness. Or whatever this was. She walked around the front and got in the passenger seat.

"How are the muscles and blisters?" Tom asked.

"Excellent," she said, surprise lacing her response. "Nothing hurts. I'm keeping the protection on my hands and, as you can see, wearing the latex gloves, but I can't believe how quickly I healed up. You should consider one of those late-night infomercials. Your magic goo and ginsu knives."

He laughed at her. "Find yourself watching a lot of late-night TV, do you?"

"A long time ago," she said. "I haven't had a TV since before my children were born."

"Ah, one of those fussy mothers—no TV to poison the little minds?"

"Not so virtuous. I can't afford a TV—that's a luxury way beyond me. But who can forget ginsu knives? I used to love those demonstrations. It wouldn't have surprised me if fingers went flying. But who knows—maybe they did and the icky stuff was cut. No pun intended," she added with a laugh.

He stared straight ahead as he drove for a few moments. Then he turned down the long drive into the orchard. "Here's what we're going to do, Nora. I'm going to wait for you where the road from town meets 36 and give you a lift. And I'll drop you off there after work."

"I told you, I don't mind—"

"I know, you don't mind walking. I give you a lot of

credit for that—you have gumption. But I'd like you to reserve your energy for work. And it's not one hundred percent safe out here at dawn and dusk. I'm not saying it's dangerous, but there are wildlife issues."

"I can run," she said. "Seriously, I'm fast."

He glanced over at her. "Seriously, you never want to try that. The only wildlife you can outrun is a turkey. Bobcats, mountain lions, bear—that's just what they're looking for—running marks you as prey and they're way faster than you could dream of being. If you come across one of them, back away slowly, making some kind of noise. Bark like a seal or something. Clap your hands. And pray." He took a breath. "I'm more than happy to give you a lift."

She sighed. "Thank you, Mr. Cavanaugh," she said. "But I'm not sure it's such a good idea for your other employees to think I'm getting special treatment."

"It's Tom," he said on a laugh. "Just Tom. If the idea doesn't sit with you, we can see if Buddy will drive you after work—he shows up sometimes after school for a couple of hours."

"Like I said, we probably shouldn't encourage Buddy...."

"You just tell him—you're twenty-three. And if he thinks about a date with an older woman, maybe say you're not over your ex-husband or something."

"But that would be a lie," she said.

He smiled. It was unmistakable—he smiled. "Well, then, you *are* over him."

"There is no ex-husband."

He shot her a look. "You're married?"

She shook her head.

"Widowed? Already? At your young age?"

"Never married. Mr. Cavanaugh." She took a steadying breath—he clearly wanted to know. "I have two children, have never had a husband, my boyfriend ran out on me and he is now in jail for assault and felony possession and I am on my own. He will not be allowed near my children again. I don't use or deal, I'm trying to get it together for my girls and myself. And I won't lie to anyone."

The big white truck actually slowed a little bit while he absorbed this. Then Tom accelerated again, getting back up to speed. "Then just tell Buddy you're twenty-three and a single mother. That should do it."

She was quiet for a moment. "I'm sure," she said softly. Of course that would discourage him. It would send any man running for his life.

"I'm going to ask him to take you to the turnoff after work and I'll meet you there before work. A mile or so walk each way is more than enough for anyone and I don't feel like having an employee mauled by a puma or bear. I've had to repair our fence a couple of times and while I haven't seen any, I suspect bears. They're usually shy and avoid people, but let's just play it safe."

She stared at his profile for a moment. "Mr. Cavanaugh, I don't want to be pitied and I don't need special treatment. I'm more than happy to do whatever it takes to work a job that pays well. I appreciate the gesture, I absolutely do, but—"

"Do you feel like fighting off a bear? Because a man was mauled not far from here. And you do have a family to think about."

"Mr.—"

"Tom!" he barked. "It's just Tom. The subject is closed."

He pulled up to the barn that held his office, turned off the truck and got out, leaving her sitting there.

She wasn't sure what it was about her that made him so angry. Alternately angry or kind or amused, that was more accurate. She tried to show him respect; she was honest with him even though it wasn't easy.

She watched him tromp up the steps and across the porch, into the house. Stubborn. And just as quickly he was out the back door and walking toward his office. He stopped by his truck and peered in the open driver's window at her. "Maxie said to tell you to come in for a cup of coffee with her."

"Oh. I wouldn't want to impose…."

"She invited you, therefore it's not an imposition."

"But I don't want to—"

"Nora! For God's sake, don't make everything so much harder than it needs to be! Just go have a cup of coffee with my grandmother."

"Should I make your coffee first?" she asked.

"I'll make it. I know how to make coffee."

A smile tickled her lips. "Ah. I didn't realize that."

And he scowled at her.

She shook her head and couldn't help it, she had to hold in a laugh. This man, who had no reason at all to be so ornery, was certainly a piece of work. As she walked across the wide yard, up the back steps and onto the porch, she found herself thinking that if she lived with this bounty, she would never have a cross day.

She gave the wooden screened door a couple of polite taps.

"Come in, Nora," Maxie said.

When she opened the door, Maxie was sitting at her kitchen table with her coffee and crossword puzzle. The yellow dog stood to greet her with a wagging tail. "Good morning, Mrs.… Maxie."

The older woman smiled and Nora was momentarily mesmerized. She was truly beautiful with her thick white hair, bright healthy teeth and rosy cheeks. "Grab a cup," Maxie said. "Sit with me a minute. Tell me about your weekend, about your sore shoulder and roughed-up hands."

Nora dressed her coffee with cream, *real* cream, and sugar. She didn't drink coffee at home—she didn't have a pot and it was expensive. And cream? Forget about it! Then she sat across from Maxie. "Everything feels great. I'm still wearing the gloves and using the goop—I don't want any trouble. I want the next chance at overtime."

Maxie laughed. "And the shoulder?"

"So much better," she said, rotating it to demonstrate. "I'm kind of embarrassed that I didn't know about something as simple as anti-inflammatory and ice. But I've never done this kind of work before."

"What kind of work did you do?"

"I waitressed in high school and worked part-time in a college bookstore. And then I became a mother."

"Yes, how are the little ones? And who's watching them for you?"

"The girls are absolutely fine—smart, good-natured, energetic. And one of my neighbors, Adie Clemens, sits with them until day care opens, then she walks them down the street. Adie is an older lady and not a ball of fire, if you get my drift. But she and the girls get along beautifully. And she wants to do this."

Maxie chuckled. "I know Adie. I've known her a long time—she's always been a little on the fragile side. We're about the same age, I think. She's a lovely woman."

Nora's mouth dropped open. The same age? Maxie was vibrant, strong and energetic. Adie seemed frail. Health problems and old age must have taken their toll, not to mention the rigors of poverty. Yet another reason to get ahead of this rough patch, Nora thought. "She is lovely," Nora finally said. "So sweet. She loves my little girls. I'm so lucky."

"And how are you getting along here, at the orchard?" Maxie asked.

"I'm not as fast as the men, but I bet I'll catch up. I'm very determined."

"And is Tom treating you well?"

She glanced away briefly before she could stop herself. She looked back instantly. "He gave me a ride from the crossroad this morning," she said.

"I know. I had an idea that's what he was up to

when he drove out of here so early. There's no reason for him to go anywhere before dawn."

"I told him it wasn't necessary," Nora said quickly. "I like walking. I do."

"You should probably carry a weapon of some kind if you're walking through the forest before dawn. It's a rare thing that a human is attacked by a cat or bear, but it's been known to happen. Sunrise and sunset are busy times for the wildlife—on their way to breakfast or off to bed, thinking they're all alone...."

Hah, she thought. She'd never spend money on a gun when she had children to feed and protect. "It was thoughtful of Tom," she said instead.

"How do you get along with him? Is he giving you trouble?"

She thought about her answer before saying, "I think I annoy him. I think he sees me as a burden, someone he's forced to look after."

"It's probably not so much that as Tom getting used to his new role here. He was raised on this orchard and knows the ropes, but he's been away. He spent the past several years in the Marine Corps. Two of those years he was deployed, first to Iraq and then to Afghanistan. He separated from the military after his second deployment—there were a lot of casualties in his command, I gather. I've noticed a kind of impatience in him that wasn't there before. Sometimes I catch him brooding and I wonder—has he lost good friends? Comrades? Taking and giving orders—that's not really the way we've been running this business, but that's what Tom was used to in the military. We're all going to have to give him time to adjust, I think. I suppose he has issues. Combat issues."

War? She hadn't been watching television coverage, obviously, so was left to her imagination and what she'd heard. And what she'd heard people say was terrible! Even with all she'd been through, she couldn't imagine the war in Afghanistan. She heard a couple of the apple pickers talking about how it had recently been the bloodiest month in Afghanistan so far with the loss of sixty-five soldiers.

And although life had held challenges, incredibly difficult challenges, she and the babies had enough to eat, were safe and warm, healthy. She vowed to never complain.

"Oh, of course," she said softly. "I had no idea. What could possibly be worse than war? Well, don't worry, Maxie. He seems perfectly normal to me. He's been very kind to me. If he's a little impatient sometimes, I suppose there's very good reason."

"One of these days, maybe on a weekend, I'd love to have you and the little girls come to the house. We could include Adie. I'd love to meet them. I hardly ever get to be around little girls. I had a son, then a grandson."

"That's so lovely, but I don't have anything like car seats," Nora said. "No car, no car seats."

"I know. Don't worry about that right now—I would never transport your children without them."

"That's very kind of you but you—"

"It's completely selfish, Nora. I love children. Especially little girls. I hope that fool grandson of mine does something about that before I die."

Nora had a great little chat with Maxie but she had to remind herself that they weren't friends. Maxie owned the orchard; Maxie was her employer. Maxie and Tom. "Are there any other family members?" she asked Buddy when they were dumping their apples one afternoon.

"Nope, that's it. I hear she raised Tom since he was a baby, but I don't know anything about why and Maxie's husband died around ten years ago or so. There's Junior—the foreman. He's been on this orchard as long as I can remember, since I was a little kid. He must be just about family." Then Buddy laughed. "Anyone Maxie cares about is usually considered family. When you know her a little better, you'll get that."

"I think I already get that," she said, thinking of this woman wanting to bring her girls and Adie out for an afternoon, though she hardly knew Nora at all.

This revelation about Tom Cavanaugh caused her to look at him a bit differently. Over the next week she found herself thinking about him and keeping an eye open to catch sight of him. While she was up in the branches of the taller apple trees, on top of her tripod ladder, she would occasionally see him and she could stare without being obvious. He spent a lot of time working with Junior, a big, muscled man of about fifty; they laughed together while they worked. And while Tom loaded large crates of apples into a delivery truck to take to grocers, straining his muscles, she couldn't help but admire his physique. He dressed the same every day, jeans, boots, his work shirt with the Cavanaugh Apples logo over the left breast pocket, sleeves rolled up, a whisper of soft brown hair on his forearms. His hands were very big and as she could attest, rough with calluses. The muscles of his upper arms, shoulders, back and legs moved under the fabric; that perfect male butt in jeans that weren't too loose or too tight drew her eyes. Sometimes he seemed to get a little worn out—the tendons in his neck stood out and after putting a crate in the truck, he'd stop to wipe his brow. Then he'd laugh with one of the guys.

She wondered what it must be like to be the kind of girl he'd smile and laugh with. What kind of girl would that be? A pretty and smart young teacher? A model or movie star who would be more than willing to leave the limelight for life on an orchard?

Now and then she'd be staring at him and imagine him in military fatigues rather than his work shirt, carrying a gun rather than a crate of apples and she'd wonder—had his losses been many? Had he been afraid, so far from home in a place of great danger? Did he miss the edge, the adrenaline rush of combat?

Or was coming home to the serene beauty of the orchard a relief? A comfort?

The following weekend Nora was able to take advantage of some overtime, and what made it even more desirable, it wasn't a ten-hour day, but just a long morning that ended in early afternoon. Adie assured her she was definitely up to the task of watching the little girls. When Nora walked back into town after work on Sunday, she found Reverend Kincaid waiting for her at Adie's house, chatting with her outside.

"Well, hello there," she said to Noah.

"How are you?" he asked.

"Excellent. Put in a good day's work and still have daylight to spend with my girls."

"They're still napping," Noah said. "Let me walk you to your house—there's something I want to talk to you about."

"Sure," she said. "Are you doing all right, Adie?"

"Fine, dear. I think the girls should be waking up in another half hour, maybe less."

"I won't keep you long," Noah told her. They walked down the street to Nora's little house and before they even went inside, Noah said, "I have information about your father. He's alive, still teaching in the Bay Area and he's been looking for you."

She was stopped on a dime. "How do you know this?"

"It was pretty quick—I went searching for Jed Crane in the missing-persons registry—my very first stop on the internet. And what I found was that Nora Crane is the one missing."

# *Four*

"I responded to the online missing-persons registry with my name and phone number and when I received a call from Jed Crane, I told him that I had known a Nora Crane in Seattle, but I told him I doubted it was the Nora Crane he was looking for—I said I thought the woman I knew was around thirty years old. And I couldn't provide an address. He was very forthcoming—he's been looking for you for a couple of years. Nora, I'm sorry to be the one to tell you this—he's trying to find you because your mother passed away. I couldn't ask for details without giving you away and there's nothing on public record about the cause of her death."

She went instantly pale. "Dead?"

He nodded gravely. "I think we should arrange a meeting with your father. Apparently he has lots of information about your mother and none about you. He said he lost custody of you when you were only four years old."

"He wanted custody?" she asked, in a state of shock.

"So he says."

"But I was six. I'm sure I was six—it was first grade. I remember exactly what I did at school that day—I came home and asked where Daddy was and my mother said she didn't know. That he'd left us." And so often over the years her mother, Therese, had added that he was no good, that they were better off. She said that getting involved with that man was the biggest mistake of her life, with no regard for how it might make Nora feel.

"I really think you have to look into this," Noah said.

"But what if he's a bad person? What if he abused me like my mother said?"

"I believe I can keep you safe. I know you're not going to throw your trust into him before you have all the evidence you need that he deserves it. If you don't want to see him on home turf, I'd be willing to take you to the Bay Area or somewhere in between to meet with him. If what he's saying is true or even partially true, he must have some documentation— marriage license, divorce papers, photos, something. Obviously without documentation, you don't neces- sarily have to believe him."

"But...but is she really dead? My mother?"

"Therese Alice Sealy Crane, age sixty two years ago?"

She nodded numbly.

"There is a public record of her death. I'm so sorry, Nora."

"She hated me," Nora said in a whisper, as though it was a shameful secret.

Noah was shaking his head. "Maybe she had a difficult time showing affection or love. Maybe there were things you didn't understand when you were a girl. Maybe her best effort at being a good mother was just not very good at all."

"Or maybe she hated me," Nora said.

"Right now you have more questions than answers. Consider looking for some of those answers. What's the worst-case scenario? That everything you think you know about your parents is true? To verify that rather than wonder—that could help set you on a path of rebuilding your life."

"I'm not that strong," she said.

Noah actually gave a little laugh. "Oh, you're by far one of the strongest women I know. And the most gentle. But I leave this entirely to you—just know that I'm here for you, willing to be your partner in this next step."

"I don't know. I'm going to have to think about it."

"Go ahead and think about it. Your father didn't hint at any urgency in contacting you...."

"There you go—urgency! What if he's only looking for me because he needs a kidney or something? What if he wants to make amends for doing terrible things to me that I was too young to remember? I'm better off not knowing, right? Because all those hard years with my mother were bad enough without adding more awful stuff...."

"Just think it over and if you want to talk about it, we can talk it through before you make a decision. The good news is we can find him easily. And he wants to be found."

Just think it over? Nora could think of nothing else the following week and picking apples was the perfect job—she could indulge in obsessive remembering while filling up her bag.

There were very few times while growing up that Nora braved her mother's emotional outbursts to ask questions about her father or express her desire to know him. It was a dicey proposition; Nora was never sure whether Therese would rage, "How can you keep putting me through this? Don't you ever think of anyone but yourself?" Or she might cry, "I've done my best for you, rescued you from a horrible father, can't you just be grateful for what you have and stop torturing me?" And there was always the chance she'd just slap her and scream, "I should've just let him take you, then you'd know what *real* abuse is!"

She had no idea the nature of this abuse her mother put on her father, but she knew exactly what kind of abuse she suffered at her mother's hands. Her mother had dramatic mood swings and she was never sure which woman was coming home from work each day. It could be the Therese in an upbeat mood with plans for a treat, like pizza for dinner and an evening of watching all their favorite TV shows or it could be the woman in a foul temper who blamed the stress of her work, a long day of listening to screwed-up crazy people's problems. Or, sadly, one of the best options was when her mother went out after work, meeting friends for dinner or a movie or shopping, friends that Nora rarely got to know because it was so seldom Therese brought them home.

She struggled to remember when she fully realized that Therese almost never had a girlfriend who lasted a whole year, and Nora understood why. Therese was difficult, selfish, short-tempered and completely unpredictable. She was also very funny at times—she could certainly make people laugh when she wasn't in a snit. She was attractive and well turned out and had a great singing voice she exercised when in a happy state. When Therese laughed and sang, Nora held her breath, afraid to let herself enjoy it.

But Nora was probably all of seven or eight when she began saying *I will not be like my mother* over and over to herself. When she found herself pregnant with Berry she was terrified that something would happen to her and she'd wake up one morning finding she hated her child, discovering she couldn't control her anger.

Noah turned up at her house after work three evenings during that week, just to give her an opportunity to talk. News of her mother's death brought out all these issues she had with her mother, which she told Noah.

"But what about this father of mine?" Nora asked. "Right in the area and never a phone call? Never any contact, any help to deflect some of my mother's more cruel moments?"

"Yet another thing to ask, to try to understand," Noah said.

"He's either a very bad man or a very negligent man," Nora said. "He had a daughter! Shouldn't he have done *something?* Was my mother right? That I was better off? Because it's hard to imagine being better off alone with her."

"When you're ready, you can ask these questions," Noah said.

"I have a full-time job, thank God," she said. "I can't leave the kids with Adie and leave town. And I'm not letting him anywhere near my children."

"All these concerns are resolvable. Once you settle on a day—a day that I can take you—I'll ask Ellie to help out with the girls. She's wonderful with babies and was a huge help to Vanessa Haggerty when she adopted a nine-month-old before her eighteen-month-old was out of diapers." Noah laughed and shook his head. "It was insane—and all turned out well. Remember Paul Haggerty? He plowed the roads in town last Christmas and sent one of his crews over to your house to seal the windows and doors."

"Listen, I don't need everyone in town knowing that Nora Crane has yet another crisis, that I'm from a crazier background than they even imagined."

"I know it sometimes seems that way, Nora—that everyone else has a normal, average, functional life and only you have stuff to work out. Believe me, I know the feeling. But really, it's not that way. I come from a pretty crazy family, and poor Ellie—she had such trials growing up, taking care of her kids alone before we met. When you get to know her better, you can ask—Ellie is very up-front about everything. For right now, let's think about the challenge you're facing. You need to see your father. Talk to him. Ask him questions. Ask for some documentation that he's really your father, that your parents were divorced and he chose not to see you, et cetera. First find out what he has to say and then let's work on understanding what happened."

"I won't put my girls at risk," she said.

"Absolutely not," Noah agreed. "Whenever you're ready."

Of course Nora told her closest girlfriends what was going on—Adie and Martha, both in their seventies, and Leslie, the much younger neighbor a few doors down. Those three women had included Nora in gab sessions on the porch and shared stories and it happened they agreed with Noah—that she should face her father with her questions.

Of course she hadn't mentioned anything at the orchard. She didn't feel close enough to anyone there to talk about her personal business. In fact she had been so preoccupied thinking about her mother's death and her father's reappearance, she did her job mechanically, the hours passing like minutes while her mind was in another place.

She showed up at the crossroad of 36 and the road to Virgin River and there sat that familiar big white truck. And there he was, leaning against it. Waiting.

"Wow," she said, stopped in her tracks.

"Hop in," Tom invited.

She went around the front of the truck and climbed up and in the cab. "I bet when your grandmother forced you to hire me, you didn't foresee taxi service."

"Is everything all right, Nora?" he asked before starting the truck.

She was startled by the question. No, things were not all right. But it was personal business. It had nothing to do with her job. "Fine," she said. "Why?"

"You've been really quiet," he said.

*He'd noticed?* she wondered. "I have?" she asked.

He nodded. "Your muscles okay? Back, shoulders, et cetera?"

"Yes. No problems. Why are you quizzing me?"

"I don't mean to pry, but I thought I should ask because... Well, you had some injuries before and kept it to yourself."

"I don't have any injuries."

"You probably don't realize it—but the first couple of weeks at the orchard, you had a hard time keeping up, but you laughed. You also hummed a lot—I kept thinking you were going to break into song or something. We could hear you all over the place. Maxie could hear you from the back porch and she said things like, 'That girl's good to have around—she's happy in her heart.' I had no idea what you had to be so happy about, but we all got used to hearing you—and then you stopped. So I thought…wondered…"

Her mouth was hanging open. It took her a moment to recover from her shock. "Wait a minute," she said. "When did you start to care if I was happy or not?"

"It's not exactly like that," he said. "I know you need the job to support your family because you told me you did and I know you go to a lot of trouble to prove yourself. And I know you've been quiet lately. I wanted to be sure you weren't hurt or sick or maybe in trouble."

"I didn't even know I did that," she said. "I was so damn relieved to have a job that actually put food on the table, I guess I was in a pretty good mood. I hum? Really? And you actually noticed?"

He hit the steering wheel with the heel of his hand in apparent frustration. "Excuse me for being sensitive," he grumbled. "I'm not a bad guy, I'm just a guy and one of my employees is—"

"Okay, okay, okay," she said. She ran her hands through her hair, removing and replacing the ponytail tie. "It's been a very strange week. I'm estranged from my parents—my father left when I was little and I fell out with my mother when I was nineteen. I just found out my mother died two years ago, cause unknown. And my missing father has been looking for me. I've had a lot on my mind. I'll try to laugh more if it'll make you feel better."

And now it was his turn to be silent. Shocked. "I'm sorry. I had no idea."

"Of course you didn't. I don't usually talk about all that personal stuff. And I'm kind of sorry I just did, to tell the truth. I'm pretty sure I have the most screwed-up family on the planet and really, I don't advertise that."

And he laughed.

"This is funny to you?" she asked.

"Not at all. Coincidental, that's all. Who would think we'd share something so bizarre—like screwed-up family?"

"I know Maxie a little bit and she is *amazing*," Nora said.

"You bet she is. When I was born my dad was a test pilot in the Air Force, out in the high desert, Edwards Air Force Base. He flew spooky new jets. My mother was at the end of her rope with the living conditions, the lifestyle, all that went with his job, plus she was really young and I guess I wasn't exactly planned. So, when I was a month old she brought me to Maxie and said, 'Here. You take care of him. This was all a mistake.' And off she went. I might know more about her except my dad was killed in a crash a couple of months later. I have no memory of either of them. So, there you go—we both have some unusual family histories. I hear my dad was a normal guy, but who knows what's in the other gene pool. I don't know anything at all about my mother." He took a pause. "But I'll tell you this—if she showed up all of a sudden, I'd have some questions."

She was speechless. Why was it that everyone else's life always seemed so easy, so flawless?

He pulled onto the road, heading for the orchard. Nora watched his profile. He was smiling. This was a hard man to read—he could be so kind, so generous and thoughtful, but she had also seen him glower as if just seconds from an outburst. Perhaps, she thought, being raised by Therese left her fearful of a frown. Surely not everyone came apart at the seams if something displeased them—that certainly wasn't the case with her.

Tom pulled up to the barn and parked. He jumped out and she followed more slowly. When he got to the door to his office, he turned and looked at her. "You okay?" he asked.

She took a breath. "That was nice of you, to tell me that. It made me feel a little less… I don't know…a little less like a loser."

He actually laughed. "How long have you lived here?"

"Eight months."

"If I hadn't told you, someone else would have. Everyone knows. And everyone talks."

"Right," she said.

He turned to walk away and she said to his back, "So what would you ask her? Your mother? If she turned up suddenly?"

He pivoted. "I guess I'd ask her if she had any regrets."

"Yeah," she said. "Makes sense."

"How about you?" he fired at her.

"What?"

"Oh, I don't know. Any regrets? About finding yourself a single, twenty-three-year-old apple-picking mother?"

Remarkably, coming from him, she took no offense. After all, they shared some difficult history. And she was going to have to get used to that very thing he said—that everyone knew and everyone talked. "About having my daughters?" She shook her head. "I could never regret having them. They're miracles. About not having them *after* being married to a handsome, rich investment banker for about six years? Yeah, that's regrettable."

That brought out his grin and she realized he had a very attractive dimple. Left cheek. "Investment banker, huh?"

"Okay, neurosurgeon. Astronaut. Computer genius. CEO of a Fortune 500 company."

He laughed. In fact, he tilted his head back and guffawed, hands on his hips. "Damn, kid—an ordinary old apple grower wouldn't stand a chance!"

She stared at him, watching him laugh at her for a long second. Then she headed for the office door. "I'll make the coffee," she said.

Well. If he'd been looking for something to take her mind off her current challenges, he'd certainly done it with that statement. He probably had no idea what a luxury it seemed to someone like her to raise a family in the healthy and pristine beauty of these mountains, in a great big house right in the middle of a delicious orchard. Or the fantasies it could inspire to think about being wanted by a man like Tom Cavanaugh.

He drove her back to the road to Virgin River after her shift. "You can't do this every day," she said. "It's too much."

"It's two miles," he replied. "And when you get a ride, you pick more fruit."

"Well, I have to admire a man who knows what he wants," she said. Then she jumped out of the truck and headed for home. Even though Adie was expecting her, she stopped at the church, looking for Reverend Kincaid.

She stood in his office doorway and waited until he looked up. "If that offer is still open, I'd like to set up a meeting with my father. If you'll contact him and go with me."

"Be happy to," he said. "Any particular day?"

"Doesn't matter to me. Weekend, if he's available and if you're available. Saturday? I could take a day off I think, but I don't want to do that to the Cavanaughs—work weekend overtime and take off on a regular pay day. But if that's the only option, I think Tom Cavanaugh would give me a break."

"I'll call him," Noah said. "Jed Crane, not Tom."

"Tell him I want some kind of evidence—that he's my father, that my mother is dead, that he's employed.... I don't know what to ask. I just want to be sure he's not a fraud. Or a creep who's just after something. I'm not sure I can remember his face."

Noah stood from behind his desk. "I'm glad you're doing this. No matter where it goes from here, you deserve some answers. I'll ask Ellie to help with your girls."

They chose a public park in Santa Rosa as a meeting place and Nora was so stressed out, she barely spoke all the way there. She did say, "Please don't leave me alone with him and don't mention that I have children." Once Noah had to pull over because she was afraid she was going to throw up. When they got to the park at noon, Nora knew Jed immediately. The memory of him came back instantly—he was the same, though older. He was very tall, his brown hair was thin over a shiny crown with a lumpy shape, his eyes kind of sad, crinkling and sagging at the corners. He had thick, graying brows, had a bit of a soft center— a paunch—and wore his pants too high. And he wore a very unfashionable short-sleeved plaid shirt with a button-down collar that she thought she recognized from the last time she saw him.

Apparently he knew her right away because he immediately took a few anxious steps toward her. And then he opened his arms to her and she instinctively stepped back, out of his reach. That just did him in— he almost broke down. A huff of air escaped him and she thought he teared up. "I'm sorry," he said. He carried a large padded envelope which he held out toward her. He swiped at invisible tears, embarrassed by this display. "I apologize, Nora," he said. "I was afraid I'd never see you again."

And what were her first words to her long-lost father? "Did you ever take me bowling? When I was too little to even think about bowling?"

Sudden laughter joined his tears. "I had no idea what a weekend father was supposed to do—so yes, I took you bowling. It was a disaster, but you seemed to have a fun time. Your ball never once made it to the pins. Here," he said, pressing the big envelope on her. "Copies of all the papers Reverend Kincaid said you'd like to have." Then he stuck out his hand to Noah. "Thank you for helping with this. Thank you so much."

But Nora said, "Weekend father?"

"Let's sit down somewhere," Jed suggested. "There's so much to catch up on."

As he turned in the direction of a picnic table, Nora put out a hand to his forearm and stopped him. "Do you…" She faltered, then took a deep breath and asked, "Do you have any regrets?"

"Nothing but regrets, Nora. I just don't know how I could've made things better for you."

They found a table in the shade of a tree and even though there were lots of people around, began to forage through the past. "My mother said the bowling never happened. I remembered bowling, planting a garden, you reading me stories, that kind of thing, but she said…"

"It's going to be so hard to explain her," Jed said, shaking his head dismally.

"What's in here?" she asked, holding up the envelope.

"Reverend Kincaid said you had no documentation at all, that you weren't even sure your mother and I divorced. It's all there—copies of the marriage license, the divorce decree, the order from the court that Therese retain custody and that I would have visitation one day a week. Then I lost even that. I had a few pictures—you as a newborn, your first birthday, a day in the park, the first day of preschool. I didn't get many."

"But *why?*" she asked. "Why did you leave us?"

He seemed to take a moment to compose himself. "I've wanted to explain and yet dreaded this moment for years," he said. "Therese and I were at terrible odds—lots of conflict. I suggested a separation, suggested we might've made a mistake and could work it out amicably, and that did it. Pushed her right over the edge. I could say she threw me out, except that I'd already suggested separation. Her anger with me was phenomenal and I left because I'd had all I could take.

"I was over forty when we met and though I was plenty mature, I wasn't exactly a ladies' man. I had so little experience with women. We weren't a young couple. We met, dated and got married too quickly because we were getting older and wanted children—your mother was forty when you were born. The sad truth is, we weren't happy for long. She was sick when she was pregnant and suffered terrible depression when you were a baby and it took about a year for her to recover. Maybe she never did—I'm not sure. Therese was a loose cannon. I never knew what might set her off. She lashed out at me constantly. I suggested maybe motherhood didn't make her as happy as she thought it might and that…" He shook his head and looked down. "I always seemed to say the wrong things."

"Were you ever happy?" Nora asked.

"I thought so," Jed answered. "At the very beginning. Then there were issues I thought had to do with pregnancy and new parenthood. But by the time a few years had passed, I knew we were doomed.

"But I thought she loved you, Nora. As long as I wasn't around, she seemed to take good care of you. When I came home after work, you sparkled. You were so happy and showed no signs of suffering. I was afraid of what a life with her might do to you in the long run, but there didn't seem to be much I could do." He shrugged. "The truth is I was afraid you could become like her—so over the years I watched from a safe distance. I checked on your school progress, went to school events to catch a glimpse, asked questions about you. When Therese got wind that I was around, she lashed out, lost her temper. I was very circumspect, but I was never far away."

"And I never saw you?"

He leaned toward her, his brows scrunched. "You might remember when your mother stopped talking to the lady next door," he said.

"They had a fight," Nora said. "I was never sure

what that was about. Mom said she'd been insulted and accused of something. They stopped talking and I was not allowed to go to their house. Sometimes after school I'd say hello or we'd talk in the yard, before Mom got home from work, but we had a pact—we'd keep it our secret."

"The fight was about me calling the neighbor and asking how you were, how things were going in my home, with my daughter. She let it slip. So, it kept Therese from talking to her neighbor, but it didn't keep the neighbor from watching, from talking to me." He swallowed hard. "She moved when you were about to graduate from high school. I lost my best connection to you."

"This isn't happening," she said. "This is my worst nightmare. She was a *therapist!*"

"I've never understood that," he said, shaking his head. "That should have guaranteed a certain level of stability. Civility. Understanding. I think she was crazier than half the people she counseled. What I've learned since is that, sadly, she was hardly the only inept counselor—they are plentiful. So are competent, helpful, talented counselors. There were times she raged at me in a way that made me think she was truly insane. Nora, there was something wrong. It's been suggested by professionals I've seen that maybe she was a borderline personality—not mentally ill, but narcissistic, hostile, perhaps a bit sociopathic. Very manipulative. Successfully manipulative. Quite functional. We were like oil and water. I wanted to take you with me but she wouldn't have it. There was something about me that set her off."

"There was something about everyone..." Nora mumbled. "You could have at least called me."

"I should have, but I didn't want to force you to lie or be secretive. There's no other way to put it— she was vengeful when she didn't have her way. That worried me."

"But you said you lost even your visitation," Nora said.

"I did, but not in a legal action. I went to pick you up for our day together and you weren't there. Things like that happened very often. And Therese started screaming at me, accusing me of terrible things and I lost my temper. I punched a hole in the wall. I don't think I ever punched anything in my life before that, or after. I'm just not that kind of person."

"I remember that hole!" Nora said. "She never fixed it!"

"She called the police and there I stood with banged-up knuckles. While you played at a friend's house, I was taken away in handcuffs."

"And then?"

He shook his head. "I knew it was bad for you, that it was never going to get better. There were so many fights and standoffs when I came to get you, I stopped coming. I didn't know what else to do, didn't know how to protect you from that anger. I saw lawyers, but I wasn't going to get custody of you and trying to see you only lit a fire in her. Therese had feuds with anyone who would talk to me. She was completely estranged from your aunts because they checked on you on my behalf. They haven't spoken since you were seven or eight years old."

"Aunts?" Nora said weakly.

"Therese was the youngest of three girls and a good many years separated them. Her eldest sister is deceased now, but Victoria is still alive, living in New Jersey. She was named in your mother's will. And I didn't know your mother had died until it came to my attention that checks I'd been sending for alimony and support weren't being cashed. I don't think there's anything you can do about her will, I'm sorry."

Nora put her head in her hands. "Checks? Will? Aunts? Oh, my God." She looked pleadingly at Noah. "This is nuts. This can't be true. She said there was no family, that there was never any support. I was on partial scholarship and I worked—my mother only paid for textbooks, nothing else."

"You could've gone to Stanford for practically nothing," Jed said. "I'm a professor there. Your mother said you had no interest."

"I only went to college for a year." She looked at Jed. "If this is true, she must have been completely insane."

"I don't think so," Jed said. "At least not clinically. I've done a lot of reading and have talked to a few professionals—there are people who lie, manipulate, hold terrible grudges who are not mentally ill but have anger problems the rest of us just don't understand. And what made her so angry? I have no idea."

"And you couldn't *do* anything?"

"Nora, she was completely functional. She held a full-time job, paid her bills, raised a child. You were clean and fed. You did all right in school. You seemed happy and had friends…unless I came around and the whole world went to hell…"

"She was a train wreck! *She* didn't have friends, at least not for long. She lied about her family, about you. There was never a single picture of you in the house, not one. And why didn't she get fired from her job? Explain that?"

"I don't think she was well liked by everyone, but you have to understand that especially in a situation like hers, an educational institution, just being difficult and slightly dysfunctional on the job wasn't going to get her fired. She knew how to do her job, and she had a great deal of seniority. I know she had problems from time to time, but for some reason there never seemed to be consequences. I can give you the names of a few coworkers—they might talk with you. In that envelope you'll find a list of the books I read, trying to understand who she was. I can't say I came to any conclusion—just a lot of guessing."

"When did you get a divorce?" she asked.

"I moved out when you were four years old and we divorced quickly."

"Why do I think I was six? That's what I remember."

"I stopped coming for you when you were six—

those two years must have been the worst of your life—your mother and I fighting every time I came, hiding you from me, refusing to let you come with me. I never went to the house without a fierce battle. So I stopped."

"I thought this might give me answers," she said. And when she said that, Noah reached for her hand, giving it a squeeze.

"I'm so sorry," Jed said. "You were used as a pawn and eventually I abandoned you, hoping that would set you free. I can't imagine the trauma. Counseling might be in order. I've had a lot of it."

"How could you trust a counselor? She was a counselor!"

"Listen, Nora—there are good and bad in every profession—doctors, lawyers, teachers—"

"Clergy," Noah put in. "Jed's right. And a lot of troubled people study counseling to try to figure out their own issues. I might've been guilty of that myself."

Her eyes filled when she looked at Noah. "I'm exhausted. I don't think I've ever been this tired in my life."

"Maybe you and your father should continue all the questions and answers over the phone or computer. Take it one swallow at a time. You can use my computer at the church—we'll set up an email account for you." Noah glanced at Jed.

"Absolutely," Jed said. "I don't want to overwhelm you. I'm just so relieved to find you alive. One thing— is there anything you need? Is your health all right?"

She gave a nod. "And you?"

"Blood pressure medicine, statins for cholesterol—everything under control."

"And you're teaching?"

"At Stanford—history. I've been there twenty years now. I'd like to hear more about what you're doing. When you're ready. Everything you need to find me is in the envelope."

"Thank you," she said, hugging it to her. And without touching him, she turned away from him, heading back toward Noah's truck. Then she stopped, turned back and said, "How did she die?"

"Complications of pneumonia. She went to the emergency room, was hospitalized and slipped away very quickly. I'm sorry, Nora."

She nodded and went to the truck.

Noah stood and spoke with Jed for a few minutes while Nora just escaped. They were under way for several miles before she spoke. "All that driving for a thirty-minute meeting. I hope you're not angry about that."

"We agreed, the meeting was to be on your terms. No one else would control it—only you. I think you accomplished a lot. What do you think?"

"I think it was surreal. And I am completely drained."

# *Five*

Noah Kincaid had become a passable detective over time and necessity—Nora wasn't the first person he'd helped thusly. He knew how to verify an address and employment and with the help of Brie Valenzuela, court documents. He reported to Nora that Jed Crane checked out and provided information on her aunt Victoria with a phone number to call when she was ready. There were three cousins—the entire family back east. All the items in the envelope were legitimate. There was one surprise included—a check. It was more money than Nora had had at one time in her life—five thousand dollars.

"What is the money for?" she asked Jed in an email sent from Noah's church office.

"I made alimony and support payments and after your mother died, checks weren't cashed. I thought maybe you could use it," he wrote back

"But I'm sure you're not rich," she fired back.

"Can you put it to good use?" he returned.

Could she! The first thing would be car seats, just in case anyone offered to take her with the girls anywhere. And they were in sore need of clothes, all of them. She'd have to get the girls outfitted for winter—secondhand was perfectly adequate, but still cost money and should be done soon. The church always threw a little something her way, but she would still have to buy things like underwear and shoes. Disposable diapers for the baby cost the earth and formula wasn't cheap. And then there was preschool and day care.

And there was one other thing that gnawed at her. She went to Noah and said, "I have a confession to make. It's about the house...."

"What house?" he asked.

"The one I'm living in." Her cheeks grew hot and rosy. "I have no idea who owns it. It was a broken-down hovel when Chad brought us here. Fay was a newborn. It didn't look like it had been lived in for years and the door was unlocked. I asked a man who was walking by with his dog who lived there and he said different renters on and off. The gas and electric were running, so we just went in. Noah—I'm squatting."

"Squatting?" he asked.

"No one knows this, but no one has collected rent. The gas and power—I don't use much, but I'm behind on the bills. Bills come in the mail to someone none of my neighbors has ever heard of and I get a money order from the Corner Store and pay a little something and miraculously, it keeps running. No one questions me. And now I have some money so I should make it right. And I'm scared. What if…"

Noah laughed. "Nora, that house was abandoned years ago—that's why it wasn't kept up. There are at least a few of them in town. Utilities are on?"

She nodded and chewed her lower lip. "Oh, my God—what if I'm evicted?"

"It's shelter," he said. "I'll try to figure out who owns it, but sometimes it's better not to ask a question if you can't stand the answer. It's probably owned by the state or bank. One tiny house with one bedroom— it can't cost much in utilities."

"But someone could notice I'm behind one of these days and shut everything off," she said. "And what if it happens in winter?"

"Call me if that happens, meanwhile use a little of this money to catch up on the utility bills as much as you can," he said with a smile. "We're there for you, Nora. We don't have much, but we always have lights and heat. You can bring the apples."

Tom had a lot of friends from high school still living in the area, many of them working on family ranches, vineyards or farms; most of them married and some already parents. He had missed his ten-year high school reunion; he'd been in Afghanistan. His Marine Corps friends were either still serving or separated and returned to homes all over the U.S. And, there were a few deceased—he kept in touch with some widows and parents of fallen marines.

As for a social life, he occasionally drove all the way to the coast for a beer where there might be datable girls. He hadn't met any particularly tempting women, however. And there was always Jack's, but Maxie was so intent on cooking up a good evening meal for him that he had to head her off before she even planned one in her head. "Friday night I think I'll go out," he'd say. "Maybe hook up with some of my old friends." Maxie was always delighted to hear that. She wanted Tom to have some fun. But what she didn't know was that he seldom hooked up with anyone.

One thing he did do was give his only female employee a ride each morning and afternoon. She had stopped protesting and he found himself looking forward to those few minutes coming and going, fascinated by the updates on her family situation. She had met her father and began either talking to him for a few minutes a day or emailing from Noah's church office.

"There's a lot to process," she told him. "It's shocking how much I have to learn about myself—how my experiences growing up influenced some of the choices I've made."

"As in bad choices?"

"Sure, some. But Reverend Kincaid has been wonderful in helping me navigate this minefield and tries to prompt me to find some of the good choices I've made. Like the choice to be a loving mother. Now, I don't know about you and your views of fatherhood, but I always thought I'd be stuck with the kind of mother I turned out to be and to tell the truth, I was afraid I'd stink at it. It never occurred to me I had a choice."

"I think some people are naturals, though," he said.

"Oh, I'm sure. Your grandmother, for example. If I could be like her one day…" And then she smiled at him with a smile that so lit up her pretty face he thought it was a miracle he didn't drive off the road.

He realized they were becoming friends, the most unlikely friends imaginable. If she were a little older and less encumbered, they might even be more than friends. That was out of the question, of course. Tom was not in the market for an instant family. He was especially unwilling to take on the kids of some unknown guy or guys.

It was too bad she had that baggage because there were things about her that really blew his whistle—like her undeniable beauty. She had rich mahogany hair—long, silky, thick. She usually kept it in a ponytail but had a habit of letting it loose, shaking it out, combing it with her fingers back into the tie that held it. And her eyes were smoky, a kind of odd brown shade that grew almost gray in the bright light. And those slim, dark brown brows—she could lift just one and it became provocative. Sexy and even suggestive. He loved that she took her breaks in the orchard rather than the break room in the barn—she said fall was her favorite season and it would be gone too soon. And it touched a place deep inside him when she said working in the orchard was like a fantasy she hadn't even dared dream of—a luxury.

Almost everything about her appealed to him. Except her past, of course. And the ready-made family— he didn't even know where they'd come from.

He would enjoy their chats, get a kick out of her sometimes teasing, sometimes challenging personality. Here she was, struggling and down on her luck, yet she didn't take any of his guff. He liked that in a girl. All that being said, he'd keep looking. He'd find the right woman one day. And he wouldn't be completely surprised if she turned out to be a little like Nora.

Until he did, he not only picked her up and drove her home, after a week of that he began to go all the way into town to get her. And he tried not to keep an eye out for her during the workday, but still managed to find things to do near wherever she was picking.

Maxie took a run over to the coast for some shopping and since she was gone, Tom went to the kitchen to make himself a huge sandwich full of meats, cheeses, lettuce, tomato and pickles. He cut it in half, wrapped it in a couple of paper towels and set off for the orchard. He went to where he'd last seen her picking, but she wasn't there. Her ladder stood abandoned. He walked deeper into the orchard and finally he thought he heard her humming and he moved toward the sound.

Very soon he realized it wasn't music—she was crying. His pace quickened as he looked for her. "Nora?" he called. But she didn't answer; her sobbing became closer and more ragged. He felt panic rise; his fear for her surpassed all other thoughts.

Finally he saw the satchel in which she carried water and lunch and the shadow of her bent knee on the far side of an apple tree. Her crying was very close. She was sitting on the ground, leaning against the tree, her face covered with her hands. Three long strides brought him to her and he instantly fell to his knees in front of her.

"God, are you hurt?" he asked.

She shook her head and turned her red, wet eyes toward him. But she didn't answer, she simply cried.

He put aside the sandwich and gently grabbed her shoulders. "Nora, talk to me. Tell me what happened, what's wrong."

She just shook her head and sobbed.

He pulled her against him and held her. He whispered to her, *shhhh* and, *it's okay*. He rocked her a little bit. And finally, through her tears she choked out, "I remember." And then she cried some more.

Tom had always hated it when girls cried. He had always thought it either weak or manipulative. But when Nora gripped the front of his shirt in her hands and held her face against his chest, weeping, he found it curious that those thoughts didn't even come to mind. His shirt was getting all wet and he didn't care. And while he wished he knew exactly what caused these tears, he was willing to soak them up until she was ready. All he wanted was to take care of her. He wanted to comfort, stop the tears, ease her worry, feed her half of his sandwich.

He held her for a long time before she took a few

deep, uneven breaths. Against his chest she said, "All of a sudden I remembered. I was up in the tree, on top of my ladder, and I remembered." Then she leaned back a little bit and still gripping his shirt with some desperation she added, "I just remembered. Jed…my father…said that he was divorced when I was four but stopped coming for his visits when I was six and for all these years I believed my parents divorced when I was six. I remembered so clearly, coming home from first grade and asking if Daddy was coming home." She shook her head. "I lost two years of my life. Two whole years. And I just got them back."

He threaded his fingers into the hair at her temples and, just as he'd seen her do at least a dozen times, he combed back her hair until it came free of the ponytail. He spread it over her shoulders and smiled into her eyes. "Does a little girl of four remember so much, anyway?"

"Yes. What I remember now is hiding under the bed, behind my mother's heavy curtains, in the closet or outside. Because when my dad came to get me, there was always a terrible fight—lots of yelling. My mother screamed at him. He was so passive—he would keep saying, 'I just want to take Nora for the day and I'll bring her back on time,' but my mother made it so horrible, so scary, that I was terrified and I shook all over. I wet my pants and she blamed my daddy. Oh, God, I remember." She swallowed convulsively. "And then when I got home, she was crazy all night, sometimes all week. I remember telling her I didn't want to go with Daddy, thinking it could make her better. I told him he shouldn't come because it made Mommy too mad and made Mommy cry. I remember." Huge tears rolled down her cheeks. "I sent him away, Tom. He never came again. Never called, never sent cards, never showed up for birthdays or holidays. And my mother used to say, 'You're better off—he was an abusive ass.'" And she dropped her head against his chest again.

Tom sat back on his heels, facing her. He ran his hands down her hair. He'd wanted to touch it for a long time, but he never imagined it would be like this.

"I used to remember things," she said. "Very small things—standing on my stool to do dishes with him in a sink that wasn't our sink. Or going bowling when the ball weighed half as much as me and Daddy laughing so hard. Or reading in a park, then going on the swings, then getting ice cream—all nice memories that didn't seem abusive to me. My mother said those things never happened and that I invented them. She said he abused me and I had buried memories." She lifted her head for a moment. "I did—but they weren't the kind my mother suggested they were."

He ran a thumb across her cheek under each eye. "Are you crying because you remember?"

"I don't know," she said. "Because suddenly I realized I hadn't remembered—that two whole years had been gone from my life. That my mother is really dead and nothing was ever worked out with her. That my father came back to tell me she was dead and that he was sorry." She sniffed. "Do you have any idea what I'd have given to hear my mother say that? That she was sorry?"

He leaned his forehead against hers and gently massaged her shoulders. "Of course I do," he said. Because he'd like to know what the hell happened between his parents and had accepted that he never would.

"Of course you do." She took a deep breath. "I have to get a grip. It's time to get back to work…"

"Not just yet," Tom said. He reached for the sandwich and opened the paper towels. "Do you have water in that?" he said, jutting his chin toward the satchel. When she nodded he asked, "Will you share it with me?"

"Sure," she said with a sniff, pulling out a big bottled water that she refilled at home every night.

He chuckled and put the sandwich on the ground on one of the paper towels, handing the other to her. "You need this for your eyes and nose. I'll share mine."

She obediently wiped the wet off her cheeks and blew her nose, but her eyes instantly filled again. "Thank you, Tom, but I don't think I can eat anything."

"I know that's what you think," he said, handing the sandwich toward her. "I want you to take a couple of bites. Maybe you'll feel a little better. Don't worry," he said with a laugh. "I can eat what you can't finish."

"Why did you do this?" she asked, taking a very small, experimental bite.

He smiled, a little naughty. "Maxie went to town

to shop. All the way to the coast. No one's watching me, making assumptions."

"Ah," she said, chewing. "You're afraid Maxie will think you like me."

"I'm sure she already thinks that. She's noticed I give you rides. She notices everything. But a ride and a lunch—I don't want her getting all worked up, like I'm taking it to the next level. Because I'm not taking it to the next level."

"Because we're employer and employee," she said, helping him out.

"Uh-huh, and friends. Come on, we're friends. Aren't we friends? I watched you blow your nose—that's very intimate. Isn't it?"

She laughed in spite of herself. She also took another bite of her sandwich. "You're a very sensitive man, underneath it all."

He gave her a serious look. He shook his head. "I don't know about sensitive—but I've been to Iraq and Afghanistan with the Marines. I've seen grown men cry for their mothers. I've promised to visit their wives if they don't make it."

She was frozen, he could see that. She coughed and nearly choked, swallowing hard. "God," she said. "I can be so selfish. What I've been through is nothing compared to war."

He gave another stroke to her long, wonderful hair, hoping he didn't get mustard or pickle juice on it. "Don't do that to yourself, Nora. You've had your own war. You're allowed to feel the weight of it. This has been traumatic for you."

Her eyes filled again, but she seemed to will them to dry right away. "See? Very understanding of you." She handed her half sandwich toward him.

"I think you took three bites. Small bites. Can you try a little harder? I really worked to build that thing."

She laughed again, but she took a bite. And she thought, *Oh, this is scary.* Because if someone like Tom could actually like her, it would be unimaginably wonderful. If a genuinely good man who happened to live inside a very large, hard, sexy body felt the slightest attraction...

But she took another bite. "It's very good, in fact."

"What's in the sandwich you bring every day?" he asked.

"What do you think? PB and J. Berry's favorite. I make her have a banana or, these days, apple slices with it. Protein, carbs and fruit."

He took a giant bite of his half. After he swallowed he said, "Teach her how to spread the peanut butter right on apple slices. Or, take some apple butter home today—peanut butter and apple butter make a mean sandwich. And let's hook you up with some cider. It might be too much for the baby, but Berry can handle the cider—so full of vitamins, it'll rock her world." He lifted his eyebrows. "Could eliminate the nap—it seems to fill little kids with energy. But it's good energy."

"You are definitely the apple man," she said.

"I love apples." He grinned and nodded toward her. "One more bite. And can I have a slug of that water?"

"Of course." She handed him the bottle. And she took yet another bite. "You have a gift here, as well," she said, nodding toward the huge sandwich.

"Are you feeling a little better?" he asked.

She nodded. "I apologize. It hit me out of nowhere. The memories, then the crying, then the anger, then grief, then… I don't know what happened. But thank you. I'm a lot better." She held the sandwich toward him. He lifted both brows and she took one more bite. "That's it," she said. "Kill it. If I get hungry again a little later, I have my PB and J."

He started on what was left of her half. "Why'd you name your daughter Berry?" he asked.

"I don't know," she said with a shrug. "I was alone, scared out of my mind and the only friends I had were the people in the drug-infested motel where I lived or the ones I met in the welfare or Medicaid lines and I just wanted a cheerful, happy name for the baby I had no idea how I would support or take care of. I liked it. The name."

He frowned. "You were in a bad place."

"Bad. Place."

"And now?"

"Good place. The nicest job I've ever had, though I might not be saying that in a couple of months when the cold sets in. The kids are happy, healthy. I support them in a town that has welcomed us in spite of the fact that we really come from nothing. I'm very grateful. Life is actually good, despite the fact that I have some issues to work through." She took a sip of water and handed it to him. "I need to get to work."

"Not yet," he said. "I think the best thing to do is for you to take the afternoon off—check in with Reverend Kincaid. Talk to him awhile…"

"I'd like to, but you pay better," she said, smiling tolerantly.

He stood up and held out a hand to help her to her feet. "The investment will be worth it," he said. "If Noah is helping you navigate this minefield, as you say, today's meltdown might be worth the time away from apple picking."

"You're probably right," she said. "That sandwich. That was nice. Even if you only did it when Maxie wouldn't know."

"Well, a guy has to be crafty when he has a grandmother like Maxie. She's a little on the pushy side. Come on, we'll swing by the house and grab some cider and apple butter and I'll give you a ride back to Virgin River."

A few days later, after talking to Noah and thinking things over, Nora phoned her father. "I remember now," she said. "I sent you away."

"You can't take responsibility for that, Nora. You were only six. And I could see how difficult our situation had become. I thought you were terrified of my visits and rightly so—not only was Therese impossible at times, I was the one who punched a hole in the wall. Our relationship was out of control. I had to leave it—I was the kerosene on the fire."

"How did you two end up together, anyway?" she asked.

"I asked myself that often enough," he said. "We met at a college fair, a large presentation to potential freshmen by area colleges. I was one of many people working the UC Berkeley booth. I was walking around the area, looking at the other presentations, and bumped into her. Your mother was a very attractive woman. She made me laugh...."

"She could be so funny," Nora remembered. "There were times, between her white-hot rages, we could laugh together. She was at times so destructive that it's hard to remember some of her good traits. But how did you end up married?"

He sighed into the phone. "We married too quickly. We had several dates, talked about the fact that here we were, older at thirty-nine and forty-four, both had wanted to marry and have a family and yet had never come close. A few months later had us running off to the courthouse to get married so we could try to get a start on that family before it was too late. And then it was living together as husband and wife that allowed me to see there was a lot more to Therese than met the eye."

"No kidding..."

"For a little while, I was on a cloud. I'm not an exciting guy, I know that—I'm a nerdy, quiet, boring history teacher. I'm excited by things very few other people care about. And then this pretty, funny, intelligent woman liked me. Liked me a lot. Wanted to be with me, have a family with me… It was such a powerful feeling. I couldn't resist—I thought I'd finally found the life I'd been waiting for. She was pregnant immediately. And then I thought a lot of the high drama and tantrums had to do with that."

"Nah," Nora said. "Trust me—the temper came out of the blue. I never knew what a day would hold. We'd go for days, sometimes weeks, and everything would seem so normal. Maybe not a happy circus, but normal. And then there'd be some incident—fight with the neighbors, disagreement at work, an argument with a friend… Once a traffic ticket had her in a state for weeks! She ranted on the phone to anyone who would listen right up to her court appearance. She performed for a traffic judge who threatened to throw her in jail. I might never have known about that, but I was with her. It was regular. Frequent. I don't know what made her so crazy."

"There were also lies—things she said people did to her, that hadn't been done. I'm sure she claimed that traffic cop abused her in some way," Jed added.

"Um, yes," Nora said. "She had an elaborate story. But there are cameras in the patrol cars. That got her in trouble…and produced a long running rage. If there was one thing Therese hated, it was being caught."

"And there you have it," Jed said. "After four years of trying to be the ballast in the drama of the day, I finally told her I couldn't take the mood swings, the anger, the crazy-making. And it wasn't always directed at me—but fifty percent of the time there was some enormous melodrama that I didn't understand and couldn't deal with. And I was the most convenient person she had to dump it on. I suggested we try a trial separation. I said I thought the pressure of working and parenting was wearing on her and I could take some of that stress off her hands. I wanted to take you. I might as well have launched a missile—she went into an immediate defensive posture. She saw a lawyer right away. We were instantly at war." He took a breath. "You'd think after the number of years I spent studying historic battles, I'd know better than to draw first blood. I'm sorry, Nora. I'm the one at fault for all of it."

"Well…apology accepted, but I know you were no more capable of making things different than I was. Life was sometimes so hard with her…."

"I'm so sorry, Nora. I'd give anything if I could've been smarter. If I'd been a better father."

"What if I inherited it? Her instability?"

"According to her sisters, whatever it was, it was there since she was a just a girl. Her sisters were older than she—larger, stronger, presumably smarter—and yet they were sometimes afraid of her. When we got married, she didn't want any family there…. Nora, I don't know what caused your mother's problems, but if you don't have those issues now… I trust you're free of it. I hate that I had to miss so much of your life."

"I have something to tell you," she said. "There are… I have…" She swallowed. "I have children. Two girls. Ten months and almost three years. And no, I haven't been married. Their names are Fay and Berry."

She heard a strange sound on the phone. "God," he said in a whisper. "Oh, my God…"

"They're very smart and beautiful," she told him.

"Can I… Will you let me meet them?"

"You can visit for an afternoon when I'm not working," she said. "Even though you're my father and we've been talking for a couple of weeks, I'm not ready to leave you unsupervised with them, so that's the best I can do. I work a lot. I'm not close to Stanford—I'm in Humboldt County. A little town called Virgin River. There are a couple of motels on the coast a good half hour away, but no guest room and no bed-and-breakfast."

He sniffed loudly. "Don't worry about that. Tell me when I can come. I'll take time off. Oh, Nora, thank you for telling me. Thank you for giving me a chance."

"Yeah, don't screw up," she said. "I've somehow survived one really mean parent. The first time it looks like it's going down that road with you, it's over."

# Six

Nora rode to the orchard with Tom and said, "I'm going to let Jed visit for a couple of hours on Sunday afternoon while I'm there."

"Jed?" Tom asked.

"It might be quite a while before I call him Dad."

"But you're going to let him meet your daughters…?"

She laughed lightly. "I'm not going to *give* him my daughters, I'm just going to let him see them. And let them meet him. I think it's the right thing to do."

"Want me to be there? Just in case you get nervous?" Tom asked.

She smiled at him. "I could have sworn you found me annoying…."

"Well, maybe I did. At first. But you're not a bad kid."

"I'm not a kid," she said with patience. "And I'm a little unsure of him, but I'm not afraid of him. My memories of him are good. Reverend Kincaid has checked him out—I guess Jed's telling the truth about everything."

"Does it feel like the truth?" Tom wanted to know.

"It does, but I'm not relying on that. I don't think I quite trust my instincts about truth versus lies. I've been wrong too much. How do you think I ended up just about penniless with two little kids and no husband or partner?"

Tom surprised her by pulling the truck to the side of the road. "As a matter of fact, I've been wondering. I didn't think it was polite to ask. But since you brought it up…"

"Curious, huh?" she said.

"I won't say anything to anyone," he said. "And if you don't want to talk about it—if it's none of my damn business…"

"It probably isn't," she said. "Your business, I mean. But, six months ago I could hardly talk about it at all. Noah has me slowly coming out of my shell. I'm starting to put things into perspective, giving myself a break sometimes. I was so hard on myself at first, but—well, here's the thing—I was a college freshman, away from home for the first time. I had only had a couple of very brief boyfriends up to that point. I never had dates or anything. I wasn't one of the popular girls in high school, so…" She shrugged. "So—I went with some friends to a baseball game. They knew a couple of the players because they'd been on the local college team and had their eyes on going to the big league. But first, the minor league. And one of them, a real handsome, athletic, talented guy flirted with me. And boy—I just bit the dust. I fell for him. Bam! Five months later, before the start of my sophomore year, I was pregnant and he was traveling with the team." She looked down and gave another shrug.

"And?" Tom said. "Then what happened?"

"Well, I held my stomach in till he was back in town. I was living in a campus apartment at UC Berkeley and I guess I thought he'd marry me or something, take me with him. But he said, 'You'll have to get your mother to look out for you—I'm on the road all the time.' So he went with me to my house. And my mother went crazy. She started throwing my stuff out the front door. She told me to get out. She said if I thought she was taking on a baby while I went to college, I was crazy. Everything went out the door, on the lawn."

"What stuff?" he asked.

"I'd already moved into my campus apartment so there wasn't a ton of stuff left at my house. But my mother said there wouldn't be any more money for school or anything. She said I was obviously not smart enough for college anyway. So, we threw it all in Chad's trunk and backseat and he said he knew a place I could stay." She made a face. "It was a terrible place, but I guess there was a part of me that felt like I deserved it—I'd made a terrible mistake in judgment. So, I moved into this awful motel in a bad section of town. I went to social services for help and medical benefits and…and Chad went back to his team. I didn't hear from him for months."

"Really?" Tom said. "He didn't call you or anything?"

"He called a few times, but it seemed like he wanted to know about other people, not me. Like a couple of his friends who lived around there. But they weren't really friends—they were guys he got pot from." She met his eyes. "Before I found out I was pregnant, which by the way I found out right away, we used to smoke a little pot. That's something I'm sure you never did…"

Tom laughed. "Oh, of course not—not a good old boy from Humboldt County! Where we grow our own."

"You mean you *did?*" she asked, stunned.

"You should keep that to yourself. Maxie wouldn't be too happy about that, even though I was just a stupid kid."

"Seriously? You did?"

"I was not a pothead, all right?" he said, somewhat indignantly. "I was a kid, a boy. There might've been a little beer, a joint. I never got in trouble." He shook his head. "Maxie would kill me. Even now."

She laughed at him. "Your secret is safe with me. And that describes my dabbling exactly. I realized I was pregnant with Berry and there hasn't been any of that since. Not anything. But Chad? I had absolutely no idea, but he was a sinking ship. Since I never saw him, how would I know? But when he came back later, when I was pregnant with Fay, his appearance had changed. He'd gotten so thin—his teeth and skin were terrible. He said they were working him to death, and I believed it, but that wasn't what it was. I found out too late—he had fallen headlong into all kinds of drugs, had been kicked off the team, was doing some dealing to cover his own habit. He was not the same guy who rang all my chimes at a baseball game when I was nineteen." She looked at Tom and just tilted her head. "I was young and dumb, no experience. I didn't know anything. And I didn't have anyone to lean on."

"And then what happened?" Tom asked.

"Then?" she said.

"Well, you have two kids...."

"Oh," she said. "Well, by the time I realized what was going on I had a one-year-old and was pregnant, living on assistance in a hovel with my useless boyfriend living off me. I was twenty-one, broke, had no family and no money and Chad said we were coming to Humboldt County because he had found work, but Fay came before. It was winter in the mountains and he left me with a newborn baby and a toddler in a house that didn't even keep the wind out. If it hadn't been for the kindness of strangers, I don't think we would have survived."

"What work did he come here to do?" Tom asked.

"He said he got a job with a farmer," she said with a rueful laugh and a slight flush. "I don't think it was your regular kind of farmer—it was Christmastime! Do farmers hire hands at Christmas when the snow is four feet deep? I think it was a grower and I think

Chad either got fired or ran or maybe even robbed the guy before he ran. He abandoned us, but he came back about six months later looking for money and the men in town caught him trying to shake some money out of me. Jack, Noah, Preacher. Mike V., the town cop, was there, the sheriff was called and Chad is now in jail. He's going to be in jail for a while. Hopefully long enough to forget about us."

Tom had turned in his driver's seat. His arm was rested on the top of the steering wheel; he balanced it on his wrist. The other arm was stretched out along the seat, toward her. He just stared at her for a long moment. Finally he said, "You've had a tough time."

She took a breath. "I wish I'd made better choices."

"You were young."

"I had girlfriends who were as young, but protected themselves much better."

"Yeah? I had friends who were better at lots of things than me. But I can grow a real pretty apple." And then he tucked a stray lock of her hair behind her ear.

"I am very impressed with your apples," she told him.

"All those things you didn't feel you had the best instincts for before? You'll be so much better at that now," he said.

"I had a very sweet maternity nurse when Berry was born," Nora said. "She was a grandmother, she said. And she felt so sorry for me that my mother wanted no part of Berry's arrival—she wouldn't have missed her daughter's delivery for the world. And she said, 'You will do so much better than that. You will.' And when she put Berry into my arms she said, 'Congratulations. This is your new best friend for life.' So now it seems like more than one person I admire believes in me."

He just looked into her eyes, silent.

"I should pick apples," she said.

He came out of his trance. "Right," he said, putting his truck in gear.

She was so young, Tom thought, to have had to learn so much. And this worldly education in life had not only been achieved with complete lack of support, at least to this point, but with a couple of helpless little kids. And he'd already known she had a messy past, but the story she told only made it sound worse than he imagined.

Throughout the day, while he tended the trees and crop, he thought about that, comparing her to himself. He was almost thirty and had just realized he was ready to settle on the orchard, take on a wife and family, and this decision that was both emotional and practical, had taken a lot of consideration. He hadn't been even near ready two years ago and five years ago it was a possibility that terrified him. But he'd left the Marine Corps knowing that was the next stage of his life.

And had come back to Virgin River? Where the hell did he think he was going to find a wife here? All the girls he thought were hot in high school were spoken for, as were most of the young women in his age range in the coastal towns. In fact, a lot of them had already been married and divorced with a kid or two. No, that wasn't what he was looking for at all. The whole kid thing scared him enough without taking on someone else's kids.

He was so preoccupied that he was relieved when Junior told him that no extra hands were needed over the weekend. And when he gave Nora her ride home, she seemed cheerful when she jumped out of the truck. "Well," she said, "I'm having a family reunion this weekend. Do you have any big plans?"

"Nothing for me," he said. But he thought maybe he should try to get out of town for a day, maybe a weekend. "Enjoy yourself. Pick you up Monday morning."

Tom sat at the kitchen table in the house, cup of coffee in front of him and his laptop open to his schedule. But rather than scrolling or typing or figuring, he tapped his finger idly. A lot of what ran through his head was asking himself how Nora could be different enough so that she'd be more right for him. No kids, for one thing. No doper ex, for another. I mean a few beers, a joint, that was one thing—but hooked up to a guy who went to prison for felony possession? A little too far into the deep and dark underworld. Yeah. And then there was her youth. Twenty-three was young, but twenty-three and been around the block a few times? He didn't expect a virgin, but for God's sake.

No one had seemed to notice his thoughtful mood.

"You're awfully quiet," Maxie said.

He smirked and looked up at his grandmother. Except her, of course. He grumbled something about having things on his mind.

"And cranky," she said. "Trees talk back today?"

"I know you think you're very funny...."

"Maybe this will perk you up," she said, pulling a slip of paper out of her pocket. She unfolded it and tried to smooth it out. "A girl called you. She'd like you to call her."

His mouth dropped open. He wasn't working on anything with any girl anywhere. He stared dumbly at his grandmother.

"Well, it didn't cheer you up but it did get your attention," she said, handing him the paper.

"Aw, this isn't a girl, this is Darla—the woman who was married to Pritchard. Bob Pritchard, a guy from the Corps who was killed in Afghanistan. She's the woman I stopped off to visit on my way home." He ran a hand over his head. "God, I hope she's all right...."

"She sounded just fine," Maxie said. "Very happy, very friendly. She told me you'd said very nice things about me."

"But what does she want?" he asked.

Maxie leaned toward him. "She'd like you to call her," she repeated softly.

He just stared at her.

"I could leave the room," she said, "But I can't make dinner anywhere else, so why don't you just go upstairs or out to the office."

He still sat there for a moment, looking up at a silver-haired grandmother who was much shorter and always seemed much taller. "Right," he finally said, picking up his laptop and heading for the office in the barn. And on the way he thought, *How do I expect to hook up with a woman when I'm so dense?*

And yet, he sat at the desk for a while before picking up the phone because the truth was, if Darla was in a place of grief and pain, he really didn't feel up to it. He still had those moments over Pritchard that clouded his eyes and closed his throat. There had been about six marines trying to get him to the helicopter when he was holding on to life by a breath.

That was a year ago. She might be lots better by now even if he wasn't. So he dialed.

"Tom!" she said excitedly.

"How did you know it was me?"

She laughed into the phone. "Caller ID, Tom. I assumed it was you and not your grandmother who was calling me. What a sweet woman, by the way."

"Sweet," he said.

"How have you been?"

"Fine. Good. Well, at least reasonable. You?" he asked with trepidation.

"Much better," she said. "Much, much better than when you were here. I think seeing you and hearing about Bob and about the war and all that—I might've been a little emotional and maybe gave the impression I was going to be a wreck forever. Bob wouldn't want that. I'm getting along very well, actually. In fact,

I'm going to be in your part of the world—I'm taking a post-grad course at UC Davis, not all that far from your little town. I'll be there for about eight weeks."

"Post-grad?"

"A pharmacy course. It's full-time and I'll have studying to do, but I don't have labs or classes on weekends and I figured while you're picking apples, I could get a little reading done. That is, if you feel like getting together. I don't want to impose."

"That's right," he said. "You're into pharmaceuticals."

She laughed. "In a good way. I have a town house lined up—my company has been sending sales reps through this course for years and has a lease on a town house I hear is nice. I'll be going back to Denver when the course is over, of course. But, I'll be there next week and don't have much going on. Want to come down? There are some nice restaurants around there."

"Aw, we're picking apples, Darla."

"Well, gee. I knew that—I searched *apple harvest in Humboldt County* on Google. I could always come to see you. I'm sure there's a motel nearby…."

*Yeah,* he thought, *I'm going to get right on the list of smoothest bachelors in the U.S.* "Darla—we have more room than we need and Maxie loves having company. Just let us know when you'll be here. It's not fancy, but it's homey. We don't have a lot of restaurants, however. No nightlife here at all, in fact, but there are some really good views and the apple pie is top-notch."

She laughed, a very musical sound, a very happy

sound. No, he decided, she wasn't coming to Virgin River to grieve and cry. She was coming to visit a friend. And Darla might be widowed, but widowed from one of the best guys he knew. And there hadn't been kids yet. And she was older—twenty-eight or so. Smart, pretty, self-sufficient.

"I love apple pie," she said.

"Do you like mountain vistas? Ocean views? Redwoods?" he asked, finding himself getting a little excited.

"I've never seen the redwoods."

"Well, if you can get away from the books for a few hours, I know where they are," he told her.

"I know it's your busy season...."

"I take a day off now and then. When can you be here?"

"I'll get to California next week. I want to unpack a few things, check my class schedule and then I might be able to head up there on Friday. It's not too far. A few hours, right?"

"Right. And cell phone reception is spotty, so don't count on it, especially in the taller trees and mountains."

"Tom," she said, kind of seriously. "I emailed you. About three times. You didn't answer. I was a little afraid to call...."

"Aw, damn, I'm so bad about that. Darla, hardly anyone emails me and it's all junk. I'm sorry. I haven't looked lately."

"But don't you do business online?"

He laughed. "We've been doing business with the same people for years. We drive the truck into town, to the stores, unload the apples and hand over a paper invoice. Maxie is on the computer more than I am."

"Well, that's a relief. I thought maybe you were avoiding me."

"Not a chance. This is one of the nicest surprises I've had in months."

Since Nora had been talking to Jed for a couple of weeks, exchanging the occasional email as well, she was comfortable that she was getting to know him and like him. But still, his first visit to her humble home was a little nerve-racking. Her phone rang at noon and he said, "Hi. I know we said afternoon and it's about one minute after, but I'm in the area. When can I come over? I don't want to intrude. I really hope to be invited back."

She smiled to herself; that was kind of cute. And that rising fear reared its ugly head—*Please don't let this all be false. Please, please let it be true.*

"You can come now," she said. "The girls are bathed, dressed and fed."

"Nuts," he said. "I was going to offer to pick up lunch."

"Not necessary, but have you eaten? Because I have a bunch of apples, apple butter, bread, but not the kind of food a man might be looking for."

"I had a late and very large breakfast. I'm completely satisfied."

"Then come. Oh, and Jed… As I mentioned before, Berry is very shy. Step softly."

"Of course. See you shortly."

And shortly it was—he must have phoned from just out of town. Fifteen minutes later, he was at the door. And he was bearing gifts—he held a bag from a toy store. "Oh, my," she said. "I shouldn't be surprised, but oh, my!"

"I couldn't stop myself," he said with a sheepish smile. "The truth is, I didn't even try."

Jed stood in the open doorway holding his big bag. Fay had been standing beside the couch but upon seeing company, she dropped to a sit and then rapidly crawled toward him. Nora swept Fay up before she flew right out the front door. Berry, on the other hand, shrank back behind the couch, just peeking at him.

"May I come in?" he asked.

"Oh," she said. "Right." And she held open the door for him.

He didn't say anything at all, but moving slowly and smiling gently, he got down on the floor with his bag and started removing toys. They were all new, something Nora had not been able to provide for her kids. They had some perfectly good toys, a whole plastic laundry basket full, but these were so much better. There was a spire that played music when the brightly colored plastic hoops were stacked on it. There was a toy that mimicked the animal noises. *A cow says moooo*…. Another toy had an arrow that pointed to a number or a letter—and this one spoke in either Spanish or English. And there were several books.

Nora sat at their small table and watched. Fay was struggling to get down off her lap.

"Let her come, Nora, it's okay—these are all safe for a one-year-old. I double-checked." Then he lifted his eyes to Berry. "These are for you and Fay, Berry," he said calmly, softly. "You can keep them and play with them." He lifted a book. "When you feel like it, we'll read a story."

"It's okay, Berry," Nora said. "This is your..." She didn't finish.

"Say grandpa, Nora. Then whatever they want to call me, that's it. My friend, Susan, who is a grandmother, her grands call me Papa."

"Berry doesn't talk very much," Nora said. "She's so shy."

"Nothing wrong with being cautious," he said easily. "I'm shy, too."

"You are, aren't you? I think I remember that about you!"

"It was always easier for me to read and write than to interact. Probably how I ended up on the faculty. I can lecture because it's prepared. I can write a great paper and defend it. I can talk to students about their work, their grades, their schedules. But when they bring me personal issues, I freeze. I'm determined to do better with you. And your children." He pulled out something else, a mesh bag of large, beautifully colored plastic blocks with letters on them. For now,

Berry could stack them; eventually she could line them up and make words. He unfolded a very small play stroller, added a little doll and a doll-size diaper bag.

Fay was immediately drawn to the bright colors and Jed showed her how to make them tinkle and sing and talk.

"How did you get up here so fast?" Nora asked. "What time did you leave this morning?"

"I came last evening. I stayed over in a motel in Fortuna. I didn't want to waste a minute." Then with a slight flush he said, "There's more, Nora."

"More what?"

"Things for the girls."

"Oh, Jed, that wasn't necessary. I don't want them to think that every time they see you there will be presents."

"I thought of that. I left everything in bags. You can put them away in a closet and when the girls are asleep, take them out and look at them, give them things when I'm not here so they don't think, you know..."

"Think what?"

"That I'm Santa Claus or something. But it was such an experience, like I've never had before. When Susan's grandchildren came, I went shopping with her and she was a crazy fool—throwing things in carts, literally losing her mind! I thought she'd gone mad." He shrugged. "Then I suddenly had grandchildren and... Lord, I couldn't stop myself. Don't think she didn't get the biggest kick out of it."

"Susan?" she asked.

"Haven't I mentioned her before today? She's a professor, but I met her fifteen years ago when she was a student. Not my student, but an older woman, finishing her degree once her children were nearly raised. Younger than I."

"And she's your girlfriend?"

He gave a nod and another slight blush. "I guess you could say. A few years after my divorce, ten years after hers, we began seeing each other. She's more a close friend than anything. We don't live together, we're not engaged. I'd like you to meet her. She's nice." Jed pulled a large, glossy book out of his bag and held it up so that Berry could see. "Princess stories," he said. "Susan's granddaughters love them. They're princesses every Halloween."

Berry came slowly forward, chewing on a finger. The brightly colored princesses on the cover got her. He let her take the book out of his hand and she immediately backed toward Nora. Leaning against her mother's legs, she opened the beautiful book.

And Nora's eyes clouded with tears. She sniffed.

Jed looked at her. "Are you crying?" he asked.

She shook her head, but she pursed her lips together tightly, not trusting herself to speak.

"What's the matter, honey?" he asked.

*That* brought the tears, calling her honey. "I don't know," she said. "Grateful, maybe. Embarrassed that I didn't amount to more. That I couldn't give my kids more. I don't know what you must think of me."

He was still on the floor, but he sat up a bit taller.

"I couldn't be more proud of you," he said. "When I think about…" He just shook his head.

She wiped away tears with her fingers and pulled Berry onto her lap. "When you think about what?" she asked.

He had trouble meeting her eyes. He took a deep breath. "If I had approached you at fifteen or sixteen, told you where I was and that I'd do whatever I could to help if you needed me, if I'd done that, things would have been so different. But I didn't."

"Why?" she said in a breath.

He shook his head again. "I thought it was for you. But maybe it was for me. Maybe it was easier to avoid the possibility of any conflict—I'm guilty of that. I learned that about myself, that I'm too passive. If I had known she would do what she—that she would throw you out… My God. Please, you must *not* blame yourself."

Nora looked at his sad eyes and thought, *I'm not sure. He could be lying to me and I wouldn't know the difference.* "We have a long way to go, you and I."

"A long way, yes, you're right about that. And part of that has to involve coming to terms with how your mother was. Nora, we can spend a lot of time talking about how much pain she caused us. We could work that like a hangnail for a lot of years, you and I. But at some point we have to let some things go. For my part, I broke her heart. I hurt her. She obviously felt abandoned, robbed, cheated. Abused. I spent years feeling the hurt she caused me by keeping you from

me, but certainly she must have felt deep hurt, as well."
He shook his head. "Who knows what that can do to
a person?"

"Well, I'll tell you what it does," Nora said. "It makes
them angry and unforgiving and unreachable."

"She made mistakes, Nora. So did I. We don't have
to keep reliving them. We can make a decision not
to repeat them. To do better." He gave her a smile.
"You're obviously doing exactly that. Your children
love and trust you. And after hardly any time at all I
can tell, you'll always be there for them."

Jed's trunk was full of stuff for his granddaughters—mostly clothes for the girls, which they needed.
There was a jumper with a butterfly appliqué on it, the
gauzy wings standing out and a few sequins sewn on
that melted Berry's heart and when she touched it she
said, "Ohhhhh." So Nora put it on her. While Berry
was a long way from letting her brand-new grandfather cuddle her, she did gently finger that butterfly
and look up at him with a slight smile.

He admitted that Susan helped with the shopping—
there were even dishes and placemats for the girls. His
gifts had not been extravagant. They were all necessities and he'd left the price tags on in case they should
be exchanged. They were inexpensive, but so nice.
And there was also a big bag of diapers, a case of formula, a box of wipes, a batch of bottles and sippy cups.

Then he took them all to Jack's Bar for Sunday
night dinner and it was the first restaurant experience

Berry and Fay had. But there could be no more perfect place because not only was the grill stocked up on high chairs, booster seats and mini-meals for children, but there were a number of families there, including Jack's. Jack shook Jed's hand excitedly. "Welcome," he boomed. "I didn't know Nora had family nearby—that's great. Nora is one of our favorites around here, just so you know. She's helped out at the clinic, at the new school—a real trouper. And this town is made of troupers."

A short time later Mel Sheridan came in with her kids and beamed when she saw Nora with her dad. Before even sitting down, she introduced herself and her children. "How fantastic you could visit! Nora's become a good friend of mine. She reaches out to everyone, helping whenever she can—a godsend."

Nora had the strangest feeling of being normal, even admired. She hadn't felt like that very often in her life.

"And you thought I wouldn't be proud of you?" Jed whispered.

What she learned after six hours with Jed was that he was neither the perfect fantasy father she had hoped nor the beast her mother had tried to prepare her for. Reverend Kincaid would no doubt be hearing a lot about this later. Jed Crane was an intellectual, a success in his field, but he was clearly not a social dynamo. Those parenting and relationship skills he now had were probably developed during the time he spent with his girlfriend, Susan. When Nora was a baby and preschooler he was a gentle and attentive parent without an angry bone in his body, but he didn't have the skills to deal with someone like Therese. In fact, Therese might have seen in him a man she could manage. If so, that would explain her many years of anger that he would leave her.

He couldn't protect Nora then. It was doubtful he could protect her now.

But he had good qualities. He was sincere, for one thing. And unless he was a truly gifted psychopath, he wasn't very deep emotionally. Nor was he malicious. And the way he acted toward Nora and the little girls was sweet and precious.

He described his days; he could read for hours. He went to Germany or England or Poland for three months out of every year—he was a World War II scholar and had published two volumes and numerous papers on the war and the reconstruction after the war. He loved his field of study as much now as he had when he began his dissertation and had no desire to ever retire, however, his schedule was not strenuous, thanks to teaching assistants.

When they were saying goodbye after a successful first family visit he said, "I'd be willing to help you with the girls if you need a babysitter on weekends when you work."

"With all due respect, I'll need to know you better before that happens," she returned.

"Completely understandable. I'd like to come back for another afternoon, as soon as you'll allow it. I'd also like to bring Susan sometime."

"Because she gives you credibility?" Nora asked.

"Well, no. She does, though. I'd like to introduce you. I'm not that great at presentation—something you no doubt have noticed. But Susan? She's a natural. She's so good around people that it makes you wonder what she sees in me. When you say it's okay, I'll bring her along—she wants to meet you."

"You can bring her whenever you like," Nora said. "But we're sticking to just afternoons. Weekend afternoons."

"I can't wait to tell her," he said. And then when he smiled, it was as if he'd transformed. All his shyness seemed gone, replaced with confidence and happiness. "Thank you for this," he said. "It was one of the best days of my life."

# *Seven*

When Nora jumped in Tom's truck early Monday morning, she was feeling pretty good about herself. And she realized before they were even out of town— she was humming.

"I get the impression the family reunion went well," he said.

"You could say so. This Jed Crane—he seems to be a nice guy. He brought the girls lots of things—clothes, toys, supplies. Since I've been needing that stuff, it felt good. It didn't get him any special privileges or anything, but I was grateful. This was the first time I've spent a whole afternoon with my father since I was a little girl. I can't tell if he's who I remember or a brand-new person."

"Maybe he's both," Tom said.

"There are things about him I never knew because my mother was too mad at him to tell me anything good. He's a Ph.D, for one thing. History." She laughed a little. "When he starts talking about history, it's almost as if he's transported to another time and place—he's fascinating. I can see how he can inspire his students to learn. And it would never have occurred to me to look in the academic or history book section of the bookstore or library, but he's very accomplished. He loves World War II—it sounds like he's an expert. Who knew?"

"Why didn't your mom tell you?"

"I don't think she wanted me to like anything about him, since he walked out on her and all. She needed it to be all his fault. And he didn't exactly defend her, but he did suggest that maybe she just wasn't capable of much more. That in leaving, he hurt her too much." She shook her head. "It's going to be a while before I get there—I'm still pretty angry with my mother. In fact, now that I know my father paid support and wanted to see me, I might be angrier. It wasn't easy growing up hearing that half of my biology was no damn good, as my mother used to say."

"She said that? Really?" Tom asked.

"Of course she did," Nora said. "But I told you that already. That's why I'm going to think of some positive things to tell the girls about their father when they start to ask."

He gave a huff of laughter. "That should be interesting. The guy's an addict in prison for dealing."

"I know," she said. "He's a tragedy, when you think about it. Here was this guy with a dream—a gifted ballplayer who had it all for a little while—a scholarship, a league contract and looks, and then something happened to him. Did he get the idea that things could be a little easier and faster and maybe more fun if he had some pharmaceutical help? Did someone give him something and wham, he was hooked? I'll never know. I guess he wouldn't be the first pro athlete to go down that road. It's an American tragedy, that's what it is."

"Nora," he said, almost shocked, "he wasn't good to you!"

"I know," she said softly. "But I don't want my kids to carry that load. That's my load. I remember when I first met him—damn, he sparkled all over. Getting involved with him when it wasn't a good idea, that was probably as much my fault as his." She turned and looked at Tom. "I had some friends, but when it got down to family, to people who would always play on my team no matter what, I was a little lacking. I was probably stupid and very lonely."

Tom took a deep breath. "I hope he stays in prison a long time."

"Oh, me, too. It's one thing to find positive things to say to the girls about their father. But let him near them?" She shook her head. "I don't think so. I *will* protect them."

He grinned. "Five feet four inches of hell on wheels."

She smiled back. "Four and a half inches!"

"But," he wanted to know, "are you lonely now?"

"Not lonely," she said, shaking her head. "The kind of friends I have now are tough. Genuine. I have Noah and his wife. There's Adie, Martha and Leslie—

three strong women who have never judged me. And there's…well, there's you."

"Me," he said. It was almost a question.

"Yes, you're the one who said we were friends. Without any effort at all, you have me telling you all my personal business so even if you don't think of me as a friend, I think of you as one. So, how was your weekend?" she asked. "Did you work the whole time?"

"Mostly. But I'm going to take a little time off next weekend. Will your father be back?"

"I'm sure of it," she said. "We haven't made specific plans yet, but he didn't seem to be bored for one minute yesterday. And I know he wants to include this lady friend he's been seeing for fifteen years." As Tom pulled up to the barn, she asked, "Do you have overtime on the weekend?"

"Possibly. But I have a friend coming and I'm going to take a little time. Junior and Maxie will be in charge."

Her eyes lit up. "A friend?"

"A woman."

"Holy cats!" she said. "You have a girlfriend?"

"Not yet," he said, turning off the ignition. "This is her first visit."

"Wow. Maybe we should shut the place down for a while, give you kids your privacy." And she winked.

"She's staying at the house, Nora. Privacy and Maxie are mutually exclusive."

"Awww," she said. "Well, take it from me—you want to move slowly. Make sure you know what you're doing."

He laughed at her. "And do you know what you're doing now, Miss Nora?"

"I absolutely do," she said with a nod. And then she thought, *Did I really* wink *at him?*

Nora happened to be picking not far from the drive into the orchard on Friday afternoon when a very classy red Caddy pulled in. She almost fell off her tripod ladder straining to see the woman get out of the car. Nora leaned so far right the ladder wobbled and she had to quickly grab on to a branch and right herself before she ended up on the ground under a pile of apples.

But wow, was this woman gorgeous. She didn't seem the type Nora would have pegged for Tom—she was very fancy in her red high-heeled boots, creased slacks, charcoal cape and multi-colored scarf. Those *red boots!* Nora almost swooned with desire—*red leather boots.* Was there anything more extravagant? And she had the kind of hair Nora had always envied—sleek, soft, shoulder-length blond that swung with her movements and yet kept its shape. As she casually slung her scarf over one shoulder, her beautiful hair moved in an almost choreographed manner. It caused Nora to touch her own hair self-consciously. The only haircuts she'd had in the past four years were the ones she gave herself.

But those clothes, those boots, that car—the woman looked like visiting royalty.

Oh, she was so happy for Tom. Surprised, but very happy. He deserved perfection.

And then he came across the orchard toward the woman, marching fast, smiling broadly. He was wearing his uniform of jeans, knee-high rubber boots, blue company shirt with the logo, sleeves rolled up, drawing attention to those muscled forearms and big hands. It was chilly in the orchard, but people who were working, like Tom and Nora, didn't need jackets. He swept off his hat just as he got near her, then pulled her into a big hug, rocking her back and forth. Then they separated quickly on a laugh; she brushed off her expensive cape. Yes, he was probably dirty. She'd watched him aerate between the trees, fix the fence and load wooden crates full of apples today.

She watched them walk across the yard and mount the porch steps, arm in arm, laughing.

*Yeah, this was what Tom deserved.* Nora went back to picking.

If someone was going to find the perfect partner, she'd rather it be Tom than almost anyone she could think of. Funny, she thought, how she began by resenting him, fearing him a little, pretty sure he didn't like her. Then she was sure that he felt stuck with her. But it hadn't taken too long for her to appreciate him, admire him. It probably started with him treating her minor injuries with such gentle understanding, then driving her to and from work. But he really scored when he brought her a sandwich and held her as she cried.

She'd had a small fantasy that she knew was idiotic, that she would never reveal to a soul, that after she'd gotten on her feet a little, after she'd proven she wasn't such a pathetic loser, that Tom might gradually develop an interest in her. She knew it couldn't happen fast, that it was really far-fetched, but hard times couldn't kill all her fantasies.

That was before she caught a glimpse of the perfect woman, of course.

A while later she happened to see Tom wrangling the woman's bags up the porch steps…her designer luggage. Now this just tears it, she thought. She had no idea which designer, but she knew—those cost a fortune. Plus, if Nora were visiting for a weekend, she'd be able to get by with a backpack. There were matching large, medium and small bags plus a rather large briefcase. Wow. She must be very important in addition to being beautiful.

She sighed. Besides secretly fantasizing about a man like Tom in her life, she also saw herself sitting at that kitchen table in a bathrobe, reading the paper, waiting for her daughters to wake up in the morning. And she saw herself cooking, baking, canning and working a little in the orchard. She wondered if Maxie kept a summer vegetable garden; Nora would if she could. But by far the most delicious fantasy she had was sitting on that porch, watching the sun set over the orchard and mountains. The beautiful, lush, full and ripe orchard.

After unloading her last big bag of apples, Nora grabbed the satchel in which she carried lunch and water and headed down the long drive to the road. She let herself out and closed the gate. She usually waited for Tom by the barn, but there seemed no question that today he was a little busy.

Never mind her silly, juvenile dreaming, when she tried to picture a woman Tom would find his perfect mate, she was a lot homier-looking than the red-Caddy blonde. Nora thought it might be a requirement that his woman could bake an apple pie to rival Maxie's. Oh, stop, she told herself harshly. There was no reason to think that magnificent creature couldn't bake a perfect pie. After all, Nora couldn't bake at all!

She heard the horn of the truck give three short blasts and she stopped and turned. She expected to give him a wave as he passed by, but he stopped. "No way," she said to herself.

"What are you doing?" he asked through the open window.

"I'm going home," she said. "Tom, you have company."

He laughed. "She's unpacking a few things. It looks like it could take several hours. I have time to take you home and get a shower and shave before dinner. Jump in."

She climbed up into the big truck. "You're so ridiculous! You could be doing something much more interesting—like helping her unpack."

"I thought you understood I was committed to getting you home," he said, laughing.

"I'm so grateful—but on days some totally classy

blonde doesn't bring her entire wardrobe for a weekend with you. This need to drive me verges on obsession."

"It does kind of look like it could be her whole wardrobe, doesn't it? When you think about it, I could put every piece of clothing I own in a duffel. Did you happen to see how many suitcases for two nights?"

"Not on purpose," she said, and when her cheeks colored he laughed at her. "It was kind of right in my line of vision. But oh, my." She sighed.

"What?"

"She's so magnificent!"

"She's pretty, I'll give you that…"

"Tom, I picked a few pretty apples today—that woman is out of this world. Have you known her long?"

He shook his head. "One of my guys was married to her. He was killed in Afghanistan and I paid her a visit on my way back to Virgin River…to be sure she was holding up all right. At that time she was still trying to get back on her feet. She's a lot better now and happens to be taking a class at UC Davis, so she came up for a visit."

"Oh, my God, I thought she was your girlfriend!"

"That's still possible, I guess. Her name is Darla and there's nothing about her not to like. I agree with the pretty, the classy and she's very nice and smart. But she sure doesn't travel light!"

Nora couldn't help it, she laughed hard. "You better look out. She looks expensive."

"She does, doesn't she?" he agreed. "I told her to

bring a pair of nice pants and boots in case we went to the coast for dinner." He shrugged. "I guess she had a hard time deciding."

"Seriously, she's the most beautiful thing I've ever seen. I'm pretty sure she'd be beautiful in a sack, but Tom—those red boots." She put a hand to her chest, let her eyes drop closed and her head tilt back.

"What?" Tom said.

She looked at him in shock. "What? Tom, red boots are like the top of the mountain, the epitome."

"They are?"

She turned slightly toward him. "If you can actually afford beautiful high-heeled leather boots, you get black, to go with everything. You only get red because you already have black and you want something indulgent, magnificent. Astonishing."

"Really?" he asked. "And you know this how?"

"Tom," she said with some impatience. "Red is special. You only have red for important things, because red doesn't go with everything. Black goes with everything so to be practical, you buy black."

He just shook his head. "Amazing, the stuff a guy can live without understanding… And did you have red boots?"

"Like those? Oh, please! I think a handful of women on earth have boots like those. I don't know who the designer is, but the soles were shiny black. They were like art. But hey, I had red patent leather pumps once, when I was fifteen, for a special high school dance…"

"There you go…"

"That I went to with my *girlfriend,*" she finished, laughing. "Trust me, I've never been in the red leather boot league!"

When he pulled into Virgin River he became a bit more solemn. "Listen, there's another reason I drove you besides my devoted friendship. We've been having some wildlife issues."

"I saw you fixing the fence again."

"Three times in a month. Seriously, we don't usually get the fence broken down. No one has seen our pest, but I suspect a bear that was pestering one of our neighbors. I caught sight of her in the orchard earlier in summer—eating green apples. She has triplets, and by now they're getting pretty big. She must be coming in early morning or evening. At least she isn't bothering the orchard while we're working. But I'm getting mighty sick of repairing the goddamn fence."

"How can you be sure it's a bear?"

"Deer won't break down a fence—they'll try to reach over it for the fruit. Mountain lions are carnivores—they're not interested in apples. They're interested in meat—the flesh of any animal they can catch."

"Oh," she said. "Feeling so much better now that I know that."

"They almost never attack a human that doesn't have them cornered."

"Way to comfort, Tom," she said.

"I think the bear and her cubs are climbing the fence to get over and breaking it down in the process and I'll be damned if I'll build a brick wall to keep them out. I'll sit up in a tree and shoot her first."

"Hey, I'm not going to lobby for her safety. I'm just thinking—are we talking lost apples or lost lives here?"

"I'm thinking broken fences," he said. "But there's a danger of running into her or the cubs and being attacked because you posed a threat."

"How could someone like me pose a threat to anything?" she asked.

He scraped off his cap and ran a hand over his head. "It's not logical, Nora. It's wildlife, trying to protect their young and their turf. She recently took a swipe at a guy who was too close and he was laying facedown, playing dead. Hurt him pretty bad."

She gave her chin a resolute drop and said, "Yep, the bear has to go. Good luck with that."

"I'll be here Monday morning. Don't walk. Are we on the same page here?"

"Of course," she said. He pulled up to her house and she grabbed the door. As she was exiting, she grinned devilishly. "Have fun with those boots."

"Get out, you little hussy."

"Hey! I think it's against the law for a boss to call an employee a hussy!"

He leaned toward her. "Sue me."

Tom went home, showered and shaved and, for once, put on clothes that did not wear the Cavanaugh logo. When he went downstairs, he found Darla sitting at the table while Maxie puttered around the kitchen, cooking and talking. Darla nursed a glass of white wine and Tom helped himself to a beer. "Junior coming to dinner?" he asked his grandmother.

"Not tonight. It's just the three of us tonight. I want a chance to get to know Darla a little bit."

"There's not too much to know. I grew up in Colorado, went to college there, got the only job I've had since with a local drug company, met my husband there. We hadn't been married long when he deployed."

"I'm so sorry for your loss, Darla," Maxie said.

"Thank you. I've moved on—that's what Bob would've wanted. I'm very close to my family and they've been a huge support."

"You live near your family?" Maxie asked.

"We all live within five miles of each other," she said. "My brother, his wife and their two kids, my mom and dad, an aunt and uncle, a couple of cousins. We watch each other's pets when we travel."

"You have a pet?" Maxie asked. She looked down at Duke who was sprawled under the table and at her look, he lifted his head. Then dropped it again in boredom.

"A little white poodle named Precious," she said. "He doesn't shed."

Tom choked on his beer. Maxie slapped him on the back. "Wrong pipe," she said. "Is your dog with you at UC Davis?"

"No, that wouldn't have worked. I didn't have friends there. He's at my parents' house where he has a close relationship with their Scottish Terrier. I travel in my job so Precious is often with my parents."

"Anything I can do to help you, Maxie?" Tom asked.

"Yes, thanks. Go to the basement and pull a pound cake and some strawberries out of the freezer. We'll have that with our coffee later."

"Oh, not for me, Maxie," Darla said. "I'm not much of a dessert person."

"No sweet tooth?" Tom heard his grandmother ask as he took the stairs to the basement.

"Not too much. It seems I'm always watching my weight."

"Pity. I guess Tom will take care of yours."

When he came back upstairs, he noticed that Darla was wearing a different pair of boots for dinner— brown suede flat boots that went over her jeans, jeans that were delightfully tight. She wore a long-sleeved fuzzy sweater that had a fairly deep V-neck and it was red. Tom was beginning to understand what Nora meant when she said red was special. There was a lovely cleavage visible.

Maxie began putting one of her best meals on the table—a standing rib roast that Tom would have the honor of carving. Twice-baked potatoes, asparagus from her own garden, fresh rolls that had risen earlier and were warm and plump with sweet cream butter from a neighboring farmer. She added salt and pepper, glasses of ice water and a small bowl of horseradish, Tom's preference.

"What a feast!" Darla said. And Maxie smiled

proudly. When they were seated and Tom was cutting the meat Darla said, "A very small piece for me, please."

"Aren't you hungry?" he asked. "You had a long drive."

"I'm not a big eater of red meat. Not a vegetarian or anything—I just eat more fish than beef."

"You'll do fine in this part of the world," he said, serving her up a small slice. "The Virgin River supplies some of the most amazing trout and salmon around here. What fish do you like?"

She was delicately cutting up her beef and asparagus into very small pieces. "Hmm, I think ahi tuna is my favorite. I'm partial to sushi. Do you like sushi?" she asked Tom.

"Sure," he said. "Did a lot of that in San Diego."

"Any good sushi bars around here?"

"On the coast, maybe…" he said. "I think this part of the state is more known for beef, wild game, hearty, meaty meals."

"Wild game?" she asked, lifting a very tiny portion of meat to her mouth.

"Duck, pheasant, goose, venison, that sort of thing. Big hunting area. Lots of hunters pass this way."

"Hunting? Ew."

He leaned toward her. "Hunting is fishing on dry land."

"I suppose," she said, sampling the asparagus. "Maxie, this is fabulous. You said you grew this?"

"Yes, ma'am. I have a small vegetable garden, and

it's almost plucked clean by now, but the broccoli and asparagus come in late."

Tom watched Darla take a little bitty bite of potatoes, then go back to the vegetable.

"So, what are your plans for the weekend?" Maxie asked.

"Well, boring as this sounds, I thought I'd take Darla for a walk through the orchard tonight, then tomorrow, if you can spare me, I'd like to take her through the redwoods and over to the coast. We could have dinner in Arcata, so you're on your own, Maxie."

"Wonderful. And what happens Sunday?"

"I have to be on the road by around noon," Darla said. "My class begins Monday morning."

"Here, sweetheart," Maxie said, lifting the bread basket toward her.

"Oh, thank you, but no—bread is not really part of my diet. I can't stay in these jeans if I eat bread. And butter is out of the question." Then she put her fork on the table and leaned back, her plate still quite full. "Maxie, that was fabulous."

"How do you know?" Maxie asked, looking at the plate.

Darla laughed. "I don't have a big appetite. And I'm careful about things like starches, fats, red meat."

"I'll remember that," Maxie said. "Can I fix you a PB and J to hold you over?"

"A what?"

"Peanut butter and jelly," Tom supplied. And he

unremorsefully kept shoveling food into his mouth, jealously eyeing Darla's still-full plate.

Darla laughed as if it were a joke. "I'm fine, really."

"What's for breakfast?" Maxie asked.

Darla tilted her head, lifted a pretty blond brow and asked, "A little granola? Plain yogurt?"

"How do you feel about All-Bran?" Maxie asked.

Darla made a face.

"We're going out for breakfast," Tom announced. "I have eggs, potatoes, sausage, bacon and toast. I'll be sure you have granola and yogurt."

"Tom," she said sincerely, "aren't you worried about your cholesterol?"

He forked a big mouthful of potatoes, full of butter, cheese and sour cream into his mouth and after swallowing he said, "I lift a couple thousand pounds of apples a day. I dare my cholesterol to keep up with that."

"I guess you have a point," she said. "I work out every morning, but the rest of my day isn't so physical. I'm in sales. I have a lot of meetings. Many of them in restaurants. If I ate everything that was put in front of me, I'd weigh two hundred pounds!"

"You look just lovely, dear," Maxie said. "You'll be fine. Now tell us about the sales job and who you sell your products to."

And cleverly, Maxie turned the table over to Darla, who was not eating and could talk while Tom and Maxie finished their dinner. And it was interesting— her work with doctors and hospitals and drug trials that might actually cure diseases and conditions that to this point rarely were successfully cured. She traveled for three to four days every other week and enjoyed her travels. She had long-term clients who had become friends because they depended on her. And there were benefits—bonus gifts she could give to her clients, and to herself, like good seats at concerts and sporting events. There were greatly discounted resort destinations—the Caribbean, Hawaii, Mexico. She had the best vacations and bonuses in the world.

During her explanation of her work, Tom and Maxie rose from the table and began to clean up dishes, careful not to ignore her. Since Maxie was letting the broiler pan soak, it didn't take long to wash up, put things in the dishwasher, wipe off the table. Maxie didn't even bother with the pound cake yet.

"Come on," Tom said, holding out his hand. "Let's find your jacket and walk off some of those calories you stuffed away at dinner."

Hopefully only Tom noticed Maxie roll her eyes.

# *Eight*

To Tom's great pleasure, it was a clear night. Cold, clear and the sky was peppered with a million stars. He walked with Darla down the lane between the two big groves, hands tucked into their jacket pockets.

"I can see why you love it here," she said. "It's so quaint and peaceful."

"I guess I never think of it as quaint. It's so much work. We move tons and tons of apples and gallons of cider."

"But you have employees," she said.

"Several. And now that I'm home I can manage the business end of things—accounts, payroll, shipping—all stuff Maxie did with Junior's help while I was gone. I think she's entitled to a slower pace. It was either run the orchard or think about selling it in the not-too-distant future."

"Sell it?" she asked.

"It's been in the Cavanaugh family since the first trees were planted—a very long time ago. I think it was my great-grandfather. I think Maxie would grieve it. I'm pretty sure I would. I can't think of anything I could do but this."

"And this is a good business?" she asked.

"Good enough to take care of all our needs year round. And in the winter when we're not planting or picking, it keeps us very well."

"Is it lucrative?" she asked.

"I guess so," he said with a shrug. The fact was, Tom didn't think like that. He wasn't comparing his orchard to anyone else's. They did very well and when there was profit left over, they always put it into the land, crop, equipment and the house. There were some savings of course, but mainly their money went back into the business. They were continually enlarging their crop. And of course they paid employees and provided benefits for all but the seasonal help.

"But what a great place to come on weekends, to get out of the rat race," she said.

"Better than Jamaica?" he asked teasingly. "Better than front-row seats at a Lakers game?"

She gave him a playful slug in the arm.

"You come up here any weekend you feel like it," he invited.

"Will you come to Davis?" she asked.

"Probably not during the harvest," he said. "I rarely take a whole weekend off between the end of August and Thanksgiving. I can wrangle a day sometimes. Or an evening."

"But you were gone for seven years and they did fine," she pointed out.

"But I'm home now and they don't have to make do."

"Am I keeping you from something important now?" she asked him.

He stopped walking and looked down at her. "This is a treat. After spending all day in the orchard, I don't usually do this. Walking through the trees at night, under a clear sky, it gives me a whole new appreciation for the place." He took a deep breath and put his hands on her waist. "So, how are you doing, really, since Bob's been gone?"

"Very well," she said. "I had my time of grief, which was so hard, but I'm better. I've even had a few dates. Nothing very promising, but hey…"

"You know, I kissed my first girl in the orchard," he said.

"I bet you've kissed a lot of them since."

"Not in the orchard." And he slowly closed in on her, cautiously meeting her lips. Her hands rested on his forearms and she tilted her chin up, offering her mouth. He moved over her lips softly, then slid his arms around her waist, pulled her against him and got serious about the kiss, deepening, demanding a bit.

Darla went along with this for a moment and then gently pulled away with a nervous laugh. He didn't let go, but watched her smile, her eyes. "Let's take this nice and slow, Tom," she said.

"Sure." Then he took her hand in his much larger

one and walked with her down the lane. "I'm surprised that you got in touch, Darla."

"Really? Because I thought you could tell when you visited—I was hoping we'd see each other again." She looked up at him. "I asked for this class, Tom. I thought it might give us a chance to get to know each other better."

"No kidding?" he replied, stunned. Then he grinned and squeezed her hand. "I'll be damned."

"You shouldn't be so surprised. You're a desirable man—handsome, accomplished, successful."

"I am?"

She laughed and leaned against him. "We're going to have a good time this weekend."

Tom enjoyed watching Darla gasp in awe at the redwoods, at the rocky coast, aiming her cell phone at scenic views for pictures and short movies. He was surprised by the amount of pleasure it gave him to answer her many questions about the area, the business of operating an orchard, how he grew up with his grandmother. He assumed she had very few questions about his time in the Corps because, after all, that was how she lost her husband.

She did say she was comfortable around him because she felt as though he knew her, having served with her husband. Tom nodded, but in fact he didn't feel like he knew her at all. Bob hadn't talked about her much, just to say things like he couldn't wait to get home, that his wife was gorgeous—no argument there. But Tom hadn't known anything more about her. Tom was a captain, Bob was first sergeant. They weren't exactly old friends, but Tom served with him in the sandbox and had a lot of respect for the guy. Bob was looking at a military career while Tom had been pretty sure he was heading out after that deployment.

Twenty-four hours into Darla's first visit to the orchard, Tom already had a very hard time picturing her as a marine sergeant's wife, especially a career marine. She was very proud of her job, loved what she did. She was passionate about her career.

He asked her if she and Bob had hoped to have children and she said they had barely talked about it. But over dinner on Saturday night, they managed to talk about more personal things. He told her about growing up an orphaned only child and she told him about growing up with one older sibling and devoted parents. It sounded like she had led a charmed life until choosing to marry a marine and being suddenly widowed. He felt bad about that; everyone had tough stuff to carry, but this pretty and successful girl shouldn't have had to go through that trauma. It made him think about how many happy, pretty young women lost their men and how many fine young men had buried their wives because of the same war.

On Sunday morning they found that Maxie had managed to provide granola and plain yogurt for Darla, something that brought a bright smile to her lips. After his usual hearty breakfast, Tom kissed her forehead and told her he'd be back after doing a quick check of the orchard.

"Please do be quick," she said, smiling sweetly. "I have to leave by noon and I don't want to go without saying goodbye. And planning when we can get together again."

And so Tom was back at the house in plenty of time. He found Maxie in the kitchen and grinned at her. "You're something, you know," he said. "How far did you have to go to find granola and yogurt?"

"Not that far," she said. "But I can't have her on my conscience. I saw her eat one asparagus spear all weekend."

"I saw her eat more than that," he said with a laugh.

"Thank God. She might not eat much, but she's got an ensemble for every hour of the day."

"I think that's the reasoning behind staying slim," Tom said, giving his grandmother a little tap on the nose with his index finger. "She'd have to file bankruptcy if she grew out of those clothes."

At least Maxie laughed. "She's packing up," she said. "Go see if you can do anything to help. And offer her lunch, although I have no idea what she'd be willing to eat. I could mow the lawn and offer her a plate of grass...."

"Don't be mean," he said, frowning. But then, chuckling to himself, he mounted the stairs and found Darla gently folding things away.

She smiled at him but he frowned. "Darla, are you folding your clothes with tissue paper?"

"Yes," she said proudly. "It absorbs any odors, helps keep wrinkles out and if there's any kind of luggage malfunction, like a hairspray or perfume spill—tissue paper is one more layer of absorbent. But really, I do it for odors and wrinkles."

"Amazing."

"I'm guessing you don't go to this much trouble," she said.

"No. A couple of clean drawers and a shaving kit—that pretty much does it for me."

"Such a guy."

There were three suitcases open on the bed. She was wearing her fourth pair of boots for the weekend—these were black with thick heels—and her fourth soft, sexy sweater. Since she was wearing boots, he assumed the fancy red boots that sat on top of the largest suitcase were traveling back to Davis. He picked one up. "Tell me about these boots," he said.

"Tell you what?" she asked.

"Well, they look like they might be special. Are they special?"

She broke into a wide smile. "You could say so. They're Jimmy Choo."

"Jimmy Who?"

"Choo. A very high-end designer."

"Okay, now tell me—do you have them because you need them, like them, love them, what?"

"What an odd question," she said, taking the boot out of his hand. "Bob used to ask questions like that, but he still liked looking at me in those boots. They're very special and they make *me* feel special. Isn't that really enough?"

"I guess," he said, "if you can afford it. I bet they're expensive. They look expensive." In fact, he thought, she looked expensive all over.

"I can afford it, Tom," she said, laughing.

"Well," he started, pushing over a suitcase to sit on the bed, "here's a question, since I have absolutely no idea what it takes to make a beautiful woman like you feel special—*how* expensive?"

"You don't really want to know," she answered, folding away a scarf that he'd never seen.

"I do. I do want to know."

She shook her head. "It's really not something you'll ever have to worry about. I never buy anything extravagant that I can't completely afford."

"Humor me," he said. "I'm curious."

She leveled her gaze on him. "Are you sure? Because I won't tolerate you judging me. I can already tell you're not interested in things like designer boots and coats and that's fine with me. But I won't have you judging me for trying to look beautiful and being willing to spend my own money to do so."

He put his hand to his heart. "Absolutely not. I like you beautiful."

She smiled very nicely. "Okay. They're a lot. Over a thousand."

He could be cool. After all, he'd been shot at—he wasn't going to cave to a woman who spent a ridiculous amount of money on clothes. "Seriously? How much over?"

She took a breath. "I got a deal. Thirteen-hundred-seventy-five."

He swallowed and let her have a small smile. "Quite the deal," he said.

"I know," she said. "It required some serious searching! I might've found some on eBay but I won't have used! If I'm going to spend the money, they have to be new."

"Absolutely," he said. But inside he was thinking, *insane*. Except they were kind of fun to look at. He could think of ways they would be more fun…. "The pharmaceutical sales business must be good."

"Oh, very. However, I did come into some money last year…" She dropped her gaze briefly and Tom nearly winced—Bob's death. "I could've paid bills, but I thought I deserved a few special things…"

"Of course," he said. "I'm sorry, I—"

"That's so wonderful of you to understand. Most men don't get it, what beautiful things mean to a woman."

He ran the knuckle of his index finger along her soft cheek. "Well, Darla, I get it. I really do."

A few minutes later, he carried the luggage out to the Cadillac. He held the driver's door for her and rather than getting in, she stood just inside the door, put her arms around his neck, gave him a full body press and openmouthed kiss. She put a little tongue into it and moaned slightly with what he could only perceive as longing.

Like Pavlov's dog, his arms went around her, pulled her in tight and bent to the task of doing that kiss justice. One hand slowly slid up her back until he was caressing the back of her neck, his thumb and forefinger moving in slow circles while he deepened the kiss. He thought about the fact that he should get back in the house so he could resuscitate Maxie before she went into full cardiac arrest, because she was certainly watching. But Maxie had had a full life.... He concentrated on the banquet before him and wondered why he hadn't tasted this passion the day before or last night when they were alone, when they could've talked about taking this a bit further.

She pulled back slowly, rubbing a hand along his chest and giving him a very sweet smile, her lids lowered seductively.

He laughed almost uncomfortably. "Where was that kiss last night? I'd have been happy to pull off the road on the way home...."

"We decided there was no rush," she said. "But if you want to know what I think, I think this friendship has potential."

"I know I'll be checking my emails more often," he said, lifting her chin for another kiss. But he kept it brief. As tempting as it was to linger, she was leaving and he didn't feel like making out in the drive between the house and barn.

"Good. I'm sure I'll see you soon. Please thank Maxie for me. She's so wonderful."

"Would you like to run inside and thank her yourself?" Tom asked.

"I said thank you this morning. And I must really be going. There's an orientation this evening."

"I'll tell her," Tom said. "How about a call later, just to let me know you made it safely."

"Sure." And she leaned in for a quick peck on the lips. "And thank you, Tom. I didn't know it was going to be so wonderful." And with that, she got in her car, executed a wide U-turn and drove away.

"Me, either," he said to himself, scrubbing off his cap and running a hand through his short hair.

And then he followed on foot so he could close the gate behind her.

It had come as no surprise to Nora that Jed wanted to come back again as soon as she would allow another visit, and that he wanted to bring Susan. He stood at the door on another Sunday afternoon with another box of gifts. "This is getting almost predictable."

"Oh, wait," the woman beside him said with a smile. "Hi, I'm Susan and I'm so happy to meet you. Thanks for letting me be included. Watching Jed discover his family has been…" She sighed, closed her eyes briefly and said, "It's a joy. It's been his dream for so many years. He's enjoyed my daughters and grandchildren, but this is a whole new thing. He's in ecstasy!"

"Susan," he said. "Don't scare her. I'm not obsessed."

Susan, a woman for whom glamour was obviously not a priority, just laughed. A woman in her fifties, she had chosen to let the gray hair in and wore no makeup. She was dressed in jeans, a T-shirt and wore a flannel shirt over it. Very plain, very down to earth, completely approachable. "He's obsessed," she confirmed. "But you don't have to be afraid."

Jed didn't waste any time—he was down on the floor with his box of goodies. Curious Fay was there in a flash, crawling up to the box while Jed slowly removed toys and books. Berry was slower, but she edged near, sitting on the floor, keeping the box between herself and Jed.

"Can I get you something to drink, Susan?" Nora asked.

"Nothing, thanks. I just want to watch Jed. But we can both do that and talk. I wanted to know if you had a major picked out when you were in school. Did you have any ideas about what you wanted to study?"

Nora sat down on the sofa and Susan joined her there. "I thought maybe education, but I had no experience. And no idea why I was drawn to the idea."

"But even if you didn't have the details, you knew your dad was a teacher."

She nodded. "And when I was little, I played teacher with the girl next door and the dolls. But that was all play...."

"Don't discount it too quickly," she said. "I used to

build villages as a child. I used flowers and toothpicks and rocks—anything at hand in the yard. Hollyhocks were my favorite people. But never dollhouses, always towns filled with people. I had great complex plays and adventures. My mother thought I'd be a playwright, my father thought I'd be an architect. Turns out I'm an anthropologist." She laughed and Nora was so taken by how beautiful this plain, unfussy woman could be. Her eyes twinkled; her smile was alive with happiness. "I watched my daughters play and I guessed them right, but they were so obvious."

"Huh?"

"Well, Lindsey was always undressing other children. She's doing her residency in family practice. Melanie tried to diaper and breastfeed her dolls—she's the one with three children and is a stay-at-home mom who still talks about college one day. We'll see."

"Holy cow. I'm going to have to watch how Berry and Fay play!"

"But what about you?" Susan asked. "What are you playing at these days?"

"I'm picking apples," she said with a laugh.

"Do you like it?"

"It's very hard, heavy, taxing work. And yes, I like it. More than that, I love being there, in the orchard. It feels…natural. Healthy. But I'm doing it because the hours and pay work for me."

"Do you ever entertain the idea of going back to school?" Susan asked.

"Susan," Jed said in a warning tone.

"He eavesdrops," Susan said with a laugh. "But do you?"

"Not for a few years," Nora admitted. "Why think about things you can't possibly manage?"

"Well—"

"Susan," Jed said in a pleading voice, cutting her off. He took a breath and looked at Nora. And while he did that, Fay crawled trustingly into his lap. "Nora, this conversation can wait, we barely know each other. And since these little girls are my granddaughters and I want them protected, I completely support your caution with anyone, including me. But what Susan is jumping into here is—that's an option for you. If you want to go back to school, complete your education, you have opportunity at Stanford."

"Jed," Nora said with humor. "It's not just tuition and books that stand in my way. I have a family to support. Even if you paid for school—"

"Most of my friends are married men and women with kids," he said. "I know what's involved. Housing, subsistence, child care, transportation—lots of expenses. I understand. But listen—you should be more sure of me, comfortable with your decision, clear on your goals. Personally, I don't care—if school doesn't interest you, maybe something else does. I just want to help."

"Haven't you helped enough?" Nora asked.

"I don't think so," he said. "For seventeen years I sent a check to Therese without knowing how it was used. That was at least fifty percent my fault—I should have found a way. But now? I want to give you the things I couldn't give you while you were growing up. And there aren't any strings attached."

"Look out, Nora," Susan said with laughter in her voice.

"Susan!" Jed said. And again, Susan laughed. "I brought a few things you obviously need," Jed said. "Things that will make your life a little easier. I want to do these things just because you're my daughter and these are my granddaughters."

"What things? Like formula and diapers?"

"And a car," Susan said.

"Oh, for the love of…" Jed rubbed his temples.

"It's used," Susan said. "It was mine—used by me and I took very good care of it. I put a lot of miles on it, but I pampered it. I was ready for a new car so Jed bought it from me rather than me trading it in. It's a few years old, in pristine condition and it comes with car seats." She smiled that lovely smile again. "My daughter knew exactly what kind to get and where to get them at the right price—she's an expert on that. The other one is an expert at saying, 'Put on this gown, please.' See, we all have our special gifts!"

Nora was speechless. A car? No, this was too much. No matter what anyone said, there had to be strings. And she wasn't ready.…

"I can't," she said, shaking her head.

"But you can," Susan said. "See, my ex-husband and I had to help my girls out with cars and with their insurance when they were sixteen or seventeen. They had jobs. We both worked and couldn't chauffeur. It was a choice between helping with the transportation or no jobs. Then there were other expenses—proms, graduation, events, and the clothing and accessories became more and more expensive. So over the years, we ponied up for stuff they needed. Lindsey needed tons of college, Melanie and her young husband needed a down payment on a house. Had Jed been around when you were going through all those stages, it wouldn't have seemed like such a windfall." She smiled at Nora. "You're very lucky. Your father wants to help and he doesn't expect anything in return except for a chance to get to know you."

Jed had Fay in his lap on the floor and Berry sitting cautiously beside him as he read the *Please and Thank You Book*.

"Really?" Nora said.

He glanced at her. "Nora, I have a lot to make up to you. Not the other way around."

# Nine

Luke Riordan was throwing trash from his cabins into the big Dumpster on his property when he heard a horn honking. He looked up and saw a big truck hauling a camper pull into the compound. There was no mistaking his old friend, Coop, two weeks early. Unsurprisingly, with no notice. He tossed his trash in the Dumpster, laughed and shook his head. Then he headed for the truck just as Coop was getting out.

"You get fired again?" Luke asked, sticking out a hand in welcome.

"I quit. You heard about that oil spill in the gulf?"

"Was that your company?" Luke asked.

"*Was* being the operative word. They were always on the edge, stupid bastards. Took way too many short-cuts and it was coming. So I quit."

"Now what?" Luke asked.

"For now, this little town in the mountains while I regroup," Coop said. And then he flashed that badass grin he was known for.

Henry Cooper, AKA Hank or Coop or Hank Cooper, had gone to helicopter training when Luke was an instructor at Ft. Rucker. He was known as a rebel. Also known as one of the best chopper pilots the Army had. He'd had a notable Army career, though he did butt heads with authority regularly. And for the past ten years Coop had flown a helicopter for oil companies to offshore wells. And no big surprise, he butted heads with them, also.

"And the paycheck?" Luke asked.

Coop ran a hand around the back of his neck. "Yeah, they didn't give me a farewell package. But hey—I socked away a few bucks before I quit. And I sold stock. While they were killing people at the pumps, my options went way up. There's no justice, right? I'm in pretty good shape. I can screw around hunting and fishing while *you* work—that suits me." And then he smiled again.

Luke had to laugh. He talked a good game, but Coop always pitched in. He was a hard worker. "And Ben?" Luke asked of the third buddy scheduled to show up for this little reunion.

"Yeah, I called him. Not only can't he come early, he might not make it when we were planning to get together. He's got some kind of cesspool or septic tank issue up at that bait shop of his. You ever been there?"

"Never," Luke admitted. "Well, at least you brought your own bed. Whatcha got there?"

"Toy hauler. I keep a Harley, a Yamaha Rhino—an

off-road vehicle—and a wave runner. Plus it's a pretty nice apartment. I sold the boat."

"You been living in that thing?"

"Yup," he said. "I'm a damn fine landlord, too."

"Some things just don't change," Luke said with a laugh. "Well, you're in luck—I have the RV park all set up with power, water and sewage and—this is big—I'm cooking tonight."

"Why is it big that you're cooking?" Coop asked, frowning.

"Well, this is top secret. My wife loves to cook. She's not necessarily any good at it. You say anything about that, you die."

"Gotcha. So, you mentioned you reproduced. Where's the result?"

"Brett's napping. You have time to park your trailer before he gets up. You'll like him—he's a tough little guy. Your slab is around back. After you handle that, I'll give you a beer."

"Obliged," Coop said. He looked around appreciatively. "This isn't ugly…"

"I don't think there's a place for that wave runner close by," Luke said. "Too many rocks in the river. Beachfront is a little rough up north here. You could head for the lake, but it's getting cold on the water. But you're going to enjoy the Rhino and the Harley—you won't find more beautiful country. Need a little help hooking up and unloading?"

"Just point me in the right direction," he said. "And Luke. Great to see you, man. How long has it been?"

"I don't know. Six years? Eight?"

"Too long," Coop said. And then he jumped back into his truck and pulled the trailer around behind the cabins.

Coop had kept in touch enough with Luke to have the facts, that he'd come up to Virgin River after retiring from the Army to check out some old cabins he and a brother had invested in. Luke had nothing better to do, so he stayed, fixed them up, met a woman, got married, et cetera.

But there was no way for Coop to prepare himself for the new Luke, or his wife.

When these two men had met some fifteen years ago or so, Coop was a kid of twenty-three and Luke was a few years older and a helicopter instructor who was just coming off a really bad marriage. When Luke got back from Somalia he'd found his wife pregnant with another man's child. And not just any other guy, but an officer in Luke's command. It screwed Luke up so bad, it was legend. Almost as big a legend as Coop's brush with disaster over a woman. But at least Coop hadn't married her. He'd merely gone to jail over her.

To say they had been a scrappy pair was putting it mildly.

And here was Luke now, a changed man. Or rather, a man changing a diaper! That was a sight Coop never expected to see. Oh, Coop had married friends here and there, but not this domesticated. And when Luke's young knockout of a wife got home from work, Coop almost passed out. Luke had said she was young; he had failed to mention she wasn't quite thirty years old and a stunner.

"You dirty old man, you," Coop said with a very large grin. "Where did you find this beauty?"

"Right here, my man," Luke replied. "Twenty-five years old and ripe for the picking."

"I thought you'd sworn off."

"Yeah, so much for big proclamations. The minute I saw her—"

Luke was cut off by the ripple of laughter coming from his wife, Shelby. "He's such a liar," she said. "He fought me every step of the way."

But Coop found this new Luke fascinating. In addition to a pretty young wife and rambunctious little kid whom he clearly adored, Luke was also the guardian to a loveable man in his thirties who had Down Syndrome—Art. While Art set the table, Luke served his wife a glass of wine and turned steaks on the grill. Brett drove his miniature quad around in the yard and the catching up on old times commenced. Then through dinner, there was more of the same. And after Brett was tucked in for the night, Luke lit a fire in the pit in front of the porch.

"What were you and Luke like in the good old days?" Shelby asked. "When you first became friends?"

Coop laughed, a tinge of embarrassment included. He was grateful Shelby wouldn't be able to see the slight stain on his cheeks. "Nothing like this," he said. "I was just a kid, that's my excuse. But you wouldn't have liked us much, I'm pretty sure. We drank too much, drove too fast, got in the occasional fight when we took a break from chasing women."

"I have no trouble seeing Luke as a womanizer," Shelby said.

"Yeah, he wasn't that slick with women," Coop told her. "One hit him over the head with a beer pitcher once. I never did find out what his offense was."

"Breathing," Luke muttered. "I was coming off a bad relationship. I might've been a little bitter...."

Coop let go a big laugh. "Ya think? At least you never went to jail!"

Shelby sat up straighter and faced Coop. "What did you do?"

"Turned out I did nothing, but since I was passed out, I wasn't much good in my own defense."

"Passed out with bruised knuckles..." Luke contributed.

"Yeah, that's the missing link, I guess. I have no idea how that happened, but there was a time I had a bad habit of losing my cool and punching a door or a wall, because, that's how intelligent I was back then. It took a few years to occur to me that didn't hurt anyone but me."

"But how did you end up in jail?"

"I had this girlfriend—Imogene. She wasn't a very good girlfriend to start with—extremely high maintenance. But beautiful, very beautiful, with a body you wouldn't believe. She was a waitress at a dive right off Ft. Benning. I used to ask her all the time why she didn't look for more upscale work and she said military men were the best tippers. Especially the ones who couldn't afford it. Hopeful, that's what I think they were—hoping for a grope or at least a phone number. We were on and off, like oil and water. But one night when we were 'off' I'd had an unfortunate amount to drink and passed out, Imogene got knocked around. So, she called this asshole marine she knew from the bar, cried for him and told him her boyfriend beat her up. Fifteen years after the fact, I think she was looking for more than sympathy from the guy."

"But you didn't, did you?" Shelby asked. "Hit her?"

He shook his head. "I still can't remember what happened to my hand, but no one turned up hurt or dead. No complaints from a door or wall. For a terrible few days I hoped to God I'd never hit a woman. I had a lot of flaws, but that wasn't one of them. Even I had my limits—I'd never do something that low. And I'd only hit a man who made me. But this asshole marine called the MP's and they threw me in jail with a promise of Leavenworth. There are two things in the military that guarantee arrest and jail time—DUI and battery domestic."

"I guess you got out of it," Shelby said.

"Not fast. I was in the brig, court marshal pending when a couple of my boys from Airborne training rounded up a few witnesses who said a customer got rough with her at the bar. She was pissed at me for not being there to defend her, or being there and not *able* to defend her. And I think she had her eye on the marine." He laughed sardonically. "He shipped out while I was still in the brig, so that didn't work out for her, I guess."

"Who was that?" Luke asked.

"I don't know his name but I'll never forget his face. Just some jarhead who'd been to that bar a few times. Thought he was a goddamn hero. It's a face I better never see again. I could forget that I stopped punching people."

"Did the woman get in trouble? For blaming you?" Shelby asked.

"Nah. She was a civilian," Coop said. "She finally allowed that it had been dark and she might've been mistaken. And she didn't point at anyone so the MP's were out of it. However, there were boys at the bar who caught up with a guy who bragged about teaching her a lesson. Problem number one—no one saw the incident occur and he might've bragged in the bar but when questioned, he knew nothing about it. They said they were real sorry when they let me out of jail. They also said if I wanted to avoid situations like that in the future, I might want to cut back on the drinking and try to date less vindictive women."

"And did you?" she asked.

Coop rubbed his jaw. "Can't remember the last time I got drunk, but I've never had great luck with women...."

"Ever married?" she asked. "Children?"

"Almost married—twice. It didn't work out. No kids. And I'm thirty-seven, kind of set in my ways.

My life has changed a lot since I was twenty-two. I've been told I march to a weird beat. I guess I'm kind of a loner."

"No family?"

"Oh, I have family," he said. "Parents still living and three married sisters, a couple of nieces, couple of nephews. My family is all in Albuquerque, where I grew up. And I've been working the past ten years in either Costa Rica or the Gulf of Mexico for Texas-based oil companies."

"That sounds like more than one company," Shelby said.

Coop gave a lame shrug. "I never had a big role in the companies, the drilling, the pricing—my job was helicopter transport to the offshore platforms. But there are things you can't help but see. When they get greedy and take chances on the people, on the wildlife and ecosystem… Let's just say I get my back up. I'm a pilot—it's safety first. Risk management. No amount of money is worth a life…"

"Absolutely not!" Shelby agreed.

"Not even the life of a duck," he said.

Luke laughed. "Coop's gotten a little liberal there."

"Can't help what I see," he said unapologetically. "I can't make the rules. I haven't been a whistle blower, at least not yet, but I'm not going to work for a company that rapes the land and the consumer and puts the employees at risk while they're doing it."

"You?" Shelby asked. "Were you at risk?"

"Oh, hell no," he said. "If they asked me to fly out

to a rig in bad conditions, I wouldn't go. They could always find someone who would go—that galls me. But I'm not a cop. Cost me a couple of jobs, but I was more than happy to let them go. I had to think for about ten seconds—let's see, job? Life? Huh?"

"And now, you're an ecologist? More or less?" she asked.

He laughed heartily at that. "I appreciate nature," he said. "I respect it. As long as we don't hurt anyone or anything by drilling, by supplying fuel, I'm good with that."

"But you hunt," she said.

"And wear leather. And fill up my tank. But I don't shave safety regulations or take advantage of hungry people who need the work to feed their kids… Aww, get me off this soapbox, Luke!"

Luke laughed. "How do you like your slab out back? You have your traveling apartment all hooked up?"

Coop grinned and looked up at the sky. "I think I'm going to like this."

Nora knew that Tom Cavanaugh would come for her on Monday morning, so she waited out in front of her little house, leaning against her five-year-old gray Nissan. She couldn't wait to see the expression on his face. He pulled up at the usual time and just sat in his truck for a minute, staring. It made her let go a big laugh.

He finally got out of his truck and looked at her quizzically. "Do you have company?" he asked.

She shook her head. "Jed gave me a car," she told him. She opened the back door. "With *car seats!*"

He pulled off his cap and scratched his head. "Just gave it to you?"

"He's trying to make up for lost time, I think. It belonged to his lady friend, Susan. And rather than trading it in for a newer car, she sold it to Jed, who wanted it for me. I was pretty shocked. I still can't believe it. And guess what? It's very nice."

"I guess that means you have a driver's license."

"Of course I do. I just haven't driven in a long time."

"Maybe you should let me drive you to the orchard until you have a couple of test drives," he suggested. "You can tell me about your visit."

"I think you're disappointed I don't need a ride," she said with a laugh.

"Nah. But I kind of got used to the updates…."

"We can talk at lunchtime. If you're not too busy."

He looked uncomfortable. She thought he actually squirmed a little, looking briefly away. "I don't want anyone to think—"

She was shaking her head. "Come on," she coaxed. "This isn't junior high, and you have a girlfriend!"

"Not quite yet."

"Oh, boy—now we *have* to talk! I want to hear all about the red boots!"

"Did you get anything else from good old Jed besides the car?" Tom asked.

She put her hands on her hips and grinned. "Did you just change the subject?"

"I wondered, that's all…"

"Walmart gift card for winter clothes, some toys for the girls and, get this, he brought dinner—roasted chicken, potatoes, vegetables. He bought it on the way."

"I guess you don't need much now.…"

"I need to know how your weekend went!" she said, laughing. "Okay, look—I'll follow you back to the orchard. I'll make your coffee. We'll have a cup while we wait for the others to come—the ones you're so careful to arrive before and leave after. You can ask me questions and then you'll tell me all about your weekend with that magnificent woman!"

"Magnificent?" he asked with a frown.

"Well, Tom, I saw her! Let's get a move on or we won't have time to talk. Because God forbid old Jerome or Junior think we're friends. Come on!"

Tom was completely unsure how this little spitfire did it to him, but he was grinning all the way to the orchard, following her as she carefully putted along the almost deserted road at dawn. And after they'd arrived and parked, he suggested they have coffee in the kitchen with Maxie.

"But Tom, I'm not going to get all the more intimate details if your grandmother is there," she said quietly.

He leaned down, close to her face. "You're not going to get intimate details anyway."

"Oh," she said, laughing, covering her mouth. "All right, then."

When they walked into the kitchen, they found Maxie leaning on a hand, elbow braced on the table, her paper and coffee in front of her. She was dozing.

"Maxie?" he said.

She jerked awake. "Oh!" Then she smiled. "Morning, Nora." And she yawned. "Good grief."

"Oh, you're tired," Nora said. "Let's go get coffee going in the office."

"You okay, Maxie?" he asked.

"Fine," she said. "I think I didn't sleep well the last couple of nights or something. So—are we having coffee?" She sipped hers and made a face. "Mine has gone cold."

"Let me fix that up for you," Nora said, taking her cup. She dumped it, dressed a new, hot one with cream and sugar while she fixed her own, then sat down at the table. "Tom has promised to tell me about his weekend."

"That should be interesting—he hasn't really told me," Maxie said.

Tom cleared his throat. "You were here," he said, pouring his own coffee.

"Yes, and I'm not sure if we had a good time or not."

"We had a great time. Darla's a city girl, a businesswoman. She loved the orchard, the redwoods, the coast. She just couldn't appreciate our country lifestyle, I think. You know what I mean—not the type to get real excited about country-fried steak and gravy. But she wants to come back."

"She does?" Maxie asked.

"She does," he confirmed, narrowing his eyes at Maxie, trusting her not to carp about the strange appetite, the many outfit changes, the fact that Darla never got out of her chair to help with dishes.

"How wonderful." Maxie looked at Nora. "She's a very beautiful and successful woman. Widowed."

"So I heard," Nora said. "Her husband served with Tom, right?"

"What was her husband like?" Maxie asked Tom.

"A good guy," Tom said.

"Oh, now I could pick him out of a crowd," his grandmother said.

"He worked for me," Tom said. "You can't usually get real cozy with the men you command, but he was a sergeant and his boys would walk into hell for him. In the end, he walked into hell for them—he lost his life saving others. But let me tell you this—he was loyal, smart, brave…and he had a great sense of humor. When he wasn't driving them hard for their safety and survival, he was making his boys laugh. Sometimes he thought rules were stupid and sometimes I agreed. He didn't exactly cross the line, but man," he said, laughing and giving his head a shake. "He ran right up to it—he was an edgy guy. He had common sense and terrific instincts. Unafraid. He didn't talk about Darla too much, at least not with me. But then, we were kind of busy."

Nora was in a trance, listening. "Busy," she repeated. Though he hadn't said, what she imagined he meant was that they were under fire. She tried to shake that off—he was home safe now. So she asked, "What's Darla like?"

"Like?" he asked, frowning. "Nice."

Maxie and Nora exchanged looks. Maxie lifted her brows.

"Okay, she's very smart and sells drugs for a pharmaceutical company," Tom said. "She has to travel a lot. She seems to like clothes and I think she must make good money. And she… She watches her weight."

Nora laughed and shook her head. "Men," she said in exasperation. "So—what does she like to do for fun? Does she hike or surf or go duck hunting? Or does she play chess, or read or paint? Is she kind to animals? What are her big goals and what are her impossible dreams? Does she have religion, speak more than one language, cook, bake, sew? Is she on Facebook? Does she tweet? Would she like to have children, and would she rather be a working mother or stay-at-home mom? Who is her best friend, and worst enemy? Who is her idol? When she lists her five most important things, what are they? And what are the three things she's most grateful for? And if she could have dinner with any famous person, dead or alive, who would it be?"

When she finished, both Maxie and Tom were staring at her, openmouthed.

"Nora, I can't answer those questions about myself," Tom said.

"I can answer four or five of them," Maxie said. "The orchard is important—my second priority after family, who is Tom. I bake and work out walking the orchard and I think canning, baking, cooking and cleaning this big house qualify as much as exercise. I was a working mother and grandmother and hope to be a working great-grandmother. I'm on Facebook—"

"You're on *Facebook?*" Tom asked, shocked.

"A little thing for me and my friends…to share pictures and news…"

Nora was fascinated. "And the famous person you'd have dinner with?"

She looked at the ceiling for an answer. Finally she said, "Hillary Rodham Clinton."

Nora was fascinated. "And what do you want to know?"

Maxie smiled. "It will have to be a long dinner…"

"Aw, jeez," Tom said. "I think it's time to harvest apples."

"Maxie, I have some news," Nora said just as she stood to leave. "I have a car! One with car seats so I can drive myself around for errands and to work. It's going on my list of the three things I'm most grateful for."

"That's such good news," Maxie said. "So—dinner on Friday? With the little girls?"

"Maxie, I think Darla will probably come up on Friday…." Tom said.

"Oh. Well, then, how about Wednesday? Can you run home and get them? Take off a couple of hours early—you always come early and stay late. Go home, change, bring the little ones. I'll make a big pot of…" She looked at Tom. "What should I make? Spaghetti?

Chicken soup? Meat loaf and mashed potatoes? We don't want steak or roast for little mouths, little teeth."

"I vote for any one of those," Nora said. "That would be so much fun. I'll bring Fay's booster chair. Thank you, Maxie!"

# *Ten*

Hank Cooper had a top-of-the-line toy hauler, perfect for a bachelor sportsman. He had parked on the RV slab behind Luke's cabins, hooked up, then lowered the rear hatch so he could remove his motorcycle, wave runner and Rhino. Once the toys were out and the hatch put up, the roomy living room furniture was pulled down from the ceiling and out from the walls. He also had a full kitchen, large bathroom and master bedroom. He never had to pack as he'd lived in this RV for a couple of years—his closets and drawers were full. The kitchen was appointed—he didn't always go to a lot of trouble, but he cooked for himself more than he went out.

His next order of business was erecting a small shelter from pipe and plastic tarp under which he could park the vehicles.

Then he pulled out an awning and set up some of his outdoor furniture. His refrigerator was still stocked—food, beer, sodas. There was a satellite dish on top that he could extend into the trees for decent TV reception and internet connection.

And he reclined on his outdoor lounge in the midst of the forest with the sound of the rushing river nearby. Those people who rented the cabins didn't know what they were missing. He had helped Luke around the cabin compound in the morning, then with a beer at his side and laptop perched on his knees, he did a little surfing.

First he checked Devlon Petroleum to see if they were in trouble. The stock had gone up since yesterday and there were no EPA investigations or crew mishaps and while there was a part of him relieved by this, he had no regrets about quitting. There had been a couple of minor spills that hadn't made big news, a couple of injuries that could've been avoided if safety measures had been followed. His last standoff with his chief pilot was when he refused to fly to drilling platforms in the Gulf during a hurricane watch that was soon to turn into a hurricane warning. If they'd been asking him to fly out there to pick up rig workers and bring them in, he would have done it. But they wanted to take more men out there even though the weather was taking a bad turn. His chief pilot was only following orders when he said, "You take this flight or take a walk."

Coop had walked.

This was probably his own damn fault. When he'd left the Army after six years in a helicopter, he had taken on high-risk jobs. After a couple of years as a mercenary in a Black Hawk in countries without their own armies, he moved on to flying between offshore oil rigs and land and found that could sometimes be as questionable. But the money had drawn him. At the time he'd merely asked himself what the difference was between flying a Black Hawk in Iraq or Mozambique, getting fired on, and flying off Costa Rica or in the Gulf of Mexico back and forth between the continent and drilling platforms.

Then he'd experienced his first major spill and it all hit him pretty hard. The carnage was horrible. Coop hadn't paid that much attention to seagulls, pelicans and fish until he'd seen them covered with oil. Hadn't worried about where he was going to get his fish until he'd seen all the fishing boats moored and unable to work. That's when he started to notice things, like a half-assed effort at cleanup, like regulations shaved too close to the bone, high fuel prices so the consumer could pay for their mistakes and company suits and stockholders wouldn't take a hit.

He'd worked for a total of four oil companies. He left each one for what he considered irresponsible drilling and transporting. He'd look around for yet one more, but he needed a change. A break. And, although it made him feel a little guilty, the same companies he disapproved of had paid him well and given him stock bonuses. He had a healthy bank account; it would afford him some time to think about what to do next. If he thought it would make those oil companies more responsible, he'd have refused the money. Instead, he made donations to nonprofit organizations dedicated to cleanups and animal rescue.

Enough. He flipped over to his email. There was one from Ben Bailey, the guy who was supposed to meet him in Virgin River. He was up to his eyeballs in mess; his septic system had died, but it had gotten real sick first. He was trying to get everything taken care of so he could make at least a fast trip to the mountains, maybe at least aim at a deer if not shoot one. It was only a five-hour drive from his place in Oregon.

Coop shot back an email. Come when you can. I'll be here awhile. I'm between jobs. Again. If you don't get down here, I'll come up. Never have seen this little business of yours.

"Ah, the infamous Coop," a voice said.

He looked over the top of his laptop. The guy was a little taller than Luke, but the resemblance was unmistakable. He winced before he said, "Does it have to be *infamous?*"

"Your reputation, like my brother's, precedes you." He stuck out a hand. "Colin Riordan. Same DNA as Luke, and roughly same locale. We're neighbors. How you doing?"

He slapped the laptop lid closed. "Doing a little relaxing. It just doesn't get any better than this."

"Yeah, I don't know how he lucked into this," Colin said, hands on his hips, looking around. "He and our brother Sean came up here hunting, found this compound all broken down with the elderly owner bedridden and dying. He stayed dying for years. But Sean and Luke put together a deal that would take care of the guy. Eventually Luke came up here and put on a restoration show—fixed everything up. I thought he'd flip it, sell, but he stayed on."

"Shelby," Coop said.

"Isn't she something? I have definitely lucked out in the sister-in-law department. Have two more winners—Aiden and Sean both married up, as my mother says."

"How many of you are there?" Coop said, standing to face Colin.

"Five Riordan sons. Luke says you flew for the Army."

"For a few years. And if I have it straight, you flew Black Hawks, too."

"I did," Colin said. "Until a freak accident retired me. We were in an exercise at Ft. Hood and a civilian plane out of control took me down." He shook his head. "All that damn war and then it was some poor bastard with a heart attack that damn near killed me. But, I ended up here for my recovery and found Jillian, a very interesting little farmer. We're not married, but we've been together over a year. And there's no end in sight."

"Does this place just spew pretty girls?"

Colin laughed. "Wouldn't you wonder?"

"Beer, Colin?" Coop asked.

"No, thanks—but I'd like to see your digs, if you don't mind. Luke was telling me about this setup… You haul your gear and still have a house."

"It's a good little operation," he said. "Come in, look around. Plenty big for me, plenty of storage and a moving garage."

Colin stepped inside, looked right toward the kitchen and a set of stairs toward the master bedroom and bath and left into a spacious living room. "Push these chairs back against the window, fold the tabletop against the wall, raise that long sofa bed to the ceiling and the entire back wall opens—it lowers into a ramp so I can drive in the toys. The wave runner is on wheels—I push it up the ramp."

Colin took it all in and laughed. "How'd I live this long without knowing about a contraption like this?"

"I originally bought it for camping, but when I took my last job in Corpus Christi, I just rented a space and lived in it. That wasn't exactly a radical move for me—I lived on my boat for a few months, and it wasn't a big boat.... But I do have a long history of not staying in one place for long."

"Or with one job? Luke mentioned something about your difference of opinion with the way the suits run things."

"Yeah, that," Coop said with a laugh. "Luke thinks I turned into a tree hugger. I'm not, I don't think. Just hate rape and pillage."

Colin laughed. "Well, I think I am a tree hugger... I only shoot animals if they're about to eat me. And Jilly? She won't even use pesticides on her vegetables. I wanna see the rest of this place." He pointed to the stairs. "What's up there?"

"That's the part of the trailer that sits over the truck bed," Coop told him. "Bedroom and bath. Go ahead."

Colin took the steps and looked into a large bathroom that contained a shower and then a bedroom with a queen-size bed and a long wall of drawers and closets. There was a nice flat screen on the wall opposite the bed. "I might have to get me one of these," Colin said.

"Have a lot of toys, do you?"

"Not yet," Colin said with a grin. "Let's fire up that Rhino of yours and I'll take you on a tour of the forest. We might even end up at Jilly's farm—really something to see."

After all the employees had left the orchard on Wednesday afternoon, once the equipment was secured and the gate closed, Tom headed for the house. As he neared, he saw a little girl sitting on the back step, a large picture book in her lap, carefully turning the pages. Even if he hadn't known Nora and her children would be joining them for dinner, he would definitely know this was her daughter. She had the same peachy complexion that would eventually freckle. Her brown hair was a lighter shade, but when she looked up at him he recognized those big brown eyes with the golden flecks.

This would be Berry. Nora had talked about her often enough.

Tom sat on the top step next to her. He pulled off the boots he'd worked in that day—they smelled of manure and Maxie didn't allow them under her dinner table in that condition. Berry scooted away a bit. Shy. Nora had said Berry was very shy. He glanced over at the page that had her attention and asked, "What animal is that?"

She didn't even favor him with a look, but she said, "Cow."

"Do you know what a cow says?"

"Moo," she said in a very, very quiet voice.

He chuckled. Berry was wearing a cute little lavender outfit, pants and a long-sleeved shirt with flowers on it, tennis shoes over her lace-trimmed socks. He had expected a ragamuffin in old, used, tattered clothes, not nice stuff like this. "If the cow was that quiet, the farmer would never be able to find her. What's next?" he asked.

She turned the page. "Guck," she said softly.

He laughed. "Or duck, depending on your preference. And what does the duck say?"

"Guack," she whispered.

"You're very smart. What's next?"

She turned the page and said, "Fog."

"And the frog says?"

"Burbbet."

"I have a pond full of frogs. Do you like frogs?"

She nodded.

"If you come a tiny bit closer to me so I can see the page, I can read it to you," he offered. She merely turned the page.

But she said, "Kitty. Mow."

"Brilliant," he said. And *he* moved a bit closer. He read, "'This is a kitten and it says meow. The kitten likes to play with a ball of string or yarn.'" He put a little feeling into his meow and she glanced up at him with a shy smile. He wondered if Nora had been like this as a little girl, shy and sweet. She wasn't shy and sweet now, but she was definitely fun at times. And he couldn't deny she was nice enough. But she stood up for herself. She was proud. Too proud. She had bravado. He got the sense she was faking that, but he liked it. In fact, if she had to summon it and it wasn't natural, he liked it even more.

Berry turned the page and he read, "'This is a puppy and he says...'"

She looked up at him and said, "Woof. Woof."

"And do puppies like kittens and frogs?" he asked her. And she nodded. "I thought so," he said. "I have a puppy," he said.

"Gook," she proudly informed him.

He laughed. Ah, so the *d*'s were *g*'s. "Yes, Duke. Not exactly a puppy. More of a gog."

"Don't mispronounce," came Nora's voice from behind him. "I know it's tempting, and fun, but really..."

They both turned, looked at her and smiled.

"She seems very smart for two," he said. "Is she?"

"She's almost three, and she is. I need to work with her more, but there's the time thing. We need to do letters, numbers and colors. We have worked on some, but just a few. Preschool, though a necessity so I can work, is also a gift. They're so focused." She gave a nod. "That's Berry's favorite book. Her grandpa gave it to her."

"Papa," Berry corrected.

Tom smiled before he could stop himself. "She likes him, I guess."

"It hasn't been quick. He's been to visit twice and she will finally let him read to her a little bit, as long as he doesn't get too close."

"Then I scored," Tom said. "I read three pages on our first date."

Nora smiled. "If you want a shower before dinner, there's time."

He made a mock gesture of sniffing his own armpit and raising questioning eyes to her.

"Cripes," she said. "Maxie said you'd want a shower. I wasn't passing judgment."

"Yeah, okay," he said. "I'll be down in a few." And he left Berry and went in stocking feet into the house.

There at the table, propped up in her booster seat with a few crackers in front of her, was Fay. For some reason he couldn't quite explain to himself, he was greatly relieved to see that the little sister looked like Nora as well—soft, light brown hair, peachy skin, golden-brown eyes. But this little one was not shy; she squealed and laughed when he walked into the kitchen and hurled a fistful of scrunched-up crackers at him. Her teeth were brand-new and in weird, adorable shapes and lengths. Happiness and confidence just rolled off her.

Maxie laughed at the scattered cracker crumbs,

completely unperturbed. In fact, if Tom had to guess, his grandmother preferred baby mess to boots and expensive sweaters and no appetite.

"I'm going to grab a quick shower," he said.

While standing under the spray, he was thinking they were cute. And although Berry seemed a little withdrawn and not easy around strangers, the family as a whole was happy. But hell, Darla was happy. Very happy! Happiest when talking about trips and clothes and money, but what was wrong with that?

Nothing at all. Nothing.

He pulled on a sweatshirt with clean jeans. He had put on boots when Darla joined them for dinner, but tonight he just slipped into his Uggs slippers, soft and warm. They were a little on the old-man-ish side, but he'd had a long, strenuous day. He'd hauled trucks full of apple crates and cases of cider. He was tired. And he was starving.

When he descended to the kitchen he found Maxie and Nora at the table, laughing over something. Berry was seated on the other side of Nora, propped up on a bunch of couch pillows covered with a towel so spaghetti sauce wouldn't stain them.

"There you are," Nora said, leaping to her feet. "Are you ready to eat or do you want a little time to unwind first? Want a beer or soda or something?"

He glanced at Berry, stuck out his belly and rubbed it. "Me want food!" he said, making her laugh. And he thought, *What the hell was that? I don't know anything about kids! Why was I playing to the kid?* But she was still grinning at him and it made him feel something inside, like a glow.

"Good," Maxie said, joining Nora at the kitchen counter. They had salads prepared in individual bowls, dressed and ready to go. There was a loaf of garlic bread that went on the table, aluminum foil opened. Maxie was rinsing the noodles while Nora was stirring the sauce.

Nora put the salads on the table, in front of each place. "Berry, eat a couple of bites so you get your nutrients," Nora said.

"Does she have any idea what nutrients are?" Tom asked.

"Absolutely none, I'm sure. But Berry will have a couple of bites and even if she didn't, she'd get the rest of dinner. I don't punish with food. We try to be grateful for good food and blessings." Then she smiled and added, "Greens are a little iffy, but I guarantee a good performance on the noodles and sauce!"

"Tom liked that best, too," Maxie said.

"When I was a girl there was big trouble over things like vegetables. My mother started giving me a plate of weird vegetables and if I wouldn't eat them all, I went without the rest of the dinner. I had to earn things like meatloaf by eating a lot of Brussels sprouts. I'm not a picky eater now, but I'm not sure that process had anything to do with it. I'm not going to do that." And Nora tended to the bowls of spaghetti for her girls while Maxie dished for the adults. "Warning, this could be a little messy," Nora said. And she made Tom trade chairs so he wasn't sitting next to one of her kids.

It was a more than a little messy, but it seemed to entertain Maxie and Nora. When Fay got the noodles and sauce in her hair, the women nearly lost it, which made Fay giggle uncontrollably. Which made her put more food in her hair. Which made the women laugh, Fay giggle, etc.

What he noticed most was that Nora, who was little and slim, had seconds. And what bothered him was that he liked the looks of those trim, buxom females who seemed perpetually beautiful but he didn't like to hang out with women who wouldn't eat. Now how can you have it both ways?

Nora sat back from the table a little and said, "Oh, my God, please excuse me, Maxie! I ate like a pig! That was amazing!"

"Never apologize for being happy at my table," Maxie said. "Do you have room for pie? You helped make the crust."

"I'm so sorry, I can't…"

"Will you take some home?"

"Yes! Absolutely! Oh, thank you! I don't think I've been wined and dined like this in my lifetime!"

*I'm partial to sushi… Do you like sushi?*

"Sans wine," Tom pointed out.

"Someday when I'm not carting small children in the car, I promise to enjoy a glass of wine—it's been a while. I don't know if you noticed, I'm not that confident a driver to start with—I need a little more practice. I'm not about to complicate that with wine, especially with my kids on board."

"Perfectly understandable. Should we roll the ball around for a while?" Maxie asked.

"No," Nora said firmly. "We're doing the dishes before Fay starts to fuss. Then I have to get the ladies home for baths and bed. I start early in the morning."

On cue, Fay wriggled in her booster chair, raising her arms and bowing her back, and sent up a loud whine.

"Oh, no, she wants a bottle. It's time... I have one ready... Save the dishes, Maxie, until I can give her a bottle. I try to hold her for it as often as I can...."

"I'll do the bottle," Tom said. And then he thought, *I am going to lose my man card here. This is not what I want.*

"Are you sure?" Nora asked.

"Sure. Be happy to," he said.

"All righty. Let me get her cleaned up." And Nora went after the little tyke's face and head and hands with a wet paper towel. She undid the safety belt on the booster chair and handed her to Tom. "Get comfortable. I'll bring you the bottle and the blanket."

Not quite sure what those instructions meant, Tom carried the tot to the living room and chose Maxie's favorite chair, a swivel rocker-recliner, which gave him a view to the kitchen. Nora was right behind him with the gear—bottle and blanket. Fay reached for them with an irritated *eh eh eh eh.* Then, holding her own bottle and soft blanket, she reclined into the crook of Tom's arm and sucked away.

He looked into the kitchen where there was much going on. Berry was standing on a step stool between Maxie and Nora, mostly splashing while they chattered like they'd known each other since birth. And wonder of wonders, Berry not only talked as much, she was loud. Nothing like on the back steps where she was shy and quiet, but loud and extremely verbal. She addressed both Maxie and her mother, turning her head and looking up at one, then the other.

They rinsed, washed, dried and put away. Although Maxie had a dishwasher, she preferred not to use it unless the cleanup was major. She said the warm water was soothing on her arthritic hands.

He looked down at Fay, who was gazing up at him. The drowsy-eyed contentment momentarily filled him with a deep sense of satisfaction and adoration, as if he'd done something other than volunteer for a job he didn't know he wanted. When she caught him looking at her, she smiled around the bottle's nipple. He smiled back, and then her eyes drifted closed. They opened, closed, opened, closed. Finally, with just a couple of ounces left, she was gonzo. And because he'd been a little insane all evening, he lowered his lips to her head and gave it a kiss.

"I knew that would happen," Nora said.

He was stricken. Had he done something bad?

"That last bottle of the day after a full tummy

# **FREE** Merchandise and a Cash Reward† are 'in the Cards' for you!

Dear Robyn Carr Fan,

*We're giving away FREE MERCHANDISE and a CASH REWARD!*

Seriously, we'd like to reward you for reading this novel by giving you **FREE MERCHANDISE** worth over $20 retail plus a CASH REWARD! And no purchase is necessary!

You see the Jack of Hearts sticker above? Paste that sticker in the box on the Free Merchandise Voucher inside. Return the Voucher today... and we'll send you Free Merchandise plus a Cash Reward!

Thanks again for reading one of our novels—and enjoy your Free Merchandise and Cash Reward with our compliments!

*Pam Powers*

Pam Powers

P.S. Look inside to see what Free Merchandise is **"in the cards"** for you!

**W**e'd like to send you two free books like the one you are enjoying now. Your two books have a combined price of over $10 retail, but they are yours to keep absolutely FREE! We'll even send you 2 wonderful surprise gifts and a Cash Reward†. You can't lose!

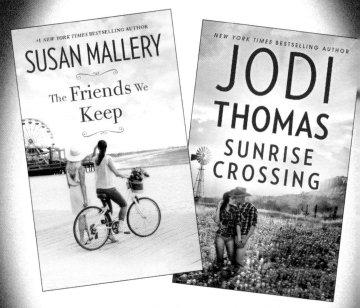

REMEMBER: Your Free Merchandise, consisting of **2 Free Books** and **2 Free Gifts**, is worth over $20 retail! Plus we'll send you a **Cash Reward** (it's a dollar) which is really the icing on the cake because it's in addition to your FREE Merchandise! No purchase is necessary, so please send for your Free Merchandise today.

### Get TWO FREE GIFTS!
We'll also send you 2 wonderful FREE GIFTS (worth about $10 retail), in addition to your 2 Free books and Cash Reward!

Visit us at:
**www.ReaderService.com**

Books received may not be as shown

▶ Detach card and mail today. No stamp needed.

# FREE MERCHANDISE VOUCHER

2 FREE
BOOKS
and
2 FREE
GIFTS

Please send my Free Merchandise, consisting of
**2 Free Books** and **2 Free Mystery Gifts** PLUS my
**Cash Reward**. I understand that I am under no
obligation to buy anything, as explained
on the back of this card.

### 194/394 MDL GLF5

*Please Print*

FIRST NAME

LAST NAME

ADDRESS

APT.#          CITY

STATE/PROV.          ZIP/POSTAL CODE

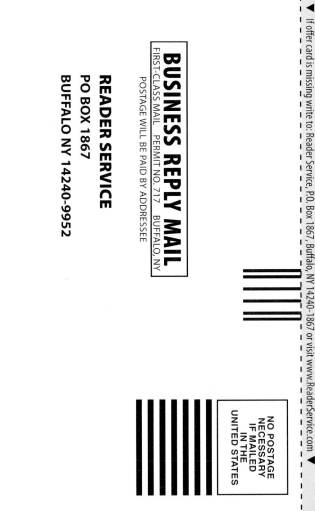

▲ If offer card is missing write to: Reader Service, P.O. Box 1867, Buffalo, NY 14240-1867 or visit www.ReaderService.com ▲

**BUSINESS REPLY MAIL**

FIRST-CLASS MAIL    PERMIT NO. 717    BUFFALO, NY

POSTAGE WILL BE PAID BY ADDRESSEE

**READER SERVICE**

PO BOX 1867

BUFFALO NY 14240-9952

NO POSTAGE
NECESSARY
IF MAILED
IN THE
UNITED STATES

knocks her out. It's a race to get the bath in before she crashes. Here, I'll take her."

"You're going to take her?" he asked.

"Home, Tom. She needs to go to bed."

"What about her bath?"

"You know what? A kid can live by missing a bath one day but you don't want to skip things like food and cuddling."

"She has spaghetti sauce in her hair and behind her ear."

"Yeah, I might give her a little spit and polish when I change her and put her in her pajamas. Not that a little red sauce will hurt her, but I don't want Adie trying to bathe her and don't want the day care to think I'm negligent. Here," she said, holding out her hands.

"I can carry her to the car," he offered. "Is the other one ready to go?"

"Yes, wearing as much dishwater as went down the drain," Nora said. She crouched and ran a gentle finger around Fay's ear. "There is nothing more precious, is there? Thanks for everything, Tom. The whole afternoon and evening—it was terrific. Someday I hope I'll be able to invite you and your family to my table."

The soft look in her eyes was so tender and sentimental he could feel it reach way down inside of him. To cover the discomfort of such emotion, he stood with Fay in his arms. He handed Nora the bottle and pulled the blanket around the baby to keep her warm.

Nora went to the kitchen to fetch Berry. Maxie was holding her on her lap, helping her into her little

hoodie, talking with her about how much fun it was to
have her to dinner. Nora put the almost-empty bottle
in the beat-up canvas tote that must serve as a diaper
bag. "I think I have everything. Berry, did you remember your book?"

Berry nodded.

"Say thank you and let's get going," she said.

The little girl said a quiet thank-you to Maxie and
in exchange got a hug. Then Maxie stood and gave
Nora a hug. "I had such fun," she said. "Promise to
bring them back."

"I would love to," Nora said. "It was so wonderful.
Now let's not wear out our welcome." She took Berry's hand and walked out to her car, Tom following.

Tom put Fay in the car seat while Nora belted Berry
in. Fay didn't even whimper; she was unconscious. He
couldn't figure out the safety straps however. Finally
Nora came around and with a chuckle, hooked up the
baby easily. Then she put her arms around his waist
for a quick hug. "Thanks again," she said.

"Give me a ride to the gate," he said. "I'll open it
for you."

"I can manage...."

"Let me," he said. "I don't want you to leave the
kids in a running car to let yourself out and close up.
I want to walk back—it's a beautiful night."

She looked up at the black sky and took a deep
breath. "When I got here, I thought I'd been thrown
into hell without a rope. Look at that sky, smell the
fall air. I had no way of knowing this was the lucki-

est break of my life. I'm sure you know how lucky you are."

"Let's go," he said, getting in the passenger side and folding up his long legs to fit. "Nice little car, Nora," he said.

"Isn't it? I'm still quite cautious of Jed, but I think it's going to be okay. I think he's a good guy. And if so, I couldn't ask for more."

*I could ask for so much more,* Tom thought. *One woman instead of two, for starters. One woman with all the right traits,* he thought.

They were at the gate in seconds and he jumped out. "Drive carefully," he said before closing the door. He was grateful he'd made the suggestion of letting her out—he needed a little time alone to think before Maxie started asking questions about how much he'd enjoyed the evening, so his walk back to the house was slow. Then he sat on the back steps for a minute, the same steps he'd shared with Berry earlier.

Tom liked a lot about Darla. He liked that she was pretty and smart and very sophisticated. He didn't mind that she made him look like a boring old farmer—he could use a little class. She had a stable and loving upbringing. She apparently had no weird, dark skeletons like an ex in jail for dealing drugs. She didn't have children yet, so no baggage. Well, there was baggage…including about a billion-dollar wardrobe, but that wasn't his problem. A wardrobe that would go to waste in a small town. So what if he'd rather vacation by camping or fishing while she was headed to the beach in the Caribbean? Lots of couples celebrated their differences rather than chafed at them and only expanded their experiences. Except he wasn't crazy about wrestling two big suitcases for every day of travel, either.

He sighed deeply.

But the things he liked about Nora were her natural, unaffected beauty, her grit and determination, her kindness, her gratitude, her humor. He even liked her kids. He hadn't wanted to take on someone else's kids, but he liked them. A lot.

# *Eleven*

Maxie sat in the living room, feet propped up in her recliner, TV on. She knew what Tom was doing—either sitting on the porch or pacing outside, wondering what the hell he was going to do. Even though he'd been gone for the past several years, she knew the boy inside and out. He was a plotter. A planner. And sometimes he got a little over the moon in his plans.

Tom didn't seem to really lament his absence of a mom and dad. That sort of thing didn't stand out that much in a place like Virgin River where extended families abounded. In a place with large family businesses like farms, vineyards, ranches and orchards, it was fairly common for the grandparents, aunts and uncles to be included in the day-to-day equation, all often present at the same dinner table. And it was also typical for small-town boys to lust after a bigger, more exciting world.

"When I grow up, I'm going to see every country in the world," Tom used to say when he was young. "I'm not going to spend my whole life on one small piece of land. I want to see things, do exciting things." Thus college and the Marine Corps, Maxie assumed. Escape to a larger world. Excitement—in spades.

She never tried to convince him of the virtues of the land. But after trying a few different majors in college, Tom had finally gotten his degree in agriculture. After the Marines, he came back to the orchard. She hadn't asked him to, but she had said that if he had no interest in the apple business, she'd sell it in a few years—she wasn't going to keep picking apples into her eighties, but she'd be more than thrilled to live in her house, on her land.

Maxie knew that deep down Tom found comfort in the beauty of simplicity, nature, wholesome living. She also knew the fastest way to scare him off the orchard was to try to sell it to him. Better he should carry lots of expensive luggage up the stairs to the guest room and give a baby a bottle. That would do more to shape him.

He'd come around. She hoped.

The screen door slammed and he walked into the living room. She patted herself on the back for her restraint. She so wanted to ask him wasn't it nice to have a dinner guest who ate and appreciated the food? Instead she said, "Pie?"

"No, thanks. I'm going to bed."

"It's seven forty-five!"

"Long day," he said. "I'll put Duke out one more time and close up for you. Come on, buddy," he said to the dog. Duke took his time getting up, as though his joints might hurt. "Any day now," Tom prodded.

It took quite a while. Since Duke hadn't been asking to go out, he wasn't in any hurry. Another ten minutes passed before the old dog ambled in and Tom trudged up the stairs.

Poor guy, Maxie thought with some humor. It was obvious he liked Nora and wanted to like Darla more. She hoped he'd be able to get some sleep. For herself, she was going to enjoy TV.

Fall was on the land and Coop was grateful that he'd lucked into one of the best setups he could imagine. Since Luke and Shelby invited him to dinner just about every night and gave him his space and trailer hookup for free, he earned his keep by helping out around the compound. He drove to the dump now and then, cleaned the occasional cabin, picked up groceries from the larger stores on the coast and did his share of grilling and cooking for them. It took a little pressure off the Riordans.

Touring the area with Colin in the little Rhino, which was like a baby Jeep or little quad, had become a favorite pastime. He'd seen much of the country by now and it was beautiful everywhere he looked. Coop was taken with Jilly's farm, the big house, the harvested garden and huge pumpkin patch, but he was mostly impressed by Colin's paintings. It was impossible to grasp that this guy wasn't a professionally trained artist, he was so gifted. "I need to have one of these paintings," Coop told Colin. "But I have no wall to hang it on and could never decide which one!"

"You'll have a wall again," Colin said with a laugh. "Once you decide what you're doing next."

Coop just shook his head. "I'm not going back to foreign wars, not going back to the oil companies and I can't paint. In fact, I don't think I can do anything but fly helicopters. Luke got lucky with the cabins— that's a decent life, I think. In a decent little town."

"You've been all over the mountains and valleys but I don't think you've seen that much of the town itself. How about a beer at Jack's?" Colin suggested. "About time you meet Jack. Luke treats himself about once a week when his chores are done and Shelby's home. Let's go get him."

Colin followed Coop back to the Riordan cabins to leave off the Rhino and grab Luke for a beer. A few minutes later, they were pulling up to Jack's bar and walked in the door.

The man behind the bar looked like he'd seen a ghost. So did Coop. And at exactly the same time they said, *"You!"*

There was nothing but silence to follow that, for at least a few stretched out seconds. Finally it was Luke who said, "What the hell…?"

Coop turned to him, his eyes ablaze. "That's him! The jarhead who had me arrested!"

"I didn't have you arrested, asshole! The woman you beat up had you arrested! I just happened to be there when she said, 'It was him!'"

"No, *you* called the MP's and told them it was me!" Coop said, advancing on the bar. "I wasn't even *there!*"

Instinctively, Colin and Luke each held one of Coop's arms. "Whoa, whoa, whoa," Colin said. "What's this?"

"This didn't really happen," Luke said, holding Coop back.

"Something happened," Jack said. "She had a funky jaw and a black eye and a bunch of other bruises and—"

"And called you? How'd she have your number? Ever ask yourself that?"

"She said she was in a bad situation and I told her if she ever needed help…"

Coop laughed cruelly. "And where were you after I got arrested, huh? Because I didn't *stay* arrested!"

"What?"

"You heard me! She was lying, did you know that? She was going to get me arrested. She was going to replace me with a jarhead!"

"I shipped out with my squad," Jack said. "I was only at Benning to get them through Airborne. She knew I was leaving—she didn't want me!"

"No, pal. She didn't want *me,*" Coop said. "And she was going to have me locked up for something I never did."

"She was beat up," Jack said emphatically.

"She got it behind the bar. There were people who knew what happened, knew it wasn't me. She blew off some guy who wanted a date, he followed her to her car and when she didn't have a change of heart, he slapped her around. She went home and called you. And even though you didn't see a goddamn thing happen, you had me arrested! Did you ever think about checking this out, since you didn't see it happen, either?" Coop shook off Luke and Colin and straightened. "Hey. I'm outta here. Ever hear that old saying, this town isn't big enough for both of us? It's today, man."

And with that, Coop turned and walked out.

Luke shook his head. "He didn't do it, Jack," he said. "We're going to have to get this straightened out. I'm not ready for Coop to drive out of here. He just got here." And then he left to join Coop and Colin in the truck.

Three men and Shelby had a beer together on Luke's front porch.

"I never would've believed it was Jack," Luke said, dropping his head, looking down. "In a way it makes sense, but that's even more reason to get this worked out."

"In what way does it make sense?" Coop demanded. "And why would I want to work it out?"

"Jack's a good guy," Colin said. "On the upside, he's got a reputation for defending the underdog. On the downside, he obviously didn't get all the facts. Or thought he had the facts when he didn't."

"The fact is, I had orders for Ft. Rucker and I wasn't taking Imogene. It would've been a disaster—she didn't really want to settle down. We hadn't been to-gether very long, definitely not long enough to be a couple… I think she just wanted a way to a new town. And so we fought, broke up what little there was to break up, I went out with some of my boys and got hammered. Not over grief at leaving Imogene—if you want the truth, I was happy to be leaving Imogene. And I'm sorry if she got hurt, but I don't know why she had to pin it on… But I do know why. She was pissed off and would rather see me sit in jail for refusing to take her to Alabama than see the guy who smacked her around punished."

"Who did beat her up?" Luke asked.

"Some sergeant who was permanent at Benning. I think she might've dated him once. I spent a few days in the brig until my boys tracked him down. And that damn Imogene wouldn't finger him! He admitted he might've slapped her." He laughed bitterly. "Might've *slapped* her. To hear the boys tell it, he punched the crap out of her. He bragged about it at the bar but wouldn't confess to the MP's. And why she wouldn't want him behind bars—I have no idea. I never saw Imogene again."

"I think we should explain, since Jack got half the story," Luke said. "The wrong half."

"I'm not explaining anything to anyone," Coop said. "I'm more inclined to move on."

"Not this time," Luke said. Luke rested his elbows on his knees and leaned a little closer to Coop. "I think there's a trait the three of us sometimes share and that's taking the easy way out—"

"You don't say that to a veteran soldier who's been to war," Coop said.

"Okay, let me put this another way," Luke said. "The place you're in right now, where it's too easy for someone to just assume the worst about you. I've been in that place more than once and it sucks. I think Colin can probably relate—"

Luke was cut off by the bark of a laugh coming from his brother. "Me?" Colin said. "The guy who got caught by his brothers chewing up oxycontin like candy? Yeah, there's been a time or two the worst was assumed about me, and a time or two they were right. I gotta agree with Luke here. We might not get it all straightened out between you and Jack, but I don't see how that matters much. Here's what I think matters— that you stand down, Coop. Hold your position—you got framed. You might've been a suspect, briefly, but you were never a convicted felon. Don't let anyone run you off."

"Please don't," Shelby said. "You don't have to make any commitment here, Coop—we understand this is a stopping off place for you. But please don't leave before you're ready just because one person doesn't understand the circumstances."

"The most respected person in town," Coop muttered.

"Jack's a good guy," Luke said. "But he's been known to run into conflicts here and there. He's also been wrong. And when he's wrong, he'll usually man up. It's worth giving Jack a little time on this."

"Maybe you didn't hear me," Coop said. "I'm not in the mood to explain myself to him, to try to make him understand. I'd rather just get my beer elsewhere."

"Sure. Reasonable. I'm just saying it's too soon to pack it in. Just because you're angry at being judged."

"*Falsely* judged," he clarified.

"Let's talk about it in a few days," Colin suggested.

Coop looked down for a moment. Then he took a pull on his bottle of beer and leaned back in his chair. "I thought I was done with this," he said.

"Any knowledge of what's happened to Imogene?" Luke asked.

He shook his head. "Nor any curiosity," Coop said. "Ever have the experience of meeting the wrong person at the wrong time and having a whole lot of stuff just go to hell?"

Luke, Shelby and Colin all looked between each other. Then it was Luke who laughed—Luke who had married pretty stupidly, got his heart really trashed, almost didn't get over it in more than a dozen years, almost didn't get over it in time to give himself to Shelby, the best thing that ever happened to him. He reached for Shelby's hand and held it. "Don't know what you're talking about, man."

Tom talked to Darla almost every evening. He told her she was more than welcome to come for the weekend, he'd love to see her, but unfortunately he'd be working both Saturday and Sunday.

"Will you have evenings free?" she asked.

"I will," he said. "I'll work all day, so I won't be a party animal, but I don't work in the dark."

She laughed at that and said, "I have so much reading to do, it might be nice to just spend the evening together. It sounds like both of us will be working hard all weekend and evenings will be ours. Should I bring some movies?"

There would be baseball. But he said, "Sure."

Tom didn't want to, but he couldn't help but notice that Maxie was a little stressed about Friday night dinner. She made salmon, rice and more asparagus from her fall harvest and although there were none of the evil things involved—like bread, potatoes, gravy, et cetera—Darla didn't seem to eat much. He supposed this was how it was with her and ignoring it would be best. After all, hadn't he already had this discussion with himself? He liked women with knockout figures and here was one. That would be hard to keep up unless you lifted apple crates all day or ate grass.

He saw his grandmother's frown of consternation. "We're going out for dinner tomorrow night," he said.

"Oh, splendid," Maxie said. "You'll have a wonderful time. Where are you going?"

"I'm not sure yet. I'll be sure to let you know. You can join us if you like."

She patted him on the cheek and smiled into his warm eyes. "Thank you, Tom. I'm sure I'll be fine."

It came as no surprise that Darla had a special little pack—leather—for her movies, her DVDs. She was kneeling in front of the TV and player. It wasn't a fancy new TV, but it was high definition—Tom bought it for his grandmother several years ago.

"I brought *Love Actually,* my favorite movie of all time, and some really special ones—*The Proposal,* which I love, and some others…"

Maxie whispered, "The Yankees are playing tonight."

"You pick the movie," Tom said. Then he stifled his yawn. "Let's watch your favorite."

Fortunately, Maxie didn't kick him. Instead, she got herself a book in progress, took her favorite chair before anyone else did and made herself comfortable.

Tom reclined on the sofa and Darla reclined on Tom. She was lounging between his legs, her back against his chest. They were positioned slightly behind Maxie's range of vision unless she turned sharply to take in the scene. It was quite decent—he couldn't even steal a kiss. She was much more casual this weekend, although it took an equal number of suitcases to be thus. And while Tom had never given a rip about the cost of things like women's jeans, he was curious. They looked damn good on her. On her feet were suede Uggs… He knew because she had told him. And she wore a fantastic, soft, loose-knit sweater he could see through. Under it was some kind of flesh-colored tank, no bra, breasts high and tight. He knew this because he was trained by the Marines in reconnaissance—there was no bra in place. He wished he could slip a hand under that sweater and figure out those breasts. She said she was twenty-nine and they were as perfect as an eighteen-year-old's....

Maxie cleared her throat and coughed; he jerked to attention as if she'd spoken aloud.

"Oh, this part always makes me cry!" Darla exclaimed.

He looked up; he had no idea what this movie was about. He slipped his arms around her waist and held her while she sniffed. And then damned if he didn't start to nod off. He came right awake again, thank goodness, because Darla turned her head and looked over her shoulder and up at him. "Tom," she whispered. "I think your grandmother is snoring!"

He almost said, "Are you sure it wasn't me?" but he caught himself. Instead he said, "Shhhh."

Every once in a while Tom stole a look at Maxie. She held her book in her lap and her head tilted down, her glasses on her nose, as though she might be reading. She didn't even bob. Every so often she'd emit a soft little snore. He had never envied a person more—he'd love to catch a little nap, or at least check the score of the baseball game. But he didn't dare.

The movie ended, Darla heaved a heavy, satisfied sigh and Maxie stretched. She closed her book, removed her glasses and while the credits were running she said, "Lovely, Darla. I'm all in. I think I'll just go ahead and head for bed." She stood up and smiled at them, so cozy on the couch. "Why don't you two enjoy another movie?"

The traitor, Tom thought. She was going to pay for that.

Darla just smiled, which was lucky for her. Tom was annoyed enough by the movie selection that if Darla had said something cheeky like *You slept through the whole thing,* Tom was never going to see her again. *He* could be perturbed with Maxie, but everyone else better mind their manners.

Then came Saturday. As Tom had explained, he had to work. He had his part-time crew in, working overtime, at least until early afternoon. He drove the tractor or truck or forklift by the barn and house several times and caught sight of his grandmother in her garden or picking apples off the small trees or lower branches. She was hearty and healthy, but they had agreed she was going to stay off ladders, at least for the most part. She baked, visited with workers, brought lemonade to the break room in the barn, put out cider for anyone who would like to take a gallon home.

Darla mainly sat on the porch lounge with a book in her lap. Well, hell, she had said she had to work as well, and this must be her work—he had no cause to judge or complain.

"We got a fence issue, Tom," Junior said.

"*Now* what?"

Junior scrubbed off his cap and wiped a rag over his thin hair. Junior had started out here over thirty years ago when he was a teenager and stayed on. He was one of their few year-round employees. Since Tom had known him he'd served a tour of duty in the Army, married and divorced and was now on his own. He had two grown children and was by far one of the finest and most dependable men Tom had known. He was damn sorry about the family issues and even more sorry Junior was mostly alone except for seeing his kids now and then.

"I just happened to see it," Junior said. "Kinda close to the house—tore down the cyclone mesh. I'd like to get it back up today. If one of Maxie's pies gets snatched off her cooling tray on the porch, she'll kill that old bitch with her bare hands."

Tom chuckled despite himself. "That bear?"

"Who else? Wunt elk or deer or bobcats." He pronounced *wasn't* as *wunt*. "Only a bear with a family is gonna go to so much trouble as that. So damn heavy, all 'em, they broke it down tryin' to get over. And wunt a person—they'd climb over, no trouble. Not like we got barbed wire on top."

"She's starting to get on my nerves," Tom said. "Costing me way too much in fencing. I see two possible solutions here—either she heads for hibernation with the kids pretty soon or I'm going to have to sit up late, catch her and shoot her. It's come down to that."

"I'll do that if you want," Junior said.

Tom grinned. "Maybe we bag that bear together?"

Junior grinned in response. "I'm into that idea."

"Buddy's working today. Pull him off the trees and get him to help on the fence—I have stuff to do."

"Sure thing."

Tom went around the perimeter to look at it even though he wasn't going to work on it. Sure thing, it wasn't torn apart so much as bent over. Same as always. It looked like a few heavy bears attempted to climb the fence and it bent under their weight. The poles that held up the cyclone fencing flattened and the metal wire collapsed. It was a bigger pain to repair than if someone had taken wire cutters to it and opened it up. With this kind of damage, more of the fencing had to be removed and replaced, more support poles replaced.

He checked more of the perimeter and saw a couple of familiar legs up on a ladder. He slowed, killed the engine and heard humming. "Hey, apple girl," he yelled.

She laughed and came down a couple of steps, her bag nearly full. "What's up, boss?"

"Got another bear scare. Damn things broke down some more fencing."

Her eyes got wide. "They aren't in here, are they?"

"Nah. One thing about bears, they're kind of hard to hide in daylight. They're big and clumsy."

"Shew. Try not to scare me."

"You're working this weekend, huh? What about Jed?"

"He's coming up tomorrow afternoon, which usually means he'll be here tonight. I think he spends the night over at the Best Western in Fortuna. I'll work till lunchtime tomorrow, then he'll come over. He wants to take the girls to the redwoods and coast on a picnic before it gets too cold."

"Nice," he said. "I guess it's working out."

"So far," she said. "I'm trying not to let the fact that he's given me so much influence my opinion of him. Know what I mean?"

Tom nodded. Her love was not for sale. "You like baseball?" he heard himself ask.

She looked a little perplexed, but nodded. "Why?"

"Red Sox played the Yankees last night," he said idly.

"Did you *see* that game?" she asked, suddenly excited.

"Did *you?*" he asked back.

"I don't have a TV, but Buddy and Jerome were talking about it—Jeter took three bases. Must have been awesome. And he put it into overtime!"

"So, you're a Yankees fan?"

"Me? I'm a California girl, it's the Giants for me."

"Well, I was raised here and I'm all about the Red Sox!" he informed her.

"I think I have a better track record, but you do what you have to do."

"Hah! Maybe you've had a little luck here and there, but better record? I beg to differ."

"What are you talking about? Giants knocked out the Sox 4-2!"

"And the next two games? Sox put 'em down!"

"Don't get cocky—it's not over."

"It's *over*—they didn't make the series!"

"They will next year—and your sucky Sox won't be there for it." She stepped closer to him even though she had a full, heavy bag of apples hanging off her shoulders. "What are you doing throwing your lot in with an East Coast team? Have you no loyalty?"

He laughed and lifted the canvas apple bag from her. She would be fun to attend a game with. Not that that would ever happen, but it would be fun. "I spent a lot of time in other places, I guess I turned." He walked to the big bin and unloaded her apples for her. Then he handed her back the bag. "I suppose you watch a lot of chick flicks," he said.

"Tom, try to keep up here—no TV. And no money for movies."

"Back when you did have a TV and went to movies…" he said.

"Some," she admitted. "But I'll tell you something if you promise not to share."

"What?" he asked.

She leaned close. "I like disaster films," she whispered. "The kind that blow up the world. I'm not fussy—it can be asteroids, aliens or Mother Nature. I think I'm a special-effects junkie."

"Yeah?" he asked, feeling like he'd suddenly grown lots more teeth in his mouth, he was smiling so big. "What was the last good one you saw?"

"It's been a while—but I think it was *Day After Tomorrow*—the glacier. I really loved that. Before that I saw New York City demolished about three times—asteroids and aliens and even volcanoes."

He laughed, hands on his hips. "Tell you what, one of these times you come out with the kids, we'll find a way to get them to sleep and watch a newer disaster movie."

She actually took a step back. Away. "That could be fun," she said. But her posture and the way she said it made it sound like anything but fun.

"What?" he asked.

"Nothing," she said.

"No really. What?"

"I'd love that," she said. "But the girls have to get baths and go to sleep after dinner and I have to get them home for that, Tom. And I get up at five. I mean, it sounds like fun, but it's not practical."

"We'll do it on a weekend," he said.

"I think you have other things to do on weekends…"

"Probably not every weekend," he said.

She gave him a smile that said she was pretty sure he was booked.

So he got a little more aggressive. "Not every weekend. We'll make it work because I love watching cities get blown up."

"You do?"

He shrugged. "As long as it's pretend. Get back to work—have to check the fence. Don't want the bear family eating all our apples!"

Nora got back to her picking, though she wasn't humming anymore. *We'll do it on a weekend* kept circulating in her brain. He must have meant that he would include her along with his new friend. But then, when she suggested he seemed to be pretty busy on the weekend, he could have clarified that, but instead said he wouldn't be busy every weekend, which almost sounded like he wanted to do something with Nora. Just Nora.

That would not be good, thinking he liked her.

When she'd thrown her life away the first time, she'd been nineteen, inexperienced, foolish and unquestionably starved for love. Now things were different—she was older, knew how bad things could get if one wasn't cautious and she didn't need the love of a young man to validate her.

She had no interest in a broken heart.

# Twelve

October in the mountains was chilly, often wet, and the busiest apple harvesting time all year. Tom had worn a slicker all day and was still wet to the skin. He was bone tired by the time he was able to make it to the house at five o'clock.

"There you are," Darla said, smiling. She jumped up from the table and Duke immediately thought she intended to pet him. He wagged and went to her and she put out her hands. "Ack! No, Duke, no! Sit. Sit." Duke tilted his head and looked confused, then forlorn. But he stopped and sat.

Then she smiled at Tom and gave her clothes a brush as if to remove his hair that wasn't there. She was decked out in a longish gray wool skirt, yet another pair of boots he didn't recognize, a woolly orange jacket over a silky black blouse. Damn, but the woman could certainly look good.

He touched the jacket. "Nice," he said.

She brushed the place he had touched, though he

had washed his hands in the barn. "Cashmere," she whispered to him. "So, when are we going out? Soon?"

"I can't think of anywhere to take you that will justify that jacket," he said. "I need a shower…"

Maxie was busy at the sink, washing up some of her baking dishes. "Long day, Tom?" she asked.

He frowned, then almost laughed at her. No one knew better than Maxie what the harvest was like. Two things occurred to him—Nora would have been helping with the dishes even though she hadn't dirtied them and Darla hadn't asked him if he was tired, if he'd had a hard day. But of course he wouldn't say that. "Give me fifteen minutes." He looked at his watch. "It's still early."

"I know," she said. "But I've been reading all day and I'm bored. I'm ready for a change of scenery."

Maxie turned from the sink. "I put your books on the stairs, Darla. Tom, since you're going up for a shower, take them upstairs for Darla."

"Oh, no, I've got them," she said.

"I can do that," Tom said.

"I'll… I'll read a little while you're showering, then I'll carry them—"

But he was already at the foot of the stairs. He picked up a stack of books—two textbooks and a paperback. He was transfixed by the paperback, the cover of which had a sexy vampire about to plunge his teeth into the neck of a beautiful woman on it. "Hmm," he said. "I guess in pharmacology you have to be ready for anything," he said.

She took the books away from him. "Sometimes I have to let my brain rest for a few minutes—what I study is pretty intense."

He put the vampire book on top. "Yeah, this looks very relaxing…" Then he watched as she went up the stairs ahead of him. He followed. He braced both hands on the door frame of the guest room, leaning in. "Fifteen minutes, Darla. Just let me get cleaned up."

"Take your time," she said sweetly. "I'll go downstairs and visit with Maxie."

Twenty minutes later Tom was back in the kitchen and when he walked in, Darla's eyes lit up as she looked him up and down. "Look at you," she said, smiling. He wondered how he'd managed to please her; he wasn't as spruced up as she was. He wore black jeans, a dark sweater and camel suede jacket. Instead of work boots, of which he had several pairs, he wore his going-out boots—polished and shiny like a good marine. She stood on her tiptoes and smoothed her hands along his shoulders. "This is a very good look on you. And I swear you must be six-five in your boots."

"I doubt it," he said. "Maxie, I don't know where we're going. You and Duke okay?"

"Oh, I think we'll manage," she said with a laugh. "Just have fun."

"Want me to bring you home a dessert?" he asked.

She shook her head. "You eat two for me."

"Let's take my car," Darla said. "That truck of yours is so high off the ground, I'm afraid I'll break my neck getting in and out." She held out her keys. "Want to drive?"

"Sure." Then with a hand on the small of her back, he escorted her to her car. "This is new," he said. "When did you get it?"

"Oh, about six months ago. Maybe nine. I can't remember."

"Nice," he said. And when he got behind the wheel, "Lots of leg room."

"You like it? You can heat your seat. Want me to show you how?"

"I'll be fine," he said with a chuckle.

This was all he had ever wanted, a woman just like this—sophisticated, accomplished, beautiful and already set up in life. A woman who would bring pride to his name, to his family. Darla was established and came from a good, strong, close family.

And yet it felt all wrong.

All the way to Arcata she told him about her current course of study, about drug trials and experiments and the FDA and the DEA and how people in her position had to be cognizant of the laws. As she had done before, she segued into the bonus perks after major sales and contracts, not to mention the generous expense account for the wining and dining of doctors and hospital administrators, as if these were the really important parts of her job. "That's one of the best parts," she admitted. "Entertaining my clients. And I'm good at it—I have one of the best client lists in the company, and I haven't been there that long."

"But what if Bob had lived?" he asked before he could stop himself. "You wouldn't have been able to stay in one place long."

"We'd been married less than a year," she said. "Before he deployed."

And it occurred to him, there was no Marine base in the Denver area. "How did you meet?" he asked.

She gave a heavy sigh, as if she'd rather not talk about it. Possibly the memories were still painful. "He was on leave, skiing with friends. I met him in Vail."

"But he wasn't stationed around there...."

"No. But I traveled so often anyway, it was easy to go to him. Like all the time. I can work from home a lot as long as I have a phone and laptop, so I sometimes spent several days in a week with him."

"But you lived in Denver?"

"Why are you asking this? Did he complain about this?"

Tom felt the icy wedge of her voice. He reached over and took her hand. "Never," he said. "I just never thought of it before, and I wondered."

"I was willing to move, to change jobs or companies, but Bob said it wasn't fair—he'd just be deploying soon anyway. He didn't want me to give up a good thing when in the end I was just going to sit alone, waiting, worrying..."

And Tom thought—*he is a much better person than I am.* If Tom fell in love and got married, he wouldn't want his wife in another state. If he was newly married and about to deploy in a few months, he wouldn't be happy about his wife not being around. Proving that he'd really screwed up by directing the conversation to her dead husband, she fell silent. He wasn't sure what was worse, the silence or the conversation about drug trials and expense accounts. Finally he pulled into the square in Arcata and found a parking place.

"The only sushi place I know about is crappy and, I guessed, probably beneath your standards. How do you feel about Mediterranean?"

"Wonderful!" she said, beaming, quiet mood gone. And she held her place in the car until he came around and opened her door for her.

Darla seemed pleased with his choice of restaurant; she appeared to be back to her bright-eyed self. After they'd ordered drinks, an appetizer and their entrees, she reached across the table and took one of his hands. "Thank you, Tom, for being such a good host, good date."

"I am?"

"You really are." She laughed. "I look forward to these weekends with you. I hope you're enjoying them as much as I am."

"Totally."

"I researched your orchard last week, in between other assignments for my class. It's very well-known, you know."

"Is it? Well-known to whom?"

"That's what I love most about you—you're so modest," she said. "You have a laptop—search Cavanaugh

Apples on Google sometime. The foodie sites love you. You'll learn a lot about yourself."

He lifted his eyebrows. "Is there anything I don't know about myself that I should know?" he asked.

The drinks came, the stuffed grape leaves. And Darla laughed at him. "I'm not sure. Do you know you have forty acres and two hundred and fifty trees with roughly twenty-eight types of apples? You've been the primary supplier in the county for twenty years. And most of your forty acres are still undeveloped and what's considered to be prime real estate. And you have a very successful local cider business going on there. Cavanaugh is leading the pack in cider. You have quite a successful business."

"Well, Maxie does," he clarified.

"I was under the impression it was a family business," she said, sipping her wine.

"It seems to be—it's been in the family a long time. I had to make a choice between the Marine Corps and the orchard. Maxie can't run it alone forever. Afghanistan helped me make the choice pretty easily."

She sipped her wine thoughtfully. "Have you ever considered selling it?"

He devoured the stuffed grape leaves; Darla was apparently satisfied with one bite, half remaining on her plate. Funny, he was getting used to that—how she barely ate. "It was going to eventually come down to that, unless I made the decision to come home and run it. Maxie won't retire till she's on her last legs, but I'm not oblivious to the fact that she's getting older. And a little slower, though not mentally," he stressed. "We had a major showdown about the ladder last year. Junior, our foreman, brought to my attention that she'd fallen a couple of times. Even though she hadn't been hurt, he could smell disaster coming and had no influence in convincing her to get an employee to climb the ladder if there was something she wanted done." He laughed to himself. "Maxie's been up on tripod ladders since she was just a kid, pregnant with my dad. She doesn't really think she needs to slow down. And it probably keeps her young."

"It's a shame," Darla said. "She deserves a much more relaxing retirement!"

"Like?" Tom asked, taking on the rest of the grape leaves.

"Like a low-maintenance home where people do all the hard stuff for you. In a nice place, like near the ocean. Where there are lots of people and activities and life is finally about fun rather than back-breaking work. But if anything should go wrong, like a fall or illness, there are trained professionals nearby. At the orchard, if Maxie falls off a ladder, it's only you or Junior to help her. Or if she, God forbid, had a stroke…"

He stopped chewing and stared at her. He had never thought of that. In this place, in the country, people got old on their land and, unless they moved away to live with their children or grandchildren, they often died on their land. If they had an accident or got sick, their family took care of them.

Darla picked up the last piece of her stuffed grape leaves and popped it in her mouth. "We put my grandmother in assisted living last year. She didn't think she wanted to go, but now she loves it. She's the community poker champ, can you beat that? And it's in a really beautiful Colorado Springs valley with glorious views, near enough we can visit her and bring her to visit us for weekends, where there are walking trails and all kinds of fun things for the residents to do. She's so grateful now."

"Is she," Tom said in passing. Many things about Darla made him wonder. And then at the risk of slowing the conversation again he said, "I have such a hard time picturing you as the wife of a career marine...."

To his surprise, Darla laughed. "Career marine? What gave you that idea?"

"Well, Bob gave me that idea when he said that was his intention...."

*"Was,"* she stressed. "When we got married he had pretty much given up that idea. I had a job all lined up for him—my dad has a golf buddy with a soft water conditioner manufacturing plant who wanted to add to his management team and Bob, being a smart, decorated marine, was perfect. Good salary, too."

Tom wondered if Bob just talked about a career in the Corps in front of his boys to encourage them when in fact he was planning to exit and get a civilian job in a factory. But Bob didn't seem like that kind of guy.

And the dinner arrived.

"Oh, my God," Darla said, looking down at her Greek salad. "Have you ever seen so much food?"

Tom knew there would be a doggie bag, and not for Duke. But that was after he had a satisfactory taste of Darla's uneaten dinner.

She lifted her fork, poised over her salad, and asked, "So, Tom, if you sold your orchard and looked for another line of work, what would you do?"

Tom had chicken kabobs—looked wonderful. He stabbed his fork into a wonderful cube of chicken and said, "Just out of curiosity, what do you have lined up for me?"

She laughed merrily. "You're so funny." She lifted one lovely light brown brow. "Well, there's that manufacturing job, still open…"

He didn't find that particularly funny. "There is nothing else I want to do."

"But it's exhausting," she counseled.

"And if it ever becomes too much work at the harvest or the planting, there are lots of people around here looking for work. But if Maxie can last seventy-four years, I can last longer."

"You could actually invest the money you earn from the sale of the orchard, watch it grow, take care of Maxie in high style *and* begin another career."

He chewed and noticed that she grinned excitedly. What had her parents invested in that smile? It was simply beautiful. He was also curious about her breasts, so large and high and delicious-looking—he wondered if he would touch them and find them not real. That wouldn't be an issue if he was in love, but he was beginning to realize he was not even close to in love. Still, he was curious.

Finally he came back to the present. He looked at her levelly and said, "I'm going to work the orchard till I drop dead."

"Why?" she asked almost desperately.

"Because I just love apples."

She made a gak sound in the back of her throat. And Tom laughed.

The drive back to Virgin River was a revisit of the drive away—a lot of talk about vacations, bonuses, expense accounts, perks. There was a little about drug trials and prescriptions thrown in there. Tom thought about introducing the topic of national health care but frankly he was tired. So he drove.

She asked him if he was happy living in an older home; she had purchased her home new with lots of upgrades like granite countertops, slate floors, cherrywood cabinetry. She could open her garage and turn on her hot tub from blocks away.

He told her he loved that old house. "I've never seen a really proper porch on a new house."

Then they came to the orchard. Tom jumped out of the car, opened the gate, pulled in, jumped out and closed the gate, and as they were driving between the groves Darla said, "Tom, I want you to know how grateful I am for your friendship. If I didn't have these little escapes to the orchard on the weekends, I don't know what I'd do."

"Huh?" he said.

"I'm lonely, so far away from my family. And with Bob gone…"

"Oh, man," he said. He'd been so busy falling out of like with her, he'd forgotten she was lonely and widowed and all that. "Well, I'm glad it's relaxing for you."

"It's a godsend, seriously. Like a rescue. And there's all the other stuff—going out, which I haven't done in so long. Home cooking. Fresh fall air. It's all just wonderful. I look forward to it all week. I've been out on a few dates, but I hadn't really expected to end up seeing a handsome, successful man with his own rather impressive business."

"I grow apples," he reminded her.

"Very popular apples," she reminded him. "If you chose to sell that orchard to a commercial grower like Del Monte, you could really make a killing. But I hope not too soon—I love coming up here every weekend. It's so lovely and quiet."

He wondered if she knew his net worth. He didn't, but he wondered if she did.

"Um, Darla. Next weekend might not be as relaxing. For a couple of weekends every October we open up the orchard for people to tour, visit, buy apples and other products. It might not seem like such a big deal, but the place is swarming. People come from everywhere. Typical of Virgin River—most of the town comes out. They shop, pick apples, bring their own

ladders even. They bring their dogs, their kids, sometimes their grills. It's big business."

"Is it lucrative?" she asked.

He paused before he said, "It works for us. But it's
madness. And there is no home-cooked meal, no going
out to dinner, no walk in the moonlight between the
groves."

"Oh, it must be so exciting!"

"You would hate it. It's not fancy. It's not presti-
gious. It's a bunch of county people on ladders, picking, tasting cider and pies and throwing softballs
around. It's barking dogs, small children, shouting
and laughing people, swarming all over the orchard,
in the barn, in the house..."

"In the house?" she asked.

"They're our friends," he said. "They're the town."

"Wonderful!" she said. "Well, if the invitation
stands, I'll see you Friday late afternoon."


Tom was up and in the orchard office by five-thirty
and even though it wouldn't be light for some time yet,
Nora was there by six.

"Good morning," she said. "I guess I thought you'd
be sleeping in or enjoying one of those big country
breakfasts. You do have company."

"I'm sure she's having sweet dreams," he said.
"What are you doing here so early on a Sunday morning?"

"Getting an early start. I'm planning to leave right
at lunchtime if you're sure you can spare me. Jed will

be coming to the house. We were talking about a picnic, but with this weather…"

He smiled. "Still Jed, is he?"

"I'm working up to Dad, but it doesn't come easy."

"I knew about your plans, Nora—we're all ready to back you up. We might have an issue with the next two weekends. If you're not going to be able to work, tell me now—we're opening up the orchard to the public. It gets chaotic."

"So I'm told. I wonder—would it be all right if Jed and Susan come and bring the girls? I promise not to get too distracted."

"Absolutely, tell them about it. Maxie would probably love it."

"I'm going to get moving before I'm caught burning daylight." She zipped up her jacket and pulled on gloves. She went past him to the break room to grab a rain slicker off a set of hooks on the wall that held a dozen or so.

"Don't you want a cup of coffee to get your engine started?" he asked her when she passed back through the office.

She grinned at him. "Now that I'm wealthy, I have coffee at home. With cream!" And off she whirled. He heard her outside as she said, "Hey, Duke, old pal—how are you this morning? Gonna be another wet one, but you like it that way, don't you? Doesn't that wet dog smell make it all worthwhile?" And then she laughed.

She was just the cutest damn thing, he found himself thinking. He wondered what she'd think of stuffed grape leaves....

It was a few hours later, the morning fog and mist beginning to give way to a bright morning sun, when Tom heard the bell from the back porch. He had asked Maxie to ring it when Darla was ready to have her luggage carried downstairs. The bell had almost never been used. Tom's grandfather had installed that bell when Maxie was very, very pregnant. It was one of those old-fashioned things with a strip of rawhide attached to the clapper. He wanted her to use it if she needed him for anything rather than walking up and down a couple of acres of trees looking for him. And what had Maxie done? She had walked through the entire orchard to find Grandpa to tell him, "I didn't want to bother you, but I've been in labor all day and now I think I have to call the midwife. Can you get her for me?"

Tom laughed to himself. He'd heard the story so many times while growing up. His grandpa had swept his grandmother up in his arms, carried her to the house, up the stairs to the bedroom and sent someone for the midwife. The midwife was from another town, of course—that long ago Virgin River wasn't much but a few farms. And the midwife didn't make it, which at the end of the day had been something of a tragedy because Maxie had a few complications that left her unable to have more children. Of course there was no guarantee that getting the midwife there on time would have mattered.

Even though his grandparents, dead in love till the day Grandpa passed away, said they'd love to have had a baker's dozen, they were also quick to say they were grateful for the bounty God gave: a son, an orchard and a woman who could bake a decent pie.

He trudged across the yard to the house. For some reason he had a picture in his head of Nora tromping through an entire orchard rather than just ringing the bell. And then, unsummoned, an image of Darla being carried on a litter by a group of Nubian slaves....

He found himself ridiculous—stuck in a box of his own making, rejecting the one who appealed and spending every weekend with the one who was not right for him, though he had desperately wished she could have been. But it was hopeless. *She* was hopeless.

She was waiting in the kitchen. "Going to get an early start?" he asked Darla.

"Since you'll be busy all day, I'll get the drive behind me. I look forward to next weekend. It sounds like such fun."

Tom mentally tried to calculate how many more weeks she'd be in Davis, close enough to spend every freaking weekend at the orchard. "Let me go up and grab your bags," he said. "Have you eaten breakfast?"

"Long ago," she said with a smile. She turned to Maxie, who was stirring a giant pot on the stove. "Thank you once again, Maxie. Your hospitality is unsurpassed."

"Always a pleasure, dear," she said. "Oh, by the

way, the next two weekends? There will be lots of company. I hope you love a crowd."

"Oh, yes," she said.

"Staying over," Maxie stressed. "Some of my girl-friends from around the mountains are coming. We'll be packed in here."

"It sounds like fun!"

"Good, then."

Tom, chuckling and shaking his head, headed up the stairs. He managed the four designer bags in two trips, loading up her trunk. He drove her to the gate, opened it while she transferred herself to the driver's side. She slipped her arms around his neck, stood on the toes of yet another pair of boots to give him a brief kiss. He was planning his email in his head—Darla, rethink this idea of spending the weekend during the apple festival. If Maxie's friends are coming, you might end up on a cot in the cider works. And if you pick at your food, they might tie you down and feed you. They're old, but they're strong and bossy.

He went back to the house, to the kitchen, having been called by wonderful smells that he hoped weren't being prepared for dinner.

"Whatcha got going there, Max?" he asked.

"Chili," she said. "It's getting so cold, so wet, I thought maybe I'd put it in the break room on a warm-ing tray along with some disposable bowls. What do you think?"

"I think I'll do that for you, after I've had a cou-ple of bowls right now. Crackers? Shredded cheese?"

She lifted one thin brow. "Side of beef to go with that?"

"Make it a big bowl," he said. "Then I'll see if I can go pick the rest of your apples for you." He waited patiently while she fished around in the cupboard for a large bowl, grabbed a bag of shredded cheddar out of the refrigerator and a box of crackers from the pantry. "I'm going to make corn bread to go with this but I sense you can't wait for that." She placed it in front of him with a spoon.

"Can't wait," he confirmed. "So? Company's coming? Who?"

"I'm not entirely sure yet," she said, sitting down at the table with him. "I never have any trouble rounding up friends."

"I see," he said, crumpling crackers on top of his cheddar-laced chili. "You haven't invited them yet."

"I'm going to do that straight away."

"Why? We're usually awful busy on apple festival weekends."

"They'll come early, help with baking, all that stuff."

"That's not why," he said. "Damn, this is good, Maxie."

"Thank you."

"So? Why?"

"I'm getting tired of Miss Picky Pants. If you marry her I'm going to kill myself."

His smile fought hard to get out, but he held it in. "What if I'm completely in love with her?"

She rolled her eyes and clasped her hands together as if praying for strength. "I've had a good life…"

He couldn't help it, he laughed. He leaned toward her. "Maxie, do you ever think about retirement?"

"Of course. This is my retirement. I don't work nearly as hard as I used to—Junior manages almost everything. At least he did until you came home."

"Ever thought about selling the orchard?" he asked.

"No, I thought about you selling it after I was dead. I felt kind of bad for Junior and the others, but by the time I'm dead, they'll be near dead anyway and I just can't manage from the grave."

"No doubt you'll try," he mumbled.

"What was that?"

"Nothing," he said.

"My hearing is perfect," she informed him.

"So," he asked, deliberately speaking very quietly. "Have you ever considered one of those homes for seniors? When you're, you know, senior?"

"I'm seventy-four," she said. "How much more senior do you expect I'll get?"

"I think some of your girlfriends live in fancy-dancy senior communities. Don't they? Where they can have the lawn taken care of for them, the cooking pretty much done every day, a little housekeeping? Some fun and games?"

"Lorna is the karaoke queen at hers…. Ever hear of such a thing?"

"Yeah, that's right," he said. "You ever lust after one of those places?"

"You need a little more privacy, Tom? Because I have places to go if you want a weekend alone or something."

He shook his head. "Darla mentioned they put her grandmother in one of those assisted-living places and she didn't want to go at first, but now she's happy about it. Loving it."

Maxie's face contorted into a very mean grimace. "Is that so?"

"So it seems."

"You might want to tell Miss Picky Pants I have a shotgun and I'm a right fine shot." She crossed her arms over her chest and leaned back.

Tom roared with laughter. "Maybe I'll just let you handle this whole thing your way."

"What whole thing?" she asked. "Is she already putting me out to pasture?"

"Uh-huh. And selling the orchard and investing the money and getting me started in a new career," he admitted. He thought about telling his grandmother what Darla had paid for her red boots, but then Maxie might stroke out and he was afraid Darla would move in to help him cope.

"For the love of God," she said.

Tom put down his spoon. His eyes became serious. "Listen, we have a situation. Her husband was one of my men, killed while he served in my command. She's lonely. She's nearby. She wants to come here… Why, I'm not entirely sure. It's not like she eats apples or wants to bake pies. But she wants to come. Maybe the service is too good...."

"I could get out the lumpy pillows and scratchy toilet paper...."

"I tried to discourage the next couple of weekends but she's planning to come even though I warned her she won't get any attention. It'll be apple-picking time. You told her you were going to fill the house up with old women and she *still* wants to come. I think, at least until she finishes this course in Davis, we're stuck with her."

"You're not mad in love with her?" Maxie asked.

He shook his head. "I want to be," he admitted. "She's very pretty." *Sexy.* "She seems smart and I gather she has a solid, functional family background, but..." *But I haven't had sex in so long I can't even remember how...and I still can't get excited about her coming for another visit... If she sprawled naked on my bed, I probably wouldn't be able to...*

"Tom, can I say something about that? About that solid, functional family background? I don't know where you got that judgmental streak or your almighty standards—maybe from your great-grandfather. Your great-grandmother was so open to possibilities, so nonjudgmental. When I stumbled into this orchard looking for work, I had come from a really rugged family—dirt-poor, had nothing, uneducated, didn't know what the term *emotional support* meant—and your grandfather took an instant liking to me anyway. I'm sure because of that your great-grandfather refused to hire me on. But your great-grandmother *did* hire me—brought me into the house, into the kitchen to help with jam, ciders, pies and housework. Tom, I had a lot of what you young people call baggage, but your grandpa didn't care. He said he loved me and wanted me no matter what my past had been like, no matter what load I was bringing along. That's never been a secret in our family—that I had burdens. Your grandpa had to take on a lot to take me. Most people have a load to carry, Tom. So do you—look at your family history! You have some amazing family history and some of it kind of strange—like the disappearing mother. You know."

"I know. You never heard from her again, did you?"

Maxie shook her head. "I would've told you. I've always told you everything."

"Many family stories," he said, very seriously.

They were both silent for a moment. Finally Maxie said, "You aren't mad in love with Miss Picky Pants?"

He shook his head.

"Then stop kissing her!" Maxie demanded.

Tom grinned. "You don't miss anything, do you?"

"You think I raised a decorated marine and made money on apples by missing things?"

# Thirteen

It wasn't unusual for busy married couples who had both children and careers that took more than the usual forty hours per week to do more communicating through phone calls, emails and during short breaks in the workday than at other times. So it was with Jack Sheridan and his wife, Mel. What was unusual was for Preacher to call Mel and ask her to drop in to the bar when things were quiet to have a chat with her husband.

"What's the matter?" she asked when she got there.

"Nothing," Jack answered. "Why?"

"Because Preacher asked me to come over if I wasn't busy. He said you needed counseling."

Jack grumbled and poured himself a cup of coffee. "He's getting worse than an old woman."

Mel stared him down for a minute, then she went to the door to the kitchen, pushed it open and said, "Preach, help me out here. I have a patient in a half hour and Jack doesn't want to talk right now." Then she went back to her stool.

Momentarily Preacher was standing beside Jack. "So," the cook said. "You haven't told her what's wrong?"

"I don't have anything to say!" he said with attitude.

Preacher faced Mel, and about that time Paige came into the bar, standing beside her husband. "About a week ago Luke brought a friend in for a beer. Old friend of Luke's from Army days—an old Black Hawk pilot. Well, it turns out Jack and Coop, the friend, knew each other way back when. Some woman accused Coop of beating her up, Jack called the MP's and Coop was locked up. But it turned out to be some kind of misunderstanding, Coop got out, Jack shipped out, the woman disappeared long ago and now what we have, with holidays and town parties coming up, is a little bad blood between the Riordans and Jack. A Riordan-Sheridan standoff over something that happened a long time ago with a lot of mixed-up details and facts."

Mel was stunned silent for a moment. Her mouth hung open, her blue eyes were wide. Finally she said, "Huh?"

Preacher took a deep breath. Then he began again. "About a week ago…"

Paige put a hand on her husband's forearm. She shook her head. "Not from the beginning, John," she said. Paige looked at her friend. "Mel, about fifteen years ago a marine and a soldier were both at the same place at the same time. Your marine was friendly with a waitress who confided she had a bad relationship. Abusive, she said. You know Jack—he offered to help if needed. He gave her a phone number and a couple of days later, she called that number and left Jack a message that she needed help."

"And I went," Jack said. "She was banged up pretty bad and crying. I tried to take her to the hospital, but she wouldn't go. So I called the police and stayed with her until they came."

Mel looked at him. "What did she want, Jack?" she asked.

"I don't know," he said with a shrug. "Moral support, I guess. I suggested she get herself away from whoever would do that to her and she said she'd go anywhere I'd take her, just to get her out of there. But I couldn't do any more—I was scheduled out on a military transport with a squad of marines. And our destination was privileged. So she told the MP's who beat her up and then, wouldn't you know, he stumbled in, half drunk, knuckles bruised, denying he'd ever touched her..."

"And Jack," Mel asked. "Who told the military police that he was the one? Was it you? Did you say, that's him?"

"He could hardly stand up! He'd been passed out and looked guilty as all hell."

Preacher made a sound. "Fortunately that sort of thing never happened to you."

"That's how I got to read his tattoos," Mel said.

"Remember that, Preach? He was completely toasted, face down on the floor and I sat up with him all night."

"All right, all right," Jack said. "Did I need an alibi? Did I have bruised knuckles?"

Mel shook her head. "My Jack," she said. "A hundred women have loved him, wanted him, been willing to lie or kill to get him…."

"Come on," he said impatiently. "She just needed some help!"

"Possibly," Mel said. "Okay, probably," she amended. "It does sound like there might be more to it, like maybe why the waitress couldn't get charges against the soldier to stick, or maybe he had an alibi besides being crocked or something. If they arrested him but let him out and he stayed in the Army, there's a piece of the puzzle missing. Don't you want to know what that piece is? On the highly improbable chance you could be wrong?"

"I heard sarcasm there," Jack said.

"Sorry," Mel said. "We have a little problem in the marriage," she said to Paige. "Two people with an overwhelming need to be right."

"I did nothing wrong," Jack insisted. "When a woman is battered and names her assailant, you call the cops."

"It's not about right or wrong, Jack—you did nothing wrong. It's about the details. Don't be so stubborn."

"That's just you," Jack accused his wife. "I'm flexible."

"Right," Preacher said. "I've seen a lot of that, just not lately."

"Look, he doesn't want to explain the circumstances to me any more than I want to hear them from him," Jack said in a sulk.

"Ducky," Mel said. "Listen, Jack, it probably doesn't matter whether you and this soldier kiss and make up. He's just a visitor. But you should work things out with Luke because he's permanent. And he's a good friend of yours."

"I haven't heard from him in a week," Jack said. "I didn't do this, you know. What would you do if you had a patient, beat up? Would you tell her not to make so much noise with all that crying?"

"Try not to be such a jackass," Paige said. He shot her a surprised look. He was at once shocked and not; Paige had been in a very scary, abusive relationship before she met John. But Paige wouldn't say shit if she had a mouthful. "Just saying," Paige added.

"I suggest you get his story and see if you can check it out for accuracy," Mel said. "Really, I tend to lean the other way—the man is always lying."

"And always guilty," Jack muttered. When he saw his wife's slow smile he actually flushed.

"Since I've been in this town, I've come up against a couple of situations with really naughty women who faked being abused by men who were the gentlest angels alive. Remember that ex-wife of Aiden Riordan's? Pretending he beat her up when he was actually with Erin in San Francisco for days? Lord help us all! So if you won't talk to the guy, why don't you ask Luke for some details? Preacher here will be happy to do a background check for you, see if the guy has any kind of record. And there's always Walt Booth if you need some Army brass on your side to find out what really happened back then."

"I guess it's possible," Jack muttered.

"We need to bury this," Preacher said. "I know Luke. If this friend of his turned out to be guilty of felony assault, he'd want to know. He'd want to be done with him. And we owe it to Luke."

"I think my work here is done," Mel said, standing up. "I wondered what was eating you," she said to her husband. "Call Luke right away—this thing has been festering long enough. I thought we were going to need counseling or something."

"You didn't see what I saw," Jack said.

"But I have, sweetheart," Mel reminded him. "I know, I know—it's never as simple as it looks. You don't know the guy but you know Luke. You should talk to him about this, then see if you can figure it out." And she leaned toward him for a kiss. Then she patted his cheek and smiled. "No wonder women fall at your feet. You're such a soft touch."

"I heard sarcasm there."

She just laughed. "I have a patient pretty soon. See you for dinner."

Things were opening up for Nora Crane in ways she had not dared hope for or imagine. First of all, she hadn't expected to ever get to know her father and here she was, spending at least one afternoon every week

with him. On almost every visit, Susan came along.
And every time they appeared, more items for Nora's
home and children arrived with them. Jed pulled a
port-a-crib and fancy stroller out of his trunk and she
had to fight tears of gratitude. Fay wouldn't have to
sleep on the mattress with her mother and sister anymore. But that was nothing to the Sunday they were
scheduled to have a picnic but were rained out; Jed
and Susan arrived pulling a trailer.

"It looks like our picnic will be another day, but I
think we'll have fun anyway," he said.

"What on earth…?"

"That old couch of yours, Nora—it just has to go!
Your table and two chairs aren't in much better shape."

And in that rented trailer were a sofa, a chair, a
side table, a lamp, small kitchen table and four chairs.

"No, you didn't," she said in a whisper. "Jed, you
have to stop this or I'll be taking care of you in your
impoverished old age!"

"I can't stop—not until I see you and the little girls
comfortable. I don't mean with extravagance—this
stuff was on sale and wasn't expensive as furniture
goes. I just want to help you get on your feet."

"But I can never repay you for this!"

"All I ever wanted was to have you in my life again,"
he said. "I never counted on the bonus of granddaughters."

When the furniture was brought into the house,
Berry was absolutely thrilled. She climbed right up

on it, her little eyes so round and happy. Fay immediately pulled herself up, too, and patted it.

Rain or not, nothing got past her neighbors. Martha and Adie were outside, checking out the delivery and from down the street Leslie and Conner arrived—Conner wanted to help Jed get the new furniture in and the old furniture out. The ratty old couch went in the U-Haul. "I'll drop this off at the dump unless you have other plans for it," Jed said.

"Nothing is thrown away around here without permission from Reverend Kincaid," Nora said. "In fact, in a couple of months I will have been here a year and without the charity of my friends and neighbors, I don't know if we'd have survived the winter."

It was hard to imagine anyone being more needy than Nora had been but sure enough, Noah wanted that couch. "I think I know just the place for it," he told her over the phone. Conner and Jed carried it through the drizzle for a block to the church where it would sit until it could be delivered further.

Her children were outfitted for the cold weather, there was new bedding, warm blankets and good food in the house. Just when Nora thought she couldn't possibly wish for more, Maxie asked her, "Nora, do you bake?"

"Welllll," she said doubtfully. "When I was a girl I made cookies, but it's been a long time."

"Do you think you'd like to?"

"If I had the time, I would," she said. "I can follow directions, I think. But Maxie, I don't have much cookware on hand."

"Here's what I'd like to do—and I've spoken to Tom about my idea. I have a couple of very big weekends coming up. If you're agreeable, you could pick apples until lunchtime, run to town and fetch Adie and the little ones and come back. We'll give them lunch and I think they'll either nap or maybe Berry will even help. I think a few of my friends will arrive later in the week—you'll like them. They're as ancient as I am, catty as can be, a little on the doting side when it comes to small children and they give Tom as much grief as they can get by with. Would you like to help me in the afternoons this week?"

"Oh, Maxie, I would love to!"

"I think Martha would rather hike than bake, but I'll leave you to extend an invitation to her, as well."

It seemed to be the natural order of things in Maxie's house that afternoon just stretched into evening—everyone gathered around her dinner table for a meal that had been started in the afternoon along with the baking. The little girls napped and when they didn't, Berry stood on a stool in the big kitchen, stirring, and Fay sat in her booster chair amidst the commotion, playing and snacking.

By dinner on Wednesday, they had accomplished a great deal—there was apple butter, apple pies stored in the root cellar where it was cool, all kinds of cookies for the weekend festivities. Nora had also learned to bake bread and make cinnamon rolls; the fall vegetables had come in, so there was zucchini bread galore.

Nora worked as hard in the kitchen as she did in the orchard. "Pace yourself," she said to Maxie. "Don't wear yourself out before your big weekend."

"Oh, darling, this doesn't tire me—it energizes me! I love feeding people."

Nora looked forward to dinnertime the most—the leaf was put in the table and everyone gathered around it, laughing, eating, telling tall tales. Adie was in her element—she couldn't do things like this at home alone and loved being with friends. And when Tom came in cold and tired after a long day in the orchard, he was not the same man Nora had met when she first applied for the job. He was cheerful and playful and she tried valiantly to tamp down fantasies of being the woman in his home when he finished his day's work.

But it was when Berry held out a cookie and said, in a voice loud and clear, "Tom! Eat dis! I maked it!" Nora just kind of went over the edge. And she had to run and hide.


"Where's Nora?" Tom asked.

The women all looked around. "Bathroom?" Adie suggested.

"No one in there," Tom said. "Keep an eye on the girls, I'll find her." He took a beer with him through the living room, dining room, even upstairs. Finally he grabbed his jacket off the hook by the door and went outside to find her huddled in a wicker chair in a far corner of the porch. Crying and shivering.

"Hey, now," he said, whipping off his jacket and wrapping it around her shoulders. He pulled a matching chair close to her. "What's with this? Why are you crying?"

"It's complicated," she said with a hiccup in her voice. "It's just that I started feeling so…so safe. So much like being a part of a big, wonderful family. And then Berry…"

"What about Berry?" he asked. "She's having fun."

"She's having *so* much fun," Nora said. She sniffed. "Honestly, what a wimp I am. I held it together through new toys, clothes and even furniture, but this week…" He reached into his pocket and pulled out a hanky, handing it to her. She looked at it cautiously and said, "You sure?"

"Blow," he said. "Then talk to me."

She blew her nose. Hard. A little laugh escaped through her tears.

"Now talk," he said.

"I don't expect you to understand, but when I was growing up and it was just my mother and I, we didn't have fun times like this. We didn't have people around. And Berry…" She crumbled again.

"What about Berry?" he pushed.

"Did you hear her? Did you hear her talk? Like she was giving orders? She's growing out of that severe shyness, Tom."

"Sure," he said, baffled. "She's getting used to all of us. She's been around us a lot lately...."

"I was so worried about her," Nora said. "I was worried about all of us—about us ever getting it together, having enough to get by, to stop being *afraid!*"

He wiped a tear from her cheek. "Were you afraid?" he asked softly.

"Oh, you have no idea...."

He smothered a chuckle. "You always act so brave," he said.

"Yeah, I act," she told him. "What else am I gonna do? Growing up I was timid, scared of everything."

"You?"

"Oh, my gosh, I was so scared of making my mother or teachers or anyone mad. And then what did I do but allow all that timidity to get me hooked up with this stupid guy who made my mother look like a day at the beach. There were times when I was pregnant..."

She was quiet for a moment and he took her hand. "Tell me. You were scared. Tell me."

"Oh, Tom, you don't want to hear all that... It's all so humiliating, so maudlin." But he nodded and she said, "Okay, I was on welfare and I worried all the time—that I'd be killed in my bed because I lived in such a scary place surrounded by gangs and dealers. Scared that I wouldn't be able to protect my children. And I thought life was hard when I lived with an angry mother, then it got so much harder. When I bake with Maxie and eat at your table, I remember those times the social worker gave me supplemental protein drinks

so I'd have enough calories for the pregnancy and I...
I just never thought I'd have this kind of life—picking
food from the garden, baking in a warm kitchen, sitting with my children at a table filled with such happiness and laughter...."

He found himself stroking the hair over her ear.
He had an unwelcome flash of Darla in her expensive
boots, picking at her meal, taking it all for granted.
He reminded himself that Darla shouldn't be ridiculed
for making something of herself. And she'd certainly
had her own heartache.

"When Chad left me in this town, even though I
didn't know how we would survive, I was so relieved
that he was gone, that I was in a place not so terrifying, and... If it hadn't been for Noah..."

Tom wrapped his hand around her upper arm. "Did
he hurt you?"

"Noah?" she asked, incredulous. "Of course not!
Noah helped, but I didn't make it easy for him. It's so
hard for me to trust anyone."

He smiled at her. "But you trust Maxie?"

"Yes," she said with a sniff and a smile. "I love
Maxie."

"And Adie?"

"Adie would never hurt a fly," she said.

"Martha?"

"Martha is strong. So good, so responsible. I love
her independence."

"Jed?" he asked.

"It's coming. I get more sure of him every week.

He's been so good to me. I'm going to let Maxie have a crack at him. If *she* trusts him…"

"Maxie has a sixth sense about things like that. I don't know where she got it. Living life, I guess. And…me?" he asked. "You trust me?"

She gave him a shy smile. "I think so, yes," she said.

"What do you think of stuffed grape leaves?" he asked.

A short burst of laughter escaped her. "I have absolutely no idea."

"I bet you'd like them. And kabobs—you'd like them, too."

"Tom, sometimes you confuse me."

"Are you better now? As in, done crying?"

"I've done more crying since I met you than I've done in the past couple of years, and the past few years were definitely cry-worthy. I don't think you bring out my best. I get so vulnerable around you. I tell you things I never tell anyone."

"I think that's okay. It means you think of me as a friend. Now here's what we have to do, Nora. You have to dry your tears and go with me back in the kitchen. You don't want the women to worry about you."

"Right," she agreed, wiping her eyes.

"Dinner's ready," he said. He held her beer toward her. "Want a sip?"

"Thanks," she said, fitting her lips to the bottle. She tilted it up and took a swallow. She stood and gave him his jacket back. "This turned out to be so much more than a job, Tom," she said. "I want you to know how much I appreciate it."

"I know. Let's get some dinner. I'm starving."

"Me, too. Even though I sampled all day long."

Dinner was some of Maxie's best stew, a salad thrown together by Adie and bread baked by Nora— her bread debut. For her efforts, she took home a batch of cinnamon rolls and promised to be back bright and early to pick apples.

After Nora, the children and Adie had been loaded up, Tom said to Maxie, "Once the festival weekends are behind us, would you be willing to babysit one evening? I think I'd like to take Nora over to Arcata for dinner."

She lifted her brows. "Really? Why?"

"I'm not sure," he said. "Because her gratitude for every little thing, even the things she has to work hardest for, is so damn charming."

"But what about Miss Picky Pants?"

"Maxie," he warned.

"I slip sometimes," she said with a shrug.

"Right.…"

"I think those little girls are divine," she said. "I'd be happy to babysit while you take their mother out. I bet she hasn't had a date in forever."

"We're just friends," he pointed out.

"I bet she hasn't had dinner out with a friend in forever. I'm going to run over to the coast and hit Costco for some movies—like Disney DVDs or something." Then she smiled very approvingly.

\* \* \*

Jack drove out to the Riordans' house and parked right in front. As luck would have it, Cooper was sitting on the porch in the late-afternoon sun. When he saw Jack he folded the *USA TODAY* on his lap. Jack got out of his truck and approached warily, putting one booted foot on the step just as Luke came to the doorway and stood there. Watching. Listening.

"Jack," Luke said in greeting.

"Hey." But then he directed his attention to Cooper. "This is a real small town."

"I've been giving you plenty of space," Coop said.

"What I came to say is—you have as much right to enjoy this town as I do. I don't know what your plans are, but just because we don't see eye to eye doesn't mean…" He paused and looked down briefly. "Look, besides you, Luke, Colin and me, only a couple of people know about our situation—my wife and my cook and his wife. And not having been there at the time, they aren't convinced you're guilty of anything, so there's no reason for you to be scarce. Know what I mean?"

"I'm not going to be around much longer," Coop said. "I'm hanging out long enough for our buddy, Ben, to show up for a little hunting. Then I guess we scatter again. And when we scatter, it takes us a while to meet up. Next time, maybe we meet somewhere else."

"Well, hunting is good here," Jack said. "Next couple of weekends the Cavanaughs have their orchard open to the public—pick your own apples, get some of their cider, hang out with friends. But this town—folks tend to gather at things like that, so even if you're not that interested in apples, it's a good way to socialize. Then there's the pumpkin patch party out at Jilly's farm the next weekend. Some people dress up. You could just go as, you know, a grump. That would work."

"What makes you think I have a sense of humor about this?" Coop asked.

"I just want to say one thing, Cooper," Jack said. "I think I did the only thing I could do back then. If what Luke thinks of you is accurate, you'd have done what I did—try to take the woman to get medical help, call the police. What happened after that was completely out of my hands. I shipped out the next day—I was just there with a Marine squad for Airborne training—we don't hang around Army posts that often. You'd have done the same thing."

"Might've," he relented. "I don't know that I would've thought the worst of someone I knew nothing about."

"Why'd she tell me she was in a bad relationship? Abusive?" Jack asked, a curious frown drawing his heavy brows together.

"Maybe because we dated for a while and fought like crazy," Coop said. "Arguing, that's all—nothing physical. She wanted to get serious, wanted to come with me to Ft. Rucker, and she also wanted to hang out with a lot of different guys, so we stopped going

out but she kept calling me and I slid back a time or
two, so—"

*"Slid back?"* Jack asked. And to add insult to injury, he laughed.

"I was twenty-two!"

Jack ran a hand around the back of his neck. "Yeah,
I vaguely remember twenty-two…" He chuckled a little. "I'm a big enough man to admit, my brain was not
between my ears."

"I never hit a woman in my life," Coop said.

"Wish I could say the same," Jack said. "I grew up
with four sisters and the two older ones… Hell, they
tortured me. If I could get one off on one of them, I
did—but that stopped when I was about twelve."

"I have two older sisters," Coop said.

"I have two younger, too."

"I have one younger," Coop said. "But she's a doll.
And I grew into the older ones eventually."

"What the hell were you doing at her house fifteen
years ago?" Jack asked. "Sliding back?"

"Hell if I know. I woke up on a picnic table in the
park across the street with the biggest headache I've
ever had. I was probably looking for any familiar place
because I was not driving anywhere. And everything
went to hell from there."

"Yeah," Jack said. "Well, hell. Listen, about these
town parties, it's a good time. Not long after Halloween it gets too cold for things like that and right up
until Christmas, we're driven inside. The Riordans
who don't already live here usually show up now and

then. You shouldn't let me keep you away. And you're welcome at the bar anytime." Jack glanced at Luke who was smiling faintly. "No need to have an escort."

"Neighborly of you," Coop said.

"But you should know," Jack went on. "I'm trying to check a few facts. If it turns out I jumped to all the wrong conclusions, an apology will be forthcoming."

Coop was quiet for a second. "I won't hold my breath."

"How'd you hurt your hand? Back then?"

"No idea," Coop said. "I hope I hurt it on the face of the son of a bitch who beat her. But the truth is, I have no idea."

"Buddy," Jack said. "You couldn't have planned that any worse."

"Tell me about it."

"It was pointed out to me, in a very sincere and sarcastic way, that I am not without flaws. Let's just hope to get it cleared up before you leave town."

"How does it matter?" Coop asked.

Jack looked at Luke. "We have mutual friends who matter." And with that he got back in his truck and drove away.

# *Fourteen*

Maxie's friends, Penny and Rosalie, arrived on Thursday afternoon. They brought very little luggage and a trunk full of sweets they'd spent the previous two days together baking at Rosalie's Santa Rosa home. Both were widowed, gray-haired, of indeterminate ages and when the three silver-haired women were together, laughing and hugging and breaking out the wine, they called themselves the Merry Widows.

Nora loved them instantly.

"Guard yourself," Tom whispered to her. "They're sharp-tongued and relentless."

Nora didn't take him seriously at all. She loved being in the kitchen with them and her children took to them immediately—both were experienced grandmothers.

When Tom was not in the house, Penny asked, "When does that woman arrive?"

Nora's ears perked up.

"Tomorrow afternoon," Maxie said. "And be very

cautious what you say around her. She can be hard to take, but Tom is very protective of her. Her husband was killed in Afghanistan in Tom's command and he feels a certain—you know—responsibility for her. If you say anything critical or offend her, he might lose his head and marry her."

"Us?" Penny said. "Critical?"

"Does she have a name other than Miss Picky Pants?" Rosalie asked.

Nora laughed suddenly. Miss what? she wondered.

"Darla," Maxie said. "Darla Pritchard."

"Is she good in the kitchen?" Penny wanted to know.

"I couldn't tell you. All I've seen her do is read, change clothes several times a day and pick at her food. If Duke gets near her, she shies away so he won't get dog hair on her."

"But wait till you see her," Nora said. The women all turned and looked at her. "She's the most beautiful thing I've ever seen."

"My dear child," Rosalie said, "have you looked in a mirror lately?"

"We should get out the old pictures," Penny said. "Show this girl we were once hot young chicks."

"Have you all been friends your whole lives?" Nora asked.

"We met when we were young mothers," Maxie said. "Right here on the orchard. Rosalie and Penny came to pick apples. Rose lived in Garberville then, Penny in Willet. And we did the one thing people never do anymore—we wrote letters to each other. And got together once, maybe twice a year."

"Maxie, did you live on the orchard all your life?"

Silence hung in the air for a moment, followed by laughter that only confused Nora.

"No, Nora—I came to the orchard when I was eighteen, looking for work. I was a dirt-poor farm girl from Idaho. I got stranded near here and this was the only place hiring."

"How'd you get stranded here?" Nora asked.

"The usual way, darling. I was following a man. A logger. He was killed in a logjam and I had no way to get home, not that home had much to offer anyway. So—I asked for work here. The old man didn't want to hire me, but his wife took me on. I started picking apples but ended up working in the house."

"Like me?"

All three women hummed and laughed under their smothered chuckles.

"Like you," she said. "Now, are you going to bring the children this weekend? Between the four of us here, we can make sure they're watched every minute."

"I thought I should ask Noah and his wife if they could help out, since I'll be needed here all weekend. And on Sunday afternoon, my father will bring them. I'm so anxious for him to meet everyone."

"And we're all looking forward to meeting him. Tell Rosalie and Penny that story, darling—of how your father came back into your life recently."

Nora gave them the quick version, trying not to

make her mother look too terrible in the telling. It wasn't long past that story that Tom came into the kitchen, ready for dinner and the family atmosphere resumed around the big kitchen table.

It was still drizzling on Friday and Tom and Junior pulled out tarps they'd erect as tents on the weekend if the weather didn't improve. On Friday afternoon Darla arrived and as the Fridays before, it was like the arrival of royalty. Tom carried her luggage up the stairs while Maxie introduced her to everyone. The women had been sitting around the table fashioning sachets out of dried apples, cinnamon sticks and cloves. They'd be given out to anyone who wanted them over the weekend festival.

"It was a long drive," she said after meeting all the women. "I'm going to change into something more comfortable."

Maxie said nothing, though she peered at her friends from under lifted brows.

Momentarily Darla returned with a rather surprised look on her face. "There seems to be a child in my bedroom."

"Oh!" Nora said, jumping to her feet. "I'm sorry, I didn't realize—"

"Is she asleep, Darla?" Maxie asked, cutting Nora off.

"On my bed," Darla said, clearly shocked.

"Then perhaps you can change clothes in my bedroom," Maxie suggested. "That's Nora's two-year-old,

Berry. She's napping. The baby is in a port-a-crib in Tom's room. Also napping."

"Will I be sharing my room with someone?" Darla asked uncomfortably.

"No, dear, Nora lives in town and will be going home after dinner. Tomorrow at naptime, I'll put Berry on my bed. I told you, we have a full house and demanding schedule during the festival weekends. It's pretty much every man for himself."

And then Darla did something that positively stunned Nora. When Nora would have expected her to ask how she could help or pull up a chair to visit, she said, "I'll grab a book and go to the other room to read. Will you tell me when the child no longer needs my room?"

"Certainly, dear," Maxie said. Then with sarcasm Darla clearly did not hear, she asked, "Can I get you anything?"

"No, thank you. I'll be fine." And she left the kitchen.

Saturday dawned bright and clear, the sun burning off the morning mist early. Nora had arrived at the orchard to help set up, having left Adie at her house until the children woke. The plan had been for her to go into town and fetch Adie and the little girls after they'd had a chance to wake up and have breakfast, but Nora was not feeling right about it.

"Maxie," she whispered, "I have a feeling my girls are going to be an imposition. It might not be too late for me to get help from Ellie Kincaid. Her daughter is nearly old enough to babysit and she loves playing with the girls."

"I want them here," Maxie said. "*They* are not the imposition."

"We all want them to come," Penny said. "And Adie looks forward to this. She's counting on being here both days this weekend and next."

"Are you absolutely sure?"

"Absolutely. Sure."

Nora actually winced. Having the kids here both days would put her in the house often, checking on them to be sure they weren't getting in the way. While that wasn't ordinarily an issue, she couldn't help feeling like a beat-up old shoe next to Darla.

On the upside, she didn't have much time to indulge her feelings of inferiority—crowds began to descend on the orchard at once. The minute Nora got Adie and the little ones back, she was needed to hand out bushel baskets, help people with ladders, pull out crates and bags for them to take their apples home.

More and more familiar faces appeared, many of them clearly intending to stay for hours. She saw some boys throwing a Frisbee through the trees and others throwing one for the dogs. The wraparound porch on the big old house was full of people and Nora caught sight of Maxie and her friends holding court. Great thermoses of tea and lemonade were set up, gallons of fresh cider opened up and tables of baked goods stood in the yard. People spread blankets in the yard to sit on and lawn chairs were pulled out of truck beds. A couple of big grills were set up and Nora saw that it was the team from Jack's bar serving up hamburgers and hot dogs while Rosalie and Penny were busily opening huge bags of chips.

Just the sight of Berry running with other small children at a town party, laughing and playing with growing confidence, filled Nora with joy. Fay spent a great deal of the morning in Nora's backpack while Nora did everything from pour cider to bagging apples.

"Break time," Tom said from behind her. And she felt the weight of the baby lifted from her shoulders. "Give me a hand here and I'll wear the baby for a while."

"Oh, Tom, I'm sure you're too busy for that!"

"We're all busy," he said, handing her the backpack to hold while he shrugged into it, then laughed as baby Fay instantly had her little hands all over his head. "Are you having fun?" he asked Nora.

"I'll let you know when I catch my breath! When you said it would be crowded, I had no idea it would be like this."

"It'll be like this all weekend and the next."

And a little while later Nora noticed Fay's little head lying on Tom's shoulder as she slept while he continued to hand out bushel baskets.

Nora took a moment to grab Berry and fix her a hot dog. They sat together on the porch steps as far away from the crowd as Nora could get them, just

long enough for Berry to devour a hot dog. She had
no sooner taken the last bite when her little one escaped yet again, and this time headed for Reverend
Kincaid's family who had gathered on a blanket in the
yard under the shade of an apple tree.

"Hey," someone said.

Nora turned to see Darla sit down on the step beside
her. "Hi. Are you enjoying the festival?"

"Oh, yes and no," she said. "It's very social, isn't
it? I've met some nice people, but two full days of
apple picking? I can think of other things I'd rather
be doing. And I get none of Tom while he's all tied up
with work." She gave a nod toward the barn. "Apparently you figured out how to tie him down for a while."

"Huh? Oh, you mean the baby? That was totally
his idea. But what a great idea—my back was killing me and it looks like Fay's getting her nap at the
same time."

"Where's your husband?" Darla asked.

Okay, she wasn't the first person to ask, Nora
thought—but why did it feel like a jab? "No husband,
Darla. Just me and the little ladies."

"Oh, sorry—did your husband die, too?"

Nora just shook her head. "No, I wasn't married.
And before you ask, there's no man in my life now,
either." Then with a guilty pang she added. "I'm very
sorry for your loss. Maxie told me."

"Thank you. Things have been so much better since
Tom came into my life. Fate is pretty strange, isn't it?

One minute I'm a grieving widow and the next I'm falling in love with the man who was comforting me."

Nora smiled at her while she fought envy. "That's wonderful. Tom is such a good man."

"Hmm, handsome, too. And look at him out there with the people! Everyone loves Tom—he's a natural salesman."

"I don't usually see him in this capacity," Nora admitted. "Around here we're all just a bunch of farmers and pickers. This is hard work, running an orchard."

"I kind of think of Tom the way I would a pro football player—the body can't do that forever. At some point a person would have to find less physically taxing work."

"Or hire the right helpers," Nora said. "Maxie is still picking apples, though Tom has tried to keep her off ladders. It's fun to watch the two of them sneaking around each other."

"I can't see Tom picking apples into his seventies. And I can't see me living on an orchard. The nearest decent restaurant is almost an hour drive."

"I guess you haven't eaten at Jack's," Nora asked.

"That bar in town?" She made a face. "I'm not big on bar food. Kind of greasy."

"Jack's has a huge reputation," Nora said. "I hear people come from all over the place. The cook, Preacher, is known for his comfort foods—meat loaf, brisket, stew, soups, breads…"

"I don't do bread," she said. She patted her flat

tummy which was snug in a pair of expensive jeans. "I can't stay in these size four jeans if I eat bread."

"Do you and Tom eat out often?" Nora asked, because she'd seen Tom at the table. He clearly wasn't worried about getting into his jeans.

"Around here? Not so much. But I'm sure that will change when the harvest is over and Tom comes to see me rather than me always traveling to the orchard. I'm only here to attend a course in Davis. I look forward to taking Tom to some of my favorite restaurants."

But Nora was no longer thinking about eating out. "When your class is done, I assume you're headed back home."

"Of course—my home is in Denver."

"But how will you see Tom then?"

Darla's eyes held an unmistakable sparkle. "Can you keep a secret?"

"Sure," Nora said. And she thought, *from whom?* She didn't exactly have a lot of confidants.

Darla circled a knee with her arms, her fingers laced together. "We've talked about the future a little bit. Like the fact that Maxie deserves a restful, indulgent retirement. Someplace where she doesn't have to work so hard or cook so much. Some sort of village for seniors where all the chores are done for her. Where she can relax and enjoy life more."

"But Maxie loves the orchard," Nora said, feeling a bit panicked at the very thought. "She loves to cook and garden and have tons of people around!"

"Please," Darla said, laughing. She threw a hand wide. "This look relaxing to you?"

Nora swallowed. "Maxie loves this. I can't imagine Tom without her here!"

"Who says Tom is staying here? Look at him out there."

He was a pure pleasure to look at, laughing with men from the town, flirting with their wives while he bagged up apples, turning so they could admire the sleeping baby on his back. Everyone was going to be bone tired when this was over, but they'd be happy to have had all their friends together, their neighbors, their town, not to mention all the folks who came from much farther away every year.

"See how great he is? Tell me something—if he can sell *apples* with that little effort, imagine what he could do with a product that brings in tons of money."

"They're his apples," Nora said quietly.

"Maybe not for long."

"What do you mean?"

"Well, we've talked about the possibilities of retiring Maxie, selling the orchard and settling in a city rather than the backwoods. With Tom's experience in business, his degree and his persuasiveness with people, he could do almost anything, but let me tell you—he'd be a natural in sales."

Nora told herself there was absolutely no excuse for feeling like she'd been sucker punched. There was nothing between her and Tom except a friendship she was very grateful for. And he deserved to have a life—

a wife, children, happiness. "So…you're getting married, then?"

"Well, we're certainly not engaged." She held out her hands, fingers splayed, demonstrating no ring. "But just between you and me, I think it's only a matter of time."

"Congratulations," Nora said, hating the weakness in her voice.

"Thank you," Darla said, straightening a bit. She was proud of that—being in love with Tom, counting the days until he asked her to marry him. "Well, look, I'm sure you have to get back to work and I have a little reading to do. And, I want to change clothes before evening."

Nora bit her tongue against asking why. Instead she told a huge lie. "Nice talking with you, Darla."

"You, too, Norma."

"No, it's Nora."

"Oh," she said on a laugh. "Right."


Sunday at the orchard was a repeat of Saturday with lots of people turning out, and in most cases not the same people. The big difference for Nora was that her dad and Susan brought the little girls, watched them, napped them, fed them and did all that while meeting half the town.

"Sunday afternoon is my regular day to visit Nora and the girls," she heard Jed tell someone. And, "Yes, you have it right—we were estranged for many years but by good fortune and Reverend Kincaid, reunited. Bitter divorce—I'm sure you've heard of such things."

She just smiled to herself when she overheard him. He didn't seem to have any shame or blame, just the facts. She admired that.

In the afternoon, people began to leave. First to go was Darla, her many suitcases carried to the red Caddy by Tom, a rather platonic kiss goodbye and off she went. A bit later Rosalie and Penny loaded up and departed and when Nora saw that, she bolted to their car to give them each a hug. "Will you be back?" she asked.

"See you on Thursday," Rosalie said.

"In the meantime, see if you can get Maxie to rest a bit before the next surge."

"I don't like rest," Maxie said. "I can rest when I'm dead."

And the three of them laughed, but Nora didn't. She carried the secret about Maxie going into retirement so Tom could sell the orchard and marry Darla.

When the October sun was lowering and the clouds moving in, Tom told her to take her kids and go. And he suggested she take her time in the morning. "It's been a long week and big weekend for everyone. We don't have to start at the crack of dawn. Sleep in if you can."

She wanted to grab him by the front of his jacket and beg him not to move Maxie into retirement, not to sell the orchard and go away. Instead, she couldn't help but smile at him. "Will you sleep in?"

"I'll try, but when Maxie starts banging around pans and Duke sticks his cold nose in my face, I usually get up. I like mornings."

She had learned to love the mornings as well, especially since she had a job to look forward to and more so now that she had a car to drive her there.

After a full afternoon of playing outdoors at the orchard, the little ladies were in dire need of a scrubbing and bed. Jed and Susan wanted to hang around awhile to talk to Nora, so she cleaned up her girls and settled them in bed. Just as she'd been completely unprepared for toys, clothes and furniture, her father managed to surprise her once more.

"Your friends at the orchard are wonderful," he said. He grabbed Susan's hand and said, "I want to make something available to you—something for you to consider for the future. And please, there's no pressure of any kind. If you have an interest in finishing your education, I have some advantages as a tenured professor. Not only is your tuition waived, after a little checking I found out I can get you into family housing. Child care on the campus is affordable. Nora, if you'd like to go back to school, I'd like to help make that happen."

She was speechless for a moment, even though he'd mentioned school at least once before. "Family housing?" she asked.

"I wouldn't presume to offer you my home, even though I'd be happy to have you and the girls move in. But I respect your boundaries. Take all the time you need, not just with me, with everyone who comes into your life. Those little girls are precious. Don't take any chances."

"It could really happen? School?"

He gave a nod. "It's not the answer to everything, Nora, I know that. This seems like a good place with good people. If it works for you here and you're satisfied, there's no need to change things. But if money is holding you back from going to school, let's not let that stand in the way. I can help. Without investing much. And Stanford is a quality school."

"My one year of college," she said. "My grades were not very good. I was a freshman and so inexperienced."

"You'd be allowed to repeat classes."

Susan grabbed his hand and stopped him for a moment. "Nora, this is only a suggestion, a possibility. I have two daughters—one went all the way through medical school and the other chose to be a stay-at-home mom. They are equally smart and equally driven with individual ideas about what makes a happy life. This is just something to consider. And the offer isn't going to expire."

*I have things to work out here,* came to her lips, but she didn't let it out. Instead she thanked them both. And once they were gone she thought about what was on her plate. First, she had to find a way to make her rent right—someone owned this little house, whether an individual or bank or the county for taxes. She couldn't steal free rent and sleep at night. And second, she had to know what was to become of Maxie.

And Tom.

# *Fifteen*

Nora had gotten a little quiet again, but Tom was not at all surprised. She hadn't had a day off in weeks, plus two full weekends of Apple Festival; besides being a hard worker, she had mothering responsibilities, as well. So he cornered her and asked, "Is your father coming up on Sunday again?"

"He wouldn't miss it."

"I want you to take the weekend off and catch up at home. Get some rest."

She drew a sigh. "I think I'll take you up on that."

"That doesn't mean you have to stay away—bring the kids to dinner," he said.

She looked surprised. "Listen, I think I've imposed on Maxie enough…."

He just laughed. "Maxie loves having you. She took most afternoons off this week and she's getting a little bristly from boredom. And since we're on the subject, why don't you take Friday afternoon off, catch a nap if you can, then bring the kids back here for Maxie to babysit. You and I will do the town."

"Do *what* town?"

"Okay, we're not going to exactly do the town—no dressing up. But there's this restaurant in Arcata. It's great. I'd like to take you. I already asked Maxie if she'll babysit and she likes the idea."

Her forehead furrowed. "Why? I mean, why?"

He scraped off his cap and scratched his head. "You don't make it easy, do you? Because you slaved for about three straight weeks, and sometimes you slaved at the orchard while carrying a baby on your back and baking with my grandmother. Come on, it's a treat. Just say yes and thank you. And then, Saturday is the pumpkin patch out at Jilly Farms and they'll have a lot to eat and drink and there will be rides on miniature ponies. I'll take you so you can pick out your pumpkin. The girls will love it."

She stared at him in shock, her mouth open. She forcibly closed her mouth and swallowed. "Um, that's very nice of you, but I'll have to take a pass."

"Why? You have a sudden aversion to fun? Or is it just me?"

"Um, look, Tom—much as I enjoy your company and as grateful as I am that Maxie would be willing to babysit for me, I'm going to have to decline."

"Why? That was a perfectly nice offer!"

"Because I don't date?" she asked as more of a question than an answer.

"Then don't think of it as a date—think of it as a

couple of friends going to dinner. My treat, as a reward for all your hard work."

She lifted an eyebrow and tilted her head. "How are you rewarding Jerome, Eduardo and Juan?"

"I'm only rewarding the pretty employees."

"Well, tempting as it all sounds, I'm still going to have to decline, with thanks."

"Are you serious? Why? I thought I was very gentlemanly."

She thought for a moment and finally said, "There is just no polite way to say this, Tom, but I made a deal with God not to lie, so I'm going to spit it out and if you hate me, I'll find a way to live with it. Just don't fire me—I need the money. I have things to work out that involve money. Here it is—I'm a little uncomfortable around Darla. She's a very nice person and all, but I feel like a peasant when I'm near her. I'm kind of Cinderella, and the glass slipper hasn't turned up yet."

"What?" he asked, dumbfounded.

"I feel a little rough around the edges when I'm with her. All sow's ear. I feel like the last kid in class to get picked for the team. You know?"

"You thought *Darla* would be coming with us?"

"She's been here every weekend. For weeks. I just assumed…"

"She's not going to be able to make it this weekend. I guess she has other plans."

"Really?"

"Now will you go out with me, Cinderella?" he asked with a grin.

"Don't make fun of me, please. I probably feel like the poor girl because I am the poor girl. Certainly not Darla's fault, but come on."

"Nora, Darla isn't coming. It's just you and me. Well, you and me and sometimes my grandmother and your children."

"Am I your stand-in date?" she asked. "Because I bet you could do better."

He growled and turned away from her. "Fine," he muttered. "I'm not going to beg you!"

"All *right,*" she said to his back. "All right, as long as it's not a date!"

He whirled back to face her. "It's dinner and a town party at the pumpkin patch. And if you relax just a little bit, it might even be fun. I'll shower before we go and I'll be nice the whole time unless you insist on baiting me."

Nora went along with Tom's plans even though she was certain this was a bad idea. It was dangerous—she had a crush on him. He was going to be her fantasy man long after he married the princess and sold the orchard. But she talked herself into it because certainly this was a once in a lifetime opportunity. Not only would Darla soon be back, the harvest would be over and Nora was going to have to move on to other things.

So—she did laundry at her neighbor's, had a wonderful blouse and vest that was a hand-me-down from Leslie down the street, dragged out a pair of boots she'd gotten from church donations and put on her best jeans—they were almost new. Everything was ironed with spray starch so she'd look crisp. No pony-tail tonight—she left her hair down and curled, some-thing she never bothered to do for work at the orchard. She added a little makeup to her lips and eyes. After baths, she dressed the girls in their pajamas, loaded a grocery bag with their night diapers, a bottle for Fay, their favorite blankets, and off she went to the orchard.

Tom might see this as a couple of friends having dinner, but for Nora it was the one date she was going to agree to this decade. But when she got to the house, she sensed a problem that hadn't occurred to her—Maxie was far too hopeful.

Well, Nora knew she wasn't fond of Darla. She'd heard the women talking about her—Miss Picky Pants. And Nora also knew that Maxie liked her, maybe be-cause they had things in common, like coming from poor roots. And they liked dogs and children and laughed at the same things. But she wanted to warn Maxie not to get excited.

But of course there was no opportunity to warn her. She kissed the girls good-night and found herself in Tom's truck, on her way to a restaurant.

"Why are you nervous?" he asked her. "It's not like we haven't had dinners together before. Lots of them."

"But this is strange," she said. "This is us going to a restaurant."

And oh, it was such a lovely restaurant—all dark wood and candles and just full of people having a good time. His hand was at the small of her back, guiding her into the restaurant and to their table—a lovely little table just slightly apart from the crowd up against some windows out of which she could see the starlight. She was at once enchanted and terrified.

The waiter handed them menus.

"Nora, have a glass of wine," Tom said. "You can indulge a little bit tonight. What do you like?"

"I have no idea," she said.

Tom looked up at the waiter. "How about a nice pinot grigio?" he asked the waiter. "And bring me a Sam Adams. Also, while we look at the menu, can you start us off with stuffed grape leaves and calamari?"

"Outstanding," the waiter said.

Nora glanced at the menu briefly. She slammed it shut suddenly and in a quiet hiss she said, "This is *far* too expensive!"

He closed his menu and looked at her over a small votive candle. "Here's what we'll do, Nora. If it's okay, I'll order for us. How about we split a Greek salad and have the chicken kabobs, unless you can brave the menu and find something you'll like better."

She just shook her head. Then she nodded and he laughed at her.

"It's okay, Nora—it's a business expense, I suppose. Taking an employee to dinner. Of course, when the harvest is over, I won't be able to deduct you anymore."

"Don't do that," she said. "Don't act like this sort of thing is going to happen again."

He closed his menu and said, "Crap. You're afraid you'll like me! Listen, take it easy on that, all right?

You hardly talked on the way over—is that the problem? You don't want to like me outside of work? Because I'd like to make it clear—that's okay with me. We get along, so why not? And get this—I actually enjoy spending time with you."

*Many, many reasons to worry about this,* she thought. *Like being devastated, for one thing.*

The wine came and he said, "Have a sip of wine. I hope you like it okay. And I hope you relax a little, otherwise you're going to suck all the fun out of this."

"Right," she said, taking a sip. She glanced up at the waiter. "This is very nice. Thank you." And then she took another sip and a deep breath. He was right; he was going to some trouble. She should be cordial.

She relaxed as much as possible, put her glass down and said, "I apologize. This is very special. I don't want to ruin it."

"Great. Now tell me, how's it going with Jed?"

"Going well," she said. "I keep trying to not be swayed by his generosity and he keeps admiring me for that. He offered to help me finish school if I'm interested. Being a professor at Stanford, I guess he can get me in and I qualify for family housing. If I wanted to do that, he could help."

"Do you want to?"

She looked down. "Eventually," she said. "Right now I have a few loose ends to work out. But that's a very good destination, don't you think? Good for my girls, too. The best thing I can do for them is set an example."

After appetizers, a little more wine and some talk about going back to college, Tom asked about those things she had to work out. Well, she wasn't about to tell him she'd like to be sure Maxie wasn't retired before she was ready.

"I haven't told anyone but Noah," she said. "Can you keep it to yourself?"

He made a face. "If it isn't going to cause death or injury," he said.

"It's about my house," she admitted. "When Chad brought me to Virgin River, I thought he'd rented it, I thought he had plans like he said. Fay was barely two weeks old and it was winter, I wasn't into asking a lot of questions. When he left us there and took off with the truck and most of our things, I expected to be evicted right away, but nothing happened. I just kept quiet and let the neighbors and the town help me out—bringing me supplies, sealing off the doors and windows so we wouldn't freeze, offering me part-time work as the snow started to melt. But months passed and no one sent me bills for rent. I paid what I could on the gas and electric bills—bills addressed to some unknown tenant. After a few months I realized Chad must've known the house was abandoned or something. I've been squatting. I owe a lot of money—to the power company for sure, though I don't exactly use much in that tiny house. And someone is due rent or something."

He stared at her in wonder.

"Oh, no," she said. "Oh, God, I've told you something you just can't imagine. Please don't lose all respect for me—I plan to make it right. I'm saving every cent I can. I'll pay the back rent, I swear I will."

"Nora. Stop. I'm shocked all right—that he didn't even take care of the safety of his own children."

She shrugged. "He's not a nice person, Tom. But before you waste any more anger on him, remember, I got myself into this mess."

"You were vulnerable. Homeless with small children. Don't let him off that easy."

"At the end of the day, he's not off easy. Last I heard, he's going to spend a long time in prison. I wish I hadn't told you so much…."

He reached for her hand across the table, giving a reassuring squeeze. "I'm glad you told me. You've come a long way, you should be proud of yourself, not beating yourself up. Is there some way I can help with this?"

A gentle smile came to her lips. "Tom Cavanaugh, you're such a good and generous man. Thank you, but no. I'm going to be fine. I have lots of options."

The salad was delivered and when the waiter left, Tom said, "I have a feeling about some of those options. You aren't going to stay here, are you?"

She thought briefly and then said, "Less than a year ago I lived in a little house that wouldn't keep out the wind, no food in the house and two babies. I wanted so little then—I just wanted to keep us warm and safe. And now I want so much more. I can get it, too, as long as I work hard and stay positive."

"What do you want, Nora?"

She bit her lip for a second. Then very quietly she said, "I want to be like Maxie." He gave her hand a little squeeze. "I'm going to do whatever is best for my children. That's what I'm going to do."

"And that, Nora, is probably more like Maxie than any other thing."

"What was it like? Growing up with her?"

He gave a little laugh. "Probably not as easy as you might think. She was strict. I got real tired of hearing about the virtues of hard work and sacrifice. I'd complain to my grandpa about how hard she was on me and he told me she'd mellowed by the time I came along. She could really drive a person hard. I think the only one she didn't get after was Grandpa. He was the sweetest man who ever lived. I don't think he ever had a bad day—not that I could tell, anyway. And Maxie adored him. But she loved me in a much tougher way—if I didn't do my chores, I didn't get a pass. If I didn't eat the green stuff on the plate, I could sit there till it grew mold. When I was sixteen, all I wanted in the world was a car so I didn't have to take the bus to school or be driven by my grandmother and you know what she said? 'I guess you'll be wanting more hours in the orchard, won't you, Tom?'"

"She paid you to work in the orchard?"

"Not the first twenty hours a week—that much was considered rent and food and clothes. I used to complain constantly about how hard she worked me. I couldn't wait to get out of Virgin River and off that tree farm. I wanted to see the world—and boy did I see it. I should've thought that through—I saw a lot of ocean and desert. And look at me, back home."

"What made you come home?"

"I was done," he said. "I went as far as I could go and I missed the damn apple trees."

"And Maxie," she said. "You missed Maxie."

"I did. It must have killed her for me to join the Marines, but she never said a word except, 'You have to do what you have to do.' And she used to always say, 'If it was easy, anyone could do it.' She was never discouraged by anything. One year we had a bad early freeze—messed up a lot of our crop and you know what Maxie said? She said the apples would be doubled and better than ever the next year—that nature suffers to fill a void. And they were.

"After four years of college and a little over six in the Corps, it finally occurred to me I might not have her forever and I came home. Some days I think that was the smartest thing I ever did. Some days I wonder if I won't die of boredom one of these years."

"Tom," she said, almost shocked, "are you *bored?*"

"It has occurred to me there might be more to life than picking apples...."

"Oh, no... I couldn't imagine a better life! I could live the rest of my life on that orchard! I could be happy forever in that big, warm kitchen."

He smiled at her. "You said you wanted a lot."

"That is a lot!"

"What makes you so sure you could be happy in that life forever?" he asked her.

"Some things you just know! I mean, I was pretty disturbed to find out I was pregnant not once but twice, but would I consider life without my girls? Never! They *are* my life!"

"What about trips to Jamaica?" he asked her. "Front-row seats at an NBA playoff game? Lots of great restaurants ten times better than this one?"

"Could that be fun?" she asked with a shrug. "I suppose so. But would it be more important, more meaningful than home cooking, soft old quilts, warm fires, fresh fruits and vegetables every day of the year?" She shook her head. "I like that I have something to show for my hard work that really endures, I guess. Lasts longer than a trip to the islands."

"Another argument for finishing college," he pointed out to her.

Right at that moment their meals arrived and the waiter lingered by the table to be sure they didn't need anything. Nora carefully cut off a tender piece of marinated chicken and popped it in her mouth. She chewed slowly. Her chin came up, her eyes softly closed and she savored it. She swallowed and opened her eyes, smiling. "And there's an argument for good restaurants. Incredible."

There might've been one or two down moments in their date, Tom thought. Especially at the onset in the quiet, nervous drive to Arcata, at the confession about owing someone money on the house she occupied, about how tough times had led her to the greater dreams of a solid, secure, stable life. But once the salads were done and the main course arrived, she was a chatterbox. She wanted to tell him everything about her experience in his grandmother's kitchen, how the girls became more animated by the minute, all that she learned from Maxie about baking, from Maxie and her girlfriends about life.

"And this apple festival thing you've got going on," she said.

"Maxie's idea," he admitted. "She convinced Grandpa to start it when my dad was a kid. Back then they drew up posters and printed flyers, took them around to businesses on the coast, nailed a few to telephone and light poles…"

"I was not even mildly prepared for what was going to happen, then when the people swarmed in, I was overwhelmed! It's more than buying apples to them, Tom—they want to be a part of what you and Maxie do. Almost every room in the house was full of people visiting, catching up with neighbors, eating, juggling each other's babies. Did I tell you I helped make about three hundred sachets with Maxie and her girls? She had dried apples, cinnamon sticks and cloves and we tied them into little bundles. And I can now bake cinnamon rolls."

"You've come a long way since terrible coffee," he said.

"I lied about how my father liked it," she admitted, laughing.

"I know that now. Good fake, though."

Although she was stuffed and he really didn't need to eat another bite, he insisted on ordering coffee and dessert. He loved the way she relished every new taste, every luxurious bite of something that for her was indulgent. One dessert of cheesecake, two forks.

"You know what I hope? I hope you always have that sense of wonder for simple things."

She just laughed at him. "Oh, I'm sure we're safe there. I'm kind of hoping to have some wonder over extraordinary things someday."

He dipped his fork into the cheesecake and held it toward her mouth. She shook her head and said, "Oh, I can't..." But he persisted until she let her lips close over the fork. Her eyes closed again, that luxury of excellence on her tongue, and he almost got aroused. His heart pumped and so many emotions swept through him—possession, adoration, titillation, excitement. Feeding her seemed to do something for him. He tried to reason with his feelings—it was a silly bite of cheesecake! But he couldn't wait to share that fork, to put his lips where hers had been.

He'd never felt like this before.

Soon they were walking across the square to his truck and he grabbed her hand, holding it. It was almost as though she hadn't noticed—she was doing a recap of the meal, the ambiance of the restaurant, the added delight of a dessert she absolutely did not need.

He listened with a smile; he found listening to her comforting. She had no idea how cute she was. And as they walked, he leaned down enough so that he could catch a whiff of her hair—sweet, flowery, clean.

There weren't too many people on the square and sidewalks, but they were hardly deserted. Still, when they got to the truck, he pulled on her hand until she faced him. She looked up at him. He put one large hand on her hip and with the other, he traced her jaw-line with a knuckle until it was under her chin. Then he lifted her chin, lowered his head and placed a very cautious kiss on those full lips.

Yeah, he liked that.

He tried that again, and again.

She put a hand against his chest and said, "Look, I don't want to upset Darla…"

"This has nothing to do with Darla. This is just you and me…"

"Okay, let me put this another way. I don't want to get in Darla's territory."

"I am not her territory. We're friends. Her husband… my squad…that whole thing. I'm just being support-ive…." And he leaned toward her mouth again.

"Wait! You know all the things I've gone through the past few years—I don't want to just get deeper in trouble."

"Huh? What?"

"I don't want to get mixed up in a situation that would hurt me…like, you know, before."

His eyes became slits. "You can't really be suggesting that I could ever do to you and your children what *he* did to you. You know I'm not that kind of person."

"You're not," she whispered. "I know."

"It's a kiss," he said. "With any luck, a good kiss. I want it. You want it."

She nodded weakly. After all, she'd made that deal with God....

"Then can you shut up and kiss me?"

Her lips were already parted, just in case she had something more to say. To her own great relief, she didn't. He came down on her mouth gently but it took only a second for it to become serious. Demanding and powerful and by the way she received it, it was very much to her liking. She'd been holding her breath and let it out slowly just as her arms slid up and around his neck. He tilted, moved, tongued open her lips, played around with her tongue. Then he lifted her a little bit, bringing her mouth up even with his and, incidentally, pinning her against his truck.

He should really care if people were walking by but he didn't. All he could think about was her small body flush against his, the taste of her mouth and the fact that after all that hedging, all those excuses, she met him with passion. He heard her whimper slightly and he took it as a little victory—she wanted him, too.

"Oh, man," he whispered.

He went back for more, covering her mouth with almost dangerous intentions. If he didn't get a handle on this, he'd be a little out of control and he couldn't remember the last time he'd had that feeling with a woman. Knowing this was where it was going to end, he forced himself to let go of her, to let her slide back onto her feet, to find some stupid thing to say to excuse it all. "That wasn't so bad, was it?" he came up with.

"It wasn't bad at all."

"Thank you. I mean for the kiss, not for the compliment. If you can call not bad a compliment."

"I hope you'll be careful with my feelings," she said, surprising him. "It wouldn't be good for either one of us if I fell for you."

"Are you sure?" he asked, leaning down and smiling against her lips.

"Pretty sure. Should we get going and relieve Maxie of her babysitting?"

"If you wanted me to, I could take you somewhere private. For more kissing," he suggested.

"Tom, I should go get my kids and get them settled in bed, because I have a long night ahead. I'm going to spend half of it thinking about what a wonderful evening I had and that fantastic kissing and the other half hoping I haven't made a big mistake."

He smiled at her and kissed her nose. "I hope you get some sleep, Nora. Because I'm taking you to the pumpkin patch tomorrow."

"I know," she said with a sigh. "And come Monday morning, I'll be waiting for the glass slipper to show up at my door."

# *Sixteen*

Tom could tell that his grandmother wanted every detail of his date with Nora. She was practically vibrating with her need to know. But Tom wasn't talking. Nora assured her that they'd had fun and the most delicious food imaginable. "Of course not better than anything that comes out of your kitchen, Maxie, but I have to admit, it was a wonderful treat. So—are we all meeting at the pumpkin patch?"

"I'm picking you up, Nora," Tom said.

"Oh. So, Maxie, are you riding with us?"

"Thank you, darling, but no—I'm going on my own steam. I may not be ready to leave when you are or I might want to leave earlier. I like having my own wheels."

"I understand," she said with a laugh.

"I'll help buckle in the girls," Tom said. "I'm going to carry Berry. You get the baby. And I'm going to follow you home to carry them inside."

"Don't be silly," Nora argued. "I can manage. It's too much trouble for you."

"It's a couple of miles," he said.

"Three-point-four," she informed him. "I know. I've walked it."

"That's why I intend to drive it," he said, tapping her cute little nose.

It was always an ordeal, transporting children, especially sleeping children. It required a committee. There were not only the kids, but a port-a-crib to collapse and stow in the trunk, supplies to gather, seat belts to fasten. It wasn't until Tom pulled up behind her that he realized he'd never been inside her house before.

He was pleasantly surprised—it was spotless and the furniture was perfectly nice. Holding Berry against his broad chest, her head on his shoulder, he whispered, "This is very nice."

"New," she said. "Compliments of Jed."

"He should get upgraded to Dad pretty soon—furniture, supplies and the offer of a college education."

She chuckled and said, "Bring Berry to my room and put her on the bed. Carefully."

Tom stepped into the only bedroom and was a little startled to find only a mattress on the floor and a very old and weathered chest of drawers. But the bed was perfectly and meticulously made up and there was a soft, thick area rug under it.

"You need a bed frame," he told her in a whisper.

"It's not a priority right now," she said. "Besides, until Jed brought the port-a-crib, we all slept together and it was safer for the kids, mattress on the floor—

if one of them rolled off, they didn't get hurt. Just lie her down, Tom, and take Fay for me so I can go get the crib."

"I'll get it," he said, gently lowering Berry to the bed.

After everything was accomplished, children settled, she was walking him the ten steps to the door. He turned toward her. "This is nice, Nora. A good little house."

"Thank you. With the help of Jed and neighbors, it's been possible to do a lot with a little. Thank you, Tom. It was such a nice night. I'll probably never forget it."

He leaned down to her and gave her a brief kiss on the mouth, just a peck. He wanted much more from her, but just couldn't tempt himself further. "I'll pick you up tomorrow at noon—will that work?"

"Sure."

"I'll bring a couple of lawn chairs and a blanket for the yard at Jilly's. You're in charge of kids' stuff, and round up some things for Fay to play with on the blanket." And then he went home to face Maxie, who had her game face on, sitting in front of the TV, not asking questions. Now, two things about this were suspicious. One—she wanted the details but didn't want to ask and give herself away. And two—by this time in the evening she was always nodding off in the chair. Tom would usually jostle her and tell her he was going to bed.

"I have nothing to say about the date," he informed her.

"I didn't ask," she told him.

"Then we understand each other. I'll be up early,

giving the orchard some time before going to Jilly's farm."

"And I'll be up early because I can't help it," Maxie said.

And he went to bed. Where he didn't sleep much.

Jack and Preacher shut down the bar. A sign was posted on the door—*Town Party at Jilly's Pumpkin Patch. Strangers welcome. Food and drink available. Fun optional.* And there were directions.

They got to the farm a little early so they could set up their grills. Jilly's sister Kelly, the chef, was in charge of the food, but Jack and Preacher were in charge of grilling. For events like this they provided big tubs of ice-cooled drinks, burgers, dogs, buns and paper products. They brought burgers and hot dogs from the bar's kitchen, but they were happy to cook up any meat brought by picnickers. They usually put out a jar for donations rather than going through the madness of ringing up for the food and beverage, and they always made out better that way.

Kelly was going to provide the rest of the food— she'd have a regular pumpkin buffet of bisque, pumpkin cheesecake, roasted pumpkin seeds, muffins and pumpkin bread. In addition she was putting out a huge potato salad plus deviled eggs, green salad, a vegetable tray with her own special dill dip and lots of chips. People in town showed up with a variety of things— some would bring a covered dish and still others would burden the food table with their own baked goods and bowls of Halloween candy. They'd stay all day and share whatever they felt like sharing. And even though many of them had gardens, they'd probably all take home a pumpkin. Some would come in costume.

Before the crowds arrived, Hank Cooper came around the corner of the big Victorian house. Alone.

"Hey," Jack said. "You bring any Riordans?"

"They'll be coming. I thought maybe I could have a second. I could help you set up, if you want my help."

"We're ahead of it here," Jack said. "What's on your mind?"

"Well, it's this. Sometimes I do unpopular things. I'm not saying that incident back at Ft. Benning—that was entirely a twenty-two-year-old mishap of me being in the wrong place at the wrong time with a wrong woman and not my fault. But I've had strong opinions about things here and there—like quitting oil companies I worked for because I disagreed with their practices, that kind of thing. You might not understand that—but then, maybe you've never seen what happens in a spill."

Preacher started scraping the char off the grill with a spatula. "In my opinion, it is not wrong to avail yourself of what the earth provides, but it is wrong to abuse and exploit and endanger it."

"Yeah," Coop said.

Jack slanted a narrow-eyed look at Preacher, who always surprised him. "*Avail* yourself?"

"You know—help yourself…"

"I know what it means," Jack said.

"So, the deal is," Coop went on, "sometimes I get

a reputation. Not always a fair one, but still. So what I do, just to make sure I can always bail myself out if I have to or get work again if I need to—I keep some records. Documentation."

"Very smart. I keep records, too," Preacher said, scraping.

"Get yourself in a lot of tight spots, do you?"

"I prefer to think of myself as a man of principle. So, I made a few copies of things from way back. There's an envelope in my truck that I'd like to transfer to your truck. It might make for interesting late-night reading. It's a record of my arrest, the results of a brief investigation, my release and honorable discharge. I did very good work for the Army, but to say the Army wasn't sorry to see me go would be an understatement." He gave a shrug. "It's been said I have trouble with authority."

Jack frowned slightly. "Why didn't you explain that sooner? That you have the proof?"

"For starters, I didn't know your name. I never forget a face, however. You don't look that much different than you did fifteen years ago." Jack stood a little taller. "Except for the gray," Coop said, brushing his fingers through his own brown hair, right at the temples.

"And you were doing so well…" Jack said. Then he added, "For starters?"

"I kept records, but it rubs me the wrong way to have to prove myself. To anyone. What happened to innocent until proven guilty?"

"That pride get in your way much?" Jack asked.

"Sometimes that's all a man's got."

"Well, I'd be happy to take that envelope off your hands. And can I just say, that's a good thing you did. For Luke and for me—you might be passing through, but we're staying here. We don't need bad blood between us, me and Luke."

"That's the thing—this place is growing on me. I might sit out some time here. And we might never be friends, you and I."

Jack gave a shrug. "Just so we're not enemies."

"Yeah," Coop said, running a hand around the back of his neck. "But just so you know, you pretty much irritate the shit outta me."

"Is that a fact?"

"You're such a goddamn know-it-all…"

Both men looked suddenly at Preacher to find him grinning like a kid. "You'll find that kind of comes and goes…." He gave a chuckle. "You'll like him better after you take some money off him at poker. He hardly ever wins."

"Funny," Jack said. Then to Coop he said, "Come on, let's go get that envelope before the crowds descend."

After tossing the envelope in his truck, Jack turned to Coop and stuck out a hand. "You irritate me, too. We might as well shake on it."

Cooper took the hand. And he laughed.

Tom was up before 5:00 a.m. and the first sound he heard was that of Junior pulling a flatbed past the house with the smallest tractor. The jingling sound it made as it rode by was the telltale jingling of metal fence posts. He pulled on his jacket and boots and said, "Crap!"

It didn't take him long to find not only Junior sitting atop the tractor, motor running like he might make a fast getaway, but the black, furry rumps of four bears ambling away from the orchard. Mother and her triplets. They were almost a hundred yards away before Junior turned off the motor.

Tom was on foot. "Did you run them off?" he asked.

"Yup. I saw one in a tree and went for the tractor. I'm going to put a post every two feet on this section now," Junior said.

"I'll help. You get coffee yet?"

"I don't need coffee to wake up. I'm pissed. That got my motor running."

By the time the fence was double repaired and half the orchard chores done, it was noon. Right now the last thing he felt like doing was spending a day with a bunch of little kids at a party on a farm, but he'd made a commitment. He'd be late to Nora's; a shower and shave was absolutely necessary. By the time he made it to her house, it was twelve-thirty. And he was exhausted.

But the second he saw her, he felt a little surge of energy.

"Sorry," he said. "I meant to be one time"

"Oh, Tom, please don't apologize—it's all right. Would you like us to go in separate cars?"

"Why?"

She gave a shrug. "Maybe you don't want to give the impression that we're, you know…"

"Friends?" he asked.

"Of course," she said and unconsciously brushed her lips with her fingers.

"We'll take your car so we don't have to move car seats to mine. I'm going to throw the chairs in the trunk."

"With the stroller, please?"

In the backseat, Berry chanted, "Punkin, punkin, punkin, punkin."

Soon the blanket was spread on a grassy spot not far from the big Victorian and Berry was pulling at Nora's hand, begging to go see the pumpkins. Someone had hooked up a few ponies for rides for the kids and there was a line for apple bobbing—apples compliments of Cavanaugh's, brought earlier by Maxie.

Maxie greeted them like old friends and took Berry right off Nora's hands.

"I'll take her around and wear her down," she said.

"Would you rather stay here with Fay?" Nora asked. "Berry's getting *fast!*"

"I think I can keep up for a little while," she said, disappearing.

Tom gave a wave to a group of men who were standing around the grill. "I'll be back," Tom assured her.

"By all means, take your time. Visit with your friends—I'll be fine."

And Nora was not without friends of her own—her neighbor Leslie wandered over and sat on the blan-

ket for a little while. Not long after, Martha joined
them. Within an hour Maxie was back with Berry
and other men and women Nora knew came visiting—Noah and Ellie Kincaid, Mel Sheridan and Paige
Middleton, Becca Timm, the schoolteacher and soon-
to-be Mrs. Cutler—she was marrying Denny, who was
farmer Jill's assistant. Kelly Holbrook introduced her
fifteen-year-old daughter, Courtney, and Courtney's
best friend, Amber—the girls put in a pitch for babysitting and as a favor, loaded Fay into the stroller and
took charge of her for a while.

From her place on her blanket, Nora kept catching sight of Tom, laughing and enjoying a beer with
a group of guys, helping to haul big pumpkins to cars
for women he knew, throwing a ball with some young
men Nora hadn't yet met.

*Friends.*

The trouble with women, she thought as she admired her handsome, sexy friend, is that when a guy
kisses us, we think he loves us. Women think kisses
make relationships when really, kisses make kisses.
And besides, was there really room in her life for a relationship? Probably not, even though there was nothing about Tom to suggest he could be as thoughtless,
irresponsible and cruel as Chad had been. Not only
were there too many differences in their characters,
she had to remember that back in the days of Chad,
he was a traveling ballplayer. She rarely saw him and
when she did, she was so overwhelmed with her crush,
she gave in to him quickly, easily.

She saw Tom every day. She spent many an evening at his dinner table. She witnessed firsthand how he cared for his grandmother. The man was nearly a prince in her eyes.

So, what if they were friends for years? Friends who had the occasional dinner out or went to a town event here and there? And what if, as good friends, there was sometimes kissing? Only one really crucial factor could make that an unappealing idea—if it wasn't good for her children. And right now everything about Tom and Maxie and the orchard had been wonderful for her children.

Of course, she couldn't be kissing him if he was also kissing someone else. The disposition of his relationship with Darla hadn't been talked about, except that she knew Darla was only supposed to be in California for two or three more weeks.

Tom brought her food—pumpkin bisque to try; pumpkin muffins and bread. A little later he brought her a soda and a couple of hot dogs—one dressed sloppy and one plain for Berry. A plate of potato salad, coleslaw, veggies and chips appeared. Then came cookies and fudge and pie.

"How's the sugar intake working out here?" Maxie said during one of her appearances on the blanket, glancing at Berry who was lying down on the blanket with a book balanced above her face.

"Berry is vibrating," Nora said. "I nearly had to tie her down. Detox tonight is going to suck."

"Want me to give Fay a bottle, since I'm here?"

And Nora smiled—if she decided to move south, to live near her father and go to school, she would miss Maxie as much as Tom. "That would be nice. She'd be more than happy to give herself a bottle, but you're only a baby once. I try to hold her whenever I can."

Maxie settled in one of the chairs Tom had brought and pulled the baby onto her lap. "Brings back such sweet memories," she said. "Nora, you remind me of a younger me. When Tom's father was a baby, I worked all the time. I worked so hard on the orchard. I can't even remember if I had to—there were Warren's parents and hired hands. But I had that baby in a sling all day while I did chores. Even picking apples."

"I think you come from a generation of hard workers," Nora said. "My generation is one of techie obsession. I'm just doing what works."

"And I was trying to justify my existence. I desperately wanted to prove that Warren hadn't made a huge mistake, marrying me."

"I can't imagine anyone would think that!"

"Oh-ho." Maxie laughed. "Warren's father didn't even want to hire me, and he was furious at the notion that Warren would marry me! I was pregnant!"

Nora frowned. "You and Warren met on the orchard, married and you got pregnant right away?" she asked.

"Oh, heavens, no! I showed up looking for work with what you young women now refer to as 'the baby bump.' I was destitute, stranded, pregnant and alone. I tried to conceal my pregnancy for as long as I could. Back in my day, you couldn't get away with illegitimacy. Single, pregnant women were hidden away and their babies were given up or taken away. It was Warren's mother who hired me." She chuckled. "This was not funny at the time—it was terrifying—but Warren's mother said to her husband, 'I'll throw you out before I'll throw this poor girl out! Can't you see she needs to support herself and her unborn child?'" Maxie shook her head, but she laughed.

Nora was completely confused. She had to concentrate to close her mouth.

"That's right, darling. I followed some useless logger from Idaho. Well, he let me come along, I guess you could say. And I lived in a logger's camp with a few other women while my logger alternately ignored me and visited me. I was just a foolish young girl who thought the right man would make everything better."

"And he was killed," Nora remembered.

"God rest his soul," she said. "We're not to speak ill of the dead, but if he hadn't gotten himself killed in a logjam, I can't imagine what would've become of me. As it turned out, I couldn't stay in the camp without his sponsorship, so to speak. I had to go looking for work. So I walked and hitchhiked all over this county and came upon the orchard at harvest time, just like you did."

"And fell in love with the owner's son...."

"To be fair, I tried very hard not to. Poor Warren— what was he thinking? I had another man's baby in me!"

"He must have been thinking how much he loved you."

"He was the most beautiful man. We had such a

good time. He could bring me out of a bad mood just by saying, 'Maxine, you're probably right but you're so damn loud!' He was a little older than me—twelve years. And we were married over forty years. We married just before my baby was born. We'd planned to have a lot of children, but it turned out we were only going to have that one. When I cried and cried and apologized that I couldn't give him his own, he shushed me and thanked me for making sure he had at least that one. 'This is my son,' he said to me. He was a wonder. Warren took after his mother, I think."

"And your son, Tom's father, died in a plane crash," Nora recalled.

Maxie inhaled sharply and gave a nod. Her eyes closed for a moment, proving you never get over burying a child. "Our children are not our possessions, Nora. They're loaned to us to raise and to be set free. From the time he could look up, he was determined to fly high and fast. I wasn't put on this earth to stomp on a young man's dreams. Although…there were times I had to ask myself if I'd have been happier if I had discouraged him in every way, even if it meant having an unhappy, bitter man alive long enough to harvest many, many years of apples. Surely not. Surely not."

Nora wanted to be her. She had to brush away a tear.

"What? You're crying? Stop at once—I've had my setbacks, but I've had the best life of anyone I know! I can't find a person I'd trade places with, and believe me, I've been looking!" Then she paused for a minute of reflection. "Maybe Penny, about once a year.

Every Christmas her son gives her a ten-day cruise, anywhere in the world. I could stand a cruise, I think."

Nora sniffed back a laugh. "If I could, I'd give you a cruise. Don't worry, Maxie—I won't ever tell anyone."

She gave a huff of laughter, a quiet laugh as Fay's mouth opened around the nipple on the bottle and her head lolled back, asleep. "Nora, this is a small town. The biggest mistake I could've made was trying to pretend to be something I'm not. Those people who were around back then knew I showed up in Virgin River pregnant, married the lord of the manor at eight months, raised a logger's son as Warren's.... Those people told the ones who came later, I expect. At least until my son's young wife gave me their baby and he died shortly thereafter...and all that became more interesting news. Nora, there aren't many secrets here. At least not for long."

Tom spent some quality time with Nora at the picnic; he introduced her to Jill who gave her a tour of the enormous Victorian house that fronted her specialty farm. Tom helped Berry pick out a pumpkin while Nora was in the house and promised to help her carve a face in it. He tried to get her to take a break by lying still on the blanket with a book, even for a little while, but she was on the move. She would have been happy to stay on the ponies for hours and, because she so often played alone, the concept of taking turns was new to her.

As long as his day had been, made a little longer by

chasing and holding small children, he was relieved when the late October sun finally began to sink behind the trees. He helped Nora pack up and take the kids home.

The day and possibly the cookies had worn on Berry. Tom had seen her fuss a little now and then, get stubborn or pouty, but the act she put on while being dragged to the car, and then on the drive home, was a shocker. Gone was the shy, mousy little girl. She screamed bloody murder and kicked her feet wildly. That had the effect of stirring Fay into a wail.

"So this is what happens when there's no nap?" Tom asked Nora.

"And Fay didn't have much of one—just a cat nap while Maxie held her. I'm going to have to get them right in the tub and into bed."

Tom helped get the girls inside for Nora. While she got them into the bath, he unloaded the trunk, put the chairs back in his truck and brought the stroller, blanket and supplies into the house. By that time Berry was in a towel, still sniffing from what had seemed an endless meltdown while Nora was drying Fay. "How can I help?" he asked.

"If you could get a bottle for Fay, that would help."

While he did that, Nora got them into pajamas. Since he was just standing around looking kind of useless with a bottle in his hand, she passed him the baby and asked, "Do you mind? I need to see if I can get this girl settled down so she can sleep. She's had way too much picnic."

"Course not," he said, hanging his jacket over a kitchen chair. And he sat in the little living room with Fay while Nora fixed Berry a glass of milk, then disappeared into the bedroom with Berry, where there was a little more crying going on. Berry fought and cried, Nora murmured.

So this was what life would be like with children, he thought. Every hand would be needed at some points. And what if there were more children? A man might get to feeling pretty neglected.

Fay took about twenty minutes with the bottle, but her eyes were drifting closed. When her eyes were open and she looked up at him, she smiled sleepily. God, she was beautiful. He wasn't that crazy about children in general, but this one and her crabby older sister, they were certainly growing on him.

He kicked off his boots to get comfortable. When she had finally fallen asleep in his arms he noticed there was quiet from the bedroom. He assumed Nora would join him in the little living room soon, but there was no hurry. Holding the baby while she slept felt surprisingly good; it made him somehow feel bigger and stronger. It was an odd feeling, as if all his resources were being called on to keep them safe.

Finally, too much time had passed without Nora joining him, so he quietly poked his head into the bedroom. Well, that explained it. Nora and Berry were cuddled on the mattress, asleep. He meant to put the baby down in the port-a-crib and gently wake Nora to say good-night.

Instead he put the baby down and lay down on the other side of Berry, who was framed by Nora and Tom. He pulled the quilt from the bottom of the mattress over all three of them and thought, *I'll just lie here for a little while*...

The bed was too small, too low, the mattress too thin, and he'd never felt better in his life. He just couldn't bring himself to move. The baby snuffled in her bed while Berry curled against him and softly snored; he could smell her sweet breath; Nora hummed in her sleep and sometimes talked, but it was in an indecipherable language. His sleep was not deep or constant—he was acutely aware of the children, of Nora.

And then he heard birds just as he felt something in his hair. He opened his eyes to predawn light breaking through the slats in the blinds and Nora was running fingers through his hair.

"I didn't think you had enough hair for bedhead," she teased in a whisper.

"I think maybe you had too much picnic, too," he whispered back. "You were going to quiet Berry and instead Berry put you to sleep."

"Children can show you a kind of tired you just didn't think possible. Did you mean to spend the night?"

"Not at first. I woke up a lot. Sometime in the night I decided I just wasn't going anywhere. I have to go now, however."

"Is Maxie going to be upset? Worried?"

He shook his head. "It's rare, but I have been known

to get in at dawn. Whatever she feels about that, she doesn't let it show."

"Can I get you a cup of coffee?" she asked.

"Will she be all right without us here?"

Nora nodded. "When she wakes up, she'll come right into the other room. I'll make coffee."

A half hour later Tom was saying goodbye at the front door. "The neighbors will all have seen my truck in front of your house all night."

"You're admired around here, Tom. I don't think my neighbors will worry that I'm getting mixed up with a bad person. And we're just friends...."

His lips curved in a lazy smile. "There are friends and there are friends," he said. Then he slipped an arm around her waist and pulled her against him. He tested her lips once, then again, then a third time and then took her mouth by storm. Her arms went around his neck to hold him close and she opened for him and God, he wanted to pass out, it felt so good.

But he made himself stop. "Gotta go," he said, and realized his voice was hoarse. "I have to work twice as hard today since I gave you a weekend off," he teased.

"If you need me to work, you know I'll come."

"I need you to rest and enjoy Jed's visit. I can't wait to hear about what he brings this time. If he's smart, he'll bring Berry a pony." Then there was a little kiss on the lips and he was gone.

# *Seventeen*

Maxie was standing in the kitchen when Tom walked in. She regarded him through narrow eyes and, lifting one brow, she asked, "Breakfast? Or have you eaten?"

"I'm starving, but if you're going to glare at me, I'll fix my own."

"I haven't said a word. Nor have I glared."

"What are you doing right now?"

"Struggling to stay awake. I didn't sleep well."

"All right, here's what happened. The little girls were train wrecks—too much sugar, not enough naps. Nora bathed them and I did a bottle while she quieted Berry and we fell asleep along with the kids. In our clothes. I shouldn't have to tell you that, Maxie. I'm old enough to sleep anywhere I want."

"Yes, you are. But I like that girl a lot and she's had some pretty impressive struggles. I'm not going to tell you not to go near her—I want you to. At least you're looking at the possibilities. But Tom, you be careful. Don't hurt Nora."

"I would never deliberately hurt anyone."

"I know, I know," she said tiredly. "It's so hard. I want you to use caution, to take your time. I also want you to get me beyond the suspense! I'm old!"

He grinned at her. "You're going to have to let me pick my own girl. But no matter what, there's no reason you can't have Nora in your life. She loves you, Maxie."

"Well, life would be a lot easier if you'd just let me tell you who to fall in love with. After all, I know more about this sort of thing than you do!"

"Fall in love? Maxie, I think you're getting way ahead of yourself."

Yet those words followed him around all day Sunday as he worked and puttered around the orchard. Certainly he wasn't falling in love—he was simply attracted. And from what he could tell, she was also attracted—and they had a nice little attraction going. He'd traveled that very road quite a few times since the age of fifteen or sixteen. Yet, he'd never been in love.

Tom told himself that the fact that he wanted to talk to her or see her all day Sunday had nothing to do with his feelings. And that Sunday was one of the longest days he'd experienced since being back from Afghanistan, but he told himself it was only about magnetism. After all, she had a special charm.

But he would not fall in love with her. Nora was encumbered, not just with small children but with a troubled past she was still struggling to overcome and understand. He was looking for something else entirely—a woman without entanglements. A woman ready to settle down and make him the center of her world.

But when Monday came, when she arrived at the orchard, he felt himself light up on the inside. He was grinning like a fool before he could control himself. She was the first of their seasonal workers to arrive as usual; she came to his office to tell him good morning and he came around from behind his desk to stand before her. He took her hands in his, looked into those golden brown eyes and said, "I've been thinking. We'd better be careful. We shouldn't get too involved, too quickly."

She tilted her head and drew her brows together. "Explain why you have such a giant smile on your face when you say that."

"I had a good time on Saturday. Friday and Saturday. But we're adults, you have a family to think about and I have a lot of responsibility. Let's not be foolish. If there's a little attraction between us, no reason we can't enjoy that for just what it is. But we don't want to fall headlong into anything real complicated. We're going to have to keep it friendly. Light. You know."

"Is this your idea of a 'no strings attached' proposal?"

"I'm just saying—I don't see friendship, even a close friendship, getting in the way of us each managing the lives we have to manage. If we let it get too deep, too fast we could regret it. We don't want complications. Or heartbreak."

She smiled at him. "Oh, you're right. We wouldn't want that."

"You understand, then?" he asked. "That we don't have to take this too seriously? The fact that we seem to get along so well?"

"Perfectly."

"And around here—we should be professional. Set an example. You know."

"Of course," she said. Then she waited. "Is that all?"

"I think so, yes."

"Then I'll get going—those apples won't pick themselves."

He gave a nod.

"I'll need the hands," she said, pulling her hands out of his.

And he immediately dropped his hands to his sides. "Right."

She was chuckling as she left his office. Well, he thought, she could laugh it off if she wanted to, but he felt much better, having said his piece. He probably should have added that he wasn't in love and wasn't going to be, but then it was easier to think she'd figure that out in no time.

The problem with his theory hit at about eleven in the morning. Junior was on the press, Jerome had offered to deliver apples to some of their local groceries, Juan and Eduardo were picking on the other side of the orchard.... And Tom found Nora. She was on a ladder, up very high, her bag holding only a few apples and not yet heavy. He climbed the tripod ladder until he was standing on the step right under the one upon which she stood so that they were face-to-face, at least partially concealed by the branches of one of the oldest, thickest of trees.

He touched her lips once, twice, then slipped his arm around her waist, pulled her against him and covered her mouth in a deep, wet kiss that lasted for over a minute.

"Whew," she said. "Is this your way of keeping things light?"

"How do you like it so far?"

She touched his face with her fingertips. "I like the way you kiss—a couple of test kisses, then a huge kiss. I have only one problem—my imagination."

"Huh?"

"If that's your version of light and playful, I'm a little curious about what happens when you are serious."

"But we're not going there," he said. "We agreed."

"Fine. Okay."

So he did it again, kissed her like a starving man, kissed her until she couldn't catch her breath. And again, and again, holding her tight against him.

"You're going to make cider out of these apples in my bag," she said.

*Just once more,* he told himself, kissing her again. But since this was going to be the last one for a good long time, he made it a very long kiss. He stopped when he started to get aroused.

He lectured himself for a while on how only a fool would allow himself that kind of contact with a woman he wanted to keep at arm's length. So—that was pleasant, he thought. And now it will officially stop. No more playing around; no more five-minute kisses in the apples.

And at two o'clock in the afternoon he found her in the orchard, slid that heavy bag full of apples off her shoulders, spun her around the thick trunk of a tree and kissed the breath out of her. Over and over.

When he let her breathe, she laughed. "I know you want me to understand that this is not passion or desire, but just friendship, but I have to be honest—I'm having a little trouble with the concept. You are very distracting."

"So are you," he accused. "I'm not really doing this because I want to be serious. I'm doing this because you taste like apples and honey and I *like* apples and honey."

"And you taste like roughly ten tons of testosterone. I am not sleeping with you."

"We could probably manage it, though. Without getting too involved."

"No," she said.

"But why? I mean, if we're trusted friends? And it doesn't interfere with our responsibilities?"

"Did that line ever actually work for you?"

"I can't remember. But it probably did—it's brilliant."

"No. Never gonna happen."

"Really?"

"Tom, how many children do you think I have to have before I figure out you get them by having sex?"

"Of course there would be protection," he offered. "Tons of it."

"No."

"Jeez. Well, then, could you stop looking so good?"

"You're pathetic," she said with a laugh. "I'm dressed for apple picking and have no makeup on and no matter what you say, I'm sure I don't smell or taste that good."

His lips instantly sought her neck; he kissed and licked. He groaned. Then he went after her lips again, kissing her stupid.

"No," she said when their lips parted. "Now, as much fun as it is to make out with the boss, I have work to do."

"Had enough of me, have you?" he asked.

"For now," she said with a smile. "Your professional behavior is killing me."

He sighed and let her go. He helped her back into the apple sack.

"Thank you," she said. "Now go do something important." And she gave him a little shove.

"All right, but I have a feeling I might be back."

"Yeah. I know."


Tom wasn't a particularly good liar and he blamed Maxie. She had always told him that lying created bad karma and that often you were stuck with the lie. She said it was God showing his sense of humor. When he was a kid in school and hadn't done his homework, she'd warn him, "Don't say you couldn't do it because your grandmother died unless you want your grandmother to die—lies have a funny way of working into truth."

However, he felt some lies, minor lies to be sure, had to be safe. So when Darla called and said, "How was hunting over the weekend?" he said, "Didn't get anything."

"Well, I missed you so much, I can't wait for this weekend. And I've been thinking, if you can break away from the orchard for a little hunting, you can break away to visit me in Davis."

"Unfortunately, I can't. I'm hunting again."

"Tom! Again?"

"It's a tradition around here and very important to community relations." He was glad she couldn't actually see him wince under the weight of the bullshit.

"I'm not going to be in Davis that much longer," she said in a pout. "And I miss you. I miss the whole orchard."

"Well, if you want to spend the weekend alone with Maxie, I'm sure she'd be more than happy to entertain you." And, just as he thought, Maxie was eavesdropping. The speed with which that old woman made it to the kitchen where he was talking on the phone was rather phenomenal and gave lie to her impending death. Her eyes were as big as apples and she bared her teeth at him. "In fact, she might be having her girlfriends for the weekend again," he said to further discourage Darla.

Maxie rolled her eyes and went back to her television program.

"Well, when exactly will you be gone?" Darla asked.

There were times it was not easy being a man, and he was proving himself to be a typical one. He could hoist up an M-16 and go after insurgents fearlessly, but he could not tell an interested woman that it was a no-go. No interest. In fact, some measure of dislike. More than some—Darla was not for him. He would far rather she finish her time in Davis, return to Denver and forget about him. "Well, I'll be leaving very early Saturday morning, we'll camp overnight and I'll be back around noon on Sunday," he said. Just coincidentally, about the time Darla would be leaving Virgin River if she came to visit.

"Well, that not only eliminates the possibility of you coming to Davis for a nice weekend we could spend *alone,* but why would I bother to come to Virgin River for one evening?"

There was definite emphasis on *alone* and he actually gulped. "Sorry, Darla, but some things are just tradition and were set in stone long before I even knew you had a class in Davis. How much longer is that class, by the way?"

"Just a couple of weeks, which is terrible because you and I have things to talk about! Like where we're going with this relationship!"

*Say it,* he told himself. *Say "nowhere."* But he said, "Aw, it's a shame that class didn't fall at a less demanding time of year...."

"Well, to say I'm unbelievably disappointed would be an understatement."

"I'm sorry, Darla, but it's all beyond my control."

There was just a bit more chat—he apologized, she sulked—and then he signed off. Then he looked into the living room and met with Maxie's glare.

"Why can't you be deaf like other old women?" Tom asked her.

"You're going to hell, you know. What did I tell you about lying?"

"What's the worst thing that could happen? I could be forced to go hunting and not shoot anything?"

"I don't even want to discuss it, except to say that you better not ever again volunteer me to entertain Darla for a weekend. Are you mad? Who would carry her bags?"

He laughed in spite of himself.

Nora was not experienced in love, not by a long shot. In fact, her limited experience was pretty much all bad. But she had developed better instincts since then and her intuition told her that she scared Tom Cavanaugh to death. He had prattled about responsibilities and friendly attraction and not getting serious all week—and yet couldn't keep his hands off her. She found him lurking around the orchard all day long, waiting for his chance to pounce. And oh, my, could he pounce.

She pushed him away and laughed at him, but inside everything in her twittered and twinkled. He might not know what he was feeling, but she did. She was falling in love with him. Now, given the fact that her only experience with love was disastrous, she was not opposed to the idea of giving this a very long time to develop, even knowing that it might not work out the way she fantasized in the end.

What she hoped in her heart was that there might come a day that Tom found her and her children worth the effort. When he took her in his arms, she went to another planet. Everything inside her quivered and lusted and became warm. She melted inside for want of him. When he held one of her children, she became almost misty with sentiment—nothing in his behavior toward her or them seemed reluctant.

For four straight days at the orchard, he had found special moments away from other eyes and whether he realized it or not, he was romancing her. For the first time in so long, she had hope about many things— about getting on her feet, taking care of her children, living in a safe place, finding a sense of family and... and possibly the love of a good man.

And then on Thursday after work, she came home to find a notice posted on her front door. In one week her house, owned by a financial institution, would be auctioned. She was expected to move out as soon as possible. She tore down the notice.

The girls were still with Adie; Adie would've seen the notice on the door. Everyone in the neighborhood probably had seen it. With fear in her heart she went inside and flicked on a light. Then she lit a burner on the stove. By some miracle, they utilities were still connected.

She went to get her girls and Adie met her with a look of alarm in her eyes. "Nora, what does it mean?"

"It was to be expected, Adie," she said bravely. "It's not my house."

"But what will you do?"

"I'm going to take the girls home, get them dinner and baths. And I'm going to think. The right answer will come to me."

Maxie was working up an outstanding roasted chicken in the house and Tom was working late in his office, going over some of his online accounts receivable on his laptop. He deftly ignored emails from dpritchard—he didn't have the time, nor the energy. He had some catching up to do—chasing a pretty woman around an orchard took time and cut into his workday.

He wanted this chase to go on forever; he was confident that sooner than later he would be able to convince her they could invest just a bit more in each other. He wanted her; no question she wanted him. He could negotiate and, what the hell, become her steady boyfriend. The thought actually made him smile just as he continued to believe he wasn't making a real commitment.

He heard a car and for a moment he thought she was back for dinner. It was entirely possible. Maxie could have seen her in the orchard earlier or even called her. Nora and the girls hadn't been to dinner all week.

He jumped up and opened the office door—a red Caddy had pulled right up to the back porch. He spun right back into the office and leaned against the wall—*no!*

He could not imagine what the devil she was doing here or how he was going to make her go away.

The door to his office pushed open and there, smiling like she'd just caged a cat, was Darla. "I thought I saw you in here."

"Darla," he said. "What are you doing here?"

"I left Davis this afternoon, early, and I'm taking tomorrow off—so I could spend a little time with you. I suppose I'll leave Saturday to go back, since you'll be busy. But really, Tom, I should think you could make a little time for me."

He scraped his cap off as he ran his hand over his head. "Darla, you shouldn't have come unannounced— I might not have been here."

She stiffened as if insulted. "First of all, I emailed you a couple of days ago. Right after we talked—which by the way was a little tense. Second, you told me I should feel welcome to come to the orchard any time I felt like it! Every weekend, if I wanted to. I don't know...." Her eyes filled with tears and she looked at him imploringly. "What's happened? You told me you were very interested in me and then— Suddenly I feel like I have a contagious rash or something!"

"Darla, Darla…"

"No," she said, backing up slightly. "I don't know what changed, but the first couple of weekends I was here, you were so attentive, so affectionate. I couldn't have imagined how passionate you were when you kissed me and frankly, I was just counting the minutes until we could spend a night under the same roof together without your grandmother in the next room…"

"I tried to explain about the harvest," he said.

"And the hunting," she added. "Did you try to explain about that, too? Or did you just drop it on me that you'd be unavailable? Tom," she said, releasing a tear. "For the first time in a year I was hopeful. Happy!"

"Stop now," he said gently, pulling her into a hug, her head against his chest. "I apologize, but there are many things we should talk about. And I'm not sure where to begin or how." He pushed her away slightly. "And dinner is almost on the table. I need a shower and you could probably stand a glass of wine."

She sniffed at wiped at her eyes. "Maybe I should just leave…."

"I'm not going to let you drive all the way back to Davis, upset and crying."

As she looked up at him, he was quite sure he'd never seen her eyes that round, that sad. But wait—of course he had. When he visited her on his way home, that visit to console her and tell her what a good man her husband had been.

"We need to go in the house," he said. "I'll get a shower, we'll have a little dinner with Maxie, then we'll find a quiet place to talk for a while. We'll get this all straightened out."

"All right," she said sadly. "Will you bring in my luggage?"

"Of course," he said and he thought, *Maxie is going to have my head for this.* "First we go inside and tell Maxie that you're here. Since I didn't get the email, she would have no idea."

"Didn't get?" she said, lifting a pale brown brow. "Or didn't read? Because that was something else you said—from now on you'd be very careful about checking your emails."

"Yeah. Some old habits are tough to change. Come on," he said, taking her elbow.

As he escorted her to the house, he noticed she was dressed as if she might be attending a very important business meeting in which she was the chairman of the board. The red boots were back, this time paired with a long black skirt with a fringe on the hem and a rich, red poncho. Who goes to classes like this? Who drives four or five hours to an orchard like this?

Life was not fair, he brooded. The woman was so beautiful and such an invasive, intrusive, demanding pain in the ass. He had a strong desire for a simple woman in worn jeans that hugged every little curve and a plain old hoodie. Even if he could dress her up in these designer clothes, he wouldn't want to. He loved her unaffected style, her lack of guile. She was pure and simple and honest and that was all he wanted.

He walked Darla across the porch and opened the kitchen door. "Maxie," he said. "Look who's here."

His grandmother turned from the stove and jumped in surprise. "Darla!" she said, her hand going to her chest.

Tom did not want to ever lose his grandmother but he did have the passing thought that if she at least fainted, it might divert Darla's attention from what was going to be a very uncomfortable evening.

"Maxie," she said, opening her arms to embrace the older woman.

"What a surprise," Maxie said, submitting to the embrace, patting Darla's back. Over Darla's shoulder she stared daggers at Tom.

"I missed you," Darla said warmly.

"Well, so nice you're here. I wish you'd have called—I'm afraid there's nothing but calories on the table tonight."

"Oh, that's good, I'm famished. And guess what? I brought a very nice, very expensive Chardonnay. I put it in the trunk in a frozen wine sleeve so it's ready to be uncorked. Will you join me in a glass while Tom brings in my luggage and takes a shower?"

Maxie lifted one eyebrow. "Perhaps more than one," she said. And while Darla may not have picked up on the sarcasm, Tom did.

Duke came into the kitchen, happily wagging his tail, because of course he assumed everyone who came to the orchard came to see him.

"No, Duke, no," Darla said, backing away with the palm of her hand out, warding him off. "You're hairy."

"Darla, he's a dog," Tom said, perhaps a little irritably. Then in order to cover his tracks, he said, "I'll get your bags."

When he came into the house again, carrying three of her four bags, he noticed that she was sitting at the kitchen table. Remaining in the trunk of her car was a fancy briefcase and her chilled bottle of wine. He found it simply remarkable that the woman didn't even bother to fetch those two lightweight items and bring them in but rather waited for him to do so. As he passed through the kitchen on his way back to her car he asked, "Just out of curiosity, how do you get the luggage *into* the trunk?"

"Oh, you just won't believe it. The nicest man lives in the condo right next door—also a student at Davis. He's been so helpful, so accommodating. All I have to do is tell him when I'll need a hand and he's right there, ready and able."

"Does he carry your books to class, too?" Tom asked.

"Why, Tom," she said, a teasing tone to her voice. "Are you possibly jealous?"

He was sure he would not have a problem telling her, tonight, that she'd better get some new ideas about her future because he was now officially off the map. The woman drove him insane. "Let me get the rest and get that shower."

"Thank you, sweetheart."

He did not dare turn around and look at his grandmother's expression.

* * *

After Darla picked her way through an amazing roast chicken, mashed potatoes and gravy, Tom helped his grandmother clear the table and take care of the dishes. Darla excused herself to change into something more comfortable.

"Thank God," he said to his grandmother. "Okay, listen, Maxie. You're going to have to disappear for a while, give me the room. I have to tell her how it is—that we are not seeing each other, not now, not ever. She's very determined, although I can't for the life of me figure out why."

"Maybe you just blow every whistle she's got," Maxie said with a sneer.

He just stared at her. "Oh, yeah, you have to leave the room. You're losing control of your filter."

"Well, I'd go into town, maybe stop off at Jack's looking for gossip, but I had to drink two glasses of her very expensive wine just to be able to sit through dinner with her. Don't you ever bring an anorexic to dinner here again! And by the way, she got screwed on the wine! Doesn't she think we country hicks know good wine? We have award-winning vineyards around here! We know our wine! If that bottle cost more than eight-ninety-nine I'll wet myself!"

He rolled his eyes. "Can you find something to do in your...room?" he asked.

"And miss the Raiders and Cowboys game?"

"If you do this for me, I'll buy you a fancy flat screen for your bedroom."

She snatched the dishtowel out of his hands and said, "I'll record the game. And read. But would you please not beat around the bush? I've had about enough of this. And for God's sake, don't lie!"

"Yeah, stupid me," he said. And then mocking himself, "What kind of trouble could a hunting lie create?"

"See? If you'd just listen to me…"

"Well, now," Darla said brightly. "I brought some movies if anyone is interested."

# *Eighteen*

Although Tom dreaded the whole idea, he was burdened with the impossible task of helping Darla understand his position, which was one of not being even slightly in love with her. Ironically what made this even more difficult was the fact that he couldn't understand what in the world made *her* want *him*. She didn't really love his world, his apple kingdom.

"Movie, Tom?" she asked. "Maybe *While You Were Sleeping?*"

"Darla, before we look at movies, we have to talk. Let's talk in the kitchen. I'll fix you up with another glass of wine," he said. "I'll have a beer with you."

She grinned devilishly. "Tom, are you trying to get me drunk?"

"No," he said, though that wasn't a bad idea. "Thing is…" Then he stopped. "Listen, how did you say you met Bob?"

"Did I say?"

"I think so. I can't remember."

"He was in Colorado Springs, snowboarding."

*In Vail, skiing.* He did so remember.

"Did you date very long?"

"Not long, no. A few months. Almost just enough time to plan a nice wedding. It was beautiful. He had his orders for deployment right before the ceremony, actually."

"Hmm," Tom pondered, rubbing his jaw. "You must've fallen in love with him the second you met him."

She sighed. "Well, what wasn't to love? Big, handsome, decorated hero. Every woman I knew envied me. Bob was very nearly famous!"

"Didn't you worry about how complicated life might be with a husband in the Corps? Hadn't he deployed before?"

"Three times before," she said with a nod. "But no—I wasn't worried. And I sure wasn't going to wait till the age of forty to be married."

"Huh?" he asked.

"I expected to be married by thirty and when that didn't happen I—"

"Huh?" he said again, interrupting her. "Bob was twenty-seven," Tom said. "He enlisted right out of high school. He had almost ten years in. He told me he wanted a career."

"That was just talk among the men," Darla said with a wave of her hand. "Bob was a little younger than me."

He leaned toward her. "How much younger?"

"A few years. But it was instant love…"

She had searched him on Google, Tom thought. Why hadn't he done the same? "How old are you?" he asked.

"Tom! Do you need to see my driver's license?"

He gave a nod. "Don't need to, but…"

"Thirty-five," she said, unmistakable annoyance in her tone. "That wasn't a problem for us!"

"And you weren't married very long when he deployed?"

"A couple of months, most of which he was with his unit and I was in Denver, but we saw each other every week. *Almost* every week."

She had said less than a year, as Tom recalled. Well, that was far less. And her couple of months was probably actually a couple of weeks.

"Why all these questions?" she asked.

"Well, we haven't known each other that long and I'm trying to figure out a few things. Like what you think our life would be like if we got serious…"

"I'm sure it would be so much fun!"

"Oh? And what fun things do we do together?" he asked.

She took a sip of her wine, her mood brightening. "Not many things, so far—but you've been very busy with the harvest. And you said the harvest doesn't last all year. I suppose when you're finally not picking apples and making cider all the time we can explore some of the fun things that revolve around my job—

the travel, the entertainment, events. I have season
tickets to the symphony."

*Kill me now,* Tom thought. He knew, beyond the
shadow of a doubt, she did not capture Bob with that
bait.

"And every now and then I get passes to the company's box at the Lakers' games—you have to like
that idea. I'm not really into sports, but I love being
in that skybox."

He reached for her hand across the kitchen table.
"Darla, have you thought about how our lives just don't
match? I like to watch sports on TV—you like ro-
mances, chick flicks. I'd rather hunt than go to a symphony. And, well, I live with my grandmother."

She laughed softly. "Tom, I *adore* Maxie, but as
this gets more serious, you wouldn't continue to live
with your grandmother. We would have to be alone
together sometime! In fact, I think it's about time we
explore what 'alone' would get us."

*It could get us laid,* he thought. And what a damn
shame. The idea of having sex wasn't far from his
mind—he wanted sex! This woman was amazing-
looking—and he didn't want her at all. He didn't even
want to kiss her and he was no longer curious about
her perfect breasts.

He'd been having very disturbing dreams for several weeks in which he was having the most delicious
sex of his life. He was taking his partner to heights
she'd never before experienced and she was satisfy-
ing him in ways he hadn't imagined. They were like

bunnies, just screwing their brains out. He could taste her, feel her breasts and hard nipples under his hands, slide into her and make her climax in seconds over and over again and he would wake up hungry for her.

And she was Nora, the woman he didn't want to want. Every goddamn last time, she was Nora. The woman with kids from a felon, the girl who was desperately down on her luck and hanging on to her dreams and her pride by a thread…

…and impressing the hell out of everyone, including him. Though she had these profound obstacles, she laughed as though life was a treat. It was only Tom who had hang-ups, who wanted the woman of the rest of his life to match some unachievable fantasy woman. What a fool. The real deal had been picking apples for him all along.

Duke wandered to the back door. He wagged and looked over his shoulder at Tom and Tom got up to let him out, welcoming the distraction.

"There are so many options for us to look at as we get to know each other better," Darla was saying. "I mean, things change, Tom. I'm sure you won't want to grow apples forever. Then again, maybe you'll want to expand, have a good team running the place while you do something else. And did you know that one of Maxie's friends lives in a very nice seniors' community?"

Just out of stubbornness he asked, "Which one?"

"Oh, I can't remember. I think it was—"

Duke started to bark ferociously, that kind of bark that Tom recognized, not just from Duke, who was ten years old, but from dogs of his youth. That wild, high-pitched cry for backup. His eyes grew big, his mouth opened. He shot to his feet just as the dog's scream came, as if he'd been attacked.

"Did you leave the gate open?" he asked Darla in a shout.

"I…ah… I don't…"

"Tom!" Maxie yelled as she came pounding down the stairs.

He had the back door open. "Duke! Duke! Come on, boy! Come, Duke!"

The dog skittered up the porch steps and into the kitchen door, tail between his legs, head down, panting in terror, shaking all over.

"Bear!" Maxie said. "I'll call Junior!"

"I'll call Junior—check Duke over. He doesn't look like he's bleeding. I hope he's just scared." He picked up the phone and punched in some numbers. "Junior— we got the bear back. I'm pretty sure the gate was left open." There was a pause. "I'll be waiting near the house so don't shoot anything that just rustles in the bushes—it could be me. I'll carry a flashlight. Let's not waste a lot of time."

He went to the living room where the locked gun closet was and pulled out a rifle and extra ammunition. He put on his jacket, gloves, hat.

"What are you going to do?" Darla said, standing uncertainly from the table.

Tom ignored her. "Duke all right?" he asked Maxie.

Duke was down on the kitchen floor, baring his

belly, Maxie beside him. "He's all right, just scared to death. You be careful, Tom."

"I'll be careful," he said.

"What are you going to do?" Darla shrieked.

"I'm going to get the goddamn bear!"

"Can't you just go close the gate?"

"And close that bear and her triplets in here for the night? Then maybe when my employees come in the morning they can meet four bears face-to-face? I don't think so. Or I could leave it open all night and have a herd of elk or deer divest me of my apples. Didn't I tell you to close the goddamn gate after you come through?"

"I don't know," she said, immediately crying. "You always did it for me!"

It was pointless. "Yeah," he said in exasperation. He looked at his grandmother. "Maxie, stay in the house. And I mean it."

"Aren't you going to tell me to stay in?" Darla asked.

"I know you're not going out there." And he left the house.

Junior and Tom took out the quads in search of bears. Typically they used the quads to pull a small flatbed with equipment or to drag soil aerating attachments when the tractor was too large to get between the trees. They could cover the orchard once in little time but it was a big job to check all the fencing, up in all the trees with flashlights and then backtrack to make sure no wildlife had slipped by them and doubled back.

They were out till three in the morning. They never saw a bear. They did see plenty of bear scat—there was no question who'd been to call.

It was probable that the bear and her cubs exited the orchard after Duke gave them a talking to, but it was impossible to know for sure. This was disconcerting for several reasons. First of all, they weren't sure whether these bears were nocturnal feeders— that wasn't necessarily the rule. Tom had always assumed they avoided the orchard while there were a lot of workers around and broke in at dawn or dusk when the gate was closed and the workers were gone and the orchard quiet, but maybe they'd been breaking down the fence at night. But there was no evidence they came daily—bear were scavengers—they loved feeding in dumps. And they had a particular fondness for fish. The river ran along the other side of the orchard. They could go around the orchard to get to the river.

"Nora's usually the first one here," Tom said.

"She doesn't come before sunup anymore," Junior said. "Not these days."

"I'm sure there's no wildlife trapped in here," Tom said as he pulled the gate closed. "Just the same…"

"I'll be here early," Junior said. "I'll go get a couple of hours and be right back."

The men shook hands, Junior got in his truck to depart and Tom went into the house. The rifle didn't go back in the gun cabinet, but leaned up against the cupboard in the kitchen.

In the living room he found Maxie in her recliner sound asleep, a crocheted throw over her. She was wearing her slippers but otherwise hadn't dressed for bed—she was still in her clothes, ready if there was any action. Beside her was Duke. He lifted his head when Tom came into the room and gave his tail a couple of thumps.

Tom scratched him under the chin and said, "Yeah, thanks, buddy. Good work." And then, without even taking off his boots, he dropped onto the couch and closed his eyes.

Nora was up, dressed for work and sitting at her table with a cup of coffee, staring at the auction notice when Adie tapped softly at her door. Nora let her in and said, "Come in. I fixed you a cup of tea—it's so cold this morning."

There was no mistaking the worry in the old woman's eyes. "Have you decided what to do?"

Nora smiled reassuringly, though she didn't feel sure of anything. "I'll think of something. I haven't even talked to anyone about this yet—maybe Reverend Kincaid has ideas. Or Jed—he might have a suggestion. Try not to worry." Or Tom, she secretly thought. What would Tom say about her being thrown out of her house?

"Did you even know this house had been foreclosed?"

Nora shook her head. "Maybe that happened a long time ago. There have been so many foreclosures in the country, I'm sure it's hard to keep up. I've heard of people living in foreclosed property for a year or more before they're actually evicted." *Like me,* she thought.

"I'll help in any way I can," Adie said. "You're always welcome in my home."

"Thank you." How like Adie, who didn't have a nickel to spare or much room under her own roof.

It was early November; Thanksgiving was just around the corner. She had been unable to suppress fantasies of how this holiday season might be spent. She would certainly be spending time with Jed, but after this past week of being chased around the apple trees and kissed on any opportunity, she rather hoped Tom might want to make some holiday plans.

But everything in her mind changed when she got to the orchard. After letting herself into the gate and closing it behind her, she pulled up to the barn. And there, parked at the rear of the house, was the red car.

Her heart plummeted. She almost couldn't breathe.

Nora gathered her mettle and got out of the car. Tom was not in his office, so she made coffee for him; likely he was sleeping a little later than usual this morning since he'd had a house guest last night. Spirit almost broken, she grabbed a bag and a ladder, pulled on her gloves and went into the trees to get to work.

Tom woke to the aroma of coffee and bacon, the sun not yet up. He hadn't moved an inch in about three hours; his feet were still on the floor. He groaned, coughed and stood up.

Maxie turned from the stove when he entered the kitchen. "Bear?"

"Never saw one," he said. "But if they were hiding in the orchard, they were damn good and quiet. We saw plenty of bear shit, though. Duke outted them."

"I heard a snore from the couch at about three-thirty...."

"I didn't even want to bother with the stairs. Did you get any sleep?"

"On and off. I kept waiting to hear a rifle shot."

"Darla?" he asked.

"She went to bed not long after you left. I guess she wasn't interested in waiting up."

He just shook his head and scratched his itching beard. "I'm going to get a shower. I'll be down in a few."

He went to his room, gathered fresh clothes to take to the bathroom and stripped to his waist. The sun was still shy, but a soft glow came from outside the bathroom window. While he shaved, he thought. While he was not the least happy about the circumstances, now dealing with Darla was going to be considerably easier. He wasn't sure how she survived in her world, but there was no way she could make it in his.

A lot of cruel things sprang to mind—like the fact that she was so self-centered she couldn't even manage to close the orchard gate much less carry her own briefcase. He wouldn't say these things, of course.

But if he didn't tell her there was no chemistry between them and send her on her way, Maxie just might. Maxie was getting more outspoken by the year.

He laughed to himself as he was pulling on clean jeans after his shower—he'd better lock up that rifle just in case Darla got the notion to try to convince Maxie it was time to pack up her things and go to some retirement home.

He'd barely pulled on his jeans in the steamy bathroom when he heard a glass-breaking female scream from the orchard.

"Nora!" he said aloud.

He ran down the stairs, taking them about three at a time. "Duke," he yelled to the dog. "Duke, show me the bear!" Though barefoot and bare-chested, he grabbed the rifle as he passed through the kitchen, Duke on his heels.

Duke, apparently over his fright from last night, got low and fast and shot into the trees, snarling. Tom ran like his life was at stake…or Nora's…and was so grateful Duke was the only one he heard growling.

She screamed again and added, "Help! Oh, God!"

Duke was way ahead and just might get the bear off Nora, even as old as Duke was. "Nora!" he yelled just so she would know he was coming. And then he turned into the trees to follow Duke, who was barking wildly. And Nora screamed again.

When he saw her, it took a second to process. Was she throwing apples at a big black bear? Screaming and throwing apples?

"Get behind the tree," he yelled, taking aim.

Nora bolted behind the nearest tree and yelled, "Tom! Behind you!"

He turned in time to see a cub behind him; damn cubs were getting big. He had the rifle trained on the mother, who stood on her hind legs, accommodating him. He was all done playing around with this one—he fired. One. Two. Three. The first one caused her to stop, the second made her stumble back, the third knocked her down. It was a lot of rifle; she wouldn't be getting up.

"Duke!" he commanded. "Come!" And the dog moved away from the dead bear, coming to Tom's side.

Tom moved slowly toward Nora and the cub ran to his dead mother, standing on all fours beside her, nudging her. He looked around for the other cubs and that was when he thought he understood what had happened. Nora's ladder was set up to take her in to the tree branches and there, in one of the big old trees, were two bear cubs.

She backed away, her hand covering her mouth, shaking like a leaf. With her back against the trunk, she slid weakly to the ground. "It's okay now," he said. "The cubs won't bother us."

She just put her hands over her face and sobbed. "God, oh, God," she kept saying.

He heard some distant sounds—Junior's truck, the slamming of the porch door, talking. Positioning himself so he could keep an eye on the mother bear to be sure she didn't rally, he put his rifle on the ground and knelt beside Nora. He gently pulled her hands away from her face. "It's all right now. It's over."

"I was on the ladder," she said, her voice shaking. "I came nose-to-nose with a bear!"

"I figured. And the mother?"

"Back in there. I screamed and fell off the ladder and she came through those trees."

"And you threw apples at her?" he asked.

She nodded. "I was going to hold her off with the ladder."

A small huff of laughter escaped him. He put a finger under her chin and lifted, giving her a small kiss. "You scared me to death," he said.

"Join the club," she said, a hiccup in her voice.

"Why didn't you come to the house when you got here?"

She gave a little shrug and looked down. "Red Caddy," she said softly.

Tom noticed Junior out of the corner of his eye, rifle in hand and pointed down, giving the dead bear a kick to see if she moved. The action caused the cub to skitter away. The ground was getting soaked with blood—that bear was done. He looked at Nora. "Yeah, that. I didn't know she was coming."

"You didn't invite her?" she asked.

"I told her I was going hunting. I didn't know it was true. Remind me to tell you some important lessons about lies." Then he swiveled toward Junior and said, "We have three cubs to round up."

"They were here all night," Junior said.

"Most likely." Then he swiveled back to Nora, ignoring Junior. "Are you going to be all right?" he asked softly.

"Eventually…"

He leaned toward her and kissed her again, this time a little more deeply. She put a hand against his bare chest and against his lips she whispered, "You must be freezing."

"Ha. Not hardly. Is steam coming off me?"

She massaged his chest a bit with one hand, right over a tattoo. "I've never been so scared."

"Come on," he said, standing and pulling her up. When she was on her feet he pulled her against him for a moment, just holding her. He kissed the top of her head. As he finally let her go, he kept an arm around her shoulders, holding her close against his side, and said, "Let's get you to the house. Then I have to help Junior with these cubs."

When he turned he saw not only Maxie standing behind him, Duke at her side, but also Darla. And Darla had a horrified look on her face, but she wasn't gazing at the dead bear. She was looking at Tom and Nora. And as she met Tom's eyes, she lifted her chin indignantly and whirled away, marching fast toward the house.

Nora looked up at him. "I think I'd rather go to the office. Or maybe just home. Is there workman's comp for bear scares?"

"Let me take you to the kitchen. Maxie will make you some tea or something, make sure you stop shaking before you go home."

"I don't feel like tangling with Darla. She looked pretty pissed."

"Yeah," he said, taking a deep breath. "I don't feel like tangling with her, either, but it has to be done."

"Good, you do it," she said, pulling away. "I'm going home to hug my children. I came a little too close to orphaning them." She allowed herself a small smile. "Thank you—you were pretty magnificent. That bear was going to eat me."

"I spent half the night looking for that damn bear and her cubs. Darla showed up just after dark and she didn't close the gate. Duke let us know there was a bear."

She gave his naked chest a pat. "Well, I'm sure she's very upset. You better go see if she's all right. I'm going home." And she walked down the lane to her car, parked by the barn. "Good luck," she said to him, giving him a wave.

Tom grabbed a shirt and jacket and went to help Junior round up the cubs, which turned out more like a game for all the orchard workers as they were on the run. The men carried rakes and shovels to try to direct the cubs into a corner where they would be trapped. The gate remained closed so they wouldn't escape into the forest; they were probably mature enough to survive, but it would be better if an expert made that decision. A couple of hours later someone from Fish and Game arrived with a flatbed attached to a big truck to take away the bear carcass; an hour after that, animal control arrived to transport the cubs to a holding facility.

All this time there was no sign of Darla and the red Caddy remained parked at the back of the house. He stood outside his office staring at that damn car. It would probably have been best if she'd gotten angry enough to leave while he was playing tag with cubs because there was little doubt in his mind she was going to be angry enough to leave after they talked.

"Girl trouble?" Junior asked him.

"What makes you say that?" Tom returned.

"Well, one charged out of here after a bear nearly ate her and in case you think no one was paying attention, she wouldn't go in the house because the other one was in there. And the other one is still in there and you keep looking at that car like you wish it would disappear."

"You're smarter than you look," Tom said.

Junior scratched his head. "I ain't that smart. I'm divorced." Then he turned back to the barn.

Tom took a breath and headed for the house. Maxie was in the kitchen, as usual. She was pouring a pot of soup into a large container.

"Where is she?" Tom asked quietly.

"In her room. Pouting."

"Okay. I'll take care of this."

"I'm leaving," Maxie said. "I'm going into town to check on Nora, bring her some soup. I'm going to stay gone for at least a couple of hours. I'd be very happy if the drama could be over when I get home."

"It will be," Tom said. But he was thinking, *Why the hell can't someone just shoot me?*

# *Nineteen*

Tom tapped on Darla's door. She bade him enter and when he opened the door, he did not see what he had hoped to see—packed luggage ready to go. Nope, she was still settled in. And she was sitting on the edge of the bed, waiting for him.

"I don't really know where to start…" he said.

"Let me help you," she returned rather curtly. "You begin with an apology. And what is that *smell?*"

He ignored the apology part and felt his neck prickling and getting red. He had a sudden curiosity—just how many times had she tricked men into marrying her? Was there any chance Bob hadn't been the first one? But then he realized, he couldn't possibly care less. "The smell is sweat, dirt and *bear.*"

"Maybe we should talk after you've had a chance to shower."

"No, we're going to talk right now, Darla. We, you and I, aren't going any further. We don't fit. It wouldn't work. It's not what I want."

"It's a bit more than that," she said, standing but keeping her distance as she wrinkled her nose. "There's another woman in the picture. You were cheating on me with one of your employees."

"That's the thing, I wasn't cheating on you because I haven't made any kind of commitment to you, not even a slight, tiny, superficial commitment. None. At all. And you and I are not dating, not seeing each other, not getting more serious. We don't want the same things, we're never going to want the same things and I'm tired of this cat and mouse."

"Then why did you lead me on?"

"Lead you on?" He frowned. "How did I do that?"

"You kissed me! You took me to dinner. You told me to visit any time I wanted to."

"Aw, Jesus—when you first showed up here, I was open to the idea of dating a beautiful woman, so sue me. I checked you out while you were checking me out—but it never got off the ground. Darla, it worked for about a day. It isn't working. We don't even like the same things!"

"I'm willing to give you another chance," she said. "Obviously you have to get rid of that female."

"You're amazing," he said, laughing in spite of himself. "Does that usually work for you? That non-listening thing you've got going on? I don't want another chance. I want us to part friends with the realization that we would have to have a lot more in common and like each other equally in order for there to be any kind of relationship beyond a very casual and very *distant* friendship. Apparently I don't have enough 'like' in this equation because I'm not interested. No more dates, no more visits, no more talking about a future that is never going to happen."

"Well," she said, a tear coming to her eye. Tom suspected they were very well-trained tears. "That was blunt to the point of cruel."

"That's how it has to be, apparently. If you could let it go at I'm not interested, we could shake hands and say a pleasant goodbye."

She seemed to shake a bit, like anger was coming to the surface. "What the hell kind of woman do you want?"

Big mistake, Darla, he thought. Big. "I want a woman who pitches in," he said. "A woman who doesn't sit and expect to be waited on while a seventy-four-year-old grandmother cooks and cleans and serves her. I want a woman who can pet the dog even if he gets a little hair on her expensive clothes. Someone who can feel special wearing boots that cost far less than a grand and I want a woman who *eats,* for God's sake! How about a woman who isn't trying to sell my family orchard out from under me and put my grandmother in a home? That would work."

She was stunned silent for a second. Finally she said, "Oh. My. *God!*"

"So here's what's going to happen," he said. "I'm going to shower while you gather your things together. Then I'll carry all your luggage to your car for the last time, shake your hand or even give you a polite hug as

I say, 'Nice seeing you, drive safely.' And then you're going to leave and we're both going to get on with our lives. Is there any part of that you don't understand?"

Another moment of silence. Then, "You are a beast. I had no idea. I barely escaped you!"

"I'll be about fifteen minutes," he said. "You take your time." And he left her.

As he showered, he thought one alternative for her, if she wanted to make a dramatic exit, was to throw her stuff in a suitcase, lug her own damn luggage down the stairs and burn rubber out of the orchard. Junior was on hand to make sure the gate would be closed behind her.

In the end, it didn't happen that way, of course. Forty-five minutes later she found him in the kitchen and, true to form, all she carried was her small pocketbook. "I'm ready," she said soberly.

"Good," he said. "I'll be happy to get your luggage."

As he loaded the last of the luggage into her trunk, he saw Junior near the barn and gave him a sign, pointing to the gate. Junior took his quad down the lane and opened it. Then Tom held the door for her as she got into her shiny car. He held out his hand and she took it.

"I'm sorry it didn't work out, Tom," she said. "I'm sorry I didn't fit into your plans. I'm very disappointed, in fact."

He gave her hand a squeeze and said, "Drive carefully." And he closed her door.

Then he watched the most superficial, manipulative woman he'd ever known leave his orchard.

\* \* \*

When there was a knock at Nora's door, it took her a while to answer. She had Fay on her hip. And there stood Maxie, holding a large container of something. "Oh, Maxie, why are you here?" she asked.

"A couple of reasons," she said. "May I come in?"

"Sure," she said, standing back.

Maxie went straight to the kitchen, just a few steps really, and put her soup on the counter. "I wanted to check on you, of course. And I brought you soup, though I really want you to come to the house for dinner tonight if you can… And I needed to leave the orchard—Tom was on a mission to send Darla away. I didn't even want to be in the house." She shook her head. "That girl…"

"Oh, Maxie, she's a beautiful girl!"

"She was pushing herself on Tom and it should have been more than clear to her that he wasn't ready for that. She's the most annoying person I've met in years, but it's not my business. I'm counting on Tom to do the right thing there."

"I just have to ask—what would the right thing be?" Nora asked.

"Make sure she doesn't trick him into more visits or whatever. He doesn't like her."

"How can he not? She told me it was just a matter of time before they got married."

"I pray she was hallucinating when she said that. But—this is not up to me. Tom is intelligent. I have to believe in him. Now, darling, how are you? You had quite a scare!"

"My God," she said. "I'm still shaking. I kept my girls home from preschool and day care—I just need to be with them. When they nap later, I'm going to have a long, hot soak in the tub. I'm frazzled, I admit it. I climbed up my ladder and picked a dozen apples before one of those cubs took a swipe at me. They had been there the whole time."

"Ah, that's what happened—you got between the treed cubs and the mother. You know they'd been in the orchard all night? Tom was out with Junior till three in the morning trying to find them and get them out. I'm sorry, Nora—this is our fault. You should be safe in our orchard."

"There's only so much you can do. I'd say hunting till three in the morning is a worthy effort, wouldn't you?" Then she let her eyes close just briefly as she remembered the sight of Tom coming through the trees, half dressed, looking a bit wild and warrior-like, holding that big gun. She hadn't known about the tattoos on his chest and biceps. She opened her eyes. "Tom was amazing. He saved my life."

"Possibly. Those black bears are usually passive and don't like to be around people, but when cubs are involved…"

"What will happen to the cubs?"

"Out of our hands," Maxie said. "Let me warm you some soup. Berry and Fay will like it—lots of soft veggies and noodles."

"Please don't go to any more trouble."

"I have to kill a couple of hours. I could watch the girls while you relax in the tub or nap?"

She just laughed. "Let's have soup together, all of us. Then I'm going to take it easy and get to bed early tonight."

"I wish you'd come to the house and let me spoil you a little. I could make your favorite meal."

But Nora had things to figure out, like what she was going to do without a home. And she was loath to ask for more help from anyone—so many had already given to her. "Everything you cook is my favorite," she said. "But I'm seriously exhausted. I'm sure it was the fright. I want to be alone with my children tonight. Maybe I'll see you tomorrow."

"Good enough," Maxie said. "Now find me a pan so I can warm up some soup for you."

They not only enjoyed a lunch of soup, they actually laughed together and reminisced about some of the more entertaining events of the past weeks. But when Maxie left her house a while later, Nora had come to a few conclusions. She was losing her home and there was no one among her acquaintances she could possibly ask for shelter. Noah had offered, but it was rather offhand and she wasn't about to stuff herself into his home. She knew Adie didn't want to lose her and would put up with anything to keep her and the girls near. Maxie and Tom would no doubt offer, but her common sense told her that Tom was simply not ready for that much—he was still wondering what to do next with her. He wanted what they shared to be casual. As far as she knew, there were no available houses in Virgin River that she could afford.

And winter was fast approaching. She'd done blistering winter here before.

There was only one place she could turn. After weeks of testing the waters it was time to let her father help her as he so wanted to do.

Friday night, after the girls went to bed, she dialed the phone. He answered and she said, "Hello, Jed? I mean... Hello, Dad?"

Tom wanted to see Nora. Not only was he running on about two hours of sleep, but she had told Maxie that she was tired and wanted to be alone with her children. Reasonable, he thought, as long as Maxie could assure him that she was all right. So he barely slept on Friday night and on Saturday morning was up early, working the orchard. That Nora wasn't there didn't faze him—he hadn't asked her to work. But the strangest thing happened—he saw his grandmother come out of the house carrying a small suitcase.

He made fast tracks to her. "What's this?" he asked.

She didn't answer until she had plopped the suitcase in the backseat of her car. "Well, Nora called this morning and said she'd like to come over later to speak to us so I talked her into dinner. She said it would just be her. Adie is going to sit with the girls and put them to bed. I've left you a casserole to warm and a small salad in the refrigerator. You know where the bread is—and for that matter, Nora knows, too. I'm going to my friend Phyllis in Ferndale. I'll spend the night, we'll have brunch in the morning and I'll be back tomorrow afternoon."

He was completely confused. "Has this been planned?"

"No, Tom," she said patiently. "I'm giving you the house. Warm the casserole—it's one of your favorites—chicken enchilada casserole. You have an opportunity to be alone to talk to Nora. Things have been a little crazy around here. I might be an older woman, but one thing I know—when children are involved, it can be a challenge to have an entire conversation. This is your chance."

"Why isn't she bringing her kids?" he asked.

"Tom," she said impatiently. "I don't know, but possibly she has things to say that shouldn't be interrupted. Or things to ask that should be asked privately. Just warm the damn dinner and *listen*."

And he thought—there were many advantages to living with a bossy, energetic grandmother. She took very good care of him and of countless details. But there were many problems with it, as well. Like this, for example. He felt flushed at the idea of being completely alone with Nora. And a little irritated at being set up to be.

Nora arrived at six looking exactly as she had on their one and only date, which he thought was beautiful. He could feel his eyes grow hot and dark. He held the door open for her, not able to say a word.

"Hi," she said, stepping inside. "Thanks for letting me come over."

"Letting?" he asked. "I wanted to see you yesterday, talk to you, make sure you were doing all right. Maxie said you asked to be left alone. I'm glad you're here."

She looked around. "Where's Maxie?"

He pulled out a kitchen chair for her. He'd gone to some trouble to set a nice table just for the two of them. "She's visiting a friend in Ferndale for the night. She'll be back tomorrow. We have dinner. Will you have a glass of wine tonight?"

"I guess so, sure. Why didn't Maxie just tell me she wouldn't be home? I wanted to explain something to both of you."

"Maybe it was last minute, but don't worry about that. I don't think I'm real clear on why you didn't bring the kids," he said, opening a bottle of pinot grigio for her.

"It's a little complicated, but I didn't want to be distracted." She waited while he gave her the glass. He sat across from her and waited expectantly. "Are you going to have wine?" she asked.

"Oh," he said. "Right." And he poured himself a glass though he wasn't the least bit interested in wine right now. He wanted *her*. Again he waited. And waited. "Should we toast something?"

She shook her head. "No, I don't think so. Maybe this is the best way to explain," she said, reaching inside her vest and withdrawing a folded piece of paper. She passed it to him.

He opened it, keeping his eyes on her face. Then he looked down and saw a notice of auction on foreclosed property—and the address was hers. He looked up. "Nora, what is this?"

"It was posted on my front door. I think we both knew something like this would happen eventually—I didn't own that house. I didn't even rent it. It was probably abandoned a few years ago."

"Auctioned next Friday?"

She nodded. "I'm sorry I can't give you notice on leaving my job. Will you be able to get by without me?"

He was on his feet. "Where are you going?"

"Well, the notice forced a decision and maybe that's a good thing. I'm going to take my dad up on his offer. I'll move to Stanford. Well, I'll move in with him until he can secure family housing for me, which might take a couple of months, given the holidays and everything. I'll go back to school. It's a very generous thing for him to do."

He was standing over her. "And what about us?"

"Us?" she asked. "I'm not sure what there is about us. I don't think you're ready for an us, Tom."

"Why do you say that?"

"Please, sit down, you're making me uncomfortable." When he went back to his chair, she continued, "You were pretty worried about me taking all that kissing too seriously."

"Come on," he said. "You must have felt what I felt."

She reached across the table and touched his hand.

"Listen, it's okay. I understand—my situation and all, it's a lot to consider. Kissing without commitment—that's much easier to handle. I'm okay about that."

"Okay, look," he said, rubbing his hand over his face, completely unsure what he was going to say next. "It's a little intimidating, I admit that. Not because there's anything wrong with having a couple of kids—they're nice kids. It's not about you—more about me. Like I should take some time to really consider whether I'm up to handling them. I don't mean *handling*...you know what I mean."

"I know what you mean," she said with a smile. "I understand. And I don't want you to think I was expecting anything more. I'm being honest."

"You weren't? Expecting more?"

She shrugged. "If by some twist of fate we ended up knowing each other longer, much longer, things might have evolved, but we haven't known each other long and—"

"A few months, Nora. Not like a day..."

"I know," she said. "I know. I really enjoyed it."

He leaned back in his chair. "I don't know what to say. All of a sudden you're leaving. Without warning."

"I'm afraid that's how it is, not really my idea. But I'm grateful, you know? At least I don't have to be afraid—Jed's a good man. The more I get to know him, the more I realize how lucky I am that we found each other after all these years. My girls will have a grandfather and I've watched them together. He's good

with them. He's like he was with me. He's so gentle.
He has the patience of a saint."

"Have you already talked to him about this idea?"

She nodded. "I had to know what I was going to do
as soon as possible."

"Did you ever think about talking to *me?*" he asked.

"Oh, Tom, I couldn't put that on you. You know—
this whole place is so wonderful—long before that notice was tacked to my door, people offered me help.
Space. Security. Noah told me to never worry. Adie
said she'd take me in, even though she lives in a tiny
house and there are three of us. I have no doubt you
and Maxie would have been willing to help me, give
me a place to stay. But I still have this crazy idea I'm
going to somehow make it on my own…"

"But your dad…"

"Is my father and he feels he has a lot to make up
for. Not only that, he keeps reminding me that if we'd
never been parted, these are the things he'd want to
do for me anyway. He tries so hard to convince me it's
acceptable—it's not extra stuff given out of guilt." She
shook her head. "I just don't want any more charity if
I can help it. I just don't want to be pitied."

"Nora," he said loudly. "I don't pity you!"

"I didn't mean you treated me with pity, Tom. I
mean I want to build a life for my girls, not rely on
someone's kindness to do it for me. I would, you know.
I have—I've had to take charity to get by. But trust me,
it feels better to stand on my own two feet."

He was quiet for a moment, then he took a slug of

wine. Not a sip but a couple of big swallows. "I'm not sure I'm ready for this," he said.

"Well, there are still a few days," she said. "I can't get out of that little house overnight. Jed is coming tomorrow. He's bringing me some sturdy boxes. I'll get us packed up early this week. He's going to come back, rent a trailer for the furniture in Fortuna and we'll drive south. I'll follow him to his house."

"Have you told anyone else?"

She shook her head. "But I'm going to take a couple of days to say goodbye, to thank people for everything they've done to help me. And I'm going to remember this, you know? I'm going to damn sure remember what it's like to need help and have a good person hold out a hand. Believe me, I'll pay that back. I might not have the luxury of paying back in Virgin River, but I'm going to be paying back the goodwill."

"I'm not getting this," he said. "It's too fast."

She started to stand up. "It's okay, Tom. I know I've blindsided you. You'll get used to the idea."

"I don't think so," he said, also standing. "Sit down—let me get the dinner out of the oven...."

"Um, if it's all the same to you, I'm not too hungry." She slid a hand over her stomach. "Telling you all this had me nervous and kind of scared my appetite away. I still have lots of Maxie's soup at home."

"Salad, then. A little something."

She shook her head. "I think now that it's out and we had a chance to talk, I'm going to just—"

"No," he said. He came around the table. "You can't just go." And he pulled her to him.

But she put her hands against his chest. "Tom, think about this. You really don't want to—"

But he pulled her harder against him and covered her mouth in a blistering kiss. No test kisses this time, just the kill. She could taste his desperation and sadly, it matched her own. She hated this at least as much as he did—she had been foolish enough to hope that given time, they might actually come together.

"Don't leave yet," he said, his voice hoarse. "Let me do something. Let me feed you. Hold you. Rub your shoulders. Change your oil. Anything, please."

She looked into his hot eyes; she was almost shaken. "Pedicure?" she asked.

He covered her mouth with his again, moving over her lips with passionate need. He licked open her lips and invaded her mouth and she welcomed him. Her arms went around his neck while his big hands slid down her back to her butt, cupping her and pulling her harder against him. He devoured her mouth and she not only cooperated, she met his fever with her own. It was a long time before he broke away. "Better than a pedicure," he said softly, making her laugh.

"I think I know what you're trying to talk me into."

"Nora, I won't let anything happen to you. I'll take care of you and you know, I care about you. You know I do. If I just wanted sex, I could find that. I need *you.* I have protection," he promised.

And so did she. She'd been caught off guard twice;

she'd been on the Pill since she started working part-time at the clinic in town. Even though she'd made the excuse that she didn't want to take chances, what she really hadn't wanted to risk was her heart. Well, hell, it was too late for that.

She met his lips again, running her fingers through his short hair, kissing him deeply and with promise. "Oh, Tom," she whispered against his lips. And he lifted her into his arms and carried her up the stairs to his bed.

# *Twenty*

This was not the setting he would have chosen for his first time with her, but there was no other place in this big house that he would have her. And if he'd had any idea it might come to this, he might have done something to make it better, but he had no idea what that could've been. "I'm sorry, this isn't ideal…" he said.

"Is this where you sleep every night?" she asked him.

"Every single night," he said. "Except for the one night at your house, I've been here every night since I came home."

"One thing I just have to know," she said. "Please tell the truth. Did Darla slip down the hall to this room when she visited?"

He withdrew from her slightly. "Never. Believe me, it never got that far with Darla."

"You kissed her, I saw you."

"Pah, it was friendly. Maybe hopeful. And that's before I realized I couldn't even be her friend. No one, Nora."

"I should have made a rule before you started chasing me around the orchard—I don't kiss boys who kiss other girls...."

His fingers went to the buttons on her blouse. "Only you."

She watched his eyes as he opened her blouse and spread it. She wore an ordinary white cotton bra that she'd had a long time and he let out his breath in a sigh, running his fingers over it gently as if it were fine French lace. "God," he said. And then his fingers found the latch and he set her free. "God," he said again, and his lips went to her neck, chest, breasts.

She tilted her head back, eyes closed. The calluses on his hands were rough, but he handled her so carefully it felt wonderful. Although he'd shaved, his cheeks and chin were scratchy, and she loved it. His lips, oh, his lips, were soft and wet and perfect on her. She held his head in her hands. And then she pushed him back. "No fair. I want a bare chest, too."

He sat back on his heels between her legs and pulled his shirt roughly out of his pants, probably springing the buttons in his haste, and over his head to cast it away. One hand reached behind his neck to grab a fistful of undershirt and rip it over his head. His haste made her laugh softly. But then she grew serious as her fingers sought out the tattoos—she'd seen the thorn branch around his biceps but had only vaguely noticed a flame that grew around his side to his right pec. She must have been too overwrought from the bear scare to look closely.

"What is this?" she asked.

"Fire," he said, whispering against her neck. "It was a firefight thing. A Marine thing. A few of us…you know… Shut up now…"

"Are there more?" she asked.

"Later," he said, slipping to her breast, taking in a nipple and making her gasp.

While he worked that nipple, his hands found the snap on her jeans and slid them down only to find they were caught on her boots. "You should plan better," she said.

"I can't think with you, I want you so bad," he said. Then he sat back again and took care of those boots and jeans, tossing them away. Which left him looking at her tiny, white bikini panties. And he growled. Then he dove for the panties, his mouth on them, his hands on her hips, causing her to gasp and her hips rose naturally. He laughed low in his throat and he pulled at those briefs, slipping them down until she was free and he went after her again, lifting her to his mouth.

And oh, God she came. The second his tongue tormented her, she was gone.

On her neck again, he whispered, "You're wonderful. You were so ready for that and I got to be there. Nora, Nora, it's like I imagined it might be with you…."

"You have to eventually get rid of the pants," she breathlessly told him.

"Pants," he said. "Right." And he sat up to divest himself of all of that, keeping behind the condom from his pocket. "And all this," he said of the vest, blouse and bra that lay open revealing her. "Let's get rid of this."

She let him pull her up so he could slide the clothing off her shoulders and leave her as naked as he was. And he took a moment to just gaze at her.

Nora knew she didn't have a perfect body; her midsection had been abused by a couple of pregnancies and she had a little potbelly and stretch marks. But Tom looked at her as though she was the most beautiful thing he'd ever seen. "Nora," he said in a whisper. "You're incredible."

He was the stunning one—sculpted, beautiful and exciting tats, six-pack belly, wide, strong shoulders and huge biceps—growing apples is not for sissies. He was a work of art. There was the smallest tuft of hair right in the center of his chest—she wanted to lick it.

He had other plans. With his hands behind her knees, he spread her legs. He put one large finger on her favorite spot and massaged, watching as her eyes rolled back. Another finger checked her to see if she was ready; she'd never been more ready. "Condom," she croaked.

She heard the package rip. He pulled her hand to him so she could feel him roll it down his length and then with his hand over hers, he rubbed it a little bit, working it. Not too much—he was as ready as she was.

When he found her, he lowered himself to her so that his mouth could be on hers as he slid into her. "I want you," he whispered.

"I want you," she whispered back.

"I want this to last."

And she thought, *How can I give him up?* "I'm ready, you're ready…."

He began to move and she moaned, her hands finding his butt to hold him inside her. He shifted a couple of times until her moan turned into a helpless squeak and when that happened, he just rode her and it happened again. BAM! She was holding him captive with all her internal muscles. "Oh, my sweet baby," he whispered against her mouth. "That is so good."

She collapsed, limp as a noodle. It took a few minutes before she could summon any real strength. "You're not done," she finally whispered.

"I know," he said. "I'm dying here."

She chuckled and gently rubbed her hands over his shoulders. "No point in that. Take your turn."

He rose up enough to look into her eyes. His were still on fire, they were so hot. "Come with me?" he asked.

"Don't know if I can," she said.

"I know where the secret spot is… I bet you can. I want to feel it again—together."

"Well, don't hold it against me if…" He started to move again. His lips brushed hers then dipped to her breast for a hearty suck. "Oh!" she cried softly. "God," she said. And he pumped for a while, hitting that favorite spot until she lost her mind, her legs wrapped around his waist, her arms around his neck, and she gave him exactly what he wanted.

And he gave it right back, bowing his back a little and letting out a deep growl of pleasure.

Tom held her against him, gently stroking her back. "Stay with me tonight," he whispered.

"You know I can't."

"Let's call Adie and tell her we need her to stay with the girls. Tell her I'll pay her a thousand dollars to stay the night with them. Two thousand."

"You're kind of cute, all desperate. No, I have to go home."

"Not yet. Please, not yet. Just give me a little more time with you like this...." He kissed her shoulder, neck, ear, lips.

"A few more minutes," she said with a sigh that sounded as helpless as Tom felt. She curled into him.

"Letting go of you tonight will be the hardest thing I've ever done. You know what we've had is special. Tell me you know that, Nora."

She put a palm against his cheek and nodded. "I am not going to cry," she said with a shaky voice. "I'm going to be grateful for every beautiful thing and I am *not* going to cry."

They made love again and Tom tried to make it as slow, as luxurious, as precious as possible. In his life, even in war, he had not felt this close to insanity—he felt as though his life was slipping away from him. When he finally relented he had to let her go, his head began to pound. He took her to her car, rode with her to the gate, kissed her hard and held her close one more time and then, with a lump in his throat, he watched her drive through the gate.

He closed the gate and gripped it, his fingers locking into the aluminum mesh, his forehead leaning onto the fence. He stood there until he was almost too cold to walk.

Jack Sheridan was manning the bar on Sunday morning when Hank Cooper walked in. "Hey," Jack said, but he didn't say it with an abundance of friendliness.

"Hey."

"Coffee?" Jack asked.

"Thanks. I came to say goodbye."

"Heading out?"

"Yeah, kind of sudden. There was a phone call last night—kind of sketchy, but the short version is our friend Ben, from up the Oregon coast—he's dead."

Jack was jolted. He damn near spilled the coffee. "Dead?"

"He was killed. He's buried already. Some old guy said Luke's phone number was written on the wall of that old store of his—and there were some personal effects for me. Well, for someone named Henry Cooper."

"Henry?" Jack asked.

"Henry. Hank. I answer to a lot of things. So, I'm headed up there…to pick up whatever it is. And to find out what happened to him."

"Aw, man, I'm sorry. Luke going?"

"He offered, but no point in both of us going. I can call him if I need him."

"And me," Jack said. "If you get up there and find out you could use a posse…"

"Decent of you," Coop said, sipping his coffee. "Thing is, I don't know when I'll get back this way, so I wanted to say…" He hesitated. "Look, I get that you did what you had to do back then. And I get that it looked bad on me and that wasn't your fault. I don't want that on my conscience."

"Consider it cleared up, but why you worrying about your conscience now? We could've settled this when you got back…."

He gave a shrug. "I have no idea what's going on, that's all. It could be complicated."

"I hope you know how to be careful," Jack said.

Coop grinned. "That's one good thing that came out of our last encounter. Careful is my middle name."

"I hope you get back this way."

Coop took another drink of his coffee, put down the cup and reached for his wallet.

"Nah, I'm not taking your money. It's just a cup of coffee between friends."

Coop put out his hand. "I think maybe that could've worked out, if we'd had more time, if we both weren't so damn stubborn. Well, if you weren't."

Jack took the hand and grinned. "I'll be checking in with Luke to find out how you're doing. And if you get back here, we'll scare up some poker."

"I'd like to beat the hell out of you at something," Coop said.

"Happy trails, man." Coop turned to go and Jack said, "Hey, Coop—that was nice, that you stopped by. Thanks for that."

"Yeah, anytime. Watch out for my friends, Jack."

"You don't even have to ask. Call if you need help."


It was early afternoon when Maxie walked into her kitchen. She found Tom sitting at the table, eating cold casserole right out of the dish. She smiled at him and asked, "Hungry?"

He pushed it away and said, "Sit down, Max—we have to talk about a couple of things. Sensitive things."

She sat warily. "Yes, I had a very nice trip, thank you for asking."

"This might be a little hard for you at first, but you're going to have figure out how to get along with the idea—I'm going to marry Nora."

Her eyes widened in shock. Her mouth hung open.

"Right away. Well, as right away as she'll go along with. Now, I know that's not what you expected me to do, marry some woman with a couple of kids—a couple of kids by some loser who's in prison—but this is how it's going to be. I think, despite the fact her life has been pretty rocky up to now, she's a solid person. She's a very moral, decent person. She might've had a few little errors in judgment along the way, but a lot of that has more to do with the hard knocks of her childhood, something I only know a little bit about...."

"Tom, I like Nora," she said.

"I know, I know. That's obvious. But liking her as an orchard worker and friend and as my wife—those are different roles. And I know that your life has been very different from hers, Maxie. You've been more mother to me than grandmother and I know the woman who raised me has a really rigid moral code...."

She straightened her spine in shock. "Rigid moral code...?"

"You were so damn strict, the apples ran for their lives! I always planned to marry a woman a lot more like you, but this one just tripped me up!"

"Tom, Nora is—"

"I'm just telling you before I go one step further, you can't judge her against your old-fashioned standards. You can't condemn her for having a couple of kids without a husband or anything related. We accept her one hundred percent, just as she is."

"Tom! You think I would judge her for that? You know that your grandfather and I—"

"I know, you had to get married—you've been honest about that. This is pretty different, but I don't care. I wouldn't care if she had six kids—I need her in my life. I'm not giving her up." Then he laughed suddenly. "Damn, doesn't this just have stalker written all over it?" He rubbed his hand down his face.

"Tom, have you not paid attention? We didn't just have to get married, we—"

"I'm telling you, it doesn't matter to me, so it can't matter to you, because I'm bringing Nora and the kids to live with us. We could get our own house but if I'm going to work this orchard, I—"

"No, Tom, I absolutely don't want you to find your own house and leave me on the orchard in this great big house," she said, but she wasn't sure he was listening to anything she said. He appeared to be just about deaf and blind and a little crazed. "Tom. Tom, look at me. Has Nora agreed to marry you?"

"No, but she will because she has to. They're kicking her out of her house and she thinks she's moving to Stanford to live with her father, but I'm not letting her go," he said. "I'll find a way to make it up to her if she wants to go back to college...."

"We do have colleges," Maxie said, mesmerized by her grandson's passion. "I've never seen you like this before."

"Probably because I've never been like this before. I knew I was falling for her but I thought I had time to get used to the idea of becoming a husband and father overnight. Man, I don't need time—I only need one thing."

"Can you slow down for just one second?" Maxie asked calmly. "Can you please listen to me?"

"Don't try to reason with me, Max, because I—"

"Tom! Shut up! Listen to me!" He sat still and focused on her. "Better. You still look a little dazed, but better."

"I didn't sleep at all, and I was already running on very little sleep."

"I understand, now please try to hear me. You have

to calm down and see if you can lose that lunatic edge. No one's going to marry you if you continue to sound completely insane."

"I might be a little insane," he said. "I sure feel that way."

"Deep breaths," she said. "I love Nora. If she'll come here as my granddaughter-in-law, I would be very happy. But you must hear me on this—if you tell her she has to, any woman with a brain would run for her life."

He was quiet for a second while he absorbed this. "Right," he finally said. But he looked confused.

"Tell her how you *feel*. Just tell her how you feel and ask her if she can lower her standards enough to take you for a spouse."

He sat back. "Very funny," he said.

She grinned. "I couldn't be more serious. And before you light out of here with a mission, make sure you're wearing boots the same color and zip your fly."

He looked down—sure enough, one black, one brown. And an open fly. How did she do that? "Sometimes you're just spooky."

"Women notice things like that. Are you done with me?"

He nodded. "I'm going to Nora's now," he said. "After I change boots."

"Good. I think I've aged ten years since I walked in the door!"

But Maxie stayed in that chair until he had attended

to his clothing and left again. Then he came back, kissed her forehead and said, "Thank you, Max!"

She sat. *My God,* she thought. She just shook her head. He really had no concept of what he was asking, what he was saying. They had talked about the fact that his grandfather was not his biological grandfather, though Tom had been much younger. Maxie thought it imperative that he hear that from her before he heard it in town or at school, surprised he hadn't already. He had only asked one question—was he his father's biological son. And Maxie had said, "There is absolutely no question—you are his twin. We'll go through pictures any time you like." Apparently he had heard that, accepted it and was at peace. The biology dating back to his grandfather and great-grandfather was so far removed in his young mind, it didn't matter.

When Tom pulled up to that small house in town that held almost all his hopes and dreams, her father's car was there. He took a deep breath. *Probably just as well.*

When he knocked at the door, she said, "Come in." And he thought, *I have no flowers, no ring, nothing.*

He opened the door and saw that Jed was sitting on the sofa, reading a picture book to the little girls. Berry looked up, gave him a little smile and her version of a wave. Tom approached Jed and stuck out a hand. "Don't get up, Jed," he said. "I'm just going to talk to Nora for a couple of minutes."

Jed just shook quickly, smiled and gave a nod before going back to his reading. Nora had a cardboard box open on the table and seemed to be filling it with folded clothes. Already? "Can I talk to you for a second?" he asked.

"Sure," she said. "I'm right here."

He walked through the very small living room and faced her. "Alone?"

"Where?" she asked. "The bathroom?"

"Maybe we could, um, go sit in the truck?" he said, but even as he said it, it sounded so dumb. And not exactly the way he wanted her to remember a marriage proposal. But then, neither was this.

She leaned toward him and whispered, "If it's about last night, there's nothing to talk about. Everything was fine. Lovely and perfect. Shhh."

He whispered back. "I want to marry you."

She almost broke her neck, it snapped up so fast. "What?" she said.

He looked over his shoulder uncomfortably. Jed was peering at him over his reading glasses.

"I love you," Tom said quietly. "I want to marry you."

She frowned and leaned toward him. "Are you drunk?" she whispered.

"No! I've never been more sober! Way too sober. Marry me. You'll learn to love me, I promise."

Nora swallowed. "Tom, this is very sudden."

"So is you packing boxes. Listen, don't go. Let me take care of you, let me—"

She was shaking her head. She *couldn't* be saying

no already! "You can't possibly have had time to think this through."

"Hours," he said. "I haven't slept a night through in days."

"You're probably just hallucinating. You don't get married just because you—" She leaned to look around Tom to her dad. "You should give yourself more time to think about this."

"I have thought about it. I don't need more time, I need you."

"But you were concerned about making sure things, you know, didn't get serious."

"Yeah, because I'm an idiot—I was falling in love with you and it scared me to death. I've never been in love before, but I am now. I want you. You and the girls. If you need more time, fine—but don't leave town. I love you."

Jed cleared his throat. They both glanced at him.

"This is too fast," she whispered. "What if it doesn't work?"

"It'll work," he said. "It has to work because I haven't ever felt like this before. In fact, I wasn't sure I even wanted to feel like this, but here it is—Nora, I swear I'll be a good husband. And father. We have Maxie to kick me around if I make stupid mistakes— she loves that job."

"I'm not sure I'm ready to cross that line, and it has nothing to do with how I feel about you. I'm crazy about you. But I—"

"I'd bet everything on us," he said. "But if you

need more time, I'll show up at the auction and buy this house. Then you can take your time, give it some thought. If you want to go back to school, I'll make sure you get to." He lifted one brow. "We do have colleges here, you know."

She laughed at him. "You can't buy a house!"

"Yes, I can. I can buy three houses and a truck. I'm not broke. I was going to plant more trees and get a new tractor, but this is more important. You can come to the orchard and find out what it's like there after the harvest."

"Or I could go to Stanford and we could talk on the phone, write and email and visit on weekends."

"We could," he said. "And be miserable apart. Or you could just marry me and let me give you everything I have."

"Listen, try to understand, my parents married too quickly and it went south very badly."

"Yeah, sorry. I know that was really hard for you as a kid. I don't know anything about how mine were together, but I know how we are together. No two people have ever been more right together."

She put a hand on her hip. "What makes you think I'm right for you?"

He laughed and grabbed her hips, pulling her closer. "Are you kidding? You're way too proud and stubborn, for one thing. And you insist on doing things yourself—such a tough little broad. I've met plenty of the other kind, but I like women like you and Maxie, women who aren't afraid of themselves, who set no

limits on what they can accomplish. Did you know
Maxie had a tough time when she was growing up?
She did," he finished, ignoring her nod. "And that
didn't keep her from being a great mother and grandmother—like you. And even though you've had a few
hard knocks in the love department, it sure didn't af-
fect your ability to *give* love. You give love so good,
a man could go blind."

"Tom!" she said. She leaned to look at her father,
but he was gone. She gasped and ran to the front door.
He was outside; he had the girls in that big stroller.
"Dad, it's cold out there!"

"We have our coats on. We'll be right on this block,
don't worry."

"Are you sure?"

"Nora, take a few minutes to talk to your... To talk
to Tom."

She came back in and closed the door and found
herself instantly in Tom's arms. He was smiling. "I'm
telling you the truth—I started to want you the second I saw you and I started to love you by the time
I'd known you for a week. I wasn't sure that was such
a good idea—you being an employee. But you just
had me. Everything about you—the way you laughed
when you had nothing to laugh about, the way you
cried when you longed for the love and trust of family... Nora, you're everything I want in my life. Nothing else much matters right now. If you need to think
it over, I'll make sure you have this house, no strings,
while you think."

"Tom…"

"I came empty-handed because I was in a panic—I had to tell you how I feel before you ran off to start a new life. But I promise if you give me a chance I'll buy you a good ring, give you any kind of wedding you want, give you all my worldly goods and bring you flowers every day."

Her eyes flooded. "I love you, Tom. And not for what you can give me. For who you are."

He ran a knuckle down her jaw. "I'll take anything you give me. Marry me or think about it awhile, but just don't leave me. I love you with everything I am."

"If you take me, you have to take the whole family," she told him. "You have to be a father to two little girls."

"I'll do my best. I think I'm up to it. They like me." He smiled. "You have to take my whole family, too. Maxie is determined to live to a hundred and twenty, and I like her chances."

"Then yes, I'll marry you."

# *Epilogue*

In early June, when the weather in the mountains was warm and sunny after a long winter, Nora sat on the porch at the orchard house. Maxie was in the kitchen making a very big dinner because Nora's father and Susan were up for the weekend. Berry and Fay were playing on the porch; they were now Cavanaughs. Tom's adoption of them had been completely uncontested.

There had been a quiet wedding in Maxie's living room right before Thanksgiving and they'd been an extended family ever since. Jed loved visiting the orchard and had become enamored of researching the apple tree species. He was helpless in the face of research—he just loved it. It was hard to keep him away during the spring planting.

She rubbed a hand over the small mound in her middle that she and Tom had planted. They started it right around Christmas, it was another girl and she would arrive in September. Tom was thrilled and hoped that she, like her sisters, would look just like Nora.

No one had ever loved Nora as selflessly as her man. Her children were thriving within his love and the attention Maxie showered on them.

And just as he crossed her mind, he crossed the yard. She laughed as she saw that he carried a stem of apple blossoms. He put a booted foot up on the porch and held them out to her.

"You have to stop doing this," she said, taking the branch. "These are unborn apples."

"I promised you flowers every day."

"And love every day, which you shower on me."

"But that's the easy part," he told her.

\* \* \* \* \*

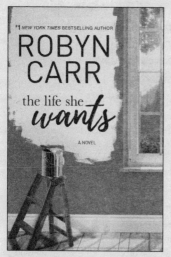

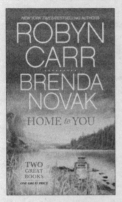

# REQUEST YOUR FREE BOOKS!

## 2 FREE NOVELS
## FROM THE ROMANCE COLLECTION,
## PLUS 2 FREE GIFTS!

**YES!** Please send me 2 FREE novels from the Romance Collection and my 2 FREE gifts (gifts are worth about $10). After receiving them, if I don't wish to receive any more books, I can return the shipping statement marked "cancel." If I don't cancel, I will receive 4 brand-new novels every month and be billed just $6.49 per book in the U.S. or $6.99 per book in Canada. That's a savings of at least 18% off the cover price. It's quite a bargain! Shipping and handling is just 50¢ per book in the U.S. and 75¢ per book in Canada.* I understand that accepting the 2 free books and gifts places me under no obligation to buy anything. I can always return a shipment and cancel at any time. Even if I never buy another book, the two free books and gifts are mine to keep forever.

194/394 MDN GH4D

Name                                  (PLEASE PRINT)

Address                                                                          Apt. #

City                          State/Prov.                          Zip/Postal Code

Signature (if under 18, a parent or guardian must sign)

### Mail to the **Reader Service:**
**IN U.S.A.:** P.O. Box 1867, Buffalo, NY 14240-1867
**IN CANADA:** P.O. Box 609, Fort Erie, Ontario L2A 5X3

**Want to try 2 free books from another line?**
**Call 1-800-873-8635 or visit www.ReaderService.com.**

*Terms and prices subject to change without notice. Prices do not include applicable taxes. Sales tax applicable in N.Y. Canadian residents will be charged applicable taxes. Offer not valid in Quebec. This offer is limited to one order per household. Not valid for current subscribers to the Romance Collection or the Romance/Suspense Collection. All orders subject to credit approval. Credit or debit balances in a customer's account(s) may be offset by any other outstanding balance owed by or to the customer. Please allow 4 to 6 weeks for delivery. Offer available while quantities last.

**Your Privacy**—The Reader Service is committed to protecting your privacy. Our Privacy Policy is available online at www.ReaderService.com or upon request from the Reader Service.

We make a portion of our mailing list available to reputable third parties that offer products we believe may interest you. If you prefer that we not exchange your name with third parties, or if you wish to clarify or modify your communication preferences, please visit us at www.ReaderService.com/consumerschoice or write to us at Reader Service Preference Service, P.O. Box 9062, Buffalo, NY 14240-9062. Include your complete name and address.

ROM15R

# ROBYN CARR

| | | | |
|---|---|---|---|
| 32931 | WILD MAN CREEK | ___$7.99 U.S. | ___$9.99 CAN. |
| 32899 | JUST OVER THE MOUNTAIN | ___$7.99 U.S. | ___$9.99 CAN. |
| 31890 | REDWOOD BEND | ___$7.99 U.S. | ___$9.99 CAN. |
| 31854 | FOUR FRIENDS | ___$7.99 U.S. | ___$8.99 CAN. |
| 31787 | A NEW HOPE | ___$8.99 U.S. | ___$9.99 CAN. |
| 31772 | ONE WISH | ___$8.99 U.S. | ___$9.99 CAN. |
| 31763 | BRING ME HOME FOR CHRISTMAS | ___$7.99 U.S. | ___$9.99 CAN. |
| 31761 | HARVEST MOON | ___$7.99 U.S. | ___$9.99 CAN. |
| 31749 | WILDEST DREAMS | ___$8.99 U.S. | ___$9.99 CAN. |
| 31742 | PROMISE CANYON | ___$7.99 U.S. | ___$8.99 CAN. |
| 31733 | MOONLIGHT ROAD | ___$7.99 U.S. | ___$8.99 CAN. |
| 31728 | A SUMMER IN SONOMA | ___$7.99 U.S. | ___$8.99 CAN. |
| 31724 | THE HOUSE ON OLIVE STREET | ___$7.99 U.S. | ___$8.99 CAN. |
| 31702 | ANGEL'S PEAK | ___$7.99 U.S. | ___$8.99 CAN. |
| 31697 | FORBIDDEN FALLS | ___$7.99 U.S. | ___$8.99 CAN. |
| 31644 | THE HOMECOMING | ___$7.99 U.S. | ___$8.99 CAN. |
| 31620 | THE PROMISE | ___$7.99 U.S. | ___$8.99 CAN. |
| 31599 | THE CHANCE | ___$7.99 U.S. | ___$8.99 CAN. |
| 31590 | PARADISE VALLEY | ___$7.99 U.S. | ___$8.99 CAN. |
| 31513 | A VIRGIN RIVER CHRISTMAS | ___$7.99 U.S. | ___$8.99 CAN. |
| 31459 | THE HERO | ___$7.99 U.S. | ___$8.99 CAN. |
| 31452 | THE NEWCOMER | ___$7.99 U.S. | ___$9.99 CAN. |
| 31447 | THE WANDERER | ___$7.99 U.S. | ___$9.99 CAN. |
| 31419 | SHELTER MOUNTAIN | ___$7.99 U.S. | ___$9.99 CAN. |
| 31415 | VIRGIN RIVER | ___$7.99 U.S. | ___$9.99 CAN. |

*(limited quantities available)*

| | |
|---|---|
| TOTAL AMOUNT | $ _____ |
| POSTAGE & HANDLING | $ _____ |
| ($1.00 for 1 book, 50¢ for each additional) | |
| APPLICABLE TAXES* | $ _____ |
| TOTAL PAYABLE | $ _____ |

*(check or money order—please do not send cash)*

To order, complete this form and send it, along with a check or money order for the total above, payable to MIRA Books, to: **In the U.S.:** 3010 Walden Avenue, P.O. Box 9077, Buffalo, NY 14269-9077; **In Canada:** P.O. Box 636, Fort Erie, Ontario, L2A 5X3.

Name: _____
Address: _____ City: _____
State/Prov.: _____ Zip/Postal Code: _____
Account Number (if applicable): _____
075 CSAS

*New York residents remit applicable sales taxes.
*Canadian residents remit applicable GST and provincial taxes.

**MIRA®**

**www.MIRABooks.com**

MRC1116BL